THE VISION

A shrill cry cut the silence. The flashing eyes of the eagle gleamed from within the sun's fiery circle. "Duuqua."

"I hear, Father of All." The words crawled up Duuqua's dry throat. His eyes never left the eagle's face as it faded, then changed shape. A woman's face filled the circle. She smiled and her dark eyes shone, soft as a doe's. His knees folded as he basked in the warmth of her smile, but it faded to fear, then froze in horror. He cried out, feeling her terror, her pain. Sorrow shadowed her face, made her eyes fill. He reached out to comfort her as a lone tear fell from her cheek. His heart lurched as he stared at the tear in the palm of his hand.

The eagle screamed once more and the woman's face faded into the sunset.

"No! Don't go." He strained toward the setting sun. "Please! Tell me how to help my people." His plea flew to an empty sky. No trace of the woman remained— except her tear. But when he opened his hand, the tear was gone. In its place lay a clear stone.

Clutching the stone to his aching heart, Duuqua fell into exhausted dreams—dreams of a journey, of sacrifice and promise, of the beautiful woman and treachery.

TIME'S CAPTIVE

KATE LYON

LOVE SPELL NEW YORK CITY

LOVE SPELL®

July 2004

Published by

Dorchester Publishing Co., Inc.
200 Madison Avenue
New York, NY 10016

ISBN 0-505-52602-6

Visit us on the web at www.dorchesterpub.com.

ACKNOWLEDGMENTS

Many thanks to Lucy Karas,
who refused to let me make my warrior a wimp,
and to Marsha Thompson for her gracious calm
and dead-on critiques. My first critique partners, their
patience with the endless rewrites was phenomenal,
and their enthusiasm for love scenes, legend.

Thanks, too, to Sabina Fox,
my first contest judge who became a close friend.
Her cheery giggle got me over some big bumps,
and her expertise kept me aiming higher.

Thanks to Jennifer Peterson and Amber McKee,
who inherited the finished product.
They saw me through the dark days
and wouldn't let me stop seeking the light.

Thanks as well to Peggy Mims and Sharon Pisacreta
for their tireless support and never-ending enthusiasm
for all things crabby.

Thanks also to my editor, Alicia Condon,
for demystifying the process and
teaching me to trust the experts!

And loving thanks to my family—
my daughters, whose enthusiasm never flagged;
my sons, who rolled their eyes but listened anyway;
and Vern, who brought the magic in the first place
and never lets me forget it.

This wouldn't have been a book without you!

TIME'S CAPTIVE

Prologue

Above the gray mists of morning, the sun climbed onto the shoulders of the hills. Fingers of light crept toward Duuqua as he placed the white-painted deerskin robe over a bed of stones.

Shadows danced across his face. Fierce satisfaction swept through him. At the top of his scalp pole, his offerings to the Great Spirit, the scalps of white buffalo hunters taken in his last raid, twisted and tangled as they danced in the wind.

He drew the sacred War Pipe from its *parfleche* and touched the bowl to his forehead. No simple pipe for this vision quest. His People's need was too great. For two suns he would smoke with the Great Spirit, who would give him strong medicine to chase away the hated buffalo hunters. He packed the pipe's blackened bowl with sweet grass and placed it on his stone bed.

Knife in hand, he stepped to the edge of the rock shelf and raised his arms to the sun. Many times he had come to this place. Each time the eagle had spoken the words of the Great Spirit in dreams that had filled him with joy and struck fear in his heart. Those visions had all come to pass. He had become war chief to the Quahadi, who awaited his return, their blood heating. The People would build a great fire and dance around it while he told the War Council his dreams and shared this vision. With the Great Spirit's help, the Quahadi would rid Mother Earth of the white buffalo hunters forever.

He closed his eyes and listened for the beat of the drums. The sun's smile warmed him, but he rejected its comfort and let the drums fill his mind. They pounded in his heart and hammered through his blood—faster, stronger—until light burst through him and his spirit broke free. One with the eagle, his brother, he floated in the arms of the wind. Clouds were his blankets. Looking down, he saw his body as the Great Spirit must see him, watched his lips move, chanting his war song. The drums and music grew louder, until he heard no more.

Suddenly his spirit swept low. Riding the wind, it hung before his body as his blade sliced into his naked chest. Blood swelled from the shallow wounds and rushed down to stain the earth.

With a screeching wail, the wind whirled him higher and higher. Light and color ran together in his mind until all the world turned red as the blood at his feet—red as the blood of his enemies, red as the sun shining through his eyelids.

"Speak, Duuqua."

His eyes flew open as the voice rumbled through him, sending his heart leaping and his thoughts flying to the sun. He reached for the voice.

"Great Spirit! You who live in the wind and the sun and all the earth, lean close and hear my prayer.

"See your People! Hear their cries! They weep for loved ones killed by the white man. They mourn the buffalo lying naked on the plains, killed by white hunters.

"Can you hear the buffalo's cry? No! For white hunters have cut out their tongues. Listen! You will hear only the wail of women and children who lie cold and hungry in the night.

"Show me how to help them, Great Spirit. Give me wisdom to lead the Quahadi against the enemies of the People.

"Hear me!"

Hear me, hear me. . . . His words echoed from the hills, but the wind blew back no answer, only wrapped cold arms around him and moaned its sorrow. His world turned black.

He awoke to the sun's kiss and a fiery throb in his chest. Leaping to his feet, he gave a triumphant shout. The Great Spirit had seen him, spoken to him. His prayer would be answered.

He lit the War Pipe and offered smoke to the Great Spirit and to Mother Earth. Singing his war song, he danced around his scalp pole, offering smoke to the four winds, knowing each step brought him closer to the vision he sought.

The new day walked on old feet. His tongue thickened with thirst, but he allowed no water to pass his lips. His stomach growled like the mountain lion; he ignored its angry voice and sang louder. Deep into the night he sang and danced, then collapsed onto his bed.

When the new sun peered over the hills, he shouted for joy. This day the Great Spirit would answer his prayers. He danced and sang and smoked as the sun stepped across the clouds to lie on the breast of the western hills. There it grew, glowing with a fire's light, filling the sky.

A shrill cry cut the silence. The flashing eyes of the eagle gleamed from within the sun's fiery circle. "Duuqua."

"I hear, Father of All." The words crawled up Duuqua's dry throat. His eyes never left the eagle's face as it faded, then changed shape. A woman's face filled the circle. She smiled and her dark eyes shone, soft as a doe's. His knees folded as he basked in the warmth of her smile, but it faded to fear, then froze in horror. He cried out, feeling her terror, her pain. Sorrow shadowed her face, made her eyes fill. He reached out to comfort her as a lone tear fell from her cheek. His heart lurched as he stared at the tear in the palm of his hand.

The eagle screamed once more and the woman's face faded into the sunset.

"No! Don't go." He strained toward the setting sun.

"Please! Tell me how to help my People." His plea flew to an empty sky. No trace of the woman remained—except her tear. But when he opened his hand, the tear was gone. In its place lay a clear stone.

Clutching the stone to his aching heart, Duuqua fell into exhausted dreams—dreams of a journey, of sacrifice and promise, of the beautiful woman and treachery.

Chapter One

Kris Baldwin paused in the last puddle of sunshine on the grassy slope of Barton Springs and ripped open the letter from the Lawton Oklahoma School District. Fingers shaking, she pulled out the single page inside and hesitated.

What if they'd rejected her? What would she do? Where would she go? She'd pinned all her hopes on this one dream.

She reached for the stone that hung from a chain around her neck, a gift from her grandmother, Powahe, a Comanche medicine woman. It throbbed against her palm, echoing her rapidly beating heart.

Be calm, Kaku. Soon you will understand. Her grandmother's voice drifted through her mind. *Read the letter.*

A shiver skittered up Kris's spine. The stone gave a skipping beat and Kris smiled. Would she ever get used to Powahe's special skills? She took a deep breath and glanced around her.

This place made her feel so alive, yet so calm, which was why she'd come here to read the letter. The Springs' swimming area wasn't much bigger than most city pools, and only waist deep. Yet she knew that beneath the placid water lay a gigantic labyrinth of channels that circulated millions of gallons of water each day. Above the rugged rock ledge on the far bank, gnarled mesquite and tangled bushes fought for dominance, in stark contrast to the fresh-mown lawns, chain-link fences and brick buildings on this side of the water.

It was the contrast that intrigued her—wild and civilized, tamed and untamed, past and present. Here the two halves of her soul—one white, the other Comanche—found harmony. Here she felt centered, at peace with herself. No matter what this letter held, good news or bad, she'd deal with it better just by being here.

Kris sucked in a deep breath and read the letter.

"They want me! I did it!" she squealed. Laughing, she twirled, arms spread wide to capture the wonderful feelings.

"Good news?" The lifeguard grinned at her from a few feet away.

"Very." She blushed, realizing the spectacle she'd just made of herself.

"Sorry to cut your festivities short, but we're closing."

"Already?" She glanced west, over the Springs' rugged far bank. Sure enough, the sun hung low in the sky. "Do I have time for a few laps?"

"Make it quick, okay?" He threw his towel over his shoulder and started toward the bathhouse. "Congratulations."

"Thanks."

She re-folded the letter and started to fit it back into its envelope, then stopped. She needed to give thanks properly, as Powahe had taught her. She'd make an offering. After making sure the return address was on the letter, she tucked it into her backpack. Then she tore the envelope into tiny pieces. Holding them tight in one hand, she moved to the edge of the Springs. With the other hand clutching her stone, she closed her eyes.

Father above, I'm thankful for this opportunity. I promise to work hard and devote myself to my mother's People. Help me to be open-minded, to listen and learn as well as teach. Please give me the understanding and knowledge I lack.

She tossed the bits of torn envelope over the water and smiled. Maybe the old custom would bring her luck. Couldn't hurt.

She ran down the stone steps into the water, arcing into a shallow dive. Her muscles tightened at the shock of the cool water. She slid into the steady rhythm that always calmed her and helped her think through her problems. Finally, pleasantly tired, she slowed and flipped onto her back. She felt so good, so incredibly content. Even dusk seemed more brilliant today.

Above her, the waning light shifted. Something flew at her. She flinched away from it, rolling to her feet as it plunked into the water beside her. Ducking under, she grabbed it before it settled on the uneven bottom.

She swiped the water off her face and opened her hand. Her heart stuttered. On her palm lay a crystal-clear stone, exactly like the one pulsing against her chest. She pulled her own stone close to compare the two. They throbbed against her fingers, echoing her heartbeat.

A breeze whispered across her skin, setting her nerve endings atingle and raising goosebumps. She jerked upright, fully alert. Someone was watching her. At first, she saw no one. Then the shadows wavered, shimmering with slivers of light that burst into brilliant, dancing color.

A man materialized on the ledge, surrounded by mist, naked except for a breechclout. She stepped deeper into the ledge's shadow, unnerved by the power he radiated. His long raven-black hair lifted on the breeze, and the tip of an eagle feather poked above his crown. He looked like a warrior from the past, like he'd just stepped from one of Powahe's stories.

Kris shook her head. She must be hallucinating. What would a warrior be doing here? She blinked hard, but when she looked again, he was still there.

He leaned forward, his gaze cutting to her like lightning

seeking a target. When their eyes met, a bolt of energy rocketed through her and the stones in her fists started a steady drumming beat that surged up her arms and pounded through her body.

He spoke, and his voice sounded like it was coming from a long distance. He seemed to be speaking Comanche. But his eyes! He'd stared right into her soul.

Suddenly, he jumped off the ledge, straight toward her. She braced against the impending splash, but it never came. He spoke again, but his words seemed stretched, garbled.

"I'm sorry." She backed away from him, shaking her head. "Can't understand you."

He frowned and stepped closer, reaching out to touch her. His hand passed right through her arm. She hadn't felt a thing. She stared up at him as a sickening sense of unreality washed over her.

"W-Who are you?" It took an effort of will not to turn and run.

He stared at his hand, then her arm, his eyes wide. He motioned for her to follow him.

"No way, mister." She kept an eye on him as she backed toward the stairs.

He started to follow, but a thick mist rose from the water, surrounding him. Then the mist dissolved into streamers that swept every trace of him away on the breeze.

"Weird!" Kris murmured, searching the shadowy bank above her, then the lawn behind her. He was gone. She felt strangely bereft, as if she'd lost something very important.

Suddenly uneasy, she turned toward the steps. The water seemed to cling to her legs. She tried to run and stumbled, almost losing her balance. Her fingers tightened over the pounding stones she still clutched in either fist. Like a live current, their energy coursed through her veins. She tried to let go of her stone, needing an arm to steady herself in the sloshing water, but she couldn't open her hands. She yanked hard and broke the chain on her stone. Both arms were free, but her hands remained fisted.

The water pitched and she stumbled again. Had the floor of the Springs moved? A low, groaning rumble surrounded her. She hadn't imagined it, the rock was moving! Panic swept through her.

"Help!" she cried, feeling the rock layers shift and slide under her feet. She screamed, struggling to stay upright. "Somebody please! Help me!"

No one answered.

A few feet away, the rock layers tilted and broke, leaving a hole several feet wide only inches from her feet. She lost her balance and fell sideways, barely managing to suck in a deep breath before her head went under. She stared in horror as water rushed into the hole, creating a strong current that dragged her to the edge. She swam as hard as she could away from it—a wasted effort with both hands fisted.

It pulled her closer. Closer! Then her feet were in it. She groaned as the jagged rock mouth scraped her thigh. A deafening roar filled her ears as the current swept her through the hole. She tried to hook an arm over the lip, but the current was too strong.

Choking, fighting panic, Kris struggled to keep sight of the fading circle of daylight above her, but the relentless current pulled her away. A silent, terrified scream rang through her head. Her chest burned.

Don't breathe! her mind screamed, but her body ignored the warning. She gasped for air and cold water surged into her lungs, chilling soul deep. Her legs and arms seemed heavy. Too heavy to move. Her eyelids slid closed.

Exhausted, she surrendered, her tears turning as cold as her watery grave.

"Come back!" Duuqua searched the still waters around him. The vision of that other place had faded and the woman was gone, as if she had never been there. How could his quest end this way? The Great Spirit had accepted his sacrifice. His vision and dream had brought him to this place, to her.

He fell to his knees, threw his head back and screamed his anguish at the sky.

He turned his face into the wind, letting it rake through his hair and cool his anger. All was not lost. He would tell his dream to Tabenanika. Maybe the old holy man could find some answers to the questions of the war council that awaited his return.

He snarled and slashed a hand through the water. Something caught on his fingers, something long and sleek and strong. Hair? He tugged on it. A body floated out of the shadow beneath the rock ledge.

"By the Sun!" He snatched his fingers free and shoved the body away. As it floated downstream, it passed through a shaft of sunlight. Something gleamed.

He moved closer and saw that the body wore a robe like the one the woman had worn. Heart pounding, he snatched a handful of hair and tugged the body closer. He flipped it over and shoved the snarled hair off its face. His breath caught in his throat. It was the woman from his vision, the one whose tear had turned to stone in his hand. But she was dead.

"No! This is not she." He remembered her standing before him, her hair black as the raven's wing, her eyes wary but shining with curiosity. Anguish clawed through him, catching his heart in its fist.

Guard her well. The words the Great Spirit had spoken in his dream whispered on the wind.

"How?" he grumbled. "She is already dead." He carried her out of the water, cursing the chill of her cold skin against his, but glad that at least he could touch her now. This was no dream.

Guard her well. The voice came again, carried by a stronger gust of wind.

He stopped and stared into her face. Was there life in her

still? His blood pounded as hope rose inside him. Quickly, he climbed to the top of the rocky bank, pushing through the bushes to a small clearing. He laid her on a patch of dry grass and pressed his ear to her chest. He heard nothing. Pain knifed through him, followed by anger.

"This cannot be the end," he shouted into the wind. "What about the buffalo hunters? What will happen to my People?"

Guard her well. The wind pushed at him.

"How can I guard her now? I am a war chief, not a medicine man."

Fight for her life. The wind screeched at him like a grieving widow.

Duuqua stared at the dead woman. Could he do such a thing? Determination flashed through him, like a fire through dry brush. If there was life inside her still, he would find it before her spirit traveled beyond range of his voice. He must force the water out of her body. He rolled her onto her stomach and knelt beside her, then pushed on her back. Fear fired his efforts, but she did not stir. Arms stiff, he pressed harder.

"Hear me, woman," he commanded. "You cannot die. Breathe!" Again and again, he pressed against her back, and while he worked over her, he prayed. But she did not stir.

Anger and sorrow warred inside him. He turned her over and shook her. "Come back," he shouted into her face. Then, ashamed, he held her tight against him. "You cannot die. My People need you."

Her spirit answered with a low growl from deep inside. Her body shuddered and water ran from her mouth and nose. He turned her to her side and held her. He could do no more. Silent and helpless, he watched her suffering. At last she fell back, her face pale, her lips as blue as fresh bruises.

Did she live? Duuqua pressed his ear to her chest. At first he could hear nothing over the pounding of his own heart. He held his breath, then heard the distant beat of a lone drum. She lived!

"Thank You, Great Spirit, for the gift of her life." Lifting her gently, he moved her to dry ground, then searched her body for broken bones. Her chest barely moved with each breath. He could see each rib through the strange robe she wore.

What kind of skin was this? He knew of no animal whose hide gave back the sun's light. He slid a finger beneath the robe near the full curve of her breast. As his finger brushed her smooth, cold skin, her nipple tightened and stood proud beneath the robe.

He snatched his finger away. His heart beat fast as heat flashed into his face. His gaze slid to her flat belly and the fleshy mound that guarded her womanhood. The heat in his face turned to flame and burned throughout his body.

Filled with shame, he tore his eyes from her beauty. This was no simple woman to share his blankets. The Great Spirit had led him to her through dream and vision. He must not look upon her with desire in his eyes and lust in his heart. He knew his punishment would be swift and strong if he used the Great Spirit's gift to satisfy the hunger of his body.

Never had he heard of a warrior receiving a woman in a vision quest. Excitement surged through him. Not even Isatai, his brother's vain new medicine man, could claim such medicine.

Pride swelled Duuqua's chest at the Great Spirit's wonderful gift. He touched the woman's arm. She was real. Not a dream. Though her skin still felt cold, her chest now lifted with each breath. He grunted, pleased by her growing strength. He stroked her limp arm down to her tight fist.

What was this? He frowned and leaned closer. Her hand should be as limp as her body, not tight as a drum. What did she hold so tightly? He lifted her hand and tried to open her fingers. They would not move. He rubbed her fingers until her skin felt warm, then pried them open. His breath hissed out and his eyes opened wide.

"The tear-stone," he whispered in awe. As he took it from her, remembered feelings flashed through him—surprise at finding it in his hand where her tear had been, regret when the eagle told him he must toss it into the sacred waters as an offering, sorrow that it was lost to him forever, and now joy that he had found it again.

He reached over her and lifted her other hand. Even in the fading light, he could see that this hand too was fisted. He once again pried her fingers open.

Another stone!

He stood, holding a stone in each hand, and held them up to see them better. Was this stone also formed from her tear? Why did it have a tiny hole near the top, and what was this thin, yellow rope hanging from it?

He closed his hands over the stones and his fingers jerked tight. His blood rushed through his body. His eyes squeezed shut as he fought the stones' strength to open his fingers.

"By the Sun!" He set them on the ground beside the woman and stared at her, seeing her with new eyes. Only a great medicine woman would possess the strength to carry these stones. Even he could not bear the power of both, but she had held them in her fists.

Had the stones brought her to him? If they had brought her here, could she use them to leave again? Did she control their power? Could she use the stones to leave before she spoke the words of the Great Spirit to the war council?

He frowned. This could not happen. He must hide them from her, let her think she had lost them in the sacred waters. Quickly, he cut a strip off his breechclout. Wrapping the stones tight, he placed them inside his medicine bundle.

The woman moaned. He touched her shoulder and frowned. She shook from cold. Her lips were still blue. Would she live to speak to the war council?

"Wake up, *pahoute*." He poked her shoulder, then rubbed her cold, limp arm.

Her chest shuddered on a deep breath. Her eyelids fluttered. He leaned closer. Would she speak? Would she tell him the message she brought? Her eyes opened. She stared at him, blinking, then her eyes widened and she tried to roll away.

He held her still. "Do not fear me," he said, relief making his voice a low growl.

"Wh-who are you?" she cried.

He stared at her, alarm ripping through him. She spoke with the tongue of his enemy!

"Taibo!" He leaped to his feet. What trick was this?

She gave a weak cry and tried to rise, but her eyes rolled back, then closed. Once again, she lay as if dead.

Lips curled in disgust, he poked her shoulder with his foot. She did not move. He paced beside her, torn and confused.

"Taibo!" The word echoed in his ears, his heart. He reached for his knife. Would a warrior carry a snake into his own lodge? No! He would end her life now. One stroke . . .

He crouched over her and yanked her head back. Her throat gleamed white in the fading light, naked beneath his blade. She lay unknowing, helpless in his hands. His breath came fast and hard. His body trembled. With a snarl, he shoved her away. He could not kill her.

He stalked away, shaking off his rage, shamed by his weakness. At the very first touch of her gaze, he had weakened. She made him want to protect her, to taste her sweetness. Her medicine was strong. What would the Great Spirit have him do with her now?

Guard her well, the wind screeched, and whipped cold arms around him.

"How?" he shouted. He pulled his blanket out of a *parfleche* and tossed it around his shoulders, glad of its warmth.

The woman moaned and shuddered. He turned to stare at her. Would her medicine power protect her from the cold?

He sniffed. The Great Spirit would not expect him to share his blanket with a *taibo*. She was a woman to be hated, not protected and warmed by his body.

She whispered something in her sleep and shuddered. His blanket felt heavy on his shoulders.

Guard her well, the wind moaned again.

His lips set in a grim line. If he did not warm her, would she die?

By the Sun! Not only could he not harm her, he could not stand by and allow harm to come to her.

He shook out the blanket, lay down beside the woman and pulled her trembling body to his side. His teeth clenched as her cold skin clung to his. He wrapped the blanket around her, then settled himself with a growl.

She moaned and turned toward him. One of her arms went over his waist, her head settled on his arm and she tossed her knee over his thigh.

He stiffened as hot blood raced through him.

"*Taibo*," he whispered, then lay stiff as a lodge pole, staring over her head into the darkness. He would warm her, but he would not look at her.

When her shivering stopped and her breath sighed easily between her lips, he eased away from her. He would do his duty as he had promised the Great Spirit. He would protect her.

Even from himself.

Gnarled, arthritic fingers swept the last tendrils of fragrant smoke from the fire. Bathing herself in its sweetness, Powahe sighed in satisfaction, savoring the last images of the vision. Her granddaughter had survived. Even now, Kris slept in the arms of the warrior who had snatched her from death. Powahe rejoiced in song, thanking the Great Spirit for His mercy.

Her entire body trembled, her small store of strength sorely taxed by this day's work, work that was not yet finished. Closing her eyes, she reached deeper into the veils and mists, her mind traveling on the last traces of smoke back to the quiet clearing where Kris and the warrior slept.

"*Kaku*." As always, Kris's nickname, the Comanche word for granddaughter, brought a smile to Powahe's lips. How strange to call a spirit so ancient "granddaughter"—but not as strange as sending her own thoughts and voice across the dark chasm that now separated them.

Kris mumbled in her sleep, then snuggled closer to the warrior. She slept deeply, not dreaming. Powahe frowned. The girl must be exhausted from her ordeal. She probed deeper into Kris's mind. The warrior's face loomed before her, barring her way.

Powahe pulled back, alarmed. So fierce, this warrior, already guarding one so recently found. Had he remembered?

Be calm, she told herself. She had seen his face many times in dreams and visions—the ancient one, Mish-awa-nee. Even his name meant wise and holy one. Yet she trembled in his presence, awed by his power, his energy even while sleeping. Why did he bar her way? Must she get past him to communicate with her granddaughter?

So be it. Powahe focused on his face, bracing herself for the contact. A low cry escaped her as she encountered the stone lying against his chest, quietly humming in response to her probing.

How had he come to possess the stone? Sweat beaded her brow. How would she communicate with Kris if she no longer wore it? She drew a deep, trembling breath and gathered her strength around her like a warm but tattered robe.

She prodded firmly, but his strong will resisted the images she sent. Did he sense the sorrow these images held for him, for her granddaughter?

"Open to me," she demanded, dangerously depleting her reserve of strength. "Open!" Then she felt it. Another stone lay in his medicine bundle. Captive, protected. Like her granddaughter in his arms.

Of course! She should have known there was another, a mate. With a gasping sigh, Powahe withdrew and collapsed beside the dying fire.

The warrior's strength of will would make her task difficult, but not impossible. There were many ways in which she could reach through the barriers. Perhaps, she mused, she might send visions, too. Interesting visions. With a pleased chuckle, she relaxed her vigil, letting her tiny fire dwindle to glowing embers as she plotted and planned. She would rest, but not too long. She must reach her granddaughter.

If she failed, Kris would never discover her destiny.

Chapter Two

Kris awakened, one nerve at a time. Every pore, every muscle cried a warning and her back and legs itched like crazy. But she was cozy and warm and the smell surrounding her was so . . . delicious. She inhaled deeply and sighed.

Mmmm. Kind of musky and a little sweaty with the tang of fresh breezes. Unfamiliar, but very interesting.

She snuggled a little closer to the warmth.

An arm tightened around her. Her eyes flew open and she realized several things at once. She lay in a man's arms, wrapped in a scratchy wool blanket. The entire length of her body was pressed to his. And her knee rested between his thighs.

She screeched, jerked her knee free and shoved against his chest. Rolling away, she tried to stand, but she was too weak. Alarm shot through her as the man leaned over her, naked but for a blood-stained breechclout.

Her gaze traveled swiftly over his lean, chiseled jaw, up sculpted hollows and high cheekbones to his bold blade of a nose, on to deep-set black eyes and a high, wide forehead. Her pulse accelerated as her gaze tangled in his long, sleek black hair. He wore a breechclout and moccasins. Incredible. Frightening. Strange. Like a character out of an old Western, only real.

Had she spent the whole night with him? She took in the single, rumpled blanket, then the blushing sky, and gulped. It certainly looked that way.

He stood and a hank of hair fell onto his chest, snagging on a blood-encrusted wound.

Memory crowded past the fear and confusion and she remembered him standing above her on the ledge at the Springs, and everything that happened after that.

"You!" Her voice came out a low croak. She winced at the pain in her throat. "It was you. At the Springs." She studied his face. It was he. She remembered the glare. At least this time he wasn't dissolving into mist.

"*Taibo.*" He growled the word, his voice low and hoarse and leaned closer, scowling into her face. "You speak with enemy tongue."

"Enemy?" she croaked. His first word had sounded Comanche, reminding her of some of the old words her grandmother sometimes used, but his English was horrible. "Who are you? Where am I?"

She reached for her stone. It was gone! "My stone!" she cried, forgetting everything else. "What happened to my stone?"

She remembered standing in the choppy water, clutching *two* stones. She must have lost them in the Springs. A horrible sense of loss swept her.

"You speak with white tongue. You enemy to my People." It was an accusation, not a question. His hot, black eyes judged her, found her guilty. He picked up a loose strand of her hair. "But you no look like white woman."

"You're Comanche?" Kris struggled to her feet when he nodded. She hoped he knew enough English to understand her questions, because she didn't know enough Comanche to carry on a conversation, just a few words and simple phrases. Her father had kept her grandmother's existence a secret; she'd found out about her accidentally when she turned seventeen. She hadn't learned the language growing up, and it wasn't included in the state university's curriculum.

"I'm Comanche, too," she told him, pointing at herself, a little surprised at the note of pride in her voice.

"You lie," he accused, punctuating each word with a finger-poke to her chest. *"Taibo."*

Outraged, she slapped his hand away. "I never lie. My father is white, but—"

He spat a low, hot word, his eyes like live coals in his face.

"—my mother was Comanche." She rubbed her stinging chest. "What does it matter, anyway? Most of us are mixed blood these days." And no one had this man's fierce pride.

"You have the blood of both people?" He grunted at her nod, then smiled—a humorless baring of strong, white teeth. "What tribe?"

"Kwerherehnuh," she said with pride. Most of the People claimed the branch that, under Quannah Parker's leadership, had been the last to surrender. But she had a right to claim it, as Quannah Parker had been her great-great grandfather.

"You lie."

She glared up at him. "I told you. I never lie." She cocked her head, considering the stubborn tilt to his chin, his arrogant stance and fierce denial of everything she said. She took a careful step backward. "Who are you?"

"Black Eagle, war chief to the Quahadi." His angry gaze raked her body. "My eyes have never seen your face."

War chief to the Quahadi? Kris almost laughed, annoyed by his air of superiority. But the look on his face stopped her. He couldn't be serious. Did she dare remind him that the elite band of warriors hadn't existed for almost a hundred and thirty years? Defeated people didn't need war chiefs.

Troubled, she reached for her stone. Its absence once again jarred her. She felt off balance, out of kilter without it. What was it Powahe had said when she'd given it to her?

"The stone is very powerful," she'd warned as she fastened it around her neck. "I do not understand it completely, but you will discover its strength."

She might be able to shake off the memory, but she remembered that she hadn't been able to release the stones after this man had disappeared, and she would never forget the horror of the swirling, icy darkness. The stones' power was as real as the relentless current that had sucked her into the Springs' underground reservoirs. She'd better find them before someone else got hold of them. The tinkle of running water spurred her into action.

"How close are we to Barton Springs?" she asked, turning toward the sound of the water. Her captor stood before a bush less than ten feet away, legs braced apart, relieving himself.

She swung away, appalled. Who was this guy? He seemed almost savage—a throwback to the nineteenth century when the Comanche roamed the plains, lords of all they surveyed. A man from a different time.

Impossible! she scoffed. She must have hit her head when the water sucked her under.

When he didn't answer, Kris examined the clearing, which looked just like the one above the Springs where she often sunbathed and daydreamed. She hurried to the tangle of bushes that should top the Springs' west ridge. Rising on tiptoe, she peered over the underbrush.

Her breath froze and her heart stopped. The rock ledge lay directly below her and she recognized the oak tree on the other bank, although it was much smaller than she remembered. But the playground, the gift shop, the little train and sloping lawns—everything was gone, as if it had been erased. All that remained of the place she knew and loved was a dirty stream of water between two rugged, rocky banks.

Shocked, she grabbed a bush to steady herself, barely noticing the thorn that pierced her palm. Had she been pulled downstream? Hearing Black Eagle approach, Kris turned to ask him, only to find him looking her over and shaking his head.

She glanced down at herself and squawked in dismay. All she wore was her swimsuit and a perky set of goosebumps. She snatched up the blanket that still lay in a heap where they'd slept, and blushed at the flattened grass beneath it. Nose in the air, she pulled the blanket around her shoulders.

"How did I get here, to this clearing?" She remembered being sucked into the vortex, but couldn't remember getting out of it.

"I carry you." He pulled a hide bag out from under the bush behind her, rummaged for a second and pulled out a handful of jerky. He took a bite and offered her one.

She declined his offer with a quick jerk of her head. "Why?"

He shrugged, thumped his chest. "You no breathe."

"I was dead?" He nodded and kept chewing. Her knees gave out and she sank to the ground with a thud. Once again, she reached for her stone and choked back a sob when she didn't find it. *Dead.* The word echoed with awful finality in her head, her soul.

"I fight for you." He reached under another bush and pulled out a bow and a quiver of arrows.

"You saved my life." Her emotions gyrated between shock, gratitude and annoyance. He acted as if he'd rescued a drowning cat. "Thank you," she murmured, knowing the simple words could never cover the debt she owed him.

He straightened and turned to face her. Their eyes met and held. Warmth surged through her body and she felt suddenly calm, as if it were right that he had been there. His harsh scowl disappeared. She smiled.

He blinked and shook his head, scowling again as he turned away.

Kris stayed where she was, still shaky, unwilling to examine her feelings too closely. She watched in amazement as he pulled on a pair of fringed buckskin leggings and a matching, loose-fitting shirt, then slung the bow and arrows over his shoulder.

Strange, she mused. *Those buckskins don't look like ceremonial costumes.* They seemed worn, hard-used. And she'd never seen anyone carry a bow and arrows, not even to a pow-wow. His easy handling of the weapons made her tense. They seemed an extension of his body, as if he always carried them and knew how to use them. Something was very wrong here.

"Do you always dress like this?"

The disgusted look he tossed over his shoulder didn't need translation. He peered over the far bushes and gave a shrill whistle. A white horse covered with huge black splotches shoved through the bushes into the clearing.

A *horse?* Kris jumped up and backed away as the animal trotted closer and butted Black Eagle in the stomach. He whispered a low, crooning singsong as he ran his hands along its neck and down its legs. It wore no harness or bridle, just a hair rope that circled its lower jaw and hung in a loop on one side before disappearing into its mane. She stared, dumbfounded, as he swung a well-worn saddle onto its back, then slid an antique rifle into a beaded leather scabbard on the animal's far side.

A horse? Bow and arrows? Buckskins? She stared in horror at the horse and Black Eagle's equipment. This was getting more and more weird every minute. It was time to get out.

Kris peered over the bushes, hoping to find a trail to spare her bare feet. Hearing a shout, she froze. About a hundred yards downstream, a crude wooden building squatted on the opposite bank. Two men stood there, staring toward her. They were dressed normally—hats, boots and khaki-colored work pants. No fringe or buckskin. She breathed a sigh of relief and waved. One of the men nudged the other, pointing toward her. Their excited voices carried on the wind as they scurried away.

"Wait!" More men came running out of the shack. They'd seen her. Help was on the way. Surely, they'd be able to get her back to the Springs.

"*Pahoute?*"

She jumped and turned to find Black Eagle close behind her. He glanced over her shoulder, his eyes sharp. "You go?"

"I'm going home," she said cheerily. She would not let him see how nervous he made her. "I really appreciate all you've done for me, but I've got to get to work this morning, and I left my bag on the lawn. Gotta run." She sounded like a chipmunk. She shoved out her hand for him to shake. "Good-bye."

His eyes narrowed. He stepped closer and grabbed her hand, but he didn't shake it and he didn't let go. Instead, he whipped a length of rawhide around her wrist.

"Wh-what are you doing?" She tried to pull away from him, even turned her shoulder into his chest, a defensive move she'd learned from a Comanche cousin. Too late. She'd only made it easy for him to grab her other wrist. Swift and sure, he tied her hands together in front of her.

"You can't do this!" She jerked at the rawhide, but he'd tied her up tight.

"Come." He turned, tugging her along behind him.

"No!" She resisted as much as she could with bare feet, which wasn't enough. "You don't understand. I have to get back to go home. I have things to do. This isn't funny, mister. Cut me loose."

"Quiet, woman." He tugged and she tumbled forward, wincing as the rawhide bit tighter. "Ouch! You're hurting me. Where do you think you're—"

Her eyes widened when he got to the horse and reached for her.

"Oh, no, you don't. Don't you dare put me on that horse!" She kicked, aiming for vital parts, missed and lost her balance. He caught her, his hands biting into her waist. Then suddenly she was airborne.

"Umph!" She slammed stomach first over the saddle. Her breath whooshed out and the pommel stabbed into her side. Seeing stars, struggling to breathe, she couldn't fight him when he pushed her upright, then mounted behind her. The horse made a tight turn and she started to slide off sideways.

"Are you crazy?" she croaked over her shoulder at him, clutching the saddle horn. "Kidnapping's against the law, you know. You may have saved my life, but that doesn't mean you own me."

"Quiet, *taibo*." He clamped an arm around her waist and pulled her back against his chest.

She tried to fall off, but he held her firmly. "Let me go!"

"Quiet!" He clapped his other hand over her mouth. "Your noise will bring my enemies."

Eyes wide, Kris realized that he now controlled the horse with his legs alone. The horse was gaining speed, heading straight for the bushes. She gasped, feeling its muscles bunch. Then they were flying! She screamed and squeezed her eyes shut.

Her teeth clunked together as the horse landed safely on the other side, slamming her back against her captor. Had he said enemies? Did he mean those men? If they were his enemies, did that make them her friends?

He shifted his hand but kept it tight over her mouth. His legs tensed, gripping the horse's barrel, keeping them centered on its back. Feeling numb, as if she'd left her brain behind in the clearing, she registered her bare thighs scraping against the saddle, the roughness of his calloused fingers crushing her lips against her teeth, his breath stirring her hair. His powerful body—all hot, straining, tensile muscle—surrounded her. Every particle of her tingled in awareness of this man who held her very senses captive. His legs flexed as he sent the horse charging uphill, then brought it to a sudden stop.

Kris forgot the man, his horse, everything but the scene before her. She felt tiny, insignificant, and—despite his overwhelming presence behind her—lost and alone. Fear escalated into terror as she stared at rolling hills bathed in mist, stretching on and on forever, finally melting into the horizon.

Where was the city? She couldn't see a single house or building! There were no roads, no power poles, not even a farm. How far downstream had the current dragged her? She'd been frightened before, but now her heart raced and her mouth went dry. This pristine wilderness scared her senseless. It was a different world, a different time.

A different time? Her mind flew, gathering bits and pieces of the puzzle: the changes to the Springs, Black Eagle himself, his horse and gear, and now this—this place.

She pinched herself hard. No, she wasn't dreaming. She was wide awake and she'd traveled back in time.

She wobbled side-to-side as Black Eagle sent the horse plunging downhill, then she watched the ground pass beneath them in a dizzying blur.

Panic tore at her. Where was he taking her? What did he want from her? She fought the hysteria, forcing herself to remain calm, and sagged against him. His hand loosened over her mouth. In a last desperate effort, she bit down, hard. He cursed and yanked his hand off her mouth. She snatched a deep breath and screamed, ignoring the searing pain in her throat.

His low curse mingled with the echoes of her cry; then his other hand clamped over her mouth.

She blinked back tears and prayed that someone had heard her.

Duuqua ignored the pain in his hand as he listened for the creak of leather, the crack of shod hooves striking rock. He heard men shouting in the distance, their voices high and excited. His heart jumped in alarm and his blood thundered through his body.

They had heard her scream. He did not know if they were enemy or friend to her, but any man who saw her in her strange robe would be driven by lust to possess her. Seeing her black hair and dark eyes, they would not believe she was half white. He must keep her safe.

He dug his heels into the horse's flanks and pushed her low over its neck, keeping his hand over her mouth.

"Stay down." He caught her braid between their bodies to keep her hair from blowing in his face. "Riders follow." When she continued to struggle, he slapped her leg in warning. "Be still. Do you want them to find us?"

"Yes!" she cried, and he almost missed the splash of water and eager shouts as the enemy found their trail and drew closer.

She struggled beneath him. He pressed tighter against her, then felt a strange pounding. The stones! His medicine bag lay between them. His breath caught in his throat as he tossed the bag over his shoulder. The stones knocked together inside and throbbed against his back. Had she felt them?

He had seen the alarm in her face when she'd searched for the stones. Did she also believe that the stones had brought her to him? If she knew he had them, would she try to steal them, then leave?

By the Sun, he vowed, he would not let her. Surely, her power told her that he would take her safely to his People, that she must speak to the chiefs in war council. So why had she tried to leave him? Would she betray them to the enemy that followed?

The wind rasped with the labored breath of hard-ridden horses. Close. They were too close. His horse would not be able to outrun them carrying two. He searched the trail ahead for a place to hide.

There, at the turn of the trail—a grove of trees and a deep shadow against a rock-faced hill. He dug his heels into the horse's flanks and leaned into each stride.

The woman squealed into the horse's mane and tossed her head in defiance. A lock of her hair escaped to beckon the enemy.

"Quiet." He captured the escaping hair and tucked it between them. "These men not know you the Great Spirit's messenger. They think you my woman. They rape you, make me watch. You beg for death long before they kill you."

She shuddered. His lips tightened. He wasn't sorry for frightening her. He spoke the truth. When she remained limp and still, he lifted his hand from her mouth, praying she would not scream.

"I'm just Kris Baldwin," she said, glaring at him over her

shoulder. "Definitely not the Great Spirit's messenger. Why would they think I'm your woman?"

Her body trembled, betraying her brave words. "You no look like their women. Hair black as night with no moon, eyes soft as doe's. They no believe you white."

A shout! Riders crested the trail behind them. A rifle barked. Duuqua ducked to the side, pulling her with him. Too slow. A bullet sliced a trail of fire across his shoulder, slamming him against her. Blood sprayed her cheek and shoulder, splattered the horse's neck.

She screamed and yanked the horse's mane. It tossed its head and slowed.

"No!" He pulled her hands free and kneed the horse around a bend, then off the trail. Digging in his heels, he sent it flying through the trees, heading for the hill's shadowed face. His enemy would not be fooled by such a simple trick for long. He leapt off, pulling the *pahoute* after him as he led the horse through a dense patch of bushes. He studied the overhanging shelf of rock that created the shadow. Would it be deep enough to hide her and the horse? It must be. He flung his blanket over the horse's back to cover its spotted hide.

"Keep him quiet." He pressed her hand over the horse's muzzle.

"Your shoulder," she whispered.

He could not stay to wipe away the guilt and regret he saw in her face. "Make no sound." He stared into her eyes, willing her to silence. Could he trust her with their lives? He had no choice. They were barely hidden. If she betrayed them, he would have to fight with his back to a rock wall and no way to escape. His jaw tightened. So be it. He would fight to the death to protect her. He prayed it would be enough.

Crouching low, he bent back branches that would tell of their passing and covered their tracks. Swiftly, he gathered dead brush to hide the woman and the horse, then slid into the shadows. He did not wait long. Five men rode back down the trail on lathered horses. Shining pieces of metal on their chests flashed in the sun. Rangers. Hatred burned inside him. These men would rather kill his People than spit on them.

He held his breath, expecting to hear the woman cry out, but she remained still as the men rode into the trees and dismounted, guns cocked and ready. His hand slid to his knife. The rock wall bit into his back. Silent as the wolf, he waited and watched.

"Damn'd injun," a big man grunted as he dismounted and led his horse closer to Duuqua's hiding place. He spat. The dark stream hit the rock near Duuqua's face and splashed into his eye. He did not move, did not blink.

"Cain't wait to git mah hands on his purty lil squaw." A skinny stick of a man grinned at the shadows as if he saw her in each one, naked.

"Think she'd be an easier ride than that bony old mare?" The big man laughed, his belly shaking. The others joined him.

Duuqua tensed at a quickly indrawn breath from the shadows behind him. The men's laughter bounced off rocks and trees, fouling the air with their stink, covering the woman's gasp.

He slid his knife from its sheath, fighting the desire to leap at the nearest man. Instead, he held his breath as they searched, poking their rifles into bushes, staring into every shadow, coming closer and closer.

"Shi-it. Ain't nothin' here." The big man's saddle groaned as he stepped into it and dragged his leg over the horse's back. He turned its nose back to the trail. The other men followed. "Slip'ry damn'd injuns. Musta cut off the trail on up ahead." They rode through the trees, searching before and behind as they passed.

Duuqua stayed hidden until he no longer heard the groan of their saddles. Lips curled in disgust, he wiped the spit off his face. Pain stabbed through his shoulder. He glanced at the wound. A crease. He grunted. It would leave a good scar.

He cleared the brush away and the woman stared up at him,

silent at last, her eyes wide, her body shaking. His eyes closed
and he tried not to think how close she had come to danger.
The thought brought a pain in his chest like none he had ever
known.

"We go," he said, and pulled her out of the shadows. The
hurt in her eyes twisted the knife in his chest. She didn't fight
him when he tossed her onto the horse's back, then led it
away from the Rangers. If they doubled back, he would send
the horse running, return their fire as long as he could, then
run a different way to draw them away from her. He kept
watch in every direction, but no one came. Finally, he jumped
on behind her and dug in his heels.

He held the woman against him to keep her from falling
off. She no longer fought him, but her body shook.

"Afraid?" he asked her. The enemy was gone. Didn't she
understand that he would protect her? "You safe."

"I don't know why I'm here, but get this straight," she said,
her eyes hot and angry. "I'm not a messenger from the Great
Spirit." She sat up straight and tossed her braid over her
shoulder, hiding her fear.

Duuqua smiled. *Taibo* or Comanche, the Great Spirit had
chosen well.

She was a warrior in a woman's body.

Chapter Three

"Who were those men?" The question tumbled from Kris's
mouth before she realized she'd voiced her stampeding
thoughts.

"Rangers," Black Eagle answered and kneed the horse into
a gallop again.

"Texas Rangers?" she asked, incredulous. Weren't Rangers

like cops back when the Comanche still lived in Texas? They
had laughed about raping her and they'd shot Black Eagle.
She'd been more afraid of them than him.

"So, why are they chasing you?" She leaned aside to look
over her shoulder at him. Just in time to catch the disgusted
look he shot her, one that didn't need interpretation.

She clung to the horse as it raced northward, her anxiety
increasing with their distance from the Springs and the
stones. She had to get back there to look for them. Without
them, she was afraid she'd never be able to return to her own
time, her own life.

They'd been riding for over two hours, judging by the hot
glare of the sun now almost directly overhead. Surely, he'd
stop soon to treat that shoulder wound. She squirmed in the
saddle, her full bladder protesting. If he didn't stop soon, she'd
embarrass herself.

She forced her thoughts away from her immediate problem.
She knew Black Eagle wouldn't take her back to the Springs,
not after being shot at by those Rangers. She'd have to find a
way to escape. She had a plan but before she put it in motion,
she wanted plenty of distance between her and the Rangers.
She didn't want to stumble into their camp alone.

"Is it safe to stop yet?" Desperation, fueled by the blur of
passing miles, gave an edge to her voice. Her plan wouldn't
work if they got too far from the Springs.

"Too soon," he grunted, but slowed the horse to a jarring
trot.

"I've got to stop." She pressed a hand to her abdomen. She
couldn't take much more of this. Dressed in nothing but a
swimsuit, she'd soon have a second-degree sunburn and
bloody thighs from rubbing against his saddle.

He abruptly kneed the horse off the trail and headed for a
clump of mesquite growing near a pile of boulders.

Perfect! Kris almost wilted in relief. She couldn't have
picked a better place.

He leaped off the horse, then reached up and pulled her

down beside him. She groaned when her feet hit the ground. He caught her before she could fall.

She jerked upright and stepped away from him, heat flooding her face. "I'm all right."

"Be quick." He dropped her hands and pointed to the bushes. "Our enemies may be near."

Our enemies? Kris glanced around as she moved into the bushes, stepping carefully to avoid injuring her bare feet. She hadn't seen a trace of another human being for hours. While she took care of her needs, she peered through the bushes, deciding which way to run.

"Uh, I think this is going to take a while," she called and rattled the nearest bush. She gave a low moan for effect. "I'm not feeling so good."

"Hurry, woman."

Finished, Kris bent forward to peer at him. He hadn't moved an inch. He stood with his back to her scanning the surrounding terrain, his head never still.

Now! her subconscious urged. She crept away, adrenaline giving her feet wings as she laid a false trail heading south, then circled north. She grinned, pleased with her progress. She'd hide in that clump of trees ahead and wait for dark, then head for the Springs. She should be able to reach them by morning.

She rounded the last boulder and glanced behind her, hearing no sound of pursuit. She'd made it!

Ker-thunk! She slammed into a wall and her foot came down on a large rock, bruising her instep.

"Ow!" she cried, hopping on her good foot.

"Lost?" Black Eagle asked. Arms crossed over his chest and legs wide spread, he frowned down at her. His horse, trailing behind him, whinnied. The sound, too much like a snicker, set her teeth on edge.

"Of course not," she blustered, her chin lifting as she faced him. She was beginning to really dislike that stoic Indian stance. What would he do to her? She'd read horrible stories of punishment the People inflicted on captives whose escape attempts failed. Her bravado faltered.

"I must have gotten turned around once I finished . . ." Her cheeks burned, but she tossed her braid over her shoulder and faced him squarely. Let him think embarrassment caused her flush, not frustration at having her plans so easily thwarted.

His cocked eyebrow and the grim set to his lips told her she hadn't fooled him. "We ride?" He turned away, ducking his head toward the horse, but not before she saw his lips twitch. He was laughing at her!

Enraged, Kris reacted without thinking. Reaching past him, she clapped her hands in his horse's face. "Hi-ya!" she shouted, then slapped its rump when it spun away from her.

Black Eagle calmly watched the horse go.

"He's getting away," Kris said, pointing. "Aren't you going after him?"

He gave her a dark look, lips pressed into a tight line, eyes black and forbidding. Then he whistled.

"Drat," she mumbled, remembering that he'd whistled for the horse that morning. Like a sprinter, she charged toward the trees. Could she make it? She had to get away from him! Breath rasping, she glanced over her shoulder.

The horse swung around mid-stride and headed straight for her captor. Just when she thought he'd be trampled, he leapt astride. Then that black, merciless gaze found her.

Damn! She jerked around and dashed for cover. She'd make it! She had to make it! Knees pumping, Kris ran like she'd never run before. She could no longer distinguish the pounding beat of the horse's hooves from her thundering heartbeat.

Suddenly the horse's shoulder brushed her, but Black Eagle's arm caught her before she could fall beneath its churning hooves. She screeched as he swung her off her feet and flung her over his saddle stomach first. Whoosh! The impact slammed every bit of air from her body.

"Let me go, you—you kidnapper!" she finally wheezed.

"Kid-napper?" He hoisted her upright in the saddle.

She shrugged off the arm he'd clamped around her waist and glared at him over her shoulder. "Now listen. You've kidnapped me, snatched me away from everything familiar and you won't even tell me where we're going. I'm not going to stop fighting until you give me some answers." Before he could stop her, she threw her right leg over the saddle horn and slid to the ground. "Talk, mister."

His mouth pressed into a thin line as he took a long look around them. He rode the horse into the shade of the trees she'd been trying to reach, then dismounted and sat crosslegged on the ground.

"You come?" he asked, and pointed to the ground beside him.

"Absolutely," she said, and hurried over to sit facing him. She waited, but he said nothing, just looked at her. "Well?"

"You ask question?"

She gritted her teeth. He was going to make her yank it out of him. *Men!*

"Where are we going?"

"Find my People."

"Where are they?" she asked, trying not to growl at him.

He shrugged and pointed. "Red River."

"They're camped somewhere on the Red River?" She frowned. She remembered something about the Red River, something that made her uneasy. "Why are you here?"

He pointed to the slash marks on his chest, hidden beneath his buckskin shirt. "I seek vision, speak to Great Spirit."

She shuddered at the reminder of his wounds. "You spoke to the Great Spirit?"

He nodded and pointed at her. "He send you."

"What?" she cried, but before she could think of a response to his ridiculous assertion, he cut her off.

"You strange medicine woman," he said, shaking his head as if very disappointed in her. "Why you not know these things? Your *puha* weak. I take you to war council, chiefs kill you."

"Now, just a minute, mister. I'm not a medicine woman.

That would be my grandmother. And how dare you drag me here, almost killing me in the process, then tell me I'm inadequate. Huh!" She jumped to her feet and paced in front of him.

He stood, too, watching her warily.

"You don't scare me, you know," she sneered, taking a careful step away from him as he slapped his arms over his chest. "That stoic-Indian stance doesn't do it for me. And what's puh-poo . . ."

"*Puha,*" he said, his voice infuriatingly calm. Had his lips twitched?

"Yeah. What's that stuff anyway?"

"Medicine. Power."

"You're right," she said, stopping to face him. "Mine is weak. Because I don't have any."

She waited for his answer. He just stared at her.

"Did you hear me?"

He nodded.

"Good." She gave a huge sigh, relieved to have reached an understanding. "Now, please take me back to the Springs. I've got to figure out how to get back to . . ."

"No." He took her arm and pulled her toward the horse.

"No?" She jerked her arm away from him. "What do you mean? I've got to go find the stones or I won't be able to return to my own time."

"No. You come. Tell war council how kill buffalo hunters. Chiefs listen. Then take you to sacred waters."

"Kill the buffalo hunters?" She stared at him, aghast, dates and events swirling through her brain. "You're taking me to a war council, on the Red River?"

He nodded and pulled her closer to the horse. "We hurry. Chiefs waiting."

"No," she said slowly. "No, I don't think I want to go there with you." She'd just remembered why his mention of the Red River made her nervous. That was what the government had dubbed the last ruckus with Quannah Parker: the Red River War. And she had no desire to be a part of it.

"Take me back to the Springs," she demanded.

"My People need you," he said. "Great Spirit tell me you have knowledge I seek."

Of all the things he could have said to her, that was the one thing sure to guarantee her cooperation. How could she refuse if there was the slightest possibility that she might be able to change history, to save lives, to reason with Quannah?

She stared up at Black Eagle, dread filling her, and nodded. "I'll come, but you have to promise that after the war council you'll bring me back to the Springs."

He nodded solemnly.

She only hoped the war council didn't kill her when they heard the bad news.

Duuqua swallowed a groan as the *pahoute*'s hips rocked against his manhood. Her braid swung between them, tickling his stomach, stoking the fire in his belly.

His jaw clenched. The sun slept and Brother Moon smiled in the dark sky. Soon he must make camp for the night, but first he must rid himself of these unwanted feelings.

He must not touch her, must not watch her body or smell the sun in her hair. She was *taibo*. He knew this. So why did his body continue to betray his heart? Desire had no place here. He must control his lust until he could satisfy his body's needs in other, welcoming arms.

Duuqua forced his gaze away from her. She was no simple woman. The stones in his medicine bag challenged his strength, reminding him of her powers. But how could she be both enemy and messenger to the Great Spirit?

He urged the tired horse uphill, glad to see the small grove of trees where he planned to camp for the night. He kneed the tired horse forward, wincing at the woman's low, pained cry. Her body would be stiff and sore. He would take care of her injuries later. First he must find a way to make their journey easier. He sniffed the air, then searched the horizon. His eyes narrowed and he smiled.

He leaped off the horse when it reached the trees, grabbed a loop of rope and pulled the woman off beside him. Closing his ears to her angry protests, he pushed her to the ground, then retied her hands behind her and tied her feet to her hands, pulling her body into a bow.

"You snake! You lying, cheating, piece of horse . . ." He gagged her with another strip sliced off his breechclout. She squealed against the gag and lurched onto her side.

He nodded in satisfaction. She would not be able to escape. She would be safe here and he would not be gone long.

She shook back her hair and glared at him. He ignored the accusations in her eyes, reminding himself of his People's need. Still, he felt small and mean. He leaped onto his horse and kneed it hard, praying that the Great Spirit would not send a lightning bolt to strike him dead as he rode.

He had to find her a horse. He prayed he could find her a blanket. He did not trust himself to sleep with her in his arms.

Kris struggled against the rawhide that forced her body into an arc, cursing Black Eagle. Her arms and shoulders throbbed from the strain, but she forced herself to breathe deeply, striving to stay calm. Darkness lay upon her like a thick, impenetrable quilt—threatening, smothering. Never had night seemed so heavy, so completely black.

A long, eerie howl froze her blood.

Was that a wolf? Her gaze darted from shadow to shadow. Another howl came, closer and louder. Something in the bushes moved. A shadow fell over her. Not a wolf. A man! A knife flashed in the moonlight. Her body snapped out of its forced arc. Another flash and her feet fell free. Would the next flash draw blood?

Kris cocked her leg and aimed a short, sharp thrust upward with all her remaining strength. She connected—right where it would hurt a man most.

Her attacker dropped the knife. With a deep groan, he staggered backward. Moonlight etched features drawn tight in agony as Black Eagle threw back his head and snarled.

Heart still racing, Kris scooted backward into a tree. Her breath came in frantic pants as she watched him and waited.

Duuqua clutched his knees and waited for his stomach to stop bucking like a wild pony. Sweat streamed off his face. She had begged him not to tie her but he had not listened. He should not have used the wolf howl to tell her of his return.

He picked up his knife and straightened, grunting at another wave of pain.

She arched away from him, pressing back against the tree.

"I will not hurt you." He spoke softly as if to a wounded animal. Approaching her warily, he cut her hands free, then untied the gag.

Her tongue came out, tracing her dry lips. She spat. Her eyes stared into his, wide and fearful, but he saw the fire burning deep inside. She was not finished fighting.

Yes, he grunted, the Great Spirit had chosen well. He said nothing, only picked up her foot and rubbed the angry marks left by the rawhide. Shame at her pain sickened him. In his weakness to resist the temptation of her body, he had tied her too tight. Never had he treated a woman so. He deserved the Great Spirit's anger.

"I—I didn't know it was you," she said.

His jaw clenched as she rubbed her wrists.

"At first I thought you were a wolf, then I didn't recognize you . . ."

Ashamed, he dropped her foot and went to fetch the dress and bonnet he'd taken from some white woman's wash line. His hands tightened on the dress, his fingers biting into the soft folds. He hoped the sight of her in a white woman's dress would kill the lust that burned through him. This thin cloth would keep her bare skin from touching his, but would it keep her safe when she lay asleep beside him?

His gaze traveled over her sun-fired face. Her tongue flicked out to wet her dry lips and his heart gave a dull thud. Struggling to still his desire for her, he kept his mind on her injuries. Her legs trembled in exhaustion, but the thin line of blood trickling down the inside of her leg spoke of greater, hidden injuries.

Guilt washed through him, but he shoved it aside with a flash of anger. How could he know that she would suffer so from one sun's ride? If she could not protect herself from the sun and the wind, how could she help his People?

True fear rose up to choke him. If she could not help them, and he and his warriors could not stop the white hunters, his People had no hope.

Duuqua tossed the dress to her, unable to speak past the tightness in his throat.

"What's this?" In the weak light cast by the rising moon, Kris untangled the folds of a full-length dress made of a light, airy fabric, the kind of plain, simple dress a pioneer woman would have worn—high-necked and long-sleeved. She sniffed it and the smell of soap and sunshine warmed her soul.

"Where did you get this?" she asked. "Is there a house nearby?" If there was a homestead nearby, maybe she could get some help. She tried to stand and sank back to her knees. Panic flicked through her. How could she escape if she couldn't walk?

"I take, you wear." He nudged the hem with his foot.

"Jeans would be more practical," she murmured, smoothing the dress in her lap and regretting the loss of the comfortable pair of jean shorts she'd left on the lawn at Barton Springs.

"Woman, you chatter like a squirrel." He stomped away from her. His moon-streaked hair swung around his shoulders like a gleaming robe. Kris's hand went to her own hair, finger-ing the loose, sloppy braid that lay across her shoulder in a tangled matt. She'd need a pitchfork to work out the snarls. Despair welled up inside her and her throat tightened. She was alone in the dark with a man she didn't know and couldn't trust, with no means of caring for herself and no defense against his superior strength.

Automatically, she reached for her stone. Her eyes squeezed shut at the empty gesture. Until today she hadn't realized how much she relied on it for reassurance. She pressed her hand over her breastbone, comforted by the steady beat of her own heart. Things could be worse, she reminded herself. If not for Black Eagle, she'd be dead.

Of course! she thought, straightening. He'd been there; he'd pulled her out of the water. Could he have seen the stones? Should she just come right out and ask him? Could she convince him to take her back to the Springs to find them without revealing their importance?

She lurched to her feet, clutching the dress to her chest and glared at Black Eagle, who had lit a small fire and was roasting something over it. She might as well wear the dress. She pulled it on over her swimsuit, sighing in relief when it fit, though it was a bit too long. She twisted an arm up behind her, wincing at the sharp twinge in her arms and shoulders as she tried to fasten the tiny buttons that closed the back.

Suddenly Black Eagle was there behind her. Brushing her hands away, he fastened the buttons, his fingers hot on her skin through the fabric.

"Thank you," she murmured, stepping away as soon as his hands stilled. She kept her gaze on the ground, fussing with the long skirt, hoping he wouldn't notice her shaking hands and unsteady breathing.

"Wait." He stepped close and tunneled a hand beneath her hair to lift it free of the high collar. His touch seared the sensitive skin of her neck. Electric pulses shot through her. For one interminable moment, their gazes locked. He stood so close she could see the smooth, fine grain of his skin, the slightly dilated pupils in his deep brown eyes. The warm aroma of man surrounded her. Her gaze slid to his lips and her breath froze in her chest.

What on earth was the matter with her?

She twirled away, tossing him a bright smile. "How do I look?"

The smoldering light in his eyes died. "Like a white woman." He returned to the fire.

Kris tossed her head and scowled at that broad back, then walked the cramps out of her legs, enjoying the cool swish of the full skirt against her bare legs. She strayed out of the fire's circle of light, but its cheerful, crackling flames and the heavenly aroma of roasting rabbit soon drew her back. Carefully, she lowered herself to the ground.

Finally, Black Eagle tore off a piece of the roasted rabbit and settled cross-legged near the dying fire. "Eat." His gleaming teeth sank into the meat.

Her stomach growled, urging her to forget everything but her food. Instead, mesmerized, she watched those strong teeth tear the meat to shreds. The hot juices soon made his chiseled lips gleam in the moonlight. He was so elemental, so powerful, so uninhibited. He frightened her.

Kris pulled a piece off its skewer. She took a tiny bite but couldn't swallow it. Her throat still hurt, probably from coughing up half the Springs when he'd revived her. She took a smaller bite, chewed it thoroughly and swallowed carefully, but it was no use. After only a few bites, the pain in her throat forced her to stop.

She poured some water onto her hands from his water bag, holding the ugly thing at arm's length, then quickly returning it to the small tripod where he'd hung it. She was sure it was some poor animal's stomach, or worse, its bladder. She sniffed her hands. The water seemed okay, no funny aroma. Sighing, she dampened a corner of her new dress and rubbed it over her teeth. She yearned for a real toothbrush and some aloe for her sunburn. Nothing would help her chafed legs but a long, hot bath. She sighed. She wasn't likely to find anything like that here. She whirled at a tap on her shoulder.

His eyes, deep as the blackest night, gleamed from his swarthy face. She backed away, one hand clutched over her pounding heart.

He frowned. "I no harm you, woman." He slapped a small gourd into her palm.

"What's this?" She wrenched a carved wooden plug off the top and sniffed, then gasped as the pungent stuff made her eyes water.

"Medicine." He pointed at his shoulder.

"Oh, no, please," she gasped. "I-I couldn't."

"Good medicine," he assured her. "Kill fire."

He's in pain, Kris realized, ashamed of herself. She poked at the torn tissue. Her stomach twisted and she almost lost what little food she'd eaten as she examined the bloody furrow the bullet had dug in the flesh of his shoulder.

"It needs to be cleaned," she murmured, then continued absently, "and you really should have stitches. Have you had a tetanus shot?"

"Hmm?" he grunted and she realized she was the only help he was going to get.

She gently swabbed the wound clean with a strip torn off the hem of her dress. Sucking in a deep breath, she dipped two fingers into the gourd, then dabbed the ointment on his torn flesh. Her bare toes curled into the grass. Her hands shook, knowing the pain she must be causing him, but he didn't flinch or utter a sound.

"Done." She stuck the cap back on the gourd and shoved it into his hand. Wiping her tingling fingers on the folds of her skirt, she sucked in a ragged breath.

He grunted, examining the wound as he rose.

"Come, *pahoute*." He was spreading his blanket—his only blanket—on the moon-silvered grass.

Her heart skipped a beat, then started thumping. Did he expect her to sleep with him again?

His gaze raked her, lingering on her legs as he started toward her. He wasn't smiling.

She gulped, backing away as he stalked her.

"Lie down, woman. Spread your legs."

Chapter Four

"What!" Kris backed away as Black Eagle advanced, her heart racing. How could she have been so naive? She should have tried harder to escape.

"Just because I said I'd speak to your war council doesn't mean you can take advantage of me." She whipped around and sprinted away from him. In a flash, he caught her by the arm and spun her back to face him. She stared up into his onyx eyes, eyes that closely guarded his secrets, and fought the urge to scream.

"Let me go," she demanded. She stumbled and glanced down. He'd backed her onto the blanket. "You don't want to do this."

"Sit, *pahoute*." He maintained his hold on her arm and gestured with the hand that still held the medicine gourd. "This will heal your injuries."

She froze, staring at the gourd. "M-my injuries?"

He yanked up her skirt and pointed at her thighs. "Good medicine."

"Oh!" she cried, staring at the thin line of blood on the inside of her right knee. It was okay. He just wanted to put some of that stuff on her legs.

On my legs? Is he out of his mind?

"I appreciate your concern," she said, pulling away. "Let go. I'll wash it. It'll be . . . Oh!" Her feet tangled in the blanket and she plopped onto her tender backside. Moaning, she slid onto one hip, all the fight washed out of her.

"Be still." He knelt and grabbed her leg, pulling her closer. "No hurt."

"I'd rather do it myself." She tried to scoot away from him as he uncorked the gourd, but his fingers tightened on her leg. He flipped her skirt up and dipped two fingers into the gourd.

She shoved her skirt down and tried to slide away, but he tossed her skirt in her face, then prodded her legs apart while she fought the clinging fabric. Her entire body jerked when he touched her swollen knee.

"Don't!" she cried, her heart beating so hard she thought it would explode. She glanced down and the sight of his dark fingers against her chafed skin held her mesmerized as gently smoothed the salve into the abrasions. His touch brought immediate relief, the cool salve absorbing the fire in her flesh.

His hand lifted. His fingers dipped into the pot of salve.

She tried to wriggle away, but he pushed her onto her back and held her there with one strong forearm while he worked on her thigh, murmuring something low and comforting. His hand holding the gourd settled low on her belly. Her stomach muscles jerked and bunched.

His fingers took one long, slow stroke from the inside of her calf to well above her knee and heat swept through her, centering in her loins. She bit back a gasp, trembling with the effort to control her reaction. Her hands fisted in the blanket. He was trying to help her, not seduce her, she knew, but his hand on her belly sent hot jolts skittering through her.

She refused to let herself respond to this man. She'd be leaving in just a few days and didn't want to leave any part of herself behind. Especially a chunk of her heart.

He gripped her jaw and forced her to look into his eyes.

She braced herself on rigid arms, flinching away from the concern in his gaze.

"What you fear?" He pressed a hand over her heart, frowning when she brushed his hand away. "Does my touch cause you pain?" His hand smoothed along the outside of her leg.

"No," she acknowledged grudgingly, even as she eased away

from his stroking fingers and reached for the gourd. "I'll fin-ish."

He placed a hand under her leg and lifted. She gasped at the red, puffy skin above her other knee that hadn't yet been treated. "I do," he said firmly. "Sun comes, much better."

She hesitated, searching his face. She saw no lust, no heat, only concern. She lay back. Eyes wide, she clutched a handful of blanket and stared unseeing at the stars glittering in the sky.

He bent her knee, dipped more salve from the gourd, then pressed her knee wide. She tried not to think about the skimpy, clinging fabric between him and her most private parts. She must have tensed because he once again murmured the low chant. He slowly stroked higher up her thigh and a low moan escaped her as the medicine left a cool trail.

Her eyelids fluttered. She had to stay awake, but she was so tired. She yawned. Her hold on his arm relaxed. She barely noticed as her hand slid to the blanket.

If only he could work this magic where it really counted. If only he could send her home.

Duuqua stared at the sleeping *pahoute*. He pulled her dress down. She would not like to awaken and find him staring at her long, beautiful legs. Why did she fear his touch? Did she not know that he would protect her until her message was safely delivered to the chiefs?

Any fool could have seen the fear in her eyes when he tried to help her. She had thought he wanted her, that he would force her to be his woman. Doubts tumbled through his mind, like sagebrush whipped across the plains by a strong wind.

Why had her medicine not protected her from the sun and these injuries? How could she protect his People if she could not protect herself? Why had she asked him where he was tak-ing her? Did she not know? He sighed. Maybe the new sun would bring answers to his many questions.

Duuqua lay beside her and wrapped the blanket tightly around them. She sighed as he pulled her into his arms but did not awaken. The tear-stones hummed against his chest, at rest inside his medicine bag. Afraid they would awaken her, he tossed the bag over his shoulder where it settled against his back.

A dream came swiftly—colors bright, emotions strong. From sunlight to shadow, childhood to manhood, it swept Duuqua through a stranger's life, filled with hardship, then blessed with love. Envy, bitter and vile, rose within his heart for the man's happiness as Duuqua watched him court and win his love.

Deeper and deeper the dream pulled him, until he felt the man's emotions as his own. He ached with the man, poised above the woman he loved, a captive of her warm arms and welcoming smile. Duuqua groaned as the man sank deep within her body, his own soul near bursting as their two hearts beat as one. Yet, her loving eyes reflected not a stranger's face, but his own. The image shifted and his reflection stared in horror as she stroked his cheek, her fingers dripping with blood. His blood.

Duuqua struggled free of the dream's grasp. The stones throbbed against his chest. The cold bite of the night air cleared his mind of the dream's sticky web. He turned to the *pahoute* sleeping beside him, ran a hand down her arm, glad of her warmth. He captured a handful of the dark hair flowing over his arm. She was so beautiful. He was not surprised that his mind had placed her face on the woman in the dream.

But she was the Great Spirit's messenger with much *puha*, or the Great Spirit would not have sent her to speak to the war council.

Guard her well. The familiar words of the Great Spirit whispered through his thoughts. He groaned. Woman or spirit, until she spoke to the war council, he must protect her.

What words would she speak? This day her words had been all for herself. She had not spoken of his People or the troubles they faced. Did she understand their needs, their fears?

Would she speak of war?

If she spoke of surrender and the reservation, would he be able to save her life?

Wearing her stolen finery, Kris waited beside the horse Black Eagle had also stolen as it slurped its fill from the river. An ocean of bluebells surrounded her, broken occasionally by a wedge of yellow wildflowers. The blossoms blended into the distant horizon so subtly that she couldn't tell where earth stopped and sky began.

Normally, the beautiful scene would have charmed her. Today she found it frightening. For seven days, she'd been awed by a world she'd previously seen only in pictures or movies. But it was an empty world, except for her, an abundance of wild animals, and her captor.

Every day Black Eagle pushed relentlessly forward, his sense of purpose clear from the pace he set. Up before dawn, they were always on their way only minutes after waking. They traveled steadily throughout the day, stopping only to relieve themselves and water the horses.

After that first day, he often left her resting in the shade of a lone tree while he rode ahead. The salve he nightly applied to her thighs had worked miracles. The angry redness had disappeared, leaving her with stiff muscles but no more bloody sores. She'd torn strips from the hem of her dress and wrapped her thighs to avoid further chafing.

The dress he'd stolen covered her from neck to wrist, protecting her from the sun, but her legs, exposed well above the knee where the dress hiked up as she rode, were burnt cinnamon, almost as dark as Black Eagle's.

The bonnet he'd provided along with the dress kept her face shaded, if not cool. Her throat still hurt occasionally when she talked, but that wasn't the worst of her problems. She was exhausted. Her body ached from the long hours on horseback. And she was scared.

Tonight she planned to confront Black Eagle. They had spoken very little as they traveled. He always rode several yards ahead and insisted on absolute silence while he maintained a careful surveillance. She respected his efforts to keep them both safe, but that didn't explain the distance he'd deliberately established between them. Even when they slept together at night, wrapped snugly in his blanket, he seemed miles away, and she was too weary to force a conversation. If only he could answer the questions that plagued her.

After seven days on the high plains of Texas, Kris could no longer doubt the bizarre reality of her circumstances. She'd traveled back in time. But why? Would her knowledge of Comanche history allow her to help her People?

And what was happening back home? Had time kept pace with her? Or would she return to the very instant she'd left? Would anyone have missed her yet? What if her landlord had contacted her father? She'd listed him as her only emergency contact on her lease.

She gasped. He'd go to Powahe to find her, and the two of them hated each other. He'd blame Powahe for her disappearance.

Kris drew a deep breath and tried to calm her jangling nerves. She couldn't even get a message to them, let them know she was alive.

"Camp here."

She jumped. She'd been so involved with her own thoughts, she hadn't heard him ride up.

"Already?" She glanced skyward. It was only midday. They never stopped riding before dark. Her body sagged in relief at the welcome change. Maybe now she could talk to him. But she'd waited so long, she'd begun to dread his answers. Somehow she suspected she wasn't going to like what he had to say. She didn't want to argue with him and make him wary. They'd come so far from the Springs that she'd given up on escaping. So far, he'd kept his word. She hoped he hadn't lied to her, that he'd take her back to the Springs after the war council. She knew she'd never find her way alone.

"Make camp up there." He nodded to a clearing above the river, then rode off without another word.

"Yes, sire." Kris saluted his back, rebelling at the thought of their nightly routine.

He hunted while she gathered firewood from the oak and mesquite thickets that had become increasingly sparse with each day's travel. When those had become nonexistent, she'd learned all about buffalo chips. A full bag, collected during the day, hung from her horse's flank.

Once he returned with the catch-of-the-day, he'd tend the horses while she skinned or plucked and roasted. She'd become pretty adept with the flint and steel and his knife, even if she did say so herself.

Then came the difficult part. Once he'd doused the fire, they slept together, wrapped in his only blanket. She often lay stiff as a board long into the night, listening to him breathe, dreading the horrible nightmares that brought him upright out of a sound sleep with fear and misery in his eyes. While still in horror's throes, he clutched her to him so tightly, she feared he might break her ribs, whispering hot, scorching words into her hair. She let him hold her until he calmed, but when he settled beside her, still holding her tightly, she knew he didn't sleep. The first morning she'd questioned him about the nightmares, but he'd just stared at her, tight-lipped, his dark eyes blazing.

She'd be glad to reach his People. At least there they could find another blanket.

Kris's horse lifted its head, jerking her out of her thoughts. It shook the water from its muzzle, sending sparkling droplets flying in a sudden rainbow of color. She laughed, momentarily forgetting her concerns.

Today they'd stopped near a river—not just a creek or a stream or a muddy trickle, a real river. Vivid red banks rose sharply on either side of wide, sluggish, silt-ridden waters.

Kris canted her head, considering the murky water. A week ago, she wouldn't have dipped a toe in such dirty water. This past week she'd learned not to be so picky. She listened for sounds of movement in the clearing behind her. Nothing. Black Eagle must be hunting.

She quickly hobbled her horse in a patch of waving grass, then slid down the steep bank to the water's edge. She grinned in anticipation, her fingers flying as she tugged off her bonnet and undid the tiny buttons up her back, stripping down to her swimsuit. She waded into the shallows and scrubbed the filthy dress against the stones at the river's edge. She didn't care if the rust-colored water stained her dress, as long as it rinsed away the aroma of horse.

A twig snapped on the bank behind her. She crouched and looked over her shoulder. Nothing moved. Probably just an animal foraging for its dinner.

Her legs quivered as she crouched in the shallow water. She could stand on her own now, which was more than she'd been able to do after the second and third day of riding astride. She sighed and sank into the clear, cool water. She needed a day or two of rest. A nice long shower would be great too. There was so much dust and grit between her body and this suit, her skin felt raw. She shot a nervous glance in the direction Black Eagle had ridden. Did she dare strip off the suit too and get really clean?

Clean? she scoffed. She didn't even have a bar of soap. Still . . .

She craned her neck, taking in her surroundings. She couldn't have had more· privacy in her tiny bathroom at home. Her swimming hole lay in a deep bend of the river. A dense thicket grew between her and their campsite. In a flash, she stripped off the suit, scrubbed it as best she could, then spread it over the same bush that her wet dress adorned.

Kris scuttled back into deeper water, scooping up handfuls of sand to scrub herself pink. Then, sighing her pleasure, she decided to swim a few lazy laps. She had plenty of time before Black Eagle returned.

The shallow river—barely waist deep—didn't begin to

compare to Barton Springs, but the exercise soothed her. Finally, breathing hard, she rolled onto her back and froze.

A strange man stood at the river's edge, staring at her. She crouched and slapped her arms over her chest, thankful for the murkiness of the water sloshing around her breasts. The man's gaze lifted from her breasts to her face. He smiled an evil, nasty smile. She loathed him on sight.

Of medium height and slender, he wore buckskins adorned with ridiculously long fringe at every seam. Small bells and bits of metal tied to each fringe set up a merry jingling in the slight breeze.

He must sound like a whole circus when he moves, she thought. How had he gotten so close without her hearing him? Brightly painted gourds and a stuffed bird hung from his belt, but his cheery outfit clashed with the sinister look in his small, beady eyes. Dread snaked up Kris's bare spine.

"Go away," she shouted, with a shooing motion.

He tensed and a look of absolute loathing twisted his features. His gaze fell to her breasts again and his lip curled. Hand on the hilt of his knife, he stepped into the water.

"Don't come any closer," Kris warned, scrambling away from him. Adrenalin pumped through her and she backed into shallower water, seeking better footing. She knew better than to run.

He said nothing, just kept coming.

She crouched and searched along the river's muddy bottom, her fingers closing over a good-sized rock. Heart pounding, she remained where she was, watching him advance.

One more step, mister, she mentally calculated. He took it and she sprang at him. Sprays of water blinded her as she swung the rock at his head. His hand closed over her arm, twisting cruelly. She cried out in pain and frustration, her weapon dropping from suddenly nerveless fingers. With a savage twist, he wheeled behind her and forced her arm up between them. His teeth sank into the tender curve between her neck and shoulder and iron-hard fingers clamped over a naked breast, brutally squeezing.

Kris's scream of rage and pain ricocheted off the silent, red banks.

Anger heated Duuqua's blood when he returned from hunting to a cold camp. No fire. No woman. Had she tried to escape again? His jaw clenched. This time when he found her, he would tie her to a tree. A woman's scream and the sound of splashing water interrupted his plans for the troublesome *pahoute*. Something was wrong.

He ran through the long grass above the river and paused on the bluff. Fury kindled a fire in him at the sight of her naked in the arms of a man whose hand clawed at her breast and whose teeth were sunk into her shoulder. Her second scream echoed the horrifying sounds in his nightmares. The man's head lifted and Duuqua snarled, enraged. Isatai. He should have known the slimy medicine man would be watching for him, lying in wait to steal whatever he could and call it his.

"Get away from her," Duuqua bellowed, sickened by the sight of the man's hands on her. He lunged down the bank and into the river.

Isatai's hand released her breast. The *pahoute* swung on him, her fists and feet a blur. He backhanded her, sending her flying. Her cry of pain as she landed on her back in the shallows sent blood-red fury pounding through Duuqua.

"*A-he!*" Isatai shouted, whirling to face him. "I claim the woman. She will be my slave."

"She belongs to me." Duuqua cursed the lie that fell from his mouth, knowing it was the only way he could protect her. Isatai would not hear the truth of this woman until Duuqua spoke to the chiefs in war council. This snake would see her as a rival and try to harm her.

"You may take her," he said as he drew his knife and

crouched in challenge, tossing the knife from hand to hand. "If you kill me first." He smiled grimly as Isatai cast one long, hot look at the woman. His gaze cooled as it followed Duuqua's flashing blade.

He spread his hands wide and eased past Duuqua, offering no challenge, his eyes never leaving the knife.

"*Pabi*," Duuqua sneered, letting him pass untouched. Only an elder sister would give up such a prize without a fight.

He turned back to the *pahoute*. Rage burned again at the angry red marks Isatai had left on her body. His fists clenched. Isatai would pay for every bruise.

"There is no fire, woman." Duuqua watched her eyes kindle, knowing how much she hated gathering chips and building fires. She could not know he spoke for Isatai's ears, to give truth to the lie that he hoped would keep her safe from the medicine man's tricks.

"Watch out!" she cried, staring past his shoulder.

Duuqua spun at her warning, leaping to one side. A knife blade shot sparks from the sun as it arced toward his back. He caught the arm that aimed it and wrenched it aside.

"You have grown bold while I have been gone seeking visions, little worm," Duuqua hissed. He grimaced, surprised at Isatai's strength. Sweat beaded his face and ran down his chest as he slowly twisted Isatai's arm. Duuqua squeezed Isatai's wrist until the knife fell from his numb fingers. The smaller man stumbled, then fell to one knee.

Duuqua kicked him in the chest, knocking him backward, out of the water. "Go, before I decide to kill you."

Isatai glared, his eyes glowing with hatred before he turned and scrambled up the bank. Duuqua grimaced at the jangling noise of his passing. His stomach tightened. In the past Isatai had worked his tricks in the shadows. Duuqua frowned. Snakes that grew this bold must be killed. But this snake had the favor of the chief.

Ever since Isatai's uncle's death at the hands of white men, Isatai's hatred had festered like a stinking wound. Fatherless, and now without his uncle's aid, Isatai would have trouble acquiring enough horses to buy himself a wife and a place in the tribe. Had his hatred grown to include his own people? Before leaving on his vision quest, Duuqua had seen that too many of the People listened to Isatai's lies. He should have known Isatai would not rest while he was gone.

His back pricked at a sound in the bushes above him. So, the snake had not yet returned to his People's nearby camp. Duuqua's hand slid to his sheathed knife. He would not sleep this night. He must protect the woman.

She stumbled into deeper water and fell to her knees. Anger burned through Duuqua and the need to hunt down Isatai warred with the woman's needs. There were no women here to help her. He must get her back to camp. He would deal with Isatai later. Let the snake watch for his coming.

He knelt beside her and began cleaning the bite on her neck. Isatai's teeth had not broken her skin, but he had left his mark. Duuqua gritted his teeth, his anger so hot he could not speak. She held both arms tight over her chest, her eyes closed. He leaned over her shoulder and saw a red streak where Isatai's finger had marked the pale skin of her breast.

"Come," he said, helping her to her feet, offering her the wet dress. She looked at him, but didn't see him. The light in her eyes had dimmed. She snatched the dress out of his hands and held it to her chest.

He lifted her into his arms, cursing under his breath when he felt her shaking. Still holding her, he tore his blanket off the horse, then stood her before him and rubbed her all over, avoiding her new wounds. Then he wrapped her in the blanket and laid her on a patch of grass. Unable to watch her suffering, he started a fire and made a drink from a pouch of bark and herbs that old Tabenanika had given him to take the heat from his wounds.

"Here." He lifted her only enough to drink the medicine. "Make pain go."

She drank, then looked up at him. Her eyes saw his face. "Thank you," she said, low and quiet, then drank more.

He laid her down again and knelt beside her. "He pay. I promise you."

"You know him?" Her eyes had gone wide; she pulled the blanket closer. "He's one of your People?"

He scowled. How to say Isatai in the white tongue? "He Rear End Of A Wolf, or Coyote Droppings."

"Coyote Droppings?" She frowned at him and struggled up on one elbow. "But all the books say he was kind, that he eased the People's transition."

"Kind? What this word, *books?*" For the first time, he wished he had listened when Chikoba taught him and Quannah the hated white tongue. He would ask Chikoba to teach him more so he could speak with this woman.

"Just a word. It's not important." She looked away from him. He knew she lied, but he would not challenge her now.

"I need to dress," she said, and struggled to sit upright. "This blanket's itchy." She scratched the arm pressed over her injured breast.

"No," he said, pressing her flat. "Dress wet. Rest."

She pushed his arm away. "I'm okay now. That man isn't going to ruin my day. Besides, I've got to find my suit." She glanced around the clearing. It must still be down at the river."

"I find. You no move." He waited for her to nod before leaving.

Kris watched him go and couldn't help smiling. Her smile faded when he returned with the suit dangling from one hand. How was she going to get it on in broad daylight with him hovering?

It was her own fault she'd been hurt. She should never have taken such a chance—stripping down to the skin in the wild. What had she been thinking? She'd been lucky Black Eagle had been close by. She shuddered, knowing exactly what would have happened.

Coyote Droppings, she mused, *Quannah's self-proclaimed Messiah.*

With a little judicious blanket juggling, she managed to get into her suit; then she draped the blanket over her shoulders while her dress dried. Black Eagle insisted on a closer look at the bite on her neck. She didn't try to resist, though she feared his reaction. The handprint over her breast was going to make an ugly bruise, but the bite throbbed with a life of its own.

"Thank you," she said, tensing as his fingers probed the bite. He said nothing as he applied the pungent salve. It stung the tender skin at first, then the throbbing eased. She trembled at the anger in his eyes. "Will the dress cover it?"

"Yes." He touched the upper slope of her breast.

Startled, she glanced down. His finger rested lightly at the tip of a blue mark that extended below her suit toward her breast.

She looked up and his gaze settled on her face. His finger lifted to gently touch her lips, the tip of her nose. Then he traced an eyebrow. A fire kindled in his eyes and was quickly extinguished.

He started to pull away, but she caught his other hand, put it on her waist, then lifted onto tiptoes and pressed her lips to his.

She hadn't planned to do this, but the instant her lips touched his, she knew she'd been fooling herself. She'd wanted to do it since that first morning, when she'd opened her eyes and found herself wrapped in his arms.

He groaned and both arms closed around her as his body pulled her into his heat. She melted against him with a gasp of need. His tongue swept deep and she met it, turning her head to give him better access, then turning again to taste more of him.

"No!" he yanked away, staring at her. "*Pahoute*. Great Spirit's messenger."

"But I'm not," she said, and reached for him.

He backed away, shaking his head. "No."

Helpless to stop him, she watched him leap onto his horse and gallop away. She couldn't remember ever being so embarrassed. How could she have made a mistake like that? She'd seen the heat in his eyes just before she kissed him. And he'd kissed her back, but only after she'd practically climbed him.

She held her face in her hands and shook her head. If she'd been thinking, she wouldn't have grabbed him. She couldn't afford to alienate him. She knew what lay ahead for the Comanche, and half-bloods, or "breeds," were not welcome among the white people of this time. She had no place here. She had to find a way home and Black Eagle was her best hope.

"Why did you kidnap me, Black Eagle?"

"Kidnap?" Duuqua choked on his last bite of rabbit. "What this word mean?"

"Am I your captive?"

Each word that came from her mouth reminded him of her white blood. He searched her face and saw little to mark her as his enemy, but she was not like the women he knew. Black wings of hair marked her brows and long, black lashes framed her soft brown eyes. He liked these differences and others as well, like the shining black bush of hair at the top of her thighs. But it troubled him that he found her more beautiful than the Comanche women he knew. He must remember her white blood and kill his desire for her. It would not please the Great Spirit.

"Answer me, please," she begged as she tried to pull the snarls out of her long hair.

"I hear you, *pahoute*." The hated taste of the white man's words in his mouth closed his ears to the plea in her voice, his eyes to the trembling of her fingers. Crossing his arms over his chest, he waited, knowing she was not through asking questions. Women could talk the life from a stone. "What you want know?"

"My name is Kris Baldwin." Her angry words, like small

stones, bounced off his chest. Annoying, but not painful. "Not *pahoute*, not woman, just plain Kris Baldwin. Can't you call me Kris?"

He shrugged. What difference did it make? She knew when he spoke that he was talking to her. Did she think he talked to his horse?

She spoke again, but he could no longer listen. Her white words stirred his blood to anger. He left to check on his horses. He heard her surprised cry, felt her eyes burning into his back, but he did not stop.

He did not understand her. She did not respect him as a woman should. She grumbled if he rested while she cooked their meat. She asked stupid questions. Why did her *puha* not give her the answers to these questions? Why had she kissed him? How could he share his blanket with her tonight?

He stayed with his horses until she called, wanting to be close in case Isatai had hidden nearby. He ate what she cooked, but when darkness came she did not join him within his blanket. With sharp, angry movements, she lay on the other side of the fire, her back to him. She put a parfleche beneath her head and her dress was her blanket.

Snug and warm in his blanket, Duuqua lay and watched her from across the fire through eyes open only a crack. She shivered and twitched at every little noise. Smoke from the fire drifted over her, making her cough. Finally, well into the night, she sat up and faced him across the dying fire, tossing her tangled hair over her shoulder.

Had her anger cooled? If she now wished to share his blanket, he would not offer it. She would have to come to him. Blood racing, jaw tense, he waited for her to speak.

"Why are you called Black Eagle?"

He raised himself up on one elbow. He would teach this woman to respect him. "I fall upon enemies like eagle. They know only darkness."

Her wide eyes and long shiver should have pleased him. Why then did he feel small and mean? When she said nothing, only lay down and turned her back to him, he gritted his teeth and stared at her back, hoping that his words kept her awake.

Taibo and Comanche. Both this *pahoute* and his adopted brother bore mixed blood. Was that why the Great Spirit had sent her to speak to the war council? Were her words meant for Quannah's ears? If so, would Quannah hear her or kill her?

He must speak to the chiefs, share with them his powerful vision. He hoped his words would save her life. If not . . . His jaw clenched and his hand closed over the handle of his knife. He would keep his promise to the Great Spirit. He would protect her with his life.

The stones in his medicine bag hummed gently. He lifted the bag, feeling their weight. Should he tell the war council about them, about the power he believed they possessed? As if in answer to his question, the stones jumped into a faster beat.

Such power must be held sacred, Duuqua decided. *Men would kill for it.*

Above all, he must keep the stones hidden from the woman.

Settling deeper into his blanket, Duuqua watched the *pahoute* squirm on the hard ground. Without her in his arms, would he sleep without waking in the clutches of the nightmare? Would the Great Spirit punish him for letting her sleep alone and cold? He sniffed. She had chosen to sleep alone and cold.

Let the heat of her anger warm her this night.

"Grandmother?" Kris jerked awake, searching the clearing for the beloved woman whose voice had floated through her dreams. She threw off the damp dress that had tangled about her shoulders and basked in the soft, early morning light that slowly erased the night's chill. She sat up cross-legged, breathing deeply. She was alone, but a soft breeze whispered through the grass, circling her, caressing her.

"Kaku," the voice called, and Kris sighed. Tears sprang to

her eyes at the sound of her nickname. She closed her eyes, listening with her heart as Powahe had taught her. Her hand closed in a fist over her breastbone, where her stone used to hang.

"Beware." The voice grew weaker with each word. "Beware, beware . . ."

Kris shook off the eerie sensation. She'd been dreaming of her grandmother, worrying about what her father would do or say if he thought Powahe was responsible for Kris's disappearance. That must be why she'd imagined Powahe's voice.

She rose and shook out the dress, a sorry excuse for a blanket, still damp and now heavy with dew. Better get a fire going, she decided, before His Majesty got back from wherever he'd disappeared to and demanded breakfast. Maybe today they'd finally reach the Kwerherehnuh.

While struggling to fall asleep last night, she'd decided to try to get to the chief before Black Eagle did. If she could convince him that Black Eagle was crazy, that she couldn't possibly be a messenger from the Great Spirit, the chief would be happy to send her back to the Springs. But she had to get to the man first.

Suddenly sensing she was no longer alone, Kris spun.

"Oh, you scared me," she sighed on a relieved breath, as Black Eagle entered the clearing. They'd both been tiptoeing around each other, pretending that kiss never happened. Kris snorted. Fine with her. Saved her the trouble of apologizing.

As usual this morning, he wore nothing but his breechclout. Water droplets sparkled on his skin, reflecting the early morning light. His hair, unbraided and slicked back, glistened with blue highlights. He stared at her for several long moments, wary and expectant, freezing her where she stood. His distrust, a tangible thing, made her long to cry out her innocence. What crime had she committed?

"What's going to happen when we get to the Kwerherehnuh?"

He scowled and a muscle jumped in his jaw. "Wash." He

jerked his head over his shoulder, indicating the river sparkling in the early morning sun.

Her chin rose as swiftly as her temper. "I bathed last night." When he just stared at her, she repeated her question. "What's going to happen?"

A disgusted grunt was her only answer as he turned away.

"What do you want from me?" She caught his arm and made him look at her.

"Only you can answer your questions, *pahoute*." He pulled his arm free and walked away without a backward glance. "You have all the answers."

"Damn!" Fuming, she turned and stomped down the hill straight into the river. Only when she stood in the center did she realize she was still holding her dress.

"Damn!" Now she'd have to ride in a wet dress. She threw it onto the bank and started swimming. What was wrong with her? She never swore. She never acted like a spoiled brat. She couldn't let that man get to her. She swam until the fury drained out of her. Finally, convinced she could be reasonable and calm, she wrung the water out of her dress and trudged back to camp.

Black Eagle glanced up, his fingers poised over the red circles he was drawing around his chest wounds. He frowned at the wet dress flung over her arm, but she hardly noticed. She couldn't quit staring. He looked like a fiend from hell. He'd painted his face and torso white, but black circles swallowed his eyes, creating deep mysterious caverns.

Proudly, he stood and faced her. Had he sensed her uneasiness? "Come." He scooped a fingerful of black paint from a small gourd. "I paint you. Take you to my People."

He wanted to paint her? Like that? Kris recoiled as he reached out to touch her face with the paint. "No, thank you."

He stepped closer, looming over her. "Paint protect you."

"From what?" She scoffed, standing firm before him, though unnerved by his frightening appearance. "I don't need protection from my own people."

He stared into her eyes for several long, silent seconds, then carefully returned the glob of paint to its small wooden container. "It will be as you say."

His words, so ominous-sounding, sent chills racing up her spine. What did he mean? Was he leaving her? Warily, she watched him gather up his bags.

"What's going on? Why all the paint? And why aren't you in a hurry to get going?" She gestured at the horses, still hobbled several yards away and contentedly munching the long grass.

"We ride no more."

"You mean we're here?" she cried, excitement and alarm rushing through her. "Where are your People?"

"Close."

Her thoughts churning, Kris yanked the wet dress over her head, shivering at its cold, clammy glide down her body. Close! They were close! She had to put her plan into action, now. "Are you sure? I haven't seen anything."

He snorted, just as she'd hoped he would.

"Show me," she urged, not having to feign the excitement in her voice.

"Over hill." He pointed. "You see soon."

She ignored him and ran to the edge of camp, closer to the horses. He came after her and caught her arm. "Stay."

"Oh, I will," she assured him, shaking off his restraining arm and turning to face him. "Just tell me one thing before we leave."

He studied her, head cocked to one side, then gave a sharp nod. "Speak."

"What are you going to tell your chief about me?"

"Truth."

"Your truth, or what I've been trying to get through your head for the last seven days?"

"I tell him you Great Spirit's messenger."

"I was afraid you'd say that." She sighed.

"Truth!"

"Who knows? You came up with that crazy notion. There's no telling what else you could dream up. You might even say that I was sent here to be with you." She snorted, slapped her fists onto her hips and glared into his face.

"I no lie to chief."

"That presents a problem," she said, smiling as she stood nose-to-nose with him. "I can't let you do it."

Still smiling, she stomped on his instep, then jabbed him in the stomach with her elbow, hit him in the nose with the heel of her hand and kneed him in the groin. Scrunched into a ball, struggling to breathe, he couldn't stop her when she stole his knife, then ran to her horse and cut its hobbles.

Grabbing a handful of mane, she pulled herself astride, then kneed the horse around, feeling a twinge of regret for Black Eagle's pain. Had she hurt him badly? He still hadn't moved.

She couldn't wait! She had to get to the chief before he did.

"Wait," he gasped, as she dug her heels into the horse's flanks. "No go! I must protect you."

"I can take care of myself," she shouted and urged the horse into a ground-devouring lope.

When she pulled up at the top of the first hill, her breath caught in her throat. Only a couple of miles away, a rusty ribbon of river dissected the grass of the plains. Hundreds of tipis lined the far bank, glowing softly in the early morning light. The smell of meat cooking drifted on the breeze as she cantered down the hill. As she galloped closer, she saw people moving between the tipis. Women crouched at the river's edge while children scampered nearby.

A dog's sharp yip alerted the camp to her presence. On this side of the river, a huge herd of horses grazed contentedly. Kris's mount whinnied and danced beneath her as she approached the river. She clutched its mane, praying it wouldn't toss her off as it picked its way across.

She'd never seen so many tipis in one place. So often she'd heard old people speak of halcyon scenes such as this and the sorrow in their voices brought tears to the eyes of grown men. No wonder they clung to their memories.

Suddenly eager to experience that life firsthand, she urged her horse up the bank.

She jerked around at the pounding beat of hooves behind her. Black Eagle was coming! She kicked the horse into its fastest gait and leaned into every stride.

"Run!" she cried. "Don't let him catch me now." She had to get to the chief first. She didn't have a message for these people. Only the chief could keep her safe.

Eerie, keening cries shattered the peaceful morning as mounted warriors erupted from all over the camp. Quickly merging into a galloping mob, they raced toward Kris. Unbound, their black hair streamed behind them in the wind; their feathers waved as they raced to her aid.

She glanced back. Black Eagle was closing on her. She rode straight for the warriors, ignoring Black Eagle's cries from behind her. They came at her, fast and furious, not even slowing as they got close. Their mouths gaped wide in mindless screeching. Alarm skittered up her spine. She slowed her horse to a trot, afraid they were going to ride her down. At the very last second, they split and circled her. She hooted in delight at the smooth maneuver which kept Black Eagle from recapturing her.

Her horse pranced beneath her, tossing its head, going nowhere. The warriors galloped around her, weaving in an intricate, double circle. Her excitement died. Their eyes were black pits of hatred that stole the light from the sky and sent terror snaking through her soul.

A rope settled over her head with a seething hiss. It bit into her arms, jerked tight, yanked her off her horse. As if the ground heaved upward, she felt herself falling. The impact slammed the air from her lungs, cutting her scream short.

Dear God, how could she have been so stupid? She hadn't escaped to safety.

She'd ridden straight into hell.

Chapter Five

The *pahoute*'s scream pierced Duuqua's heart like an enemy lance. He tried to work his horse through the warriors surrounding her, but they rode knee-to-knee and kept him out.

"Do not harm her," he shouted, but he could not be heard over the warriors' excited cries.

Someone rode behind him, but Duuqua could not tear his eyes from the *pahoute* being dragged into camp. Suddenly, he was hit. He reeled in the saddle as white-hot pain burst behind his eyes. He hit the ground face first.

Before the darkness swallowed him, he heard the high tinkle of tiny bells and a triumphant laugh. Isatai.

Duuqua's frustrated cry roared through the threatening darkness. He could not fail! He must protect the *pahoute*. If she fell into Isatai's hands, the Great Spirit's message would never reach the war council.

A hard foot slammed into Kris's hip, stopping her face down in dirt. The rope fell slack. She groaned and lay still, holding her breath as she waited for the wave of pain soon to come. Fear and anger warred for dominance. And regret. How could she have been so stupid? She should have known the warriors would see her as a threat.

She opened her eyes. Surprised to find the pain manageable, she shook her head and blinked away the dirt stuck in her lashes, then spit it from her mouth. Thank God she'd been close to camp when they'd roped her.

A hideous noise filled the air. She stiffened, near choking on her fear—sharp and metallic as bile. What would they do to her now? Could Black Eagle get her out of this? Would he even try, after what she'd just done to him?

Something sharp jabbed her in the side. She jerked away with a surprised cry and struggled to her feet. A screaming horde of angry women armed with pointed sticks and clubs surrounded her. They attacked, prodding and jabbing, dancing close to kick her. She staggered and fell to one knee. A cry of outrage caught in her fear-clenched throat. Her attackers shrieked in triumph and became bolder.

Infuriated by their abuse, Kris grabbed the rope still hanging about her waist and whipped it at them, driving them back.

"*Haint!*" she cried in their language, trying to reach through their hatred. "I'm a friend." But the fiends kept dancing around her, darting forward to stab at her, keeping her spinning in a futile effort to avoid their blows. She flinched when they connected, but refused them the satisfaction of hearing her cry out.

The circle widened and Kris realized they were playing with her. They could have killed her at any time, if they'd really wanted to. What were they waiting for?

Dropping the rope, she raised her hands in surrender, sure that they would close around her and beat her to a bloody pulp. To her amazement, the circle parted. The fleeting whisper of hope in her heart died as Kris faced an old crone holding a burning branch. The woman's lips parted in an evil, toothless grin.

"Get away," Kris ordered, taking a careful step back only to be seized from behind. The crone cackled as strong hands wrenched Kris's arms back, holding her fast. She cried out in agony. Suddenly, the crowd fell silent. A path opened through them and a man appeared.

Him! The monster who had attacked her at the river. She should have known she hadn't seen the last of him. His buckskins jingled in merry counterpoint to his sinister leer. Kris couldn't remember his name, only the insult Black Eagle had tossed after him at his less than courageous departure.

"*Pabi,*" she sneered and spit on him. The mob gasped as one.

Fury twisted his features. His lips curled in a parody of a smile, then he slapped her. Kris could barely hear the mob's jeers over the ringing in her ears. He stepped close, rattling a gourd and staring into her eyes like a snake mesmerizing its prey. He gave a shriek and began an eerie chant. The crowd matched it, quickly picking up his rhythm.

A knife appeared in his hand, though Kris hadn't seen his hand move. She stared at the huge blade, dazzled by the sun glinting off its honed edge. She glared at him. He didn't fool her, this little rooster of a man. Everything he did was for effect.

"What are you waiting for?" she challenged. Her knees trembled, but she held perfectly still, refusing to fuel the frenzy with her fear.

His eyes widened and she detected a glimmer of curiosity. Then, like a hood sliding over a snake's hissing head, his eyes cooled.

Her breath congealed as he laid the flat of the blade against her cheek, then trailed it down her neck. Slicing away her dress, it settled into her cleavage. Kris shuddered.

He snickered. Her gaze flashed up to find his eyes smoldering, their black, soulless pits lit only by a tiny prick of red, dead center, as if the fires of hell itself burned inside him. She sucked in a deep breath as those fires flared brighter. The knife turned. With one swift stroke he severed her dress and the swimsuit beneath it to her waist without shedding a single drop of blood.

The fabric snapped wide and her breasts burst free. "Not bad," she said, giving him a nod. To the crowd, she added, "Nothing you haven't all seen before." She kept her head high, trying to catch the women's eyes. Many dropped their gazes, looked away muttering, "*Pasa.*"

"What's next?" she asked Coyote Droppings, and smiled.

The brute behind her gave a high, ululating cry. The men in the crowd echoed it and lurched forward, pushing the women aside.

They quickly stripped off her ruined clothes and slammed her to her back, knocking her breathless. They pulled her arms taut, yanked her legs wide and staked her down. The men's yipping screams grew to a fever pitch.

"No!" she screeched, bucking against her bonds. "I'm Nemene, damn it! I'm Comanche!"

The old crone laughed gleefully and thrust the burning torch at her face.

"No!" Kris twisted away as the sizzling wood loomed closer. Coyote Droppings danced beside her, chanting. Another man crouched between her thighs.

Kris lunged beneath him, tossing and twisting, but the crackling, fiery branch moved closer, limiting her movements. The man poised himself to penetrate and grunted at the old woman. Kris's very soul blanched. They intended to rape and burn her—simultaneously. Terror erupted from her in a single word.

"Duuqua!"

Before her lips closed, the branch flew out of the hag's hand, kicked by a sure foot. The man between her legs was flung aside. A shadow fell over her and a familiar voice—loud and angry—sent the crowd scurrying back. A blessed silence fell.

Like a rag doll without its stuffing, Kris sagged as Black Eagle crouched over her, holding back the threatening crowd with just his knife. Tears of relief started in her eyes, but she furiously blinked them back.

"Where the hell have you been?"

"You know my name!"

Black Eagle scowled down at the *pahoute*, his heart still thundering. He hardly heard his own words for the noise it made in his ears. His People had almost hurt her, raped her. The *pahoute* deserved the sting of the women's taunts for fleeing him, but the Great Spirit would not forgive his messenger being raped or burned. If he had not arrived when he did . . .

A chill spread through him. He had brought her here to help his People, not seal their fate.

"What?" she cried, staring at him as if he'd grown another head. "Cut me loose!"

"Quiet, woman," he warned, glancing warily at the angry mob. His arms swung over her, his knife flashing from hand to hand, threatening her attackers. He must protect her, even from her own stupidity. He now knew she was a true medicine woman. She had screamed his Comanche name. Never had he spoken it to her. Only through her *puha* could she have known it.

"Where were you?" she demanded, again. "Why didn't you stop them sooner?"

He looked away, her words starting a fire in his cheeks. Her eyes widened as she saw the fresh blood on his neck and shoulder. "You're hurt."

He cut the thong on her left wrist. "Come, I will take you to someone who can keep you safe."

"What happened? I didn't do that, did I?" She tried to get a better look at the back of his head.

"Hit from behind." The heat in his face burned brighter. He freed her other wrist, and looked away as she groaned and pulled her arms over her breasts. She sighed as he freed her legs. Swiftly, she tucked them close to her body. He waited, letting her move slowly though he wanted to get her to safety. He glared at the grumbling crowd still circling them, for the first time feeling less than proud of his People.

"Go back to your homes," he called to them in their tongue. "There is nothing here for you to see."

"Tell me again why you brought me here," she asked, accepting his help to stand.

"My People need your wisdom. The Great Spirit sent you to protect them. Do not hate them. Much anger burns in their hearts for the white man. Soon, you love them as I do. Come, I take you to the chief."

He would give her to Quannah. He had failed the Great Spirit. His doubts had almost killed her.

"Where are you taking me?" Kris's body protested each jarring step as she stumbled along behind Black Eagle, dodging yapping dogs, wincing when she stepped on sharp bones and debris. As Black Eagle stopped before a huge tipi, she clutched the severed edges of her dress together, struggling to conceal her nakedness.

"*Ehaitsma*," he called and rattled a bunch of bones and sticks tied beside the door. At an answering call from within, he shoved her into the huge tipi ahead of him with a hand splayed across her buttock.

Kris squawked and swatted away his offensive hand. She blinked in the dim light inside the tipi, straining to see. Somewhere in this musty clutter there had to be a blanket. With a glad cry, she spotted one, snatched it up and swept it around her. The acrid stench of old woodsmoke and unwashed bodies rose from the coarse weave to sting her eyes. She almost threw the stinky thing back, but another odor hit her nostrils. A heavy, musky scent. Prickles of awareness danced up her spine. She froze and searched the shadows.

A man lay in a pile of furs across the tipi. Kris's eyes widened as he tossed aside a fur and rose. In the deep shadows, he seemed immense—tall, broad, and rigid with anger. And it seemed to be directed at her. Most of his face lay in shadow, but his black eyes bored into hers. Her gaze skittered downward as he secured a breechclout over his erect, glistening manhood. She gasped and tried to duck back outside.

Black Eagle caught her arm.

"This isn't a good time to visit," she hissed out of the corner of her mouth.

"Stay, *pahoute*," Black Eagle warned her, his jaw clenching as something moved in the pile of robes. Black Eagle's jaw clenched.

Her gaze collided with the scalding stare of a naked woman lying amid the mound of furs. The woman stretched sinuously, her liquid chocolate gaze settling on Black Eagle. Her legs opened and she slid her fingers over the swollen lips of her womanhood and smiled.

Coolly ignoring the woman, Black Eagle returned his attention to the man, speaking rapidly in Comanche and gesturing at Kris.

Laughing low in her throat, the woman toyed with herself as she listened. Shame and embarrassment scorching her cheeks, Kris looked away only to encounter the other man's heated stare.

His black gaze scorched the high curves of her breasts, visible above the dirty blanket, then ranged lower. Mortified, Kris clutched the blanket closer.

Abruptly, Black Eagle stopped speaking and followed the man's stare. Lips pressed tight, he stepped between him and Kris.

She sagged in relief. With every fiber of her being, she longed to run from the tangible undercurrents between the other three occupants of the tipi.

Black Eagle barked something in Comanche and jerked his head at the woman lounging on the furs.

"Kiyani." The other man gave a sharp nod toward the entrance.

The woman glared, but slid sensuously into her skirt and loose-fitting top, her eyes never leaving Black Eagle. She paused beside him, bumping Kris out of her way with a sharp thrust of her hip. Kris retreated in disgust as the woman ran a hand up Black Eagle's naked thigh.

Face set, Black Eagle stared over the woman's head at the other man, whose features seemed to tighten. With a deft dip of the wrist, the woman's fingers slipped inside his breechclout. His chest lifted on a swiftly indrawn breath. The woman's greedy smile and low, sultry laugh rang in Kris's ears.

The muscle jerking in his jaw told Kris he didn't appreciate being publicly fondled. So why didn't he stop her? Why did he just stand there, his gaze locked with the other man's while the woman made free with his body?

Outraged, Kris yanked the woman's hand away, shoved her at the exit flap and, with a foot strategically placed against her broad butt, sent the slut flying headfirst out of the tipi.

"And stay out, slut!" she called after her.

The other man chuckled as if at some outrageous joke. The muscles flexed in Black Eagle's jaw, but he didn't look at her. Kris turned her back on both men, shutting out the angry screeching outside the tipi. She had a feeling she hadn't seen the last of the slut.

So, her father hadn't lied about the Comanche's lustful nature. *You must fight it, Kris. It's in your blood.* She shuddered as his warning words rang with a clarity they'd previously lacked.

I'm not like them, she told herself. *Especially not her.* The denial became a litany in her head, drowning out Black Eagle's voice as he spoke to the other man.

Determined to think of something else, she examined the tipi. It was huge, probably more than twenty-five feet across at its widest point. Curious, she touched the tipi wall, surprised to find it was made of hides. Buffalo hide. Quickly she counted twenty hides. Her mouth fell open as she remembered the hundreds of tipis surrounding this one. The sheer number of hides necessary for their creation staggered her. No wonder the People despised the buffalo hunters.

Her gaze soared up the lodge poles and she clutched her throat, nearly gagging at the many brightly painted scalps dancing in the escaping smoke.

Sickened, she gaped at the man half-heartedly listening to Black Eagle. Who was this savage brute? The man's black gaze followed her movements with a searing heat that made her pulse pound in her ears.

"Quannah." Black Eagle shot an exasperated glance over his shoulder in her direction.

Quannah? Kris stared at the man's shadowed face as everything else receded into oblivion. *Quannah Parker?* Could it really be he, the last great chief of the Comanche, the last chief to surrender and move onto the reservation?

He certainly carried himself arrogantly enough, his physique impressive, his body lean but well-muscled. He flashed her a smile, aware of her scrutiny.

She groaned. Oh, God, she'd seen his . . . She clutched a hand over her eyes. She'd just ogled her great-great-whatever grandfather!

He stepped closer, passing through a shaft of sunlight, and she could no longer deny the truth. It was he! She recognized him from the pictures her grandmother had shown her. Revered by the remnant of the Comanche nation, he had fought like a demon, driven by bitter hatred for the white men who had kidnapped his mother and little sister. Their deaths as captives of his mother's white relatives had only fueled his hatred. But something had changed his mind. Historians couldn't account for his change of heart. They still couldn't understand why he'd surrendered, moved his people onto the reservation, then guided them through the terrible transition from their free-ranging lifestyle into the humiliation of reservation life.

How she hated him! Her father had used him as an example of what *not* to be, drumming disgust for the man into her heart. She hated the very mention of his name.

"Oh, Lord," Kris cried, backing away from both men. "How can this be possible? What kind of madness is this? You're dead!"

"Dead?" Quannah thumped his chest. "Heart still beats. Not dead."

Kris stared into his furious face, knowing she walked a fine line. His temper was famous—even in her time. "Just tell me one thing," she implored, and took a deep, sustaining breath.

"Why?" She glared at Black Eagle, gratified to see him recoil. "Why have you done this to me? What did I ever do to you? Why didn't you just leave me where you found me?"

Heart racing, feeling like she was teetering on the edge of

an abyss, she squeezed her eyes shut, frantically trying to control the hysteria, only to confront the memory of the dark, icy waters of Barton Springs. Her horror mounted as she relived the drag of the current, the shock of awakening in Black Eagle's arms. Scenes from the last week flashed through her brain: the startling aberrations in his dress, his behavior; the very landscape that had made her more and more uneasy with each passing day.

The absolute reality of her situation penetrated with a horrendous thud that took her stomach clear to the floor then back up again to lodge somewhere in her throat. Denial exploded inside her.

"No!" She launched herself at Quannah, scratching, clawing and sobbing. "This isn't real! It can't be happening to me!"

Black Eagle pulled her off him.

"It's not true," Kris screamed as she fought Black Eagle's hold. "It's a dream, a lie."

Quannah was shouting, but Kris barely heard him as she sagged against Black Eagle. Her mind had gone numb. She couldn't seem to make it work, even when Quannah yanked his blanket off her and shoved her out of his tipi.

Once again, she found herself facing a sea of angry faces. Numb with fear, shaking in reaction, she turned her back to them, clutching her dress closed. Warily, she watched them over her shoulder, expecting them to attack her again. They stayed put, glaring at her, more interested in eavesdropping on the two men shouting at each other inside the tipi.

Kris studied them—their clothing, their hair, their faces, the naked children hanging onto their mothers' buckskin-clad legs. She absorbed the minute details, as if her conscious mind was determined to convince her once and for all. Besides the obvious, something was different here, different from the homes of the People she'd visited with her grandmother. It wasn't tangible, more of a feeling.

The realization came like a blow to the chest, quieting her clamoring brain. It wasn't their clothes or tipis or hairstyles, it was the the anxiety burning in their eyes—a low hum beneath the surface, a desperate hopefulness. In her own time, there was no hope, only silence.

Once again her gaze scanned the serene camp, greedily absorbing the halcyon setting. Tears misted her vision. This was what her People missed, what they yearned for, what each would gladly die to know again. Not just the tipis and the buckskin and the lost lifestyle they represented, but the freedom to live unhampered upon the land they loved.

Freedom. No wonder they mourned. No wonder their sad, unspoken lament.

Kris swallowed the keening moan building inside her. By some weird coincidence, she was here, alive, in the past.

Why? The question assailed her. Nothing like this ever happened without a reason.

Have I been sent here for a reason? To do something miraculous, to save my People or change history?

But what could she possibly do? Help them to understand and adjust?

She snorted. The Comanche she'd known in her own time still hadn't adjusted, and they'd had over a century to do it. She could only pray that her studies, the research she'd done, would help her survive the ordeal ahead. Did she dare try to change things, to help them? What if she made things worse? How would it affect the people in her own time?

Black Eagle stomped out of the tipi and grabbed her arm. Kris barely flinched, her mind still involved with her dilemma. She stumbled along behind him to a smaller tipi nearby, noting its beautiful decoration. He flung up the circular entrance flap and pushed her inside. Stumbling dangerously near the small fire smoldering in the center of the tipi, she swung on him.

"Quit pushing me around," she shouted, her heart pounding at the close call. "Just point to where you want me to go and I'll go there." She sucked in a deep breath, feeling lightheaded, losing steam. Her body ached fiercely and tears of anger and frustration threatened. But she forced them back. No one would see her cry. Not even Black Eagle.

"Why did you bring me here?"

"I have told you, woman, the Great Spirit sent you to help my People."

"I can't help them," she whispered, shaking her head.

Black Eagle's face darkened. "Speak the Great Spirit's words." He ducked out of the tipi, letting the flap slap shut behind him.

Kris sank onto a pile of furs and pressed her head to her knees.

Grandmother, help me, she pleaded silently, finally allowing the pent-up tears to fall. *What do I do now?*

Only silence answered her.

"Padaponi!"

"I come, I come."

Duuqua smiled as his aunt puffed and waddled to the tipi as fast as her short, fat legs would carry her. She held medicine gourds from Tabenanika, the People's healer. No wonder he had not been able to find her.

"I will see to your *pahoute*," she promised as she ducked into the tipi. "You go now."

He started to follow her, but she shooed him away. "Leave us. She will find no peace if you are near."

His heart felt like a stone in his chest. She spoke the truth. His gaze settled on the sleeping woman, his heart wrenched by the wet trail of tears on her cheek. He had caused her suffering. "You will treat her wounds?"

"Yes." Padaponi shoved him out of the tipi. "Then I will treat yours." She shuddered as her hand touched one of his chest wounds.

"The need of our People will not be lessened by the spilling of our own blood." Her black eyes snapped as she glared up at him. "You must remain strong for the battles ahead."

"Yes, aunt, but we cannot hope to win without the help of

the Great Spirit." Duuqua smiled at her, refusing to let her make him angry, or to let her tell him how to be a warrior. Each refused to lose the running battle between them.

Her lips tightened into a thin line. "The prayers of a Quahadi war chief are not enough?"

"Not anymore." He smiled down at her again. "But see what my vision quest has brought us? This woman has great *puha*. She will speak the words of the Great Spirit to the war council this night."

"Humph," Padaponi snorted, tossing a glance over her shoulder at the sleeping woman. "I see only a frightened young woman in need of this medicine." She nodded to several warriors who waited to speak with him. "Explain your actions this day, if you can, before more harm is done. Isatai already talks to the people."

"Isatai is a little cloud trying to blow up a big storm." Duuqua shrugged off her warning, not letting her see his concern. "I will return soon." He nodded toward Kris. "You will prepare her to speak to the war council? She must look like one of the People. The chiefs must hear her words, not be blinded by differences in her hair or dress."

"I will do my best, but I can do nothing while I stand here talking to you." Padaponi shoved him out, then pulled the entrance flap closed, only to raise it again. "Do not return until the sun sets. Then I will feed you. Go now."

The flap shut, then opened again. "Wash that wound."

The flap shut again.

Duuqua folded his arms across his chest and waited, grinning, knowing Padaponi had not finished shouting orders at him. How he loved this busy little woman who mothered him and Quannah as if they were still boys. She was the only mother he remembered. His own mother had been killed in a raid by Mexican bandits when he was still in a cradleboard. Padaponi had hidden him, then fled to safety. He'd been adopted by Noconi, Quannah's father. But Quannah's mother and small sister had been stolen many summers before by white soldiers. Only recently had Quannah learned that his mother and sister had died of a fever, prisoners of his mother's white family. Then Noconi also died of the white man's fever and Padaponi had become mother to both Duuqua and Quannah.

Duuqua's heart swelled with love and pride. He would not have survived without her.

Padaponi stuck her face out again and shot him a naughty grin. "If you are hungry now, Kiyani will feed you."

Her words reminded him of Kiyani's hands on his body while the *pahoute* watched. Anger burned in his chest. Kiyani would seek revenge for the *pahoute*'s insult, yet he could not help smiling as he remembered.

"Well," Padaponi demanded. "What are you waiting for?"

Duuqua shrugged. "I am not that hungry."

Padaponi clucked her tongue at him. "She is your brother's wife, and your . . ."

"Duty," Duuqua growled. "She never lets me forget." He turned to the waiting warriors. Why had Kiyani's actions angered him? Why did he care that the *pahoute* had seen? Padaponi was right: Kiyani was Quannah's wife, which made her his wife as well. His duty. The *pahoute* must learn to accept the People's ways.

Duuqua scowled, unable to answer the questions racing through his head. He only knew that the thought of lying with Kiyani, as he knew she would soon demand, left him feeling unclean. A betrayal of the woman who had warmed his robes the last seven suns. He had not taken her body, but he remembered her warmth in his arms. Suddenly, he knew he could never sleep with another woman without remembering the *pahoute*. Would he always wonder if the *pahoute*'s body would bring him greater satisfaction than the body in his arms?

Betrayal? He snorted, tossing off the disturbing thoughts. How could he betray a woman who had never been, never would be, his?

Chapter Six

Angry people surrounded Kris, hissing and jeering, poking at her with sharp sticks.

"No!" she cried, abruptly awakening. She lurched to her feet, arms swinging. Her enemy, a lone woman, lay sprawled at her feet.

"Aiyee!" Muttering angrily, the woman shoved her hair out of her face and rolled to her feet, eyeing Kris from across the fire.

Kris collapsed back onto the pile of furs, dismayed at the agony the simple movement caused. She glanced down to find the source of her pain and gasped. She was naked. Cheeks flushing, she yanked a buffalo robe out from under her and pulled it around her.

The woman across the fire watched. She didn't seem threatening, only surprised and annoyed. She wasn't carrying a stick and no anger lurked in her deep-set brown eyes. Tentatively, she approached. She touched a cut on Kris's arm, shook her head and muttered. Seeing only kindness and concern in the woman's eyes, Kris stood with her assistance.

With calm efficiency, the woman picked up a gourd of ointment and began applying it to Kris's injuries. Kris gasped at its sting and tried to stop her, but the determined woman slapped her hand away. To Kris's surprise, the sting quickly eased.

Kris tried to shrug off her embarrassment as the woman treated her wounds, but when she poked at the healing welts on the inside of Kris's knees, Kris snatched the gourd from her hand. She'd had enough help with those. She gestured that she'd do it herself and was surprised when the woman acquiesced. If only Black Eagle had been as reasonable.

His face lingered in her mind, tormenting her as she dabbed

her thighs with the salve. She dreaded seeing him again, knowing the time would soon come when he would expect her to deliver the message he believed she'd brought from the Great Spirit to the war council. What on earth could she say? What if she didn't say what they wanted to hear? How would they react? Had he rescued her from torture this morning only to thrust her into danger again?

His assertion that his People needed her rang false. She sighed, realizing she'd never find out unless she got to know them better. And she'd better quit feeling sorry for herself and take charge of the situation. Right now.

She handed back the medicine gourd, and pointed to herself. "Kris."

The woman frowned.

Kris patted herself on the chest. "Kris." She tapped the other woman's chest and cocked her head questioningly.

A wide smile split the woman's round face. "Padaponi," she said and thumped her chest.

"Pad-a-poni?" Kris echoed.

Padaponi bobbed her head vigorously, very pleased. She poked Kris in the chest, staring up at her expectantly.

Kris pronounced her name slowly.

"Ka-ris?"

Kris laughed. "Kris."

"Ka-ris," Padaponi mimed happily. Then she jumped up and crossed the tipi. From a small hide container hanging from one of the tipi poles, she extracted a wide-bladed knife.

Kris's smile froze on her face.

Padaponi's hand dipped into the bag again to pull out an odd-looking stick about six inches long with sharp spines on one end. She walked toward Kris, raking the crude brush through her chin-length black hair. The knife dangled from her other hand.

"A hairbrush?" Kris dove at it with a joyous cry. It was nothing more than a strip of quill-studded hide secured over a

smooth stick of wood with leather thongs. Kris dragged the
crude brush through her tangled hair. It caught in a snarl.

Padaponi helped her free the brush as Kris became increasingly frustrated. She'd never get all the snarls out. She might
as well cut her hair short like Padaponi's.

As if she'd read her mind, Padaponi offered the knife and
cocked her head.

"No," Kris said, eyeing the ragged ends of Padaponi's hair.
She didn't want to look like these women with their chopped-
off hair and the harsh streak of red paint in the center part.
She wanted to stay just as she was, who she was. She struggled
to work the snarls out of her hair, but the brush was soon
hopelessly entangled.

With a sighing sob, Kris released it. She tossed the tangled
mass of hair over her back and nodded to Padaponi. At the
first rasping pass of the knife, the tears she'd held at bay so
long slipped from beneath her lashes.

While Padaponi gathered the severed snarls, Kris fingered   •
the ragged edges of her new bob, feeling more naked than
ever. She dashed the tears from her cheeks. How ridiculous,
after all she'd been through, to sit here crying over her hair.

Padaponi chattered merrily across the tipi as if Kris understood every word. Kris avoided looking at her. One glimpse of
the little woman's sympathetic smile and Kris knew she'd lose
her tentative grip on her seething emotions. Instead, she con-
centrated on working the snarls out of her remaining hair.

Padaponi knelt beside her and laid a beautiful, beaded
parfleche in her lap. Kris stared in awe at the bag's workman-
ship. The intricate beading was identical to the design
painted on the tipi. The same colors were repeated in
Padaponi's clothing and, she suddenly realized, in the beading
on Black Eagle's worn mocassins.

"It's beautiful," Kris murmured as she traced the beadwork,
awed by the skill and patience required to create the elaborate
design. A blue section wove through the center, warmed by
yellow rays from above. Bits of bone and quill formed trees

and rock formations. Kris's throat tightened and she almost clutched the bag to her chest. The long gray section above the blue reminded her of the rock ledge at Barton Springs. She returned it reluctantly. "Thank you for showing it to me."

Padaponi shoved the parfleche back onto Kris's lap and motioned for her to open it.

"For me?" Kris gaped in disbelief, searching Padaponi's eyes. Such a gift would only be given to an honored guest.

Padaponi nodded, smiling.

"Oh, but I couldn't . . ." Kris shook her head in protest, but stopped at the hurt in Padaponi's eyes. A thrill of pleasure swept over her and she smiled at her hostess.

Padaponi's answering smile brightened the tipi like a hundred-watt lightbulb. Eagerly, she untied the thongs that held the bag closed. Kris's breath caught as Padaponi withdrew a beautiful buckskin skirt and blouse made of a supple hide tanned to a soft cream shade. Long rows of fringe adorned each sleeve and the same beautiful design on the container was repeated along the skirt's hem. Padaponi pressed it to Kris's chest, checking its fit.

"It's beautiful, my friend."

"*Haint.*" Padaponi patted her chest, pointed at Kris, then herself.

Kris started. Padaponi had understood her, had called her friend in Comanche. Elated, Kris extended her hand for Padaponi to shake. "*Haint.*"

Padaponi stared, obviously not understanding the gesture, so Kris took her hand and shook it firmly. When she tried to let go, the little woman kept shaking until Kris's ears rattled.

Sharing a grin with her new friend, Kris eased her hand free. She'd make many more friends here, she promised herself.

She just hoped she survived the process.

Duuqua paused at the entrance to his tipi. His heart pounded in dread.

Why? he asked himself. He was war chief of the Quahadi. He feared nothing and no one. So why did he stand trembling outside his own tipi?

Because she waited inside, the messenger of the Great Spirit, the woman his People had beaten. He had failed to protect her. He had tried to find her another protector, but word of how she had kicked Kiyani out of her own tipi had traveled swiftly. No man would take her. Quannah said she was *pasa*.

He hoped the *pahoute* had not made trouble for Padaponi. Would she be happy to see him or angry as a wounded buffalo? Curiosity at last drove him inside.

His eyes swept the tipi for her and found her seated amid the furs of his bed, smiling up at him, her eyes warm with welcome. As he stared, her lips parted and she blushed. His breath stopped, as if he had been kicked in the chest. His gaze followed the movement of her hand to her hair. He jerked and stared. Her long, shining hair had been chopped off just below her ears. He cursed the loss under his breath.

The *pahoute*'s smile died. Her hand fell to her lap and her lips pressed tight together.

What had Padaponi done? At least she had not painted the *pahoute*'s face red, nor plucked out the dark wings over her eyes.

By the Sun! She wore the dress Padaponi had made for the wife she hoped he would soon bring her. Desire lanced through him. Dressed as his wife, seated on his furs, the *pahoute* waited for him. Anger swelled as he realized what Padaponi had done. He struggled to control his anger as the *pahoute* stared up at him, her doe-brown eyes wide and questioning. Hurt gleamed bright before she turned from him.

"Padaponi," Duuqua growled, and sucked in a deep breath to cool the lust raging through him. His aunt had much to answer for this night.

"Yes, *tua?*" She remained kneeling with her back to him, preparing their evening meal.

"How many times must I tell you? As long as I am war chief to the Quahadi, I will never take a wife! I want no weeping woman waiting for me to return from raiding, never knowing if I am alive or dead. I must be free to lead my warriors without that burden."

His eyes again sought the *pahoute*. Her questioning gaze flashed between him and Padaponi. His heart burned at the sight of her. He felt scalded by her beauty.

Duuqua threw back his shoulders, inhaling deeply. Never would he let desire for a woman keep him from his duties. The needs of the People were great; he must remain strong, fearless.

"Padaponi," he barked, "why did you cut off her hair?"

At last Padaponi turned to face him, puffing out her chest like an outraged bird protecting her nest. "It could not be untangled."

He grunted, unable to deny the truth in her words. It had become a tangled mess, but he remembered its soft touch as they rode, its warmth flowing over his arm and shoulder like dark water as she slept in his arms. He would miss it.

"Now she looks like one of the People," Padaponi said, reminding him of his earlier instructions. "Is that not what you wanted?"

With her short hair and buckskin dress, the *pahoute* did look more like a Comanche woman. He tried to look at her as the chiefs would. "You are right," he grudgingly admitted. "The chiefs will hear her words, if they can see past her beauty."

But he had not forgotten Padaponi's other trick. "Why does she wear that dress? And why is she seated on my furs?"

"She sits there because that is where I found her and where I thought you had put her." Padaponi's fists settled on her hips as she faced him. "What would you have her wear? One of my dresses? Can you not see that she is taller and not so round as me? Would you have her go about naked, filling the young men with lust?"

"No." Duuqua flinched at the fire in his swift response.

"Then ask for a give-away. I have nothing else for her to wear."

Duuqua shut his mouth. The dress would have to do for now. Why had his heart betrayed him at seeing her dressed as his wife and waiting for him on his bed?

What would he do with her after the war council? Would the Great Spirit send her back to the sacred waters? Would the stones take her away? As if answering his thoughts, the stones began to hum inside his medicine bag. Could he bear to let her go?

The thought of her leaving filled his heart with shadows. He shook his head, feeling as if he were drowning in her troubled eyes. His heartbeat thundered in his ears. He could not breathe. He must leave!

He ducked out of the tipi and walked swiftly away.

"*Tua!*" Padaponi called after him. "Son of my sister! You have not eaten."

He did not answer. What was happening to him? How could he feed his body when his soul cried in torment? He must stay away from the *pahoute*. Her *puha* stole his thoughts.

As he stomped away, his heart laughed. What did it matter if he stayed away? She filled his thoughts wherever he went.

He could not escape her even in his dreams.

Kris forced herself to stop trembling after Black Eagle stormed out of the tipi. Dear God! If only she had a mirror. She must look worse than she'd thought for him to act so fierce, so disappointed.

Why had he hated her beautiful clothes? Did he hate seeing her, an enemy, dressed like one of the People? Her chin inched upward and she welcomed the flash of anger that calmed her. Next time she saw him, she'd remind him that his People had destroyed her own clothes.

Padaponi slapped the entrance flap closed, jerking Kris from her thoughts. She watched as the little woman returned to kneel by the fire, keeping her head averted. But Kris caught the sheen of tears in her eyes. Her jaw clenched. That man had been so hateful to Padaponi and all she'd done was try to help.

Kris rose, stroking the beautiful buckskin skirt as it slid down her legs. How could anything so beautiful cause so much anguish? She bent and squeezed Padaponi's shoulders, then motioned toward the bloody flag of meat she was roasting over the fire. She didn't know what kind of meat it was, but it smelled heavenly. Padaponi had also prepared some kind of ground corn mixture.

Padaponi gave her a watery smile and motioned for Kris to seat herself. She sliced off a thick chunk of meat, then used it to scoop up some corn and shoved the whole thing into her mouth. She stabbed the knife into the meat and nodded for Kris to take a turn.

Kris tugged the knife out, then, gulping, she followed Padaponi's example. They ate in complete silence. Afterward Kris congratulated herself that her thoughts had only slipped to Black Eagle three times.

A deep male voice called Padaponi's name from outside the tipi. She jumped to her feet and ushered in their guest with a flourish.

Burnished mahogany hair glinted red in the firelight as the man ducked inside. A white man? Kris's pulse accelerated, until he straightened to his full height and crossed his arms over his chest. His supple buckskins bore witness of a loving hand, but were unadorned, except for the long fringe along the seams. A beaded belt circled his waist and a matching sheath lay against his abdomen. His hair hung in braided, hide-covered plaits over the kind of chest men in her own time paid good money to develop. Was that belligerent stance a prerequisite for all warriors? she wondered. Comanche 101? Despite his hair and the blue eyes flashing over her, this was definitely a Comanche warrior.

This man stood as tall as Black Eagle, but there the resemblance ended. Though lean, his body was more heavily muscled, his legs as massive as tree trunks, not lean and wiry like Black Eagle's. Kris scowled. Since when had Black Eagle become the measure by which she judged other men?

"You're white," Kris blurted, overcome by the contrasts in this man—the brilliance of his blue eyes, the height of his patrician forehead and the purity of his long, straight nose juxtaposed against the hostility in his cool, measuring stare.

Kris cocked her head as his lips pressed into a thin line. Something about him seemed familiar. She shrugged. Must be the frown.

"I am Chikoba." His chin lifted and his lips settled back into that thin line, as if he disliked speaking English. "Duuqua sent me for you."

"Kris Baldwin," she said, rising to extend her hand. "I'm glad to meet you." She let her hand fall to her side when he just glared at it. Though white, she doubted Chikoba could be persuaded to help her escape. He didn't look helpful or even friendly.

He spoke sharply to Padaponi in fluid Comanche. Kris blanched at the heat in his words. Padaponi's head bobbed as he spoke, then she pulled Kris to her feet and shooed her toward the door.

"Wait a minute," Kris insisted, digging in her heels. She wasn't ready to leave the relative safety of Padaponi's company on the say-so of this tight-lipped stranger. "Why didn't Black Eagle come for me?"

"He waits with the war council." Chikoba's terse tone told her she'd get no further information from him.

She sighed and ducked out of the tipi, followed by Padaponi. Chikoba's long stride had already carried him past the nearest tipi when she called, "Wait!"

He paused, his eyes glittering. "Before we go, would you thank Padaponi for helping me?" She brushed her hands over the soft buckskin skirt.

Chikoba growled a few guttural sounds then cocked his head. "Come."

Kris gave Padaponi a hug, then rubbed her stomach and grinned. "Ask her what kind of meat we had for dinner."

"You did not like it?" Chikoba's scowl disappeared. His lips formed a lopsided grin.

Kris's stomach clenched. "What was it?"

"Horse."

Kris gave Padaponi a weak smile and stumbled away, fighting a wave of nausea. Chikoba gripped her elbow and propelled her ahead of him. Forced to trot to stay ahead of him, Kris yanked her arm away and stepped out of his path.

"I know how to jog, thank you." She slowed her pace to a brisk walk.

A huge tipi glowed ahead. Recognizing it as the one where she'd met Quannah, Kris came to an abrupt halt. It was much too soon to face the angry man she'd attacked only hours earlier.

"Quannah is no longer angry." Chikoba lifted the entrance flap. "Come. The chiefs wait."

Kris hesitated, swamped by emotions—anxiety, dismay, dread and uncertainty. But by far the strongest was fear.

What did Black Eagle expect her to say to these men?

"Come." Chikoba motioned for her to enter ahead of him.

Heart thundering, Kris ducked inside, stumbling a little as Chikoba pushed in behind her. It was a full house. She blinked at the solemn circle of men seated around the fire as Chikoba nudged her to the right and pushed her to her knees.

"*Ehaitsma*." He greeted everyone with a general nod. Kris tensed as he seated himself between her and the exit.

The other men's responding grunts resounded in her ears as she sought Black Eagle's face. He smiled, his eyes telegraphing encouragement and a warning.

She straightened indignantly. What was he warning her against? Chin up, she returned his stare, then met the stares of the other men, feigning a calm she was far from feeling. She tried hard not to gape or shudder at their attire—full warbonnets and elaborate headgear made from the severed heads of wolves and even a bear. Most of the men's eyes were lit only by curiosity, but some seemed questioning and clearly skeptical. Eagle feathers abounded, swaying in the fragrant smoke that wafted from the small fire and the heavily-adorned pipe that lay on the altar before Quannah. She lifted her chin higher. She might be quaking inside, but she would not let these men see her tremble.

Her eyes watered from the stench of liberally-applied bear grease to unwashed bodies. If not for the fragrant smoke, she'd have retched. That would have made a wonderful first impression.

Her gaze ricocheted off Quannah to the lecherous leer of Isatai, peering at her over Quannah's shoulder. As his hot, beady eyes traveled down her body, Kris fought the urge to cover herself. This time, thank God, she was dressed. She didn't miss the triumphant sneer the medicine man shot at Black Eagle.

Oh, Grandmother, she begged silently. *I need your help! Now more than ever.*

Quannah rose and addressed the men in Comanche. Chikoba leaned closer and translated Quannah's words to English in a whisper. If Chikoba hadn't been so nasty, she would have hugged him.

"Welcome, fellow chiefs. Thank you for joining me in the war council."

War council. What was she, a woman of the twenty-first century, doing in a place like this? Her attention skittered from face to face, her fear mounting until her gaze collided with Black Eagle's. He smiled and miraculously, the fear became manageable.

"If the buffalo hunters are not stopped, the People will have no hides for their tipis, no robes to keep them warm when the ice and snow come, no food. We will all die."

She listened nervously as Quannah outlined the People's grievances, stunned by the virulence of his hatred for the white man. Was this the same man who had eased his People's transition into reservation life? The man who had gained fame as a half-white chief? Was he trying to incite a riot? Her scalp tingled as her nerves tightened.

"This day my brother has returned from a vision quest." Quannah laid a hand on Black Eagle's shoulder.

"The Great Spirit spoke to me with the voice of the eagle, telling me to go to the sacred waters. There, I was told, His messenger would come to me."

Kris stared at him, astonished to hear how he'd come to be at the Springs. She felt his gaze settle on her with smoldering intensity, filled with a reverence and respect that stole her breath and made her heart slam.

"When I came there, I threw an offering into the water."

The stone! He'd thrown it! It hadn't just come out of nowhere. He glanced her way and her breath caught at the warning she once again saw in his gaze. Why wasn't he telling the chiefs about the stone?

"A woman appeared to me. The same woman I had seen in dreams during my vision quest. I reached out to her, but she disappeared like mist burned away by the rising sun. I searched and found her floating in the water. Dead."

The chiefs gasped and turned as one to stare at Kris, horror widening their eyes. Remembering their superstitious natures, especially their fear of ghosts, Kris coughed and rubbed her nose, hoping the normal everyday gesture would reassure them.

Go on, go on, she mentally urged him. How did he save her life? Surely, he didn't know how to give mouth-to-mouth, let alone CPR. So, how had he done it?

"I fought death for her."

Kris's throat tightened and she couldn't seem to breathe as he continued.

"The Great Spirit answered my prayers and turned her

spirit back from its journey." His arm lifted, his finger pointed. "She is that woman; the messenger of the Great Spirit."

Kris's gaze flicked from face to face. Heavens! Hearing his story, she almost believed him herself, and she could see that the chiefs were convinced. She wanted to shout at them not to be so gullible!

Black Eagle had found her near-dead in the Springs and he'd managed to revive her. A common, everyday occurrence in her time. Anybody could take a one-day class and learn how to do it! It was not a reason to deify some poor, unsuspecting woman. But these men faced a desperate situation. They would clutch at any straw, believe anything they hoped might save them. She wished she dared to tell them the truth—that there was no hope, that surrender to life on the reservation was inevitable for all of them. They'd kill her if she blurted out the truth and never even ask how she knew.

Quannah rose and pinned her with a stern gaze. "Woman, speak the words of the Great Spirit."

The eyes of the chiefs shone with the same wary optimism she'd noticed earlier in the eyes of their People. Her mind was a total blank. She couldn't formulate a coherent thought, let alone a speech to save her life. Sweat beaded her brow, her upper lip, trickled down her spine.

Grandmother! her soul screamed. *Help me!*

Duuqua felt as if his body hung upon the wind, as if he lived inside a dream. His most powerful vision quest was being fulfilled before his eyes and the eyes of all the chiefs. All eyes were on the *pahoute*, all waited for her to speak the words that would give his People new hope, new purpose. She would tell them where to strike their enemies, how to chase the hated *taibo* from their lands forever. Once again, the People would live free.

Her eyes, deep and dark with fear, met his. What did she fear? "Speak, woman," he urged her. "None here will harm you. Tell us what the Great Spirit would have us know." Why did she hesitate?

He watched her gaze fly from chief to chief. His gut tightened as her tongue shot out to lick her dry lips. What did she seek in the faces of the chiefs? Why did she not speak? His breath coiled inside him like a snake waiting to strike.

Much depended on this meeting. The lives of the People of many nations hung on her words. Did she understand? Was that the reason for the fear in her eyes? Should he have asked her what she would say before bringing her before the chiefs? No, her words were for all, not for him alone. But would the words she spoke be her own, or the Great Spirit's?

Duuqua had waited long to hear her message. In his heart, he would know if she spoke truly.

Kris waited, praying for inspiration, her hands clenched in her lap. Her gaze circled the chiefs and came to rest on Isatai, lurking in the shadows behind Quannah. Prickles of excitement danced along her skin.

Who is he? The softly whispered question turned the prickles into goosebumps.

Just Coyote Droppings, she thought, in response. *Who cares? Help me, Grandmother!*

Look closer. The whisper intensified, filling her mind.

She didn't question it. "Would you ask Isatai to step forward?" she asked Chikoba and waited tensely for him to respond.

"Why? Say something, woman," Chikoba hissed, glancing around the quiet circle of solemn faces. "The chiefs become impatient."

"It's important," Kris hissed back.

Chikoba rolled his eyes, but translated her request.

Coyote Droppings scowled, but stepped out from behind Quannah, into the light of the fire. He'd painted his whole body a brilliant yellow.

"Ah-ha!" Kris cried, as historic dates and events jangled through her head with all the noise and elusiveness of a Las Vegas slot machine. Her gaze flicked over the assembled chiefs—seeing past her fear to recognize faces familiar from her history books. Arapaho, Cheyenne, Kiowa, Comanche. Only once had the Comanche held such a war council. It marked the beginning of the Red River War, the beginning of the end for the Comanche. Suddenly, she knew exactly what lay ahead. In less than a year, the U.S. Army would force them to surrender and move onto the reservation.

God help her, she'd landed right in the hottest part of the fire!

"False prophet," she hissed and shot Coyote Droppings a venomous glare as she recalled his part in the Comanche's demise.

She nodded at the chiefs' chuckles as Coyote Droppings' cheeks flushed. She cast one last glance around the circle. These men weren't going to like anything she had to say. None of it was good. Within a year, two at the outside, most of them would be dead. The rest would be wards of the government.

What could she say to persuade them to forego the attack they were here to plan against the white buffalo hunters now camped at Adobe Walls? She had to stress survival, impress on them the importance of protecting their women and children. If they didn't survive, there would never be any grandchildren, let alone great-grandchildren. The thought sent a cold chill sliding down her spine.

"She knows nothing. Let us kill her now and be done with it," Coyote Droppings shouted, still flushed.

Kris glared at him. "My people call you the false prophet."

"You lie to save your own scalp, woman," Coyote Droppings sneered.

"Don't trust his medicine," she urged the chiefs. "His paint won't protect you from the white men's bullets."

"The paint was given to me in a vision," Coyote Droppings shouted.

"A vision or a hallucination?" Kris challenged. "Can you prove it?"

"I have nothing to prove to a woman."

"Then prove it to me." Black Eagle interrupted, smiling. "You are painted now. Quannah, give me a gun and I will shoot him."

Kris bit back a grin as the chiefs murmured agreement, glad of the opportunity to gather her thoughts. How much should she tell them? Too much and they'd slit her throat; too little and lives would be lost. Thousands of people relied on these men for guidance. She chose her words carefully.

"Many of the People have already signed treaties and moved onto the reservations. This is wise, for the white men will not stop coming. If you shoot one, two more will take his place. There are so many you could never count them. And they are greedy. They will not rest until they steal all your land and they will kill you for it—man, woman and child."

"These are the words of a woman," cried Coyote Droppings. "The Great Spirit would not tell His warriors to surrender without a fight!"

Kris shouted to be heard above the angry shouts of agreement. "If you attack Adobe Walls, many warriors will die. You will anger the white man's government. Soldiers will swarm over the plains like ants, burning and killing. If you stand and fight, you will die. If you surrender and move onto the reservations, you will lose your pride—but not your lives. Negotiate with the soldiers now. You'll get better terms, more food and blankets for your families."

Angry shouts erupted. "We are warriors."

"Death before surrender!"

"Kill the woman!"

Knife blades flashed in the firelight.

"Think of your People," Kris cried over the furor. Her anguished pleas, torn from her very soul, fell unheard. "Pride won't save your children."

Black Eagle leaped across the fire and shoved her out of the tipi ahead of him. Chikoba backed out behind him, knife drawn.

"Take her!" he ordered and Chikoba swept her away from the tipi into the safety of darkness.

"Wait!" she cried, straining against Chikoba's tight hold on her arm. "We can't leave him to face them alone." Over her shoulder she saw Coyote Droppings emerge from the tipi, snarling when Black Eagle shoved him back inside.

"No!" She fought Chikoba. Vivid images flashed through her mind—a knife slashing downward, sinking deep into a broad, unprotected back; blood spewing out to soak into the thirsty ground. She saw herself kneeling beside the man she loved, a man with death in his eyes. Black Eagle's eyes.

No! Duuqua! she screamed. *Not again!*

Then Chikoba's fist met her chin. Lightning flashed behind her eyes and she tumbled backward into the darkness.

Chapter Seven

Duuqua blocked the tipi entrance, ignoring the chiefs' angry shouts until they returned to the circle, until he could no longer hear Chikoba's footsteps, until the wind no longer cried his name. Until he knew the *pahoute* was safe. His heart bled.

Like his fellow war chiefs, he too longed to shout his anger. Her words had been hard. And he had brought those words to the People. He felt shame for his part. Why had the Great Spirit sent this woman to speak poison to the war council?

Would you have accepted His words if he had spoken them in your vision? The still, calm voice filled Duuqua's soul.

No, he answered honestly. Though he listened intently,

the voice said no more. He wanted to scream in denial. This could not be.

"The woman lies," Isatai shouted, facing the grumbling chiefs.

Duuqua flinched, hearing his own thoughts fall from Isatai's lips.

"She must die. Her false medicine will poison our plans." Isatai cast a triumphant look at Duuqua.

"No!" Duuqua's shout stopped their cries. "Would you kill the Great Spirit's messenger because you don't like His message?" He stared at each chief in turn.

"She has no medicine," Isatai shouted.

"You said she did," Duuqua reminded him.

"Bad medicine."

"How can we know if it is good or bad?" Duuqua asked. "She said your medicine was false. Who should we believe?"

"Do not risk our plans because of the words of a lying woman," Isatai pleaded, turning from Duuqua to appeal to the chiefs. "The warriors who hear her words will ride into battle with doubt poisoning their minds. Fill them with strength. Light a fire in them with her blood."

"Does she have medicine?" The quiet voice of Little Wolf, Old Man Chief of the Cheyenne, calmed the others.

"You have seen it for yourselves," Duuqua replied.

"We have seen nothing but a frightened woman lying to save her own scalp," Isatai hissed.

"Did you tell her of our plan to attack Adobe Walls?" Duuqua looked first to Isatai, then Quannah.

"I told her nothing."

"She has big ears, not big medicine."

"Are you sure?"

Quannah silenced Isatai with a sharp gesture and laid a hand on Duuqua's shoulder. "My brother has spent seven suns with this woman. If he says she has *puha*, I believe him."

Duuqua held his breath as the chiefs considered Quannah's words, murmuring among themselves.

"She is brave," Little Wolf said. "When she looked in my eyes, I saw that she knew we would not like her words. She was not afraid."

Duuqua sheathed his knife as the other chiefs nodded.

"She is only a woman." Isatai faced Duuqua across the fire. "I, too, have seen a vision. But not of food and blankets. I have seen guns and bullets and war. Not frightened women and old men." He sneered at Duuqua.

Duuqua reached for his knife, but when Quannah's hand settled on his shoulder, he rested his hand on the hilt. He glared at Isatai but kept his angry words behind his teeth. The woman had spoken. He must now let Isatai speak.

Since his uncle had been killed in a raid, Isatai had pushed himself forward. Claiming to have seen visions, to have spoken with the Great Spirit, he had wormed his way into Quannah's favor and then into the war council. Duuqua did not believe his lies, but Quannah did, so Duuqua kept his doubts to himself. He would watch and listen.

Isatai lifted the war pipe and drew its smoke deep. "I have seen a vision of our warriors fighting white men, shot with the white men's guns. But they did not die."

The chiefs murmured excitedly. Duuqua scowled as Isatai, the puffed-up weasel, sent him a triumphant smile while he waited for the chiefs to quiet.

"The Great Spirit has given me a special paint that turns away the white man's bullets. The woman is jealous that I have been given this strong medicine, not her. Any man wearing it will not be killed."

Duuqua snorted, outraged that Isatai would risk the lives of Quahadi warriors to advance himself in the tribe. Each man would have to pay Isatai for the privilege of wearing this paint and could lose his life in the bargain. Once again, he threw the *pahoute*'s challenge in Isatai's face. "Show us. Paint yourself and I will shoot you. Then we will know if your medicine is true."

Isatai only smiled, then tossed something on the fire and

began chanting. Sparks flew as heavy smoke filled the tipi. Duuqua's eyelids felt heavy. He heard Isatai praying, but could not understand his words.

An arrow appeared in Isatai's hand where before there had been nothing. It disappeared and three arrows appeared and disappeared, then a rifle. Moaning, Isatai fell to his knees. His whole body shuddered as he belched forth rifle cartridges, then swallowed them. Finally he staggered to his feet and faced the awed chiefs. "The white men cannot hurt you. My medicine will stop their bullets."

The chiefs leaped to their feet, shouting their war cries. Duuqua was the last to stand. His vision quest and the *pahoute* were forgotten. Only Quannah noticed that he did not also raise his voice. His hand went to his medicine bag where the stones lay, pounding. Should he show them to the chiefs, tell them how he received the first one, how it was returned to him? The stones would silence these men's doubts.

No! A voice cried in the darkness of his mind and warm, sweet air swirled around him. *Keep them safe. Tell no one.* The voice faded.

Duuqua shook his head to clear the haze left by Isatai's smoke. He turned to find Isatai staring at the medicine bag.

By the Sun, Duuqua cursed. Had he, too, heard the voice? Isatai's greed for power made him dangerous. He would kill for the powerful stones. Duuqua did not care to think of them in Isatai's hands. His own hands fisted at his sides as he fought the urge to hide the medicine bag from Isatai's greedy gaze. Inside, the stones drummed against his chest.

Isatai stared at Duuqua. His eyes narrowed and he smiled.

Quannah raised his arms and the chiefs quieted. "We will drive the hated white men out of our country," he promised, "starting with the buffalo hunters at Adobe Walls."

Every chief cried agreement.

"Do you fight?" Quannah challenged Duuqua. "Or do you choose the woman?"

Duuqua stiffened at the insult offered by his own brother. "I will fight until I die." He gave a loud, long war cry. Answering cries and the smoke of the War Pipe filled the tipi as the chiefs planned the attack on Adobe Walls.

"It is a good plan," Quannah finally said, then added, "but we will all wear Isatai's paint."

"After it is proven." Little Wolf's words brought shouts of laughter.

"A Sun Dance will protect our plans against the woman's false words." Isatai's words drew excited nods from the chiefs.

"The Comanche have never held a Sun Dance," Duuqua protested. He did not wish to anger the other chiefs who held the Sun Dance often by saying that Quahadi warriors had no need of such medicine.

"They have never before needed one." Isatai's reply brought many scowls.

"Agreed." Quannah nodded. "But no eagle claws. Only rope."

"Are the Comanche afraid of the eagle's medicine?" challenged Little Wolf.

"I would not have my warriors weakened before battle," Quannah responded calmly. "We will use ropes, not claws."

"Rope?" Isatai's shoulders slumped.

Duuqua shouldered Isatai aside. His thirst for Comanche blood angered Duuqua. He should thirst for the blood of the enemy, not that of his own People.

Kris snapped awake, her eyes flaring as they focused on the slumbering flames of the tipi fire. A noisy rumble cut across the silence. Ah—she grinned into the darkness—*Padaponi snores.*

Wide awake now, Kris stared into the dancing shadows, recalling the smoky tipi and the war chiefs and the tumult her warnings had caused. Thank goodness Black Eagle had planned for that contingency.

She shuddered, remembering the images that had come to

her outside the tipi and her horror when she saw Coyote Droppings behind Black Eagle with his knife drawn.

The images had been so real! So had the emotions that flooded her. She could almost believe she'd actually experienced the things she'd seen. Even now, she felt an aching sadness, as if someone she dearly loved had died.

She rubbed the tender point of her chin, shaking off her troubling thoughts. Chikoba must have carried her back here. She frowned as pain shot through her chin and up her jaw. Had it been necessary to hit her so hard? She'd gone down like a stone.

Tension and a feeling of impending doom brought details of the war council flooding back. She hadn't intended to say so much, but she didn't want the chiefs to cling to the ridiculous notion that she was the Great Spirit's messenger. What would happen to her now?

She knew she'd made an enemy of Coyote Droppings. How far would he go to make the chiefs listen to him, not her?

And what about Black Eagle? Should she warn him? Would he believe her if she told him about the images she'd seen tonight? Could she leave, knowing he might be in danger? She might as well face the facts. The stones were gone. Lost. Could she go back to her own time again, even if she found her way back to the Springs?

She was thinking of staying here, she realized. She couldn't do that. It was too soon to give up hope. She'd find a way back to the Springs and from there to her own time and place.

The direction of her thoughts left her restless and edgy—too tense to sleep. She threw back the heavy buffalo robe, relieved to find she still wore the buckskin outfit. She frowned. It wouldn't be beautiful for long if she had to wear it day and night.

Smoke from the small fire stung her eyes, reminding her of the heavy smoke in Quannah's tipi. Her head started pounding again; her stomach rolled. She needed some fresh air.

Moving cautiously so as not to awaken Padaponi, Kris crept to the tipi flap and slipped out.

She knew the danger in going out alone at night, but she needed to think and the smoke of the war council still clouded her brain. A sliver of moon lit her way through the tipis. The river sparkled like a silver necklace on a bed of black velvet, beckoning to her.

Keeping to the shadows of the trees on the bank above the river, she headed for a small, grassy clearing overlooking the water. Hearing voices—soft pleading, a low growl—Kris froze.

A couple stood in the clearing. The man watched the woman drop her buckskin skirt, then yank her shirt off. Shocked, Kris stared as the woman twined around him, her hand sliding down his back, then coming around to slip between their bodies. He stiffened and his moan echoed on the still, hot air.

Moonlight silvered their straining limbs. Shadows defined the man's flexing muscles as he yanked the woman flush against him and bent his head to ravage her lips. Kris flinched at the woman's full-throated moan, her own body leaping to awareness. She knew she should leave—now!—but the scene mesmerized her. Heart pounding in her ears, she gulped as the woman's head fell back, baring her neck. The woman arched, her breasts lifting in offering. Kris's own nipples throbbed in awareness as the man's lips captured one of her breasts. He drew it into his mouth as he clutched the woman's buttocks and snatched her hips to his. Kris pressed the back of her hand over her mouth to keep from echoing the woman's high moan. Heat slammed through her own loins as the woman ground herself against him, her head lolled back, her face turned toward Kris.

"Kiyani." Recognition, like an icy shower, stole the heat from Kris's body.

Go! Get out of here! she chastened herself, cursing her stupidity in speaking Kiyani's name aloud. *Leave them alone.*

Kiyani's eyes opened, focused on Kris and she smiled, a

supremely self-satisfied sneer. She clutched the man's head, pressing him closer, her smile widening, almost gloating.

Sickened by the heat, the lust glowing in Kiyani's eyes, Kris told herself to back away. She didn't want to know who Kiyani clutched in her arms. But Kris's body wasn't listening to her head.

Suddenly the images reappeared, only this time there was no fear, only fire as she clutched the dark head at her breast, pressing closer as his lips and tongue seared her.

Oh, the heat! Her back arched and a low moan escaped her.

The man's head lifted, his fiery gaze fastened on her face.

"Duuqua!" Kris's eyes snapped open as her anguish shredded the silence.

Black Eagle stared back at her from within the circle of Kiyani's arms. Time hung suspended in the moonlight.

"No!" Kris cried, struggling to wrench free of the lethargy left by the images in her traitorous brain. His black gaze speared her and the heat in his eyes sullied her soul. At last, her heart slammed into motion. Pain tore through her chest.

She fled, hounded by Kiyani's laughter.

Stumbling and cursing, she raced back to the tipi, taking a few wrong turns, her heart beating so hard it thundered in her ears in counterpoint to Kiyani's laughter. She'd never forget that ugly, triumphant laugh, or the lust in Black Eagle's eyes. Lust for another woman.

Why did that hurt so badly? She had no claim on him. Why did she feel as if she were bleeding inside? Why did his Comanche name keep popping into her head? And where did those startling images come from?

Dear God, she had to get out of here and away from him, get back to the Springs before she lost her mind completely, or something worse happened.

Duuqua watched the *pahoute* run from him, disgusted with himself for his weakness. Kiyani's loud laughter stripped the night of its peace, its silence. He shoved her away from him.

How many years had he shared Quannah's burden, shared the meat of the hunt, protected Quannah's three wives when he went raiding? Why, when Quannah made Kiyani his fourth wife, had Duuqua's responsibilities changed to include satisfying her? Duuqua knew Kiyani's blood ran hot. He had tasted pleasure in her arms long before she set her sights on Quannah. But when Duuqua had refused to take her to wife, she had chased Quannah with a heat that sickened Duuqua. After Quannah took her to his robes, she wasted little time making her interest in Duuqua known to her husband. Finally, Quannah had come to him, asked him to share *this* responsibility also, but only for this fourth wife, only Kiyani. Duuqua had agreed, only because Quannah asked it of him. He pleasured Kiyani, but took great satisfaction in denying her a child of his loins. Only a wife of his own choosing would bear his sons.

This night would have been like so many others, except for the *pahoute*. Why had her cry knifed through him? Why, looking at Kiyani now, did he feel nothing but disgust?

Had the long days and nights spent with the *pahoute* made him think she belonged to him, that he might have her? He knew it could not be. He had thought he had controlled the lust he felt for her. But had he? She belonged to the Great Spirit, and as war chief he had vowed never to take a wife. He would not risk sharing his furs with the *pahoute*, for fear of drawing the wrath of the Great Spirit down upon the heads of his People.

By the Sun, he cursed. Did he no longer know his own mind? He pushed free of Kiyani and stomped toward the river. He needed to wash himself.

"Where do you go?" Kiyani caught his arm, her nails biting deep. "Did that woman's ugly face make your manhood small? I know what it likes." Her thick tongue slid over her lips.

"No." Duuqua shoved away the hand that reached between them.

"Not tonight?" Kiyani stuck out her bottom lip in a child's pout, but her eyes flashed.

"No. Never again." He watched her eyes narrow. Quannah would not be pleased when his newest wife complained that Duuqua had refused her this night. Duuqua sighed. He knew his brother could be persuaded, but it would cost him many horses.

He smiled. The *pahoute* would be surprised to know she had helped him this night, giving him a reason to end this unpleasant duty to Kiyani without losing face or offending Quannah.

Kiyani hissed, seeing his smile. "You cannot refuse me."

Duuqua swatted her wide buttocks and turned away. "I just did."

"I won't let you do this."

He faced her, fighting to keep his anger hidden. "How do you plan to stop me?"

Kiyani's smile chilled his blood. "You know I only married Quannah because you used me, then would not have me for wife."

Duuqua's stomach jumped. "You used our chief to force me to share your furs?"

"It worked," she crowed, her grin making him feel even dirtier.

Duuqua spat at her feet. "You disgust me."

"Oh, no, my husband's brother." Her smile turned knowing. "I excite you."

"No more than any other woman." Vivid memories of himself and this woman mating flashed through his mind, but they stirred him to shame, not lust.

"You lie," Kiyani cried. "You love me. I have seen it in your eyes."

"What do you see there now, woman?" He let his shame, his disgust for her and for himself, fill his face.

She searched his face and paused. For a moment, he

thought she might share his feelings, but then she shrugged. "You are angry." She stepped close and again reached for his manhood. "You will change your mind."

He twisted her hand away from his body as she tried to force it closer.

She cried out in pain and leaped away from him, rubbing her wrist.

"Never touch me again." He headed for the water, hoping he could wash himself clean.

Kiyani's laughter followed him. He grunted. Let her laugh. Never again would he part her thighs. He waded into the river and scrubbed his body again and again with handfuls of sand. Only when his teeth chattered like the squirrel's did he leave the water.

His steps became hurried as he returned to his tipi and the *pahoute*. His manhood lifted and began to harden, remembering her as she had looked earlier that day, wearing the clothing intended for his wife, waiting for him on his bed. She had stolen the breath from his chest. Now he felt unworthy to touch her clothes, let alone the woman in them.

Sly Padaponi. She wanted him to take a wife, wanted grandchildren to spoil. She had used the *pahoute* to remind him of his duty. Did she think he could be so easily persuaded? Yet her trickery stayed in his mind. He cursed Padaponi's meddling but could not hate the image that remained.

He entered the tipi and stumbled over a pile of furs where none had been before. The *pahoute* slept beside Padaponi in furs she must have stolen from his bed. One shoulder peeked out of the furs. The buckskin covering it glowed in the soft light of the dying fire.

Ah, he realized with a grin. *She sleeps in her clothes, not wanting to be naked, at a disadvantage*. He smiled, admiring her spirit. She had not spoken a word, but her buckskin-clad shoulder and the distance between their two beds told him much. She did not want him to touch her.

Swiftly, he turned from the woman and settled himself in

his furs, watching her, listening to her breathe. The stones hummed inside his medicine bag, dragging his mind toward sleep. He resisted their pull, dreading the nightmares that filled his nights. Each night the dreams became stronger, more vivid. Each night he saw more of the life that the dream man and woman had shared. Their love made him feel empty, aching for such a love for himself.

But he would not trade his present lonely life for the sorrow they had suffered. The terror in the woman's eyes haunted Duuqua day and night. Her face flashed before him often, at unexpected moments, stealing his breath. In his dreams last night, he had seen something move in the darkness behind her as she wept over him. Someone had jerked her head back and Duuqua had seen the flash of a knife as fear and resignation filled her eyes. He had awakened, his body shaking like that of an old man. Only after he had checked to see that the *pahoute* was safe had his heart slowed its rapid pace. But sleep had escaped him.

Duuqua eyed the medicine bag containing the stones. Could they be causing the nightmares? The first dream had come the night he found her in the sacred waters, the first night he had placed the stones in his medicine bag.

Would the dreams not come if he did not wear the stones? Holding it by its thong, he lifted the medicine bag off his chest. A wave of relief flooded him. He felt his body stretch, lengthen and relax. He removed the bag, tucking it safely under the bottom fur. Then he slept and, for the first time in many suns, he did not dream.

Powahe sighed wearily and relaxed her vigil. It was no use. She could not reach the warrior this night. What a shame. She had planned to show him a little more of his past, though she knew he had probably already guessed it.

Were the dreams helping? She snorted. How could she tell? She could send Kris her thoughts and some images, but she got nothing back. How would she know if she succeeded?

Rising with a low groan—old bones were not meant to sit so long on the cold ground—she poured some water over her fire. She must rest. Perhaps the warrior had simply removed the stones. Yes, that was all. She must not lose hope.

As the last ember of her fire died, darkness enveloped her—a deeper darkness than usual, a dark without sound.

Powahe froze, listening, using her inner eye to search the silence. *He* was here; she felt his cold hand upon her heart.

Quickly, she began a prayer chant, letting it rise to fill her mind and break the silence. A low groan swirled around her. The darkness moved, circling the tipi, looking for an exit. The groan swelled until it filled the tipi with roaring menace. The air around her grew biting cold. She sang louder, raising her arms high. She gave a glad cry and her fire burst into flame again.

With a shrill screech, the darkness spiraled out the smoke-hole, leaving the tipi rocking on its frame, but suddenly still, calm.

Powahe stood panting, sweat rolling down her face. The evil that had destroyed Kris's first life had found her. But he had not yet found her granddaughter. She must be more vigilant; Kris's warrior was not yet ready to deal with him.

"Wake up."

Kris started awake at the loud command and scooted away from the sturdy legs beside her bed. "Leave me alone," she said, slapping away the hand that shook her shoulder.

A snort followed her request. Chikoba stood over her, glowering.

"You're up early." She glanced toward Black Eagle's bed, relieved to find it empty.

"The sun is already high in the sky, lazy one. Dress yourself." He nodded over his shoulder. "I have brought my wife. She has a gift for you."

Kris shoved her buckskin skirt down over her knees then flipped back the fur covering her. She grimaced at the surprise in Chikoba's eyes as he saw she was fully dressed. She wanted to kick him when he shot a speculative glance toward Black Eagle's empty furs.

Chikoba extended a hand to the tiny woman waiting by the entrance and smiled. He pulled her to his side and placed a beefy arm around her shoulders, beaming down at her. "My wife, Ekararo."

Any animosity Kris had felt for this stern man dissolved in the warmth of the smile he bestowed on his wife. At first glance, Ekararo had seemed very young, but Kris could see now that she was just very petite. Ekararo's soft copper cheeks blushed a becoming pink and she turned her face into Chikoba's chest.

"What does Ekararo mean?" Kris asked, hoping to ease the young woman's embarrassment.

"She Blushes." Chikoba answered with a chuckle and smiled wider as the pink in his wife's cheeks intensified. "She has the pinkest cheeks in camp."

"Go, my *kumaxp*," Ekararo scolded with a soft smile. "We be fine."

Chikoba's sternness returned. "You will be kind to her? She carries my child."

"Of course," Kris promised, surprised at his blunt question.

"Go," Ekararo repeated, adding a swift comment in Comanche that made both Padaponi and Chikoba blush before he hastily departed.

"You speak English?" Kris asked happily.

"*Si*," Ekararo nodded. "I mean, yes. I no speak as well as Duuqua, but he learns many years and my husband is a good teacher." Again, her cheeks pinkened.

"Has Chikoba taught others too?" Kris demanded, elated. At last she'd get the answers she'd been craving. When Ekararo nodded, Kris fired off another question. "What does *kumaxp* mean? and *pahoute*? and *herbi*? and—"

Ekararo laughed and held up a hand to stop her. "No more, please! *Kumaxp* is husband. You are *pahoute* and we"—she gestured to include Padaponi with herself and Kris—"*herbi*."

"Women?" Kris clarified, and Ekararo nodded. "What does *pahoute* mean?"

"A *pahoute* possesses *puha*," Ekararo explained. "Strong medicine."

Kris frowned. Black Eagle had called her *pahoute* from the very first. What made him think she had strong medicine?

"This is not good?" Ekararo looked troubled.

Kris hastened to reassure her. "I'm having trouble understanding."

Ekararo nodded, apparently satisfied with the vague explanation.

"I'm so glad to meet you," Kris said, hugging her impulsively. "Can you teach me Comanche, tell me what's happening, and why?"

Ekararo chuckled. "I will try, if you help me know your words."

"You don't understand me?"

"Speak slow and use small words." Ekararo demonstrated with thumb and index finger.

"Deal." Kris extended her hand. When Ekararo just looked at her, Kris grabbed her hand and pumped it. Padaponi, recognizing the action, grabbed Kris's free hand, then Ekararo's and shook until both women begged her to stop.

"Now, what can you tell me about—" Kris began eagerly.

"Wait," Ekararo held up a hand, laughing. "I bring you gift." She placed a small beaded bag in Kris's hands.

"Oh, it's lovely," Kris exclaimed, turning the bag over and over, delighted by the intricate design.

Padaponi chuckled and opened the bag for her. Kris caught the glint of familiar fabric and gasped. It was her swimsuit, cleaned and mended with strips of the softest leather sewn along the severed center, which was now laced together with long, rawhide ties. Tears filled her eyes as she fingered the tiny, neat stitches. She'd thought it was ruined, lost like her stone.

"You do not like?" Ekararo's worried voice penetrated Kris's thoughts.

"Oh, I like it very much." Kris swiped away the tears. "You've made it beautiful again. Thank you."

Ekararo blushed a deep pink, but was spared a response by the arrival of several women. Kris remembered some of them with sticks in their hands. She laid aside the swimsuit and rose to stand beside Padaponi. "What do they want?"

"*Nenewerke*," Ekararo explained.

"What's that?" Kris blanched at the long line of curious faces outside the tipi.

"How you say? Payment for damage done?"

"Payment for damages?" Kris echoed, intrigued. What an interesting idea. How did these women propose to pay for her pain?

With hesitant smiles a steady stream of women entered the tipi. They plunked blankets, a buckskin skirt and shirt, a pair of moccasins, pots of paint, several items Kris couldn't identify, and—wonder of wonders—a piece of broken mirror into Padaponi's outstretched arms, then left without a word. Padaponi grunted and nodded at each one. Ekararo stayed beside Kris, offering a name for each face. Once the gift was given, each woman hurriedly left, but not without a curious glance at Kris.

Those glances, some remorseful, some sullen, but all glowing with hope, tore at Kris's heart. She longed to tell these women that she couldn't help them. She had no special powers, and she definitely wasn't a messenger from the Great Spirit.

The flap lifted one last time and Kiyani sauntered into the tipi. Blood rushed up Kris's neck into her face; her cheeks burned. Was she imagining it, or did Kiyani's smile seem gloating? The woman's tongue darted out to slowly lick her lips. Kris blanched at the malice in her smile.

Ekararo placed a hand on Kris's arm. "What is it? What upsets you?"

Kris ignored Kiyani and smiled at Ekararo, feigning an indifference she was far from feeling. "Nothing at all."

Padaponi frowned as Kiyani slapped a gourd into her hand. Padaponi wrenched off the carved wooden plug, gave one sniff and bristled angrily. Ekararo stiffened. Kris longed to demand to know what was wrong, but kept her gaze locked on Kiyani's insolent face.

Kiyani's nasty laugh echoed in the tipi long after she flounced out.

"What is it?" Kris demanded.

Ekararo's blush turned her cheeks dark sienna. "It is from Tabenanika, the medicine man," she explained without looking at Kris. "It makes a man hungry for his woman."

"What do you mean, hungry?"

"It makes a man's . . ." Ekararo hesitated, then muttered a Comanche word, glancing at Padaponi and pointing low at her own body. "A woman rubs this on her man and it makes him like the buffalo bull."

Kris felt the sting of the insult as surely as if Kiyani had slapped her face. She'd as much as shouted that Kris would need all the help she could get to arouse a man. Had Kiyani used this stuff on Black Eagle last night? Kris's cheeks heated again, nearly matching Ekararo's blush.

Scowling, Padaponi bustled across the tipi and shoved the gourd into a large hide bag, muttering words that made Ekararo flinch, her eyes widening.

"Come, forget Kiyani." Ekararo turned to Kris with a tentative smile. "She is jealous."

"Jealous?" Kris demanded, stunned.

"I am guessing," Ekararo hedged. "She may think you wish to steal Black Eagle from her."

"What?" Incredulous, Kris stared at Ekararo. She was mistaken; she had to be. How could Black Eagle belong to Kiyani when she was married to Quannah?

Ekararo shushed her. "She may be listening."

"She's married to Quannah. What hold does she have on Black Eagle?"

Ekararo frowned, her lips pursed. "I do not know this word. What is married?"

"It's when a man and woman live together, promise to love only each other," Kris replied, unsure how to explain. "Married."

"Your men take only one wife?"

Kris nodded.

"What if the man's wife has sisters? Do they belong to him too?"

"No," Kris reiterated firmly. "One wife, sisters or not."

"Too bad." Ekararo shook her head sadly. "Too much work for one woman."

"Are Kiyani and Black Eagle married?"

"Kiyani is wife to Quannah, but Black Eagle is his brother."

"What do you mean?" An uneasy, sickening feeling radiated upward from Kris's stomach.

"She is Quannah's wife," Ekararo explained patiently. "Black Eagle is Quannah's brother; he helps Quannah care for his wives."

"*Care* for them?" Kris echoed, horrified at the extent of the caring she'd witnessed last night.

"If Quannah is away, Black Eagle meets their needs."

"You're saying Black Eagle sleeps with them? All of them?"

"That is his right," Ekararo nodded simply. "It is our way."

"What if Quannah was killed? What then?"

"Black Eagle would care for them until they found other husbands."

"Oh, God," Kris moaned, sinking onto the nearest pile of furs, her arms clutched across her abdomen. Black Eagle was married. For six nights, she'd slept with a married man. And last night she'd intruded on a married couple. Kris suddenly felt very dirty.

"I need a bath." Snatching up her mended swimsuit, she hurried out of the tipi.

* * *

Duuqua watched Padaponi and Ekararo chase the angry *pahoute*. Laughter threatened to spill from his lips as they struggled to keep up with her, but he did not want the women to see him hiding in the tipi's shadow. He had been listening as they talked, and so had Kiyani, but she had left when she'd seen him.

He decided to follow the *pahoute*. He did not trust Isatai to leave her alone. She walked swiftly through the tipis, not looking at anyone, showing no fear. The People moved from her path, then stared after her. If she would only look in their faces she would see their admiration. What did she think of his People? Could she come to love them as he did?

As he had expected, the *pahoute* went to the river. He chuckled. She had told him she carried the blood of both the People and their enemy, but he knew she must also carry the blood of a fish, or maybe an otter.

He settled into the shadows of a tree and waited while she hid in the bushes. His breath caught when she walked out wearing her strange robe, her stubborn chin high as she waded into the center of the river. He was glad the robe had not been destroyed when Isatai cut it off her. He liked the way it clung to her body, revealing every curve, even her nipples which hardened as the cool water swirled above her waist. His body heated, tightening as he watched her. Her sleek robe, shining in the sun, reminded him of an otter's fur as she glided through the water.

"What does she do?" Duuqua heard Padaponi ask as she clutched Ekararo's arm. "Does she mean to clean her body?" She gasped when the *pahoute* disappeared headfirst beneath the water. Padaponi cried out in alarm when the *pahoute* appeared again, swimming swiftly downstream. "She is escaping!"

"No." Duuqua stepped up behind the two women, startling them. "She swims like the otter. I have seen her do this before. Watch, she will flip over and return."

Padaponi gasped as the *pahoute* did what he had said. Her arms flashed in and out of the water, bringing her swiftly back up the river against the lazy current.

Duuqua watched the *pahoute* spend her anger on the water, her robe gleaming in the sun. "*Tomanoakuno*," he whispered.

"Sleek Otter?" Padaponi turned to Ekararo, who nodded, smiling.

Duuqua turned to leave, but Padaponi's words stopped him. "You do not fool me, *tua*, son of my sister."

"I do not?" Duuqua parried with a smile.

"Tomanoakuno will give you many fine children." With a merry laugh, she crossed her arms over her wide middle. "They will comfort me in my old age."

"If you live that long," Duuqua grumbled as he made his escape.

Chapter Eight

"Tomanoakuno." A group of women and children who'd been seated on the river's bank whispered the strange word as Kris stepped out of the bushes after changing back into her buckskins.

"What does that mean?" Kris asked Ekararo.

"It is the name Black Eagle has given you. It means Sleek Otter."

"Black Eagle gave it to me?" Kris knew it was an honor to be given a new name, but she liked her old one. She felt herself shedding more pieces of her identity with each passing day. Why hadn't he told her?

Ekararo nodded slowly, her excitement fading in the face of Kris's frown. "He was here, watching you in the water."

Kris looked around, but there was no sign of him. Why

hadn't he waited to tell her this news himself? She reminded herself she'd vowed to stay away from him.

Padaponi yanked on Kris's arm, urging her to start the climb up the bluff back to camp.

"Tomanoakuno." Another voice, a man's voice, gave the name an ugly sound. A cold finger of fear slid down Kris's spine. She spun in the direction of the voice. No one was there, but she recognized the menace in its tone. Coyote Droppings. She felt him watching her. She pulled the fur tighter around her shoulders as Padaponi whispered nervously to Ekararo.

Ekararo nodded. "We hurry back to tipi."

Padaponi again tugged on Kris's arm, glancing about her.

Kris took her time climbing up the bank behind Padaponi and Ekararo. She would not give that slimy worm the satisfaction of seeing her run from him.

"Tomanoakuno," he called from behind them as they neared the camp.

Kris turned to face him, not surprised that he'd waited until there were more people around to confront her.

"Isatai," Padaponi hissed, and added something low and sharp.

He ignored the little woman, fixing his attention on Ekararo whose face flushed dark red.

His words were clipped as he shoved past Padaponi and stepped boldly up to Kris. He gripped her chin and turned it as if to examine her face.

"Get your slimy hands off me." Kris slapped his hand away.

Padaponi grabbed Kris and bulldozed past him, scolding him severely. Though Kris didn't understand what she said, her delivery alone should have warned him away. But Coyote Droppings only smiled.

Padaponi dragged her toward the tipi, casting anxious glances over her shoulder. When Ekararo tried to slip past him, Coyote Droppings snatched her arm.

Kris pulled up, tensing as he whispered something low and

harsh. Ekararo shook her head frantically and tried to break away.

He spoke again, cruelly squeezing Ekararo's arm and staring into her paling face. The poor girl seemed scared to death.

"Let her go," Kris shouted, and started toward them.

Coyote Droppings continued whispering. Ekararo gasped. Her eyes widened and she clutched a protective hand over her pregnant belly. His gaze slid to her hand. He smiled an ugly little smile.

Anger rose in Kris like a red haze. If she got hold of him, she'd scratch his slimy eyes out. "What's going on?" Kris pushed Ekararo behind her just as Padaponi stepped into the middle of the crowd, issuing orders in a tone that sent most of the women, and some of the men, scurrying out of her reach.

"Isatai says tell you his words." Ekararo whispered.

"No, Ekararo," Kris said, trying to see the girl's face. "You don't have to obey him."

"I'm sorry, Kris." Her hand slipped down over her belly again. "I must."

What hold did this man have on Ekararo to make her do his bidding? Wasn't he afraid Chikoba would grind him into dust?

With a pleased smile, Coyote Droppings stared at Kris. She glared back, showing no fear as he slowly circled her, though his hot gaze made her skin crawl.

"Do you think you can become one of the People by cutting your hair and wearing new clothes?" He snickered as Ekararo translated for him. "You are *taibo*, enemy to the Comanche."

Kris's heart thudded in her chest, beating out its own drum solo as she ignored his taunt. She returned his intense perusal, gauging his size, his weight. She considered the trick she'd learned from a Comanche cousin. His moves had worked on Black Eagle, who was a much larger man than this little weasel. Did she dare try it? Her heartbeat accelerated. She'd have to get closer. Catch him off guard.

"What manner of man are you?" Kris prayed he would hear her taunt, not the quaver in her voice. "You're not a warrior.

Comanche warriors don't attack defenseless women. You must be a worm."

Ekararo translated, her voice dull, lifeless.

Coyote Droppings jerked as if she'd slapped him. He gave Kris an astonished once-over, as if remeasuring his opponent. Recovering, he snarled and lifted a hand to strike her. "You are no *pahoute*. You have no words to speak to the war council. Duuqua's vision is false. The chiefs will soon see this." He dropped his hand but stepped closer, his words seething with hatred. "Then you will die."

"Don't plan on it," Kris spat. Recognizing her moment, she tucked her leg behind his knees and yanked his feet out from under him, at the same time slamming her hands against his chest. It worked! She didn't know which of them was more surprised when he went down. Quickly, she scowled to cover her amazement.

The crowd laughed and hooted. Kris turned and walked away with Padaponi clearing a path through the crowd.

Kris knew word of the incident would reach Black Eagle. Were women allowed to strike warriors? A little late to think of consequences—after the deed was done.

What was Coyote Droppings' strange hold over Ekararo? She couldn't question Ekararo. The poor thing seemed totally stressed out. Kris didn't want to add to her anguish. She'd talk to Black Eagle about this herself, make sure he got the story straight.

Coyote Droppings made her uneasy. Something lurked beneath his surface, an energy she didn't trust. As if he were capable of true evil.

Back in the tipi, the women set about putting away the many gifts Kris had received.

Kris was overwhelmed by the generosity of the women who only yesterday had done their best to hurt her. She felt warmed by their gesture, almost welcomed. What could she do to repay them?

Look beyond your own heart, your own feelings, a quiet voice admonished. *Think of their needs before your own.*

Kris's hand stilled as shame nipped at her conscience. She had been thinking of herself too much. She hoped she wouldn't be here much longer, but while she was here she should look for ways to help these people. She didn't dare hope that she could change their destiny, yet she longed to try. But what gave her the right? And how would she go about it? Why had she been sent back in time instead of someone who could really benefit them?

And who better, came the softly whispered reply, *than you with your knowledge of their history, your love and concern for those whose blood you share?*

Chastened, Kris considered the quiet words. Her grandmother had encouraged her in her struggle to reach her goal of teaching the People's children. And now, here she was, plunked into the midst of the People. If she couldn't change their destiny, perhaps she could help them face it.

"Ekararo?" Kris began hesitantly, not sure how to begin acting on her new resolutions. "Would you answer some questions for me?"

"What do you wish to know?" Ekararo explained Kris's request to Padaponi, who nodded and continued packing Kris's new belongings into her own *natsakena*, a special wardrobe case, another gift from the *nenewerke*.

"Last night, many chiefs from different nations attended the war council."

"Yes!" Ekararo ticked off the different tribes represented on her fingers.

"Did Quannah send for them?"

"Yes, he sent messengers. The chiefs worry because the iron horse has brought many white hunters with long guns. Fighting together, our warriors will soon chase the white men off our hunting grounds."

"Haven't some of the People already moved onto the reservations?"

"Only the weak and the frightened." Ekararo sniffed and Padaponi nodded sharply in agreement. "Better to die than live like sheep."

"But don't you see?" Kris reasoned, trying to keep her alarm out of her voice while at the same time anxious to make them understand. "That's exactly what will happen. If Quannah doesn't surrender, all the People will be killed by soldiers or die of starvation."

"Quannah will never surrender." Ekararo turned to Padaponi, swiftly translating. Padaponi's head jerked up and her eyes narrowed. Her low comment stung.

"She says—"

"No need," Kris interrupted. "I see how she feels." Hurt and anger burned in the other women's eyes. Kris felt them withdrawing from her. They had opened their hearts and homes to her and she had just told them to give up, to meekly accept the government's plans for their future.

Padaponi spoke in a low, steady voice, strength and sincerity evident in every word.

"My heart filled with joy when I looked upon your face. I knew that you had come to do good to me and to my people. But your words are bitter to me.

"I was born upon the prairie, where the wind blew free and there was nothing to break the light of the sun. There were no enclosures and everything drew a free breath. I want to die there and not within walls.

"Do not ask us to leave the rivers and the sun and the wind and live in houses. Do not ask us to give up the buffalo for the sheep. This talk makes us sad and angry. Do not speak of it more."

"I'm sorry," Kris whispered, hoping they would not mistake her compassion for pity. These proud women would not accept pity. Before the tears brimming in her eyes could fall, she rushed from the tipi, seeking a quiet place where she could ponder Padaponi's words.

How could she do as Padaponi asked? Convincing Quannah and his People to surrender was the only way she knew of to help them.

If she hadn't been sent here to help them, why was she here at all?

It was time for her to leave. She'd ask Quannah for a guide to return her to the Springs as soon as possible.

"Maybe you please my wife too well."

Quannah's words burned Duuqua's ears as he strode away from his brother's tipi. His attempt to speak with Quannah before Kiyani could turn his brother's heart had not been successful.

He had found Kiyani serving Quannah his first meal of the day and had been asked to eat with them. His blood boiled as he remembered Kiyani nudging his shoulder with her breasts as she served him, seizing every opportunity to rub against him.

He knew that she taunted him with his vow never to touch her again. But she had forgotten to serve Quannah, who had become angry and sent Duuqua away.

Duuqua swore under his breath. She had done it maliciously, to bring anger between him and his brother. This sun he must tell Quannah what was in his heart.

Nearing his tipi, Duuqua drew to a halt, staring in surprise as the *pahoute* rushed past him. She did not see him for the tears filling her eyes.

"I cannot believe it!" Padaponi grumbled from inside the tipi. Duuqua listened, anxious to hear what had upset the *pahoute*. "Duuqua says she has much medicine, but I do not see it. A medicine woman would not tell us to surrender."

Frowning, he followed the *pahoute* down the path to the river. "*Pahoute*," he said, catching her arm and turning her to face him when she tried to keep her eyes from his. "What brings these to your eyes?" He lifted a tear off her cheek with his finger, remembering another tear that had fallen from her eyes to become one of the stones he now bore. As if in response to his thoughts, both stones began quietly humming.

"It's silly." She wiped the back of her hand across her cheeks and looked away from him. "Nothing for you to worry about."

"Did Padaponi or Ekararo hurt you with their words?" After hearing her speak to the war council, he could guess what she had said to his aunt, but Duuqua wanted to hear the story from her own lips. Her tears made him weak. He wanted to hold her, to comfort her. Never had he felt so toward a woman, but he liked the feeling.

"No." She gave a dry chuckle and shook her head. "I'm afraid it was something I said." Her lips trembled and the tears flowed down her cheeks.

No longer able to bear her suffering, Duuqua pulled her into his arms, tucked her head beneath his chin and held her while she cried. He rubbed her back, her hair, her arms. His own eyes squeezed tight against the pain that ripped through his chest.

"You safe. No one harm you." He wanted to keep on holding her, to never let her go, but her pride soon stopped the tears and she stepped out of his arms.

"I can't believe I did that," she murmured and ducked her head, hiding her face from him.

When he tried to tip her chin up, she pulled away, covering her face. "I look awful when I cry."

"You beautiful," he told her. He gently lifted her chin to close her gaping mouth and smiled.

"You're just saying that to make me feel better."

"Do you say I lie?" He deliberately puffed out his chest. "You call Duuqua, Quahadi war chief, liar?"

"No! I . . ." When her eyes met his, he smiled as her eyes narrowed in suspicion.

"You tease." She gave him a push, then stilled when he captured her hands against his chest.

"Tell me." He pressed her hands to him when she would have pulled away. He wished she were still in his arms, but the fires once again burned in her eyes. He knew she would fight him if he tried to hold her now. "I hear Padaponi talk to Ekararo."

She looked up and blushed, then caught her bottom lip between her teeth. Duuqua almost groaned at the urge to lean down and free her lip, then capture it himself. He forced his thoughts to safer ground.

"At war council, you tell chiefs to surrender. You say same to Padaponi and Ekararo. Is this message from Great Spirit or your words?"

"I've told you before, I'm not the Great Spirit's messenger," she said, her eyes glinting with fire. "I'm just plain Kris Baldwin. I'm not important. I'm nobody from a place so far away you couldn't begin to imagine it. I don't belong here."

"You sent to me." He squeezed her hands. He must make her understand the power of his vision. Never had his visions been so powerful, so clear. "I see your face in dream before you came to sacred waters. Great Spirit send you."

"I know what you believe." She pulled her hands free, but did not turn away. "I can't explain how all that happened, but I assure you, I'm not some divine messenger. I can't tell you or the other chiefs what to do. All I can tell you is that I know many people will die if Quannah does not surrender. You say I was sent by the Great Spirit, but you reject my words. Don't you want me to help your people?"

"Give them hope! Tell me how to chase white man away forever."

"You can't," she whispered. "Nothing I say, nothing you do will stop them."

"Then why you here?" Duuqua demanded, catching her by the shoulders.

"I don't know," she cried and shrugged off his hands. "I was hoping you could tell me. Don't you see? I can't help them. Now will you please take me back to the Springs?"

"Not until we know if you speak truth at war council," he said, shaking his head.

"I understand." She turned back to camp, walking slowly,

her shoulders slumped as if she had lost a battle. He watched her go, his heart heavy and his head filled with questions.

Surrender. How he hated the taste of that word on his tongue. He would rather die! And his warriors and all the chiefs felt the same.

He could not believe this was the message the Great Spirit had sent her to speak. Her words were too hard. She would make the people angry. Did the Great Spirit not care for her safety? Had He sent her here to be killed?

Chapter Nine

"The *pahoute* did not say what you expected to hear."

Duuqua sank to the ground beside Quannah, who sat looking over the river. "Her words were hard." His brother's words stung, but Duuqua knew he must let no one see his own doubts, not even Quannah. "She spoke from her heart without the tricks Isatai would have us believe are medicine."

"You have seen too many visions, brother. You begin to see wolves in the shadows."

"And you, my brother, often do not see the threat until the wolf is at your throat."

"Enough. It is done. After the Sun Dance we will ride against Adobe Walls. Then we will know if she speaks the truth."

Duuqua stared at the sunset, considering Quannah's words. There might be another way. If he were to heed the *pahoute*, he must believe this battle was lost before it was fought. Could she also tell him why it was lost? Could she tell him how to win it? He would ask, but this was not why he had sought Quannah. "I would speak to you about Kiyani."

"Your return pleased her."

"Yes." The memory of Kiyani's intimate caress before the *pahoute* filled Duuqua with new anger.

"She was upset that you did not—"

"Enough." Duuqua did not like to discuss Kiyani with his brother, her husband. "She talks too much."

"Kiyani married me because you refused her. It was the only way she could have you."

Duuqua met Quannah's gaze. For the first time, he saw jealousy in his brother's eyes. "You believe she does not care for you?"

"She does not come to my bed when you are in camp."

The pain in his brother's eyes loosened Duuqua's tongue and the words he had held back, not wanting to hurt Quannah, tumbled from his lips. "Release me from this duty. We are not blood brothers. I no longer wish to share this burden with you."

Quannah smiled.

"You are pleased?" Duuqua stared at Quannah in surprise. "You love her."

"Yes," Quannah said simply. "She has not allowed me to give her a child. Perhaps now, she will change her mind."

"You should have spoken of this to me before." Duuqua clasped his brother's arm, glad now that he had refused to give Kiyani his child. "I would not cause you pain."

"You have not. It was not your doing." Quannah smiled and rose, pulling Duuqua to his feet with him. "No woman can come between us."

Duuqua hoped Quannah was right, but he knew Kiyani liked to have her own way.

"Go. Speak to the *pahoute*." Quannah pushed him, looking sly as a weasel. "Find out what we must do to win this fight."

Duuqua's eyes widened. "Have you too become a medicine man? Can you now read my thoughts?"

"Only when you think of her. She is a beautiful woman."

"Is that all you see when you look at a woman?"

"What more should I see?" Quannah asked with a wide grin.

"What if her words are true?" Duuqua stared at his brother. His lack of vision made Duuqua want to grind his teeth.

"What do you care? It will not change her in any way that is important to a man," Quannah teased with a shrug. "Soon we will know if her words are true. Will it matter? Will you love her less?"

"I do not love her," Duuqua said.

"I would stay to listen to your denials, brother, but I must find Kiyani and tell her you no longer wish to bed her."

"I have told her."

"Yes." Quannah thumped Duuqua on the back. "Now I must console her."

Duuqua shook his head as he watched Quannah swagger back to camp. Never would he let himself fall in love with a woman, he vowed.

Kris spun at the sound of footsteps behind her. She squinted to make out the face of the person coming through the trees toward her. Chikoba. She sighed. She'd hoped to have a few minutes alone to brace herself for another torturous night sleeping across the fire from Black Eagle. So near, yet so far. She'd hoped to get control of her wayward emotions.

What did Chikoba want, she wondered, watching him approach with a feeling of dread. He'd been very withdrawn since the war council. Could he have found out about Coyote Droppings' treatment of Ekararo?

"Who are you?" His softly spoken words caught Kris off guard.

"Who am I?"

"What is your real name?" She flinched at the distrust in his ice-blue gaze. "You seem white, but you are not like the white women I remember from my youth—my mother, my aunts, my sister." A shudder shook his big frame.

Apparently, his memories were painful. Kris stifled an expression of sympathy, knowing he would reject it.

"You do not dress like them, talk like them. You don't even walk like them. Who are you?"

"Just a woman." What more could she say that wouldn't be a blatant lie?

"Where did Black Eagle find you?" His voice had risen.

Kris took a deep breath, trying to stay calm, to keep her voice level and not let him hear her fear. "He found me at Barton . . . at the sacred waters."

"What do you hide, woman? Where did he find you?"

"At the sacred waters. I swear it." Though he kept his distance, Kris sensed Chikoba's growing anger. She took a wary step back. "My people call the sacred waters Barton Springs."

"What lies did you tell him to get him to bring you here?" The cool blue of his eyes belied the heat in his words—not so his hands, which were fisted at his sides.

"None!" she said, bristling at his accusations. "He didn't ask me to come. Actually, he didn't give me much choice." She laughed, a huff of air completely devoid of humor. "You heard all this in the war council. Why would I lie? What do I have to gain?"

"I do not know, nor do I care," Chikoba hissed. "But I have much to lose."

"What do you have that I could take from you?"

"I have made a place for myself here among people I once hated."

"Black Eagle . . . ?"

Chikoba shook his head and stepped past Kris. He stared into the sky as he answered. "He bought me from a band of Kiowa. White Bear's band." A shudder wracked his strong, broad shoulders. "But I was never Duuqua's slave. He taught me to be a man, a warrior. He gave me back my pride. And now there's Ekararo."

"I like Ekararo," Kris told him, hoping to dispel his suspicious attitude. "I'm no threat to you, Chikoba." She briefly considered telling him that Coyote Droppings was the real threat to his happiness, but she couldn't bring herself to betray Ekararo. If Ekararo wanted her husband's help, she'd have to be the one to ask for it.

His head swung around and his gaze fastened on her face. He didn't blink; his eyes never left her face. And in his eyes she saw determination and fear. What was wrong with him? What had she done to make him so angry?

"You spoke at the war council of death, of burning and rape, and the reservations. How do you know these things will happen?" He became impatient when she didn't immediately respond. "Tell me woman. How do you know these things?"

"I know the future," Kris whispered, desperately trying to think of an explanation he could understand, accept. "You must believe me. That's all I can tell you."

It was the wrong thing to say. She knew it as soon as the words tumbled from her lips. She whirled to run, but she wasn't fast enough.

Chikoba caught her arm and shoved her, knocking her flat. He followed her down, pinning her with his massive body. She struggled, but she was no match for him. His hands circled her neck and he began to squeeze. "Tell me the truth. I know you are not Kris Baldwin. You cannot be. I saw her die."

Kris forgot to struggle, just lay frozen, staring into his hard face.

"A half-breed let them into the stockade, showed them where to find us." His fingers tightened.

Oh, God, help me! Kris moaned as she pried at his fingers. "I'd never betray my People," she croaked. "You've got to believe me. I could never do something like that."

"I watched them kill her. They took a lot longer than I will take with you."

"Please, don't do this," she whispered.

"Who are you?" He shook her, letting her head thump against the hard ground. "Why have you stolen her name? Do you work for the soldiers? Will you tell them where we are?"

She cried out at the pain, but not a sound escaped her. *I'm Kris Baldwin,* she tried to answer, but couldn't squeeze the words past the strong fingers tightening around her throat. She squeezed her eyes shut. She couldn't bear the hatred burning in his. Bright spots flashed behind her eyelids like flashbulbs exploding in the darkness.

She seemed weightless. Her fingers slipped off his hands.

"Let go, Chikoba."

Dear God, she was hallucinating. She thought she heard Black Eagle's voice.

It took all her strength to push back the darkness, to open her eyes to search for him. She wasn't hallucinating. Black Eagle had come.

"Would you kill the Great Spirit's messenger?"

Hurry, hurry! A tiny cry of distress escaped the vise around her throat. *Didn't he realize she was dying here?*

"You want the People to suffer for her death?"

Chikoba's hands loosened slightly. Greedily, Kris gasped for air. Not enough! She couldn't get a good breath. She needed more. Much more. She moaned and clawed at Chikoba's fingers.

"She is not His messenger, Duuqua," Chikoba shouted and flung himself off her. "You are blinded by her beauty. I have seen the lust in your eyes when you look at her."

Kris rolled onto her side, away from the two men. Clutching her aching throat, she gasped the sweet, cool air. The two men switched to Comanche. Their words, at first loud and angry, soon became quieter. She glanced over her shoulder and gaped in astonishment as Black Eagle clasped Chikoba's arm. After one long, chilling look at her, Chikoba left. He hadn't believed a word she said. And he didn't trust her. In seconds, the thunder of his horse's hooves filled the silence.

Would he keep Ekararo away from her? Tears stung Kris's eyes. Even after only a day, the thought of losing her friendship hurt. Kris needed Ekararo, needed someone to talk to, to help her understand this strange life, the ways of the People.

She sat up, but was still too shaken to stand. Shudders raced up and down her body. She rubbed her arms, trying to generate some heat, knowing it wouldn't reach deep enough.

Black Eagle crouched down beside her. "Are you hurt?" He tipped her head up and examined her throat. An angry hiss escaped him and his lips thinned.

She tried to answer him, but her teeth began chattering.

Black Eagle left her sitting there and, though she ached at being left alone, not a sound came from her lips. She trembled in relief when he returned with a blanket and wrapped it around her, then sat and pulled her onto his lap. Only then did the tears come, accompanied by huge, painful sobs as her hungry lungs fought to replace her body's depleted store of oxygen. Through it all, he held her tight, keeping her warm.

When she finally stopped sobbing, he brushed stray hairs off her forehead. "You were very brave last night."

She shook her head firmly. "Scared," she whispered, relieved to notice that speaking became easier with each word.

Black Eagle smiled. "The heart of a warrior beats in your body."

Kris ducked her head, missing the curtain of long hair that used to hide her heating cheeks. She was stunned by his compliment.

His finger traced down her cheek, then tipped her chin up. He kissed the tip of her nose. His warm breath fanned her cheek. He smelled faintly of woodsmoke and that singular scent that was his alone and that made her feel safe, protected.

Dear God! This man was more dangerous than Chikoba. She became uncomfortably aware of the vulnerability of her position and recalled Chikoba's taunt about the lust in Black Eagle's eyes when he looked at her.

"Thank you for saving my life—again," she whispered when she could breathe without that tiny hitch in her chest.

"You must stop getting into trouble."

Nerves jangling, Kris slid off his lap, anxious to put some

distance between them. She pulled the blanket tight against the chills that still wracked her. The darkness around them seemed deep and threatening.

She'd thought she was safe with Chikoba and look what he'd done to her. She scooted farther away from Black Eagle. Could she still trust him?

His chest lifted on a deep sigh. "You change my life, woman. Nothing the same."

"Oh? And mine hasn't changed? At least I didn't drag you off into the wilderness and refuse to tell you where I was taking you. And this business of me being the Great Spirit's messenger. What a bunch of hogwash."

"Hog wash?"

"Exactly."

He cocked his head. "White men wash hogs?"

"What?" Kris stared up at him, unaware that her mouth had fallen open.

He closed it with a finger beneath her chin and smiled. "You the Great Spirit's messenger."

She stared into the deep, dark pools of his eyes, suddenly speechless from the heat of his finger stroking her jawline. If he kept this up, he might even convince her. She gulped. What was he up to?

"No, I'm not. You brought me here, remember. I didn't just drop from the sky." *But you have been dragged back through time*, she reminded herself.

"How you know about Isatai's paint and Adobe Walls?" He gripped her chin and forced her to meet his probing gaze. "How you know things no one speaks of outside war council?"

"I can't explain." Kris jerked free of his gentle restraint. "But it's not because I'm some sort of holy messenger."

"Tell me how you know," he commanded, gripping her shoulders when she would have turned away. "I will protect you."

"And who will protect me from you?"

"I already have, many times."

She couldn't—wouldn't—consider what he meant by that. Neither could she stop the response his words sent surging through her. Kris backed away from the heat in his eyes as he stepped closer. His gaze slid to her lips.

Instinctively, her tongue flicked out to moisten them. She blushed. Why had she done that? He'd think it was an invitation to kiss her.

"You are safe with me."

Could the man read her mind? "Then why are you stalking me?"

"Why do you keep backing away?"

"You make me nervous."

"You fear me or yourself?"

He *could* read her mind.

"Come," he ordered, settling on a wide, flat rock. "Sit."

He didn't glance up as she weighed his request, then sat more than an arm's length away.

"I no attack you."

"Hmph." She snorted, but scooted a little closer, still not touching him.

He cast a disgusted glance at the distance she'd left between them—more than a hand's breadth.

"Well?" she asked.

"What?"

"I know you didn't ask me over here because you can't bear to be away from me."

He grinned.

"What do you want to know?" she asked, oddly pleased that he appreciated her sarcasm.

"You very wise."

"No. I've just got you figured out."

"Huh," he snorted. "I do have questions."

"Fire."

"What?"

"Where I come from it means 'Shoot.' Start asking your questions."

He shook his head, but fired. "Your words to war council hard. The chiefs worry. Difficult for them to listen to your words."

She sighed. "I told them the truth. I couldn't lie and tell them everything would be okay."

"How we win at Adobe Walls?"

She froze, disappointed by his telling question. He didn't completely believe her, but just in case she did know, he wanted to hedge his bets. Only now did she realize how desperately she'd hoped that he, at least, would believe her. She should have known better.

"You stare into darkness. What you see, woman?"

"You're going ahead with the raid in spite of what I told you. And you want me to tell you how to win? Am I supposed to prove myself?" She gave a scornful laugh when he refused to meet her eyes. At least he had the good grace to look away. "You wouldn't believe me if I told you."

"Tell me how to destroy white buffalo hunters." Black Eagle repeated the question, leaning over her, his gaze burning into hers as he waited for an answer.

Kris knew that the only way she could positively impact this situation was to convince them not to fight. Apparently, that wasn't a possibility. What would a modern mercenary do? She answered her own futile question without realizing she'd spoken aloud. "Steal a tank, enough Uzi's for every warrior, a bunch of grenades and send in the Marines."

"What are these things?"

"Weapons my people use in warfare."

"Speak words I understand, woman."

"I'm sorry," she whispered. How could she make him understand? "It's so frustrating! I know what's going to happen, but I can't prevent it."

"What can we do?"

"Don't use Coyote Droppings' paint."

"We will prove it before we use it."

"Only fair." Kris mulled over their tactical options. "You

won't be able to surprise them." The pole supporting the roof of the main building at Adobe Walls had broken in the middle of the night. The hunters were up most of the night fixing it. They'd just gone back to bed when the Comanche attacked at dawn.

What was she thinking? How could she sit here helping him figure out how to kill white men? But why not? If she didn't, those white men would kill his warriors—and him. She clutched her head. She was caught in the middle. Damned if she helped, damned if she didn't. Where did her allegiance lie?

She had to admit that right now she leaned toward the Comanche. She'd always favored the underdog. But could she make a difference? Would her advice help? Should she tamper with history? Was that what she'd been sent here to do?

"Can't you just forget this battle?" She gripped his arm in frustration. "Don't you see? Win or lose at Adobe Walls, the soldiers will come. Your people will die for nothing."

"The Quahadi are warriors." He shook off her hand. "If the soldiers want us, let them come and find us."

She stared at him, his words ringing in her ears. She'd thought Quannah had said that. Either the history books weren't accurate or he was repeating something he'd heard Quannah say. Were the history books wrong? Could she do more than push the Comanche to surrender? How could she ask Black Eagle to relinquish the fierce pride, the determination that was such a huge part of him?

"Do not speak of surrender," he warned in a cold whisper. "I would rather die."

Kris no longer questioned his ability to anticipate what she would say, guess what she was thinking. She prayed she could convince his People to surrender before that could happen.

"We must return to camp." He helped her to her feet. His touch, gentle as always, suddenly seemed impersonal, and was quickly withdrawn.

Her heart ached. She wanted him to hold her again, to

comfort her and tell her everything would be all right, that he wouldn't be injured or killed in the raid. She peeked a glance at him through her lashes. In spite of her resolve, her gaze settled on his lips. They'd felt soft and smooth against her cheek, her forehead when he'd held her while she cried. How would they feel against her mouth? How would he taste?

How would he kiss when his heart was in it?

She remembered their brief kiss. This man had taken her mouth with hunger, his tongue had searched out her secrets, his breath had filled her soul while his arms held her captive.

She'd been sorry when he let her go.

Kris tossed her head, shaking off the torrid thoughts, deeply ashamed of herself. As if sensing her turmoil, he glanced over at her and her heart slammed to a stop. Had he guessed what she'd been thinking? The moonlight kissed his broad brow, sharpened the blade of his nose and turned his eyes mysterious, deep and full of shadows. She longed to trace the lethal edge of his jaw, explore the weathered lines beside his mobile mouth. He searched her gaze and Kris shuddered, wanting to warm herself at the banked fire in his eyes. If she reached out, touched him, would he once again shove her away?

She told herself he wasn't what she wanted.

Hah! she scoffed at herself. She'd looked long and hard and she'd never found a man like him. She'd had to fall through some abyss, backward in time, to find a man who touched a chord deep in her heart, only to realize she could never have him. He was taken.

Vividly, she remembered the torrid scene she'd interrupted the night before, saw another woman in those strong arms, another woman writhing beneath his drugging kisses.

She straightened, pulling her gaze from his, amazed at her own strength of will. She would not be another Kiyani to this man.

His gaze cooled. He turned from her.

Fool, she called herself. *Why do you look for feelings that sim-*

ply aren't there? This man is, for all intents and purposes, married—and to more than one woman.

He strode ahead of her, his long hair lifting on the breeze, his shoulders broad and strong, tapering sharply into lean, narrow hips and long legs. Beautiful. Deadly.

The wind embraced her, chilling her marrow deep. Her heart seemed nothing more than a dull ache in her chest. Even the warm blanket she clutched tighter around her, couldn't warm her. This chill couldn't be warmed. It even had a name: despair.

Chapter Ten

Duuqua whipped a rawhide thong around a joint in the framework of the Sun Dance lodge and yanked it tight. Sweat streamed off his chest and back. His body ached from a day spent chopping trees and gathering brush to build the lodge.

Pride will not feed your children.

No matter how hard he worked, the words continued to run through his head like a chant. It did not matter that he had no children. Since the war council, every time he looked at a child, any child, he imagined it injured, dying.

For three days he had seen the *pahoute* only at a distance, but he remembered her body in his arms the night he rescued her from Chikoba. The sweet taste of her lingered on his lips, her cool skin burned his aching fingers. He no longer slept in his tipi, for the sight of her, the scent of her, drove him mad.

By the Sun! The woman had cursed him. Because of her, he sweated over the building of this lodge. One of the older men could have directed its building, but Duuqua had asked to do it, so he could avoid her. He could not be near her without touching her, but every time he did, he remembered she was the Great Spirit's messenger.

"Hurry." He shouted at a woman bringing the next bundle of brush to be tied onto the lodge wall.

"Don't take your frustration out on her."

There was her voice again. The *pahoute's* voice. Was he never to know peace?

"It's me you're mad at, so yell at me, not her."

Duuqua dropped his ball of rawhide and jerked around. His breath caught and his heart started a war dance. Had it only been three days since he had stood this close to her? He had missed her. The thought made him scowl.

"What you want, woman?" Duuqua drew her away from the eager ears surrounding them. He released her quickly; her skin scorched his fingers. Shame heated his cheeks. His dark temper became even blacker. Could he not even touch this woman without lusting after her?

"I want to help." Bright color burned in her cheeks. "And you seem to be the man in charge. What can I do?"

"No." He scooped up the fallen rawhide, his fingers clenching over the tight ball. He could not spend his days with her, could not work beside her. Nothing would get done.

"No? Just like that? What, no explanations, no phoney excuses? No discussion?" She kicked at a stone. It flipped up, hit his arm.

Soft chuckles broke the silence around them. Duuqua flicked a glance at the people who had stopped working to watch. Though they did not speak the white man's words, they understood the *pahoute's* actions. He grunted and rubbed his stinging arm.

He turned slowly. The *pahoute* had covered her mouth with one hand, but her eyes danced. "You not fear my anger?"

"I'm not afraid of you." Though she spoke bravely, she backed away as he stepped closer. Her eyes popped wide when he grabbed her arm. "Let me go."

He pulled her with him as he walked away from the lodge,

ignoring her attempts to free herself. His problems would not fill the old women's mouths.

Glancing over his shoulder, he sighed. The men who had been working on the lodge had already settled in the shade. The women would soon join them. He sighed again. It was more than one man could do. He did need help, but not the *pahoute*'s.

He sat cross-legged in the shade of the nearest tree. "Speak, woman. But do not take all day. I have work to do."

"Of all the pig-headed, rude, inconsiderate . . ."

"You waste sunlight."

She spun to leave and the fringe on her skirt flipped up and stung his cheek.

Wincing, he caught her skirt and yanked.

"Oooh!" She flew backward and slammed against his chest, knocking the wind out of him as she slid into his lap.

The warm curve of her bottom settled over his manhood. He gritted his teeth to keep from moaning as he felt himself swell and grow.

With a cry of outrage, she lashed out. Her fists hit him in the chest, knocking him flat on his back. His badly frayed temper broke loose.

Dust flew as he rolled on top of her, pinning her arms down with his elbows while she yelled and twisted beneath him. Would she never shut up? His breath caught in his throat as his manhood pressed between her thighs. He stared at her open mouth and sighed. There was only one way to silence a woman.

He watched her lips, waiting for the right moment.

"Oh, no you don't." She bucked, trying to throw him off. "I see what you're trying to do. Don't you dare kiss me just to shut me up, you—you womanizer."

He gritted his teeth, praying she would stop bucking before he lost control. He must kiss her soon, or . . .

What was he thinking? He could not kiss the Great Spirit's messenger right here before all the People. Even to shut her up.

"Silence, woman," he roared in frustration. He rolled to his feet, yanked her up and gave her a firm shove to send her on her way.

"Quit!" She swatted away his hands, then faced him, her eyes big and glistening.

Duuqua groaned. She was not finished making him miserable.

"I just asked if I could help." She ducked her head and shook the dirt off her skirt, but he saw the bright color in her cheeks, felt an answering heat in his own. "And you throw me in the dirt and humiliate me."

Duuqua flinched as a tear rolled down her cheek. "Do not cry." His hands curled into fists. He would not touch her. His life had not been the same since wiping the tears off her face.

She swiped away the tear with the back of her hand, leaving a dirty streak.

He brushed the dirt from her cheek. He could not keep from touching her. He tucked his hands under his arms. "The chiefs think you bring bad medicine on our plans."

"Bad medicine?" She sniffed, frowned up at him.

A knife stabbed him in the heart.

"Is that why Ekararo won't talk to me? She scurries away if I even look at her."

"Chikoba . . ."

"I know she's just following his orders. But it hurts."

The knife twisted. Duuqua clenched his teeth. He tried to look away again, but could not. He wanted to snatch her into his arms and stroke her hair and kiss her cheeks and whisper that everything would be all right, always. Instead, he snapped at her. "It is not your concern."

She winced at his sharp answer and her eyes became deep pools of misery. The knife in his chest drew blood. He could take no more! He must get away from her before he forgot she was the Great Spirit's messenger, before he grabbed her and ravaged that full, trembling mouth.

He turned his back on her, but flinched at the soft sob she tried to cover as she ran from him.

"Kris." Duuqua looked up to find Padaponi staring after the *pahoute*.

"Let her go." He squirmed under his aunt's scowl. "It is better this way."

"Better for who?" Padaponi sniffed. "For you? Did you not see her tears?"

"I cannot help her." Duuqua turned away from her anger.

"Cannot or will not?" Padaponi looked him up and down as if he were a stranger, not her sister's son. "Why did you bring her here?"

"I did not bring her here, *pia*," he reminded gently, calling her mother to show his respect and cool her anger. It did not help. "The Great Spirit sent her to us."

"Your quiet words will not calm my tongue, *tehnap*."

"Yes, I am a grown man," he said, acknowledging her reminder. "I do not need to be told what to do."

"Someone must tell you."

Duuqua waited, knowing he would have no peace until she had spoken the words in her heart.

"The People grumble that you cannot be pleased. They call you Big Grizzly."

"There is much to do." He had too much on his mind to worry what the People said behind his back.

"Never before has work made your spirit ugly."

He flinched at her words. "It is the woman." He turned a shoulder to her. His workers still sat in the shade. Could his aunt not see that he had work to do? "But she does not matter."

"Why did you bring her here only to throw her away like a much-gnawed bone?"

"I have not thrown her away."

"You call her a gift of the Great Spirit, but you treat her worse than an enemy."

"Worse than an enemy? She is fed, clothed—"

"At least the enemy knows what you think of him."

"Her words were hard. She caused much fear, much anger."

"When you took her up before you on your horse, did you ask if her words would be hard or soft? No. You asked only that she speak the words of the Great Spirit. His words are not always easy to hear."

"No, *pia*. They are not." Was Padaponi right? Had he been punishing the *pahoute* because he did not like her message?

"She has not changed. When my eyes touch her face, I see the same frightened woman I saw the first day you threw her into your tipi." Padaponi's eyes narrowed as she turned to the river where the *pahoute* had run. "What do you see?"

Duuqua searched his mind and found the *pahoute*—battling the water, angry and annoyed. At him. He smiled, remembering how she moved in the water—like the otter, sleek and shining. "Tomanoakuno." The name slipped from his lips.

"Perhaps a better name would be Lost One."

He could not look in Padaponi's face. She would see the lust in his eyes and the longing in his heart for this woman he had sworn to protect. "What do you wish me to see?" No words could say what he saw, what he felt when he looked on the *pahoute*. His aunt's words pricked like thorns. If she did not stop soon, he would bleed.

"Love," she snapped, her eyes boring into his. "Do not turn from it."

He watched his aunt walk away from him, feeling shame at her bowed shoulders, her shaking head. His mind fled back to the river and he watched Tomanoakuno walk out of the water, weary and silent. He could not tell his aunt that when he looked on this woman he saw only one thing—pain.

Pain made him drive his helpers to finish the lodge. Duuqua's heart ached. How could he fulfill his duty to his People and satisfy his desire for this woman?

How could he give his heart to a woman the Great Spirit would soon tear from his arms?

* * *

Kris squeezed the water from her hair then smoothed it back from her face. As always, the rigorous exercise had helped to clear her head.

She couldn't go on like this. She had to concentrate on how to get back to the Springs and why she'd been sent here. Was there something she needed to accomplish? She had to figure it out, and soon, before she made a complete fool of herself over Black Eagle.

Over the last few days, she'd had a lot of time to think. She'd almost convinced herself she was here to persuade Quannah to surrender. She'd remembered that no historian had ever been able to explain why Quannah had changed from a warrior hell-bent on killing every white man he found to a concerned, forward-thinking chief determined to help his People adapt to the white man's reservation. His about-face had been so sudden and so complete that historians said it was as though he suddenly forgot he had Comanche blood. But the People, even in her time, believed it had all been a front, an elaborate trick to deceive the enemy and win concessions for his People. Still, Kris had always wondered what made him change.

Was she the catalyst, the missing link in the chain of events? She sucked in a deep breath at the thought.

Uncertain as she found her situation, she knew she could do nothing until after the battle at Adobe Walls. Once the battle had been lost, they would realize she'd told them the truth. Then they'd come looking for her and she'd make them listen. She could explain everything, convince them to surrender, then return to the Springs to search for her stones and return to her own time.

She felt comfortable with her reasoning, with one tiny exception. If she was here to help Quannah, why hadn't he been there when she traveled back through time? How did Black Eagle fit into this? And why did she keep having those disturbing bouts of déjà vú? The images that kept flashing through her head seemed so real, so frightening.

Involved in her troubling thoughts, Kris walked slowly back to Padaponi's tipi. She sighed. She knew she was the reason Black Eagle spent so little time there lately. She'd suspected he was avoiding her. It hurt to know she was right.

She glanced around her at the People scurrying about, happy smiles on every face, purpose in each step. Coyote Droppings had convinced them they couldn't lose. They seemed eager for the coming battle, almost giddy with anticipation.

Until she approached.

Bad medicine. Black Eagle's explanation stung. Skunks got better treatment. Did they really believe one woman could jinx their plans? Did Black Eagle still believe that the People needed her? Or had she become a nuisance, a humiliating reminder to him that his vision was a failure?

She ducked her head, overwhelmed and frustrated, and plowed headlong into someone.

Too late, Kris reached out to catch the person she'd sent flying, startled by a glimpse of staring blue eyes and flying blond hair. "Excuse me."

A young white woman stumbled and fell. Her buckskin skirt flew up and she twisted, yanking it back over her legs, but not before Kris saw the bruises—some fading into gray-green, some fresh purple. Before Kris could recover, the woman gasped, clawing at a rope around her neck. Secured by a slip-knot, it had tightened when she fell.

"I'm so sorry." Face aflame with embarrassment, Kris fumbled the knot loose. "Let me help you."

"No." The woman shoved her hands away. "Do not try to help me." She sent a fearful glance past Kris, then curled into a ball, her arms covering her head.

"No, let me help. I'm such a klutz . . ." Kris didn't understand the woman's actions until she turned. White Bear, one of the war chiefs, stood behind her, scowling. His mean eyes slid over her breasts, then narrowed to slits as he turned his attention to the blond woman. His arm lifted and

slashed swiftly down again. Kris caught only a blur of movement, like a snake hissing through the air. The woman
lurched, crying out in pain. A long red welt took shape on
her leg.

Horrified, Kris jumped between White Bear and the woman
before he could strike again. "Stop that!"

"Get away or he'll whip you too, no matter who owns you,"
the woman warned, without releasing her head.

"You're a captive?" Kris stared, dumbfounded, as White
Bear used the rope around her neck to yank the woman to her
feet, and gave Kris a shove that sent her flying. She landed
hard. Stunned, she struggled to catch her breath, watching in
horror as White Bear whipped the young woman in earnest,
driving her to her knees. The seams of his soldier coat
strained under his heaving muscles. A hideous smile curved
his lips and lit his eyes.

Kris staggered to her feet and struggled closer, pushing aside
the people who had gathered to watch. Furious, she moved to
once again step between White Bear and the woman but a
firm hand stopped her.

"She spoke the truth. It will be easier for her if you do not
interfere. You must not risk yourself, Messenger."

Kris glared into the sad eyes of Little Wolf, the Cheyenne
chief, also a member of the war council. "Ah, good. You speak
English." She gave him a grim smile. "Translate for me. I want
that animal to understand every word I say."

"Do not." Once again, Little Wolf tried to stop her. "She
belongs to White Bear. It is his right to punish her."

"She's a human being." Kris shook off Little Wolf's hand
and once again stepped between White Bear and his captive,
who cowered beneath the slashing whip.

"Stop. Now." Kris yanked the rope out of White Bear's
hand. Absolute silence fell, broken only by a soft whimper
from the woman, who lay still on the ground behind Kris.

Kris loathed the touch of White Bear's foul gaze, but she
faced him squarely, ignoring her heart's erratic rhythm. "It

wasn't her fault; it was an accident. I knocked her down. I wasn't watching where I was going."

Fire and fury flashed in White Bear's eyes and with a roar he raised the whip. Time suddenly hung suspended as the leather strands flashed toward her. She had no time to defend herself, no time to duck the blow. She couldn't breathe, couldn't think, couldn't hear anything but the thunder of her own heartbeat in her ears.

With a seething hiss, time and sound resumed as an arm appeared from out of nowhere and took the blow meant for her. She stared, mesmerized, as the lash snapped around the upraised arm, drawing blood.

"The *pahoute* asked you to stop." Black Eagle's voice, low and chilling, belied the murderous fire in his eyes as he placed himself between Kris and White Bear. With the injured arm, he yanked the whip from White Bear's hand. Little Wolf stepped up beside Black Eagle.

Appalled at how close she'd come to feeling that lash rip her flesh, Kris trembled in aftershock. If Black Eagle hadn't stepped in when he had . . .

Black Eagle! Kris jerked back to awareness. She'd started this. She couldn't let him take the heat for her actions. But first she glanced back to make sure the woman was safe.

The sight that greeted her sent her to her knees with a hand clutched over her mouth. White Bear had shredded the woman's buckskin blouse. Her exposed back was covered by raised weals, some oozing blood. But the livid bruises and un-healed stripes beneath those freshly laid kindled a fire in Kris's breast.

Hearing a sharply indrawn breath, she glanced up. A muscle flexed in Black Eagle's taut jaw as his gaze moved from the woman to her, searching for injury. Kris blanched at the fury in his eyes as he drew her to her feet. He tried to put her behind him, to shield her with his body, but Kris wedged herself between him and Little Wolf. Together, the three of them barred White Bear from his captive.

White Bear shouted, his hand hovering over his knife, his face purple with rage. Calmly, Black Eagle uncoiled the lash, exposing a wound that circled from wrist to elbow. Blood dripped from his fingers. Kris reeled, assaulted by a sensation of white-hot pain. That wound would have been hers and it had been aimed at her chest! Her vision narrowed until White Bear was all she could see. Her fingers curled into claws. Black Eagle's arm circled her waist, holding her back.

White Bear eyed Black Eagle, then barked a command.

Little Wolf replied, his voice even, controlled, not a shred of anger evident.

White Bear's ugly laugh and angry words blistered the air. People around them gasped.

"What did he say?" Kris's skin crawled as his hot eyes traveled up her body, measuring, weighing.

Little Wolf shrugged. "I asked him how much he wanted for her."

"Brilliant." If the woman wasn't White Bear's captive, he couldn't mistreat her. "What did he say?"

"He said he'd trade her for you and three horses."

Kris's stomach pitched. Bile stung the back of her throat at White Bear's lust-filled leer. Knowing he wouldn't understand a word she said, she spat in his face.

Enraged, White Bear drew back his fist, then hesitated at a low command from Black Eagle. White Bear glared his hatred at both of them, but he dropped his fist, his lips curling in a sneer. He said something, but stopped when Black Eagle's hand flashed to his knife.

Kris's heart thudded in her chest. How had this gotten so far out of hand? Why hadn't she just watched where she was going? She couldn't bear to look at Black Eagle's wound, knowing her carelessness, her clumsiness, had caused his pain. And the woman . . . Kris felt sick at heart, but she couldn't give in to her emotions. Not yet.

She welcomed the sound of Little Wolf's calm, reasonable voice. But he spoke only one, maybe two words.

White Bear's eyes narrowed and he answered in kind. Few words, sharply delivered.

Little Wolf beckoned two young braves out of the crowd.

Kris stared between Black Eagle and Little Wolf. "What happened?"

White Bear shouted, gesturing at the lash Black Eagle held in his hand.

Black Eagle studied the lash for a moment, as if it were something he'd like to kill. He looked back at White Bear and shook his head.

This time White Bear reached for his knife. Black Eagle and Little Wolf tensed; their knives flashed from their sheaths, points down and ready. White Bear stared at the two men, then shrugged and stomped away.

Kris heaved a sigh of relief. "Will someone please tell me what's going on?"

"My wives are going to be busy and a little jealous, I think," Little Wolf said, grinning as if the possibility pleased him.

"I feel responsible for this whole mess. What can I do to help her? Surely there's something I can do."

Little Wolf gestured and one of the braves lifted the semi-conscious woman and laid her over the other man's shoulder. Her head lolled on his shoulder, her feet swinging well above the ground. Clamping an arm about her hips for support, the warrior carried the woman away.

Kris clutched a hand to her chest, aching at each low moan the woman uttered. "What will happen to her?"

"She belongs to me now. She is no longer your concern."

Kris sucked in a horrified breath. Had the poor woman traded one monster for another?

Little Wolf stiffened, as if he'd read her thoughts. His eyes flashed. "She will be well treated. I will take her into my tipi, but not to use her as White Bear has done. My name will protect her."

"I'm sorry." Kris blushed, ashamed of the slur she'd unwittingly delivered. "I meant no insult."

Little Wolf relaxed enough to smile. "When she is healed, I will barter with the soldiers for her release."

"Sell her? Again?"

Little Wolf grinned, then nodded at Black Eagle. "You explain."

Black Eagle spoke quickly, his words tense and edgy. "New blankets and pretty beads will reward his wives for the care they give her."

Kris nodded and turned to Black Eagle. "Thank you for taking that." She nodded at his bloody arm. "I'll go with you to find Padaponi and get it taken care of." He must be in a great deal of pain, judging by his black frown. "It's going to leave a nasty scar."

"Better my arm than your face."

"No, White Bear aimed for my chest, the same place his eyes always seem to settle."

A muscle twitched in Black Eagle's jaw. "It would have flipped upward and laid your cheek open."

"You can't know that . . ." Kris was staggered by the malice behind such an act.

"I have seen White Bear do this before."

Kris's knees shook as she fully realized the danger she'd faced. Black Eagle's hand slipped under her arm and she almost sagged against him.

"Thank you." She gave him a shaky smile, then straightened as Little Wolf's astute gaze slid between them.

"You wish to repay me for helping the woman?"

"Yes," Kris answered eagerly. "What can I do?"

Little Wolf addressed his request to Black Eagle. "I have questions to ask the Great Spirit's messenger about my own People, the Cheyenne."

"But I'm not—"

Black Eagle squeezed her shoulder, silencing her.

Kris gave Little Wolf a considering glance. The hope in his eyes seared her soul. She'd read about the Cheyenne, about Little Wolf especially. The bleakness in his eyes told her that he would not be surprised by anything she told him.

She nodded. "I will answer your questions if I can."

Little Wolf nodded gravely. "I will send for you." He glanced at Black Eagle. "Guard her well."

Guard her well. The words of the Great Spirit on Little Wolf's tongue condemned Duuqua, stirring him to anger.

The *pahoute* shot him a nervous glance. "I think I'll go find Padaponi."

He laid a hand on her shoulder to keep her from leaving. Sick anguish filled him as he remembered White Bear's whip streaking toward her.

"Never do that again, woman." In his anguish, he lashed out at her.

"Do what?" She turned on him, her eyes on fire. "Defend a fellow human being from brutality? What would you have done? Let him beat her?"

"It was his right."

"Well, I'm sorry, I don't believe anyone has the right to treat another person like that."

Though he didn't understand her words, her anger was clear. "You could have been hurt."

"You don't understand."

He understood very well and it made his stomach clench. She had been threatened and he had not been there to protect her.

"I couldn't just stand by and watch. It was my fault."

He turned her to face him, determined to make her understand. "I no always be with you. You protect self too. Never step before whip."

"You don't understand." She leaned closer and he forgot all but her nearness, her warmth, her body so close to his. "That could have been me."

"Almost was you, woman."

"I'm surprised you care, Black Eagle." She laughed, but there was no joy in the sound.

Hot blood rushed through him. "You think I no care?"

He had stayed away from her so that she would not sense his confusion. He had let his own feelings come before his responsibility to protect her. "I care, *pahoute*. If the People hurt you, make Great Spirit angry."

"You brought me here to speak to your war council, but when I didn't say what you wanted to hear, you cast me aside like so much trash."

Trash? He did not know this word, but sensed that it was not good. There was anger in her words, but no fire. Had he hurt her so badly?

The sadness in her eyes tore at his heart. "I want to go home. Would you take me back to the place where you found me?"

"No." The refusal jumped from his lips, surprising him, even as the stones started throbbing. Why did she keep asking this? He stopped his hand before it touched his medicine bundle and stepped away from her. Could she sense the stones pounding as fast and hard as his heart at her words?

"You know I'm not a messenger from the Great Spirit. Take me back, or if you can't, find someone else to do it."

"The People need you."

"They hate me. Coyote Droppings wants me dead. You don't believe anything I've said. If you're so determined to protect me, take me back where you found me. I'm not safe here."

"I will not take you back, woman," he growled, bending low so that she could not miss his words, his anger. "You stay here, with me. Do not ask again."

She said nothing, only stared at him for a long moment, then walked away.

The stones pounded against his chest as he watched her go. Would she try to escape? He would have Padaponi watch her.

He must hope she had learned a lesson today and would be more careful in her dealings with his People.

"Duuqua?" A young Cheyenne brave approached. "Little Wolf asks you to share his sweat lodge after the sun sets."

"Tell Little Wolf I am honored."

"He asks that you bring the medicine woman."

"To share the sweat lodge?"

The brave chuckled. "No, to see the woman whose life she saved this day."

"She did not save the woman's life."

The brave shrugged off Duuqua's denial. "My people believe she did. The woman was badly injured."

"I will bring the *pahoute*," Duuqua agreed, though he disliked this young man's manners.

"No," the Cheyenne corrected. "Little Wolf says she is to choose."

Duuqua grimaced as he watched the brave walk away. So, Little Wolf thought he understood the *pahoute*. Duuqua snorted. Would Little Wolf like to have the Great Spirit's messenger living in *his* tipi?

By the Sun! Duuqua vowed. She had been sent to help *him*, not Little Wolf.

He would not let her go until she had done what he had brought her here to do.

"You're sure I look all right?" Kris stopped Black Eagle for the third time as they walked to the Cheyenne encampment. "Should I have worn the white buckskins?" Even in the twilight, she saw the muscle in his jaw clench. What was his problem? They were on their way to visit a chief. What was wrong with wanting to look her best?

"Who do you seek to please?" Kris jerked her face back when he shoved his close to hers. "Little Wolf?"

"Are you jealous?"

"Of Little Wolf?" Black Eagle snorted. "He is old enough to

be your father, and he already has two wives. This captive he bought today will make three women in his tipi."

"He doesn't seem so old. He's a man in his prime." Kris assured herself she wasn't baiting Black Eagle. She was simply confused about why he seemed jealous.

"His prime?" Black Eagle turned on her, nostrils flaring, brows drawn together in a black scowl. "What this mean?"

"He's strong, virile. He may be a little weathered, especially around the eyes, but that's not altogether unattractive in a man . . ." She *was* baiting him. She mentally chastised herself, but couldn't seem to stop. Black Eagle was magnificent anytime, but angry . . . He drew a deep breath and his magnificent chest lifted, filled. The planes and angles of his face seemed more finely etched. His whole body tightened. All that fire, directed at her. Of course, she trusted him to control it. He'd never hurt her.

She trusted him. She stopped short, then smiled.

Black Eagle gave up waiting for an answer. Cursing under his breath, he stomped ahead.

"What's wrong? Was it something I said?" Kris grinned, unable to resist delivering one last salvo. "But, of course, he doesn't compare to the younger warriors."

"Enough, woman."　　　•

He was jealous. But why? He didn't care for her, he'd made that clear both on the trail and here at camp. So why did it make him mad that she noticed other men?

"*Ehaitsma.*" Little Wolf welcomed them before a beautifully painted tipi. His smile warmed Kris, softening the harsh lines of his face—the brutally square jaw and thin lips, the proud nose and high, regal forehead. If the eyes were the well of the soul, Kris mused, his was deep and pure.

And yet, as a man, he left her cold. She tested her responses to him, comparing her reaction to Black Eagle. Nothing stretched between them, no thrill of awareness, no sense of connection as between herself and Black Eagle. Odd that she hadn't been completely aware of her responses to Black Eagle until she'd noticed the lack of them for another man.

"The woman is inside." Little Wolf lifted the entrance flap and waited for Kris to precede him.

The warmth of the tipi struck her, not from the small fire, but from the hominess, the comfort, the beautiful backrests beckoning beside beds of glistening furs. The air, heavy with the lingering aroma of the evening meal, yet spicy from the colorful bunches of wildflowers hanging about, suggested peace and contentment. Kris breathed it all in, even as her gaze flew to the woman who rested on her stomach in a nest of furs near the door. Her bare, wounded back glistened in the soft firelight.

Kris sank to her knees by the woman's side.

"You came." The woman reached out to clutch Kris's hand, wincing as the movement pulled the wounds in her back.

"Shhh," Kris soothed, squeezing her trembling fingers. "Don't move."

Black Eagle laid a hand on her shoulder. "We go to sweat lodge."

Surprised to find that he and Little Wolf had already shed their shirts and leggings, Kris nodded, unable to speak, overwhelmed by an alarming flash of intense heat. Black Eagle's body gleamed in the soft light, his taut muscles sharply delineated. When he turned to leave, his breechclout flared away from his body, exposing one long, lean flank.

"Uh, my hand." The injured woman gasped and tried to pull it back.

"Sorry." Hot color flooded Kris's cheeks. "How are you feeling?"

"Much better." The woman tried to move and gave a low moan. "Little Wolf has been very kind. He's very different from White Bear."

"Let's not talk about that brute," Kris whispered. "That's over. Put it behind you."

"It will never be over." A tremor ran through the hand Kris held. Sweat broke out on the woman's upper lip and her eyes squeezed shut.

An ache started in Kris's chest, tightening her throat, making her clench her teeth against the realization of the woman's agony. She stroked the woman's bright hair, pushing it behind her ear.

The woman gasped and would have pulled away if she'd been able.

Shocked, Kris dropped the woman's hand, clutching her chest in horror. The top of the woman's ear had been burned away. The small remaining portion of the upper earlobe was horribly disfigured.

Kris's stomach pitched and the face of the old crone waving a hissing torch seared her mind. *This is what they would have done to me!*

"Please, cover it," the woman pleaded, gripping Kris's hand tightly. "I'm sorry. I didn't want you to see . . ."

"There," Kris whispered, covering the damaged ear. "You know, I don't even know your name."

"Caroline Whitley."

"Kris Baldwin." Gently, Kris squeezed Caroline's hand. "Pleased to meet you."

A tiny grin lifted the corner of Caroline's mouth and a sparkle lit her blue eyes. "The pleasure is all mine."

"How can you say that?" Kris gasped, stunned by Caroline's wry humor. "It's my fault you're hurt."

"No. You saved my life. He would have killed me. If not then, later."

Kris glanced at Caroline's back and couldn't deny the truth of her statement. "What do you think of Little Wolf? I can see that he's taken good care of you."

Caroline sighed. "It's been like stepping out of a cave into the sunshine. I'm still blinking."

"Has he told you his plans for you?"

"No." Caroline tensed. "Do you know?"

"I don't think I should speak for him." Would Little Wolf make her his third wife, even if only for her protection? Was such a move really necessary? For the first time, Kris studied the woman before her, seeing past the abuse to the beauty beneath.

Caroline's golden-blond hair, though dull and unkempt now, would gleam like pure sunlight once she was well. She shouldn't have any trouble devising a hairstyle to cover her scarred ear. Hardship may have made her skinny and frail, but her hand gripped firmly and intelligence shone in her clear blue eyes.

Beneath the surface, Kris detected a strong will, and a determination that would see Caroline through her suffering. Hadn't she pleaded with Kris not to interfere when White Bear was beating her? She'd tried to protect her. Little Wolf must have admired Caroline's spirit.

Kris cocked her head, suddenly wondering if protection had been Little Wolf's only motive.

Chapter Eleven

Duuqua sat tall and straight beside Little Wolf in the sweat lodge as his host poured the fourth bowl of water over the heated stones. The other two Cheyenne warriors invited to share this sweat had already folded their heads into their laps, seeking the cooler air near the ground. Only Duuqua and Little Wolf remained upright.

Duuqua inhaled, drawing the heavy mist deep into his body, determined to outlast this Old Man Chief of the Cheyenne. He squinted at Little Wolf, uncomfortable with the tight smile that played around Little Wolf's eyes as he bathed himself in the mist, taking short, shallow breaths.

"Go, my brothers," Little Wolf told the other two men, who

then crawled out the low entrance, quickly closing it tight behind them.

"Good lodge," Duuqua complimented his host. His chest burned as he drew another deep breath.

Little Wolf smiled, closed his eyes. Nodded. Continued bathing himself in steam. "You have nothing to prove to me, Duuqua."

Duuqua bristled, but Little Wolf did not even open his eyes, just kept stroking the steam from head to chest. "The *pahoute* has eyes only for you."

"She is not my woman."

"Ah, yes. She is the messenger of the Great Spirit." Little Wolf smiled. "But she is a beautiful woman with a true heart. And she lives in your tipi."

"This is true." Duuqua too bathed himself in the heavy mist, some of the stiffness leaving his shoulders at Little Wolf's understanding words. "And it is killing me."

Little Wolf chuckled sympathetically. "Does she know you desire her?"

Duuqua flinched. How had Little Wolf guessed what he could not even admit to himself? "I must guard my feelings more carefully."

"Maybe I see more clearly than most."

"I hope that is the way of it." Even now Duuqua could hear the People laughing at him behind his back. He sighed. "I have fought battles that were easier than dealing with this woman."

"You will dance in the Sun Dance?"

"I will seek the Great Spirit's guidance for the battle."

"May I ask about the vision quest that brought her to you?"

Duuqua tensed, watching Little Wolf bathe himself in the thick steam as calmly as if they were discussing horses. But they were not, and Duuqua sensed that Little Wolf's questions had been well considered. "What would you like to know?"

"What did the Great Spirit say when He presented her to you?"

"He did not present her to me." Duuqua repeated his vision for Little Wolf in more detail than he had given the war council.

"The Great Spirit's messenger," Little Wolf murmured. "And yet, I see just a woman. This is a heavy responsibility for you to bear, and the woman also. Did the eagle say she had been sent to speak to the war council?"

Duuqua grunted. "The eagle told me my prayers would be answered."

"What did you pray for?"

"Do you question my vision?"

Little Wolf turned to him, surprise in his eyes. "I seek only to understand. Have none of the other war chiefs asked you these questions?"

"No." Duuqua drew a deep breath, determined to keep his dismay at that fact to himself. "Why should they?"

Little Wolf chuckled. "It is not every day that the Great Spirit honors His People with a messenger. Does the woman believe she is His messenger?"

"She has been difficult." Duuqua said no more. He did not want Little Wolf to think he found the *pahoute* a burden.

"A heavy responsibility."

Duuqua stiffened, no longer deceived. Little Wolf did not understand his problem. No, the Old Man Chief of the Cheyenne sought to relieve him of it.

"Perhaps you should fast and pray to better understand her." Little Wolf turned to face Duuqua, his eyes keen as the hawk's. "We would not like the Great Spirit to think the People do not appreciate His generous gift." Without another word, he left.

Duuqua watched him crawl out of the sweat lodge, then sank forward, resting his arms on his knees, his head hanging as he gulped the cooler air.

Did Little Wolf think he did not appreciate the Great Spirit's gift of the *pahoute*? Duuqua did not have to remember his every word, every deed to know he had not treated her as he should have.

Guard her well. Strange that Little Wolf had spoken the same words the Great Spirit had spoken. Had he been sent to take her from him? This must not happen. Duuqua vowed to do better, even if it meant the torture of staying close to her. He must be strong and pray for understanding.

Even though it stung a little, it was good to have the advice of an older, wiser man. How he missed Pete Noconi, his adopted father, who had died of the white man's fever when he and Quannah had only eight summers.

When he became a father, Duuqua vowed, he would share his wisdom with his sons and daughters, just as Little Wolf had done with him this night. He smiled, imagining his children—strong, daring boys and shy, sweet girls with their mother's smile and her bird-like wings above their laughing brown eyes.

He sat straight up. Hot steam slammed into his face like a fist, as another fist hit his gut, doubling him over again. He had just put the *pahoute's* face on his children. What children? He did not plan to have children, not wanting them to suffer through the troubles facing the People. He had told Padaponi he would never marry and he had never even imagined having children. Until now. Why could he now see them in his mind—and so many?

Suddenly, he could not breathe. The sweat that had beaded his face now ran down his neck and streamed down his chest. Sweat not caused by the hot mist of the lodge.

Duuqua crawled out and walked into the river, not stopping until he reached the deep water in the middle. He plunged below the surface and stayed there, crouched in the water, until his body shook with cold.

But it wasn't the cold water that made him tremble long after he rushed the *pahoute* back to his tipi, even after he crawled under his furs. He lay awake, staring into the faces of his strong sons and beautiful daughters.

Little Wolf was right, Duuqua told himself. Tomorrow he must fast and pray.

For deliverance.

* * *

The pounding beat of the drums echoed Kris's pulse as she slipped from tipi to tipi, hiding, hoping to escape notice. It shouldn't be hard, she reasoned, with all the noise from the drums and the chanting and the occasional scream of a dancer. Those screams had finally forced her to act.

Black Eagle had been dancing for three days now.

She steeled herself, determined to get into the Sun Dance lodge. It wouldn't hurt for her to relieve Padaponi so the little woman could get some rest. Would it?

Get real, she admonished herself. She had no intention of relieving Padaponi. She meant to satisfy her own curiosity and make sure it wasn't Black Eagle making those horrible noises. And if it was? She trembled, tucked the blanket tighter around her. She was strong; if the rest of the People could handle it, she could too.

Kris chose her next hiding place, a bundle of brush propped against a tree. But to get to it, she had to cross an open stretch. She pulled the blanket over her head and stepped out into the open, fighting to keep her steps even, unhurried, so as not to arouse suspicion. Three feet from the tree, she broke into a run, slipped behind the brush and waited, holding her breath.

She'd made it. She glanced around the tree. Only a short dash and she'd be in the shadow of the gigantic brush shelter Black Eagle had built for the Sun Dance. How she wished she'd been able to help, to participate. And she'd never get another chance. This was the only Sun Dance the Comanche would ever hold. The sacred ritual was supposed to bring big medicine to bear on their plans. After the results of this one, the Comanche would never bother with it again.

Annoyance thrummed through Kris. So close, but forced to miss the spectacle because of the People's silly superstitions. *Huh,* she snorted. *Bad medicine, indeed.*

Sure of her cover, Kris darted to the east wall of the Sun Dance lodge and crouched at the base, hovering in the long shadow cast by the setting sun. She glanced around to make sure she hadn't been seen, then scooted to a break in the brush wall.

She couldn't see. Too many people lined the shelter inside. She'd have to work her way to the opening and try to slip inside. Her heart in her throat, Kris tugged her blanket over her head and started circling the lodge, slipping from shadow to shadow. Though only seconds, it seemed like hours before she finally reached the entrance and slipped inside, keeping the blanket pulled well over her face.

Like a blast from a furnace, light and heat smote her face as she peered through the crowd. The same sickeningly sweet smoke that had made her so nauseous at the war council filled the air, which was already heavy with the smell of so many unwashed bodies crowded into too small a space. Her pulse pounded in her temples, heralding the onset of a nasty headache. Kris shook off her discomfort, determined to experience as much as possible before she was discovered.

The center of the lodge was open to the sky and an enormous buffalo effigy hung from the top of the central pole. She quickly spotted Black Eagle among about ten other dancers, each attached to the roof of the lodge by a rope that passed around his chest and under his arms. Prancing to the beat of the drum and chanting, they lifted their faces to the effigy every few steps and sagged against the rope.

Kris sagged too, relieved to see that the dancers hadn't pierced their breasts with the bone skewers that must be ripped through the skin before their ordeal was over. Unlike other Sun Dances she'd read about, the Comanche Sun Dance wasn't an ordeal of pain, but more of a vision quest.

The anguished cries of several women drew her attention across the lodge. A dancer had collapsed. Swiftly, his ropes were removed and he was carried out the other end of the lodge. Kris pressed the back of her hand over her mouth as her gaze fastened on Black Eagle. His three days of fasting had taken a heavy toll, leaving his ribs clearly visible beneath his glistening skin. The muscles in his back and legs leaped into sharp relief each time he sagged against the rope.

Luckily she didn't have a knife, for she'd be sorely tempted to cut him free of this torment, even knowing he wouldn't thank her for her mercy. Could she avoid discovery as long as it would take for him to reach the point of collapse? Could she bear to wait and watch it happen?

Realizing the precariousness of her position at the entrance, Kris slid deeper into the crowd lining the walls, keeping her blanket close around her face to avoid recognition. Her eyes rarely left Black Eagle, and she bit her lip to keep from crying out as he threw himself back against the ropes. She didn't know how long she watched before his movements slowed, becoming almost lethargic, and he stared up at the opening in the ceiling of the lodge. Tears stung her eyes. How could he do this to himself?

She tore her anguished gaze from Black Eagle and searched the crowd, spotting Padaponi in the forefront of the circle of watchers. Not far in front of Padaponi, Pakawa, the brave who had almost raped Kris, stood silent and watchful, arms crossed over his chest as he watched.

Black Eagle stumbled and Padaponi cried out. Pakawa silenced her with a slash of his hand, but did not move from his wide-legged stance. Black Eagle recovered and resumed his dancing.

Her heart in her throat, Kris clutched the blanket tighter, crying inside as Black Eagle threw himself against the ropes again and again. Why did his vigil cause her such pain? Why did she feel those ropes cut into her own shoulders every time they pulled against his? She had to get control of herself. No, she had to get out of here. She'd been wrong to think she could watch without being affected. But she couldn't make herself leave; nor could she stop the tears she suddenly realized were streaming down her cheeks.

* * *

Duuqua focused on the buffalo, on his hatred for the white hunters and their slaughter, but the *pahoute's* face kept getting in the way. He danced and prayed and chanted, but when he closed his eyes, she was there, waiting.

"Duty," Padoponi had said. No, Kiyani was duty; Quannah was duty. His People were duty. Tomanoakuno was desire. But he could not touch her, had sworn to protect her, even from himself and the desire he felt for her.

He cursed his inability to keep his thoughts on the Sun Dance, on his People, on his enemies, on duty. Not desire.

He danced, throwing himself into the chant, the steps, renewing his prayers. He did not see the faces of the People crowded inside the lodge; he spoke to Pakawa without knowing what he said. The stones in his medicine bag pounded against his skin. She was here; he did not need to see her to know that. He remembered how she had looked when he found her standing in the sacred waters, her face and hair kissed by sunlight and her body's secrets hidden in shadow, darkness and light. A woman of contrasts.

The beat of the drums filled the lodge, thundering in his head, in his heart, echoing through him, around him. Day had become night and then day again as he danced, unknowing, uncaring, his mind torn between duty and desire. Du-ty, du-ty, du-ty . . .

By the Sun! He was sick of duty. He wanted a life of his own not ruled by duty. He wanted his own wife, not one shared with Quannah. He wanted his own children. Wanted to know his seed, planted in love, brought them life. He stumbled, righted himself, kept dancing. Du-ty, du-ty, du-ty . . .

Duuqua jerked back against the ropes, closing his eyes tight, and let his spirit fly free. Higher and higher he flew, rising toward the Sun, soaring . . . The eagle screamed.

Duuqua.

Its hooked beak and beady eyes filled the circle of light. Its piercing scream filled his soul. He matched its call.

I have felt your anguish, my Son.

The woman, Father, Duuqua cried. *She fills my mind. I can think of nothing, of no one else. But she is your Messenger . . .*

She is woman first, messenger second. The eagle's cry stretched along the wind.

Duuqua fell against the ropes and surrendered to the darkness.

Kris's gaze darted upward and she gasped with the rest of the crowd as she saw what had made Black Eagle cry out and stop dancing, sagging onto the ropes, his eyes wide and staring. The drums fell silent.

A huge eagle hovered over the center pole, its wings widespread, its eyes flashing as it settled regally onto the buffalo effigy. Its talons pierced the buffalo's hide and its unlidded eyes focused on Black Eagle.

Run! Get away from it before it attacks! Kris bit her lip to keep the screams inside. Incredulous, she watched Black Eagle raise his arms to the bird. In unison, the two screamed, their cries identical. An eerie sense of calm filled her.

Man and bird, together in voice, united in spirit. Warriors, both, threatened by extinction.

With one final, piercing cry, the eagle departed, its wings shutting out the light. The People cowered in the sudden darkness and Black Eagle collapsed against the ropes, his head hanging forward.

Kris sagged with him. Her knees gave out and she bumped the people ahead of her. She recovered quickly, lurching upright and spinning away as she pulled the blanket closer around her face. Too late.

"Ai-yeee!" The old crone who had tormented her with the burning branch that first day had spotted her.

"No, please." Kris placed a finger over her lips, begging the old woman for silence. But there was no mercy in the woman's beady little eyes.

Others, drawn by her cry, crowded around Kris, shoving, poking, pushing her out of the lodge.

"No, please. I need to see what's happening." Kris tried to make them understand. Beyond them she caught glimpses of Pakawa freeing Black Eagle from the ropes and laying him on the ground, of Padaponi hovering over him.

Awash in pain, Kris fled the lodge, not needing the old crone dogging her heels to hasten her departure. Once outside, she dashed into the open, gulping the fresh air.

A shadow fell over her and she glanced up, then cringed in fear. The eagle circled the clearing, not far above her.

Kris Baldwin. Its terrible voice echoed through her like thunder in the mountains, rooting her where she stood. The people cried out. Covering their ears, they fell to the ground.

Kris froze, standing very still as the majestic bird soared lower and swept so close its wings passed mere inches from her trembling shoulders. Strangely, she was not afraid, only awed by its fierce beauty.

Stand tall and strong. Wings extended, it caught an updraft. *Be not afraid. Speak your heart to My People.*

Dear God, Kris groaned, watching it soar into the sky and pass from view. What was in the smoke in that lodge? Some sort of hallucinogenic? She'd imagined it. That eagle hadn't really spoken to her. Had it?

Help My People. Like an answering taunt, the command drifted over her as a long, white-tipped feather floated out of the sky and settled at her feet. She stared at it, awestruck, then picked it up tentatively, as if it might be hot. The thick spine of the feather extended well past her palm, up her forearm, more than a foot long. Black at the base, the feather gradually lightened to white, delicate tendrils at the tip that caught each whisper of the breeze, tickling her hand.

"How?" she cried, staring skyward, searching for a glimpse of the eagle. "What can I do?"

Use your knowledge.

Kris blanched at the selfish question that surfaced in her brain, hesitated to ask it, still not certain who or what she was addressing, but she had to know. "How will I get home?"

Your heart is home.

Stunned, Kris waited for more, but the voice remained silent. What on earth did that mean? That this was where she'd wanted to be? Impossible. She hadn't wanted to come here, hadn't even known it was possible. How could this be home? Did this mean she'd never see her real home again? What about her grandmother? Her father? Tears gathered in her eyes.

She glanced at the crowd of people hanging back, staring at her. Coyote Droppings glowered at her from the fringes of the crowd, his eyes glittering with malice before he turned and walked quickly away.

Kris moaned. He must have seen the eagle. Had he heard it speak, or had he just seen her talking to it? What would he make of this? Instinctively, she knew he'd find a way to use it against her, to turn it to his advantage. But the People had seen too, and word traveled fast. Already heads were bobbing together, eyes glued on her with awe and suspicion.

Confusion roiled inside her. Was she supposed to accept this experience as confirmation of Black Eagle's assertions that she was the Great Spirit's messenger? She didn't want to be a Messenger; didn't want the responsibility. Couldn't she just be plain, simple Kris Baldwin?

Just then the crowd parted and four braves stepped through carrying Black Eagle. Tears started in her eyes as he was carried past her, unconscious. She felt almost breathless with dismay at seeing him like this. He always seemed so vital, so utterly invincible. And yet, he was human. Vulnerable. Kris tried to follow, but a strong hand held her back.

"He will be fine." Chikoba's hand tightened on her shoulder.

Kris shook it off. "Let me go."

"Did you think that speaking to the eagle would make the People believe you, woman?"

Kris faced him, scorched by the contempt in his eyes, hating to ask, but desperate to know. "You didn't hear it?"

His laugh was dry, mirthless. "You would have me believe it spoke to you?"

He hadn't heard it. Kris cursed the heat climbing into her cheeks, knowing he would see this as proof that he had caught her lying.

"It would take more than an eagle to convince me that you spoke the truth."

Kris ducked her head, unwilling to let him see her disappointment. "No, you'd need something more drastic, wouldn't you?" He'd killed her newfound hope that maybe, having seen the eagle speak to her, the People would be more willing to accept her, or at least be more tolerant of her presence among them. She shook her head as she walked away from Chikoba. If Chikoba was a typical warrior, what made her think Black Eagle and Quannah would listen to her warnings, even after Adobe Walls?

What would it take to make them listen?

She knew the battle at Adobe Walls would prove she hadn't lied to the war council, but would the war council blame her for their failure? Had she said too much? Would she inadvertently change the course of history? For instance, she thought, if she didn't warn Duuqua to watch Quannah, because she remembered he'd be shot in the battle, would Quannah be seriously injured, possibly even die? Or would Duuqua be shot instead? Did she have the power to alter the future? And if she did, would it be better or worse?

Hah. She scoffed at her imaginings. She played a very small role here. She was an encyclopedia, nothing more, probably even less. At least people searching an encyclopedia believed what they read. She could no more prevent deaths than cause them. Still, she'd play it safe and warn Duuqua to watch Quannah's back.

She kicked a rock out of her path and headed back to the river, the only place where she felt at ease, at home. But tonight she was too drained to swim. She settled on a grassy knoll and stared at the water, stroking the eagle feather.

Your heart is home. The words rang through her like a death knell.

If they were true, her heart had betrayed her.

"That is something many warriors will envy."

Kris started from her ruminations, nearly dropping the feather as she jerked around to see who had crept up behind her.

She sighed, recognizing Little Wolf. She scooted over and he settled beside her on the rock. "I am sorry to have frightened you. May I?" He reached for the feather.

Kris gave it to him, surprised at her reluctance to part with it.

"This is a fine one, longer than any in my warbonnet." He handed it back with a reverence Kris understood. "The words of the People are like a prairie fire tonight."

"Oh?" Kris laid the feather in her lap and focused on the sun settling onto a fiery horizon. "What are they saying?"

"They speak of your bravery. Some say the eagle flew so close its wings touched you."

"It did," Kris confirmed with a shrug. "But it was fear that kept me still, not courage. It was magnificent. I could feel its power, feel the wind that supported it swirl around my body. Incredible."

"Those with ears to hear say it spoke to you."

Kris started, looked up to find his eyes fixed on her face, reminding her abruptly of the huge bird of prey. Suddenly hesitant to share more of her experience, she shrugged and fastened her own gaze on the feather in her lap. "Chikoba didn't hear it."

"Chikoba could not hear if it sat on his head. What did it say?"

Kris started to rise, uncomfortable with his prying questions. His hand on her arm stopped her. She stiffened, shot him a questioning look.

"Forgive me for prying." Little Wolf looked almost sheepish. "It is not every day that the Great Spirit sends a messenger like you. But you are not happy here. You wish to return to your home. I will send two of my best warriors to take you there."

Jubilation. Kris's heart leaped into triple time. Her lips moved, but nothing came out of her mouth. She didn't know what to say. She couldn't decide whether to hug Little Wolf or run for the nearest horse. She gathered herself, prepared to jump to her feet, but stopped, staring at the feather in her hand.

The Great Spirit's messenger. She stroked the feather. *Could it be true?* If it was, she couldn't just walk away. The People did need her, though they hadn't realized it yet. She still wasn't entirely convinced, but it was becoming harder and harder to deny.

"Thank you for the offer, but I think I'll stay a little longer." She smiled, searching his face. "It's not that I'm unhappy here. I'm just confused. Uncertain." She glanced away. His gaze seemed too knowing, too intent. "You understand?"

He said nothing, only watched her soberly.

Feeling uncomfortable with his earlier questions and now his silence, Kris paused to consider his motive. Why was he asking so many questions? What did he want? Ah, yes, she remembered. "You have questions for me."

Little Wolf sobered even more. His gaze lifted to the sky. "I would know what lies ahead for my people, the Cheyenne."

Kris sighed and let her head fall to her upraised knees as a wave of pain washed over her. Would it always hurt so to be faced with questions she'd rather not answer? What was it the eagle had said? *Be not ashamed . . .* It wasn't shame that made her hesitate, but pity.

Little Wolf's stern, proud face filled her mind. He wouldn't want her pity any more than Black Eagle or Quannah did. She sighed and faced him.

"What would you like to know? How many of your People will die, how much you will suffer, or simply that—in the end—you will be allowed to live where you wish?"

"Allowed?"

Kris nodded, bracing against the pain, the anger that flashed through Little Wolf's eyes. Would he, too, deny her words, pronounce them too hard to bear, decry her knowledge? And then she read acceptance in his tight lips, even as sorrow seeped into his eyes.

God, this hurts, she cried inside, her heart breaking at his torment. *Why can't I do more? Why can't I change their destiny? Why?* she railed, barely suppressing her anguished cry. *Why have You abandoned your People?*

A sudden sensation of warmth surrounded Kris, silencing the anguish, stealing her pain. *I have not abandoned them. I have sent them you.*

"Then tell me how to help them!" Kris cried. When she heard her words, realized she had spoken aloud, she leaped to her feet and ran into the deepening shadows, desperate to escape the burden laid on her shoulders, frantic to escape the voice in her head, heedless of Little Wolf's calls.

Duuqua awoke with a start, his heart thundering like the drums still pounding in his head. His hand gripped his knife. The *pahoute* was in danger. Her cry had stabbed through the darkness to awaken him.

He rose, swayed unsteadily for a moment, then turned to leave.

"Where do you go?" Padaponi caught his arm, tried to pull him back. "You must rest."

Duuqua shook her off. "I have to find her."

"Who? Tomanoakuno?" Padaponi yanked him backward. "She is at the river, as always."

"Why?" Duuqua demanded. He hadn't done anything recently to cause her to flee to the river to work off her anger and frustration. Had someone else made her angry? He remembered sensing that she was at the Sun Dance before the darkness claimed him. Had someone seen her there, hurt her?

"She probably went there to think." Padaponi shrugged.

Releasing his arm, she turned away to fuss with the stew she was preparing.

"Tell me," Duuqua growled, too familiar with his aunt's ways not to know she hid something from him.

"The People are talking."

"This is new?"

Padaponi tssked at him, frowning. "They say the eagle spoke to her and she answered."

"The eagle?"

"Your eagle."

"I did not know I had an eagle."

Padaponi gave a disgusted huff and handed him a bowl of stew. "Eat," she ordered.

Duuqua ate like a hungry wolf while she told him what had happened—both what she had seen and what she had heard. Duuqua handed her the empty bowl and turned to leave long before she finished her story, his heart racing. The eagle had spoken to her. No longer could she deny that she was the Great Spirit's messenger. At last, he would have the truth from her.

"She is safe. Little Wolf is with her."

At Padaponi's words, he began to run.

Kris sensed him behind her as she enviously watched the peacefully grazing horses, knew he watched her before she whispered his name. "Black Eagle?"

"Yes." His hands gripped her shoulders and he pulled her back against him. His breath stirred her hair.

She spun out of his hold to face him, determined to ignore the heat that leaped between them. "You've recovered?"

"What did Little Wolf want?"

Irritation and disappointment made her blunt. "He offered to take me home."

"I will kill him."

"No, you won't." Kris sighed. She'd made her decision. She

wouldn't second-guess herself now by sending Black Eagle after Little Wolf in a rage. "I told him I couldn't go. Not yet."

Black Eagle's gaze traveled over her, as if he were drinking her in, noting every detail.

Heat burned her cheeks and she blessed the darkness. She flinched away when he reached for her again. "Better not. I might spoil the effects of your Sun Dance."

"Hush, woman." He stepped nearer. "It is good you make this choice. I leave soon, but I wanted to see you."

"You haven't wanted to see me for days." Kris strained away from him. She knew what would happen if her breasts pressed against the hard, hot wall of his chest. Her nipples would tighten, and he would know that she couldn't control her response to him.

"Tell me about the eagle." Black Eagle smiled.

"The eagle?" She blinked up at him, forgetting her fear of his embrace. Word certainly did travel fast around here, and not a single telephone in sight. "It swooped down and flew around me." She shrugged, not wanting him to make too much of the incident, yet knowing he would. "That's all."

"What did it say?"

"Who told you it spoke to me?"

He grinned.

Damn it. Too late Kris realized she'd just confirmed whatever rumor he'd heard.

"Tell me, woman."

"Oh, all right." Grudgingly, she told him everything. She watched his face brighten and, in spite of her pique, his wide smile dazzled her.

"No longer can you deny that you are the Great Spirit's messenger," he gloated when she finished. "You must tell me the truth now."

She gave him the look she reserved for spiders and telemarketers. "The truth?" What did he think she'd been telling him? "About what?"

He gave her an urgent shake. "Tell me what the Comanche must do to chase the *taibo* from our land forever."

Kris bristled. "Your silly eagle changes nothing. There's nothing you can do. It's not going to happen." She broke off as a black scowl creased his forehead and his hands tightened on her shoulders. "You're hurting me."

He released her. His eyes burned a trail down her body and back to her face.

"I told you the truth. You will not win the battle at Adobe Walls. Those buffalo hunters have Sharps rifles." She trembled at the heat in his gaze as he continued to stare at her. Why was he looking at her mouth?

"Don't you understand?" She groped for a way to explain it to him. "They're high caliber. They can shoot long distances. Are you listening to me?"

He crossed his arms over his chest and shook his head. "Even now, seven hundred warriors prepare to ride against Adobe Walls with the sun's first light. Isatai has proven that his paint can stop bullets. He painted a dog and shot it and the dog looked up at him and barked. We are going into battle and the enemy's bullets cannot hurt us."

"Don't be foolish," Kris cried. "Don't trust your life to Isatai's magic. It doesn't work. You'll be killed."

"I am only foolish when I think of you." His eyes scorched her as he hauled her up against him.

Her mouth was open wide in astonishment when his lips came down over hers. His tongue swept boldly inside; his arms held her captive.

Stunned, caught completely off guard, Kris didn't—couldn't—react at first, and then her body took over. Her heart leaped into motion and her breasts, flattened against the hot muscular wall of his chest, swelled. Her nipples hardened.

In spite of her body's reaction, her mind rebelled. This was no kiss. It was invasive, violent. Was he punishing her for her harsh words? Was this how he kissed Kiyani? Well, she'd remind him that she was different. She shoved at his chest, his arms, pounded her fists against him.

He didn't budge, only groaned low in his throat. His head turned, deepening the kiss. His tongue plundered her mouth.

She struggled, twisting in his arms. She couldn't breathe.

Suddenly, his tongue withdrew and she found herself inhaling deeply. His lips gentled, lingering, nibbling, tasting, tempting—and she was lost. The scent of woodsmoke clung to his hair and his warm breath fanned her cheek, she tasted the salt of perspiration on his skin, the flavor of Padaponi's stew, and some essence that was his and his alone. New and yet so familiar. She surged closer, her lips answering his demand, making demands of her own.

His lips fit hers perfectly, so firm, yet soft. Never had a kiss stolen her very thoughts, tempting her to forget all in the wash of pleasure that sent warmth spiraling through her body to settle in a moist flood at the apex of her thighs. She sagged against him with a low moan.

Dear God, how I have missed him.

Her eyes flashed open. Kris jerked away from his tantalizing mouth and staggered back to stare at him in horrified silence. What was she thinking? Missed him? Somehow she didn't think the thought referred to the distance he'd imposed between them over the last week. Where had such a thought come from?

She pressed a trembling hand against her throbbing lips. She'd been kissing him back. Heat still radiated through her and her heart pounded so hard she could barely breathe. Was her resolve so weak? She'd almost surrendered, would have, if not for that errant thought. How could she succumb so totally to his embrace? What must he think of her?

"Tomanoakuno." He stroked a stray hair off her cheek.

"What?" She dodged his hand, grudgingly touched by the gentle gesture. She couldn't let him get to her.

"My name is Kris Baldwin," she told him pertly, trying to

step out of his arms. But he wasn't letting her go. "I wish you'd remember it. It's not really that hard to say. Much more practical than Tomano . . ."

". . . akuno." He laughed, his teeth gleaming in the darkness. His smile stole her breath, sending images flashing through her brain of him laughing, teasing, loving. She blinked, shook her head sharply.

"I suppose it's better than *pahoute* or"—she grimaced—"*taibo*, or woman, but I prefer my own name."

He studied her. "You do not like my name for you?"

"It's very pretty, and I'm flattered, but I like my own name." Kris couldn't bring herself to tell him how empty she felt at the thought of giving up her name. She'd have nothing left of herself, her previous life, but her memories.

"A new name is an honor, not a curse."

"Oh, I should be grateful that you're taking away another piece of my identity." She shook her head. "I'd prefer to keep my name. Is it absolutely necessary for me to have a new one?"

"What does Kris Baldwin mean? Does it tell about you, who you are?"

"No, but it's the name my grandfather—my father's father—insisted I carry. He said I'm named after a great-great aunt who died very young." She shrugged, hoping he would understand and not take offense. "It's special to me."

"Then I will try to use it." He seemed so serious, then he smiled. "I might call you Tomanoakuno sometimes, because it is the way I like to think of you, sleek as the otter, slicing through the water."

Kris couldn't resist his smile. "I do spend a lot of time swimming, don't I? It helps me think through my problems. In fact, I could use a good hard swim right now."

Black Eagle tipped her chin up, his black gaze once again intense. "All will go well in the battle, you will see."

"You still don't believe me, do you?" Kris pulled her chin from his hold.

"*Pahoute* . . ."

"Kris. Call me Kris. You don't believe I'm a medicine woman any more than Coyote Droppings does." She turned her back to him, ashamed of the tears that filled her eyes.

He stepped close behind her and laid his hands on her shoulders. She knew she should shrug off his hands, but her skin came alive beneath his fingers as he rubbed her shoulders. "Do not send me away with the memory of your tears—Kris."

She dashed tears from her cheeks and forced a smile. "See? That wasn't so hard."

He smiled, caught a tear she'd missed on the tip of his finger. "I not believe all your words, but I also not trust Isatai's paint. Dog is not warrior."

"I guess that will have to be enough." Quannah's face flashed through her thoughts, reminding her of her decision to warn Black Eagle of the danger to his brother. "Stay close to Quannah, keep an eye on him."

He stiffened. "You want I protect Quannah? He is great warrior; can protect himself."

Surprised, she searched his suddenly hostile eyes. Jealousy, again? Ridiculous. "Not against an enemy he can't see." She regretted her cryptic warning, knowing she should tell Black Eagle that Quannah would be wounded by a ricochet. If Black Eagle knew, he would move heaven and earth to keep Quannah from being wounded, possibly even step in the bullet's path. She couldn't bear that responsibility. Not because of her would Black Eagle take a bullet destined for Quannah, even if the man was her great-great grandfather.

He studied her face and she let him, not ashamed of the concern he would find there. "I watch Quannah," he finally told her with a grudging nod.

"Come, Kris." He took her arm gently, urging her to move ahead of him back toward camp. "We help Padaponi prepare for the journey."

In silence, they walked back to the tipi, only to find everything in readiness. Later, Kris found sleep elusive, knowing

Black Eagle would leave in the morning. Tears welled in her eyes and her heart pounded in alarm. What was happening to her? He'd kissed her and her mind hadn't screamed a warning. How had he snuck past her defenses?

Chapter Twelve

Duuqua crouched on the brow of a hill overlooking the squat, ugly adobe buildings he had come to attack. Drums pounded in his brain and deep inside his mind the flute wailed his war song. The flames of the War Dance lit the darkness behind his closed eyes and the night's chants echoed through his mind. In his medicine bag, the stones took up the rhythm, throbbing so hard he pressed the trembling bag against his chest. Their strength flowed through his fingers. Caught in his pounding blood, their energy swept through him. Behind him, seven hundred warriors waited for his signal to begin the raid.

He crooked his finger and, like a moving shadow, the warriors eased over the crest of the hill, drawing ever nearer to the sleeping enemy. They crept up to a wagon in their path and swiftly silenced the two enemies sleeping beneath it. Before their screams reached their throats, the men's dripping hair hung from Quahadi knives.

Not a sound broke the morning stillness. Nothing moved between them and their target. From the shelter of a grove of trees, Duuqua signaled again and his warriors slid onto their horses. They lay on the horses' necks, watching, waiting, then moved out of the trees, staying in the shadows. Duuqua glanced at the hill behind him, waiting for the sun to shoot its fiery, blinding light across its brow straight into the eyes of the enemy. Until then, his warriors must stay hidden.

An enemy rolled out from under a wagon near the closest

building, propped his rifle against a wheel and began rolling up his blanket.

Duuqua's breath caught in his chest. The warriors froze. The enemy was awake! His warriors would not club the sleeping enemy to death as Isatai had promised. The bright paint on his chest mocked Duuqua. How many other false prophecies had Isatai given them?

The *pahoute's* face rose before him. *You will not be able to surprise them. Watch Quannah.*

Duuqua silenced the grumbling murmurs of his warriors. They must trust Isatai's magic. They had seen the paint's strength, watched it turn away bullets. They would need that strength to kill their enemy.

The white man tossed his bedroll into the wagon, then paused to study the hillside, the milling horses. Duuqua did not breathe until the man turned back to his saddlebags. But the man picked up his rifle and again searched the hillside. Did he sense death waiting in the shadows? Moving slowly, he turned his back and tied his horse to the wagon.

Duuqua signaled and his warriors fanned across the face of the hill. His muscles tensed. His horse tossed its head. His blood boiled as he waited, stiff and silent. Then the sun crested the hill. He thrust his rifle at the sky and screamed his hatred of this foe. An answering scream of rage burst from seven hundred throats as his warriors charged Adobe Walls.

War whoops and thundering hooves shattered the morning silence, bouncing off trees and rocks, rumbling down the hill to blast the enemy and hurtle the staring white man toward the adobe buildings. He crouched and shot but his bullets flew wild. He ran to the biggest building, shouting and beating on the door when it did not open. Long rifle barrels poked through deep, narrow slits in the walls, belching smoke and death.

Duuqua charged the door, heading for the white man pounding on it. Bullets whistled by, but none caught him. The door opened a crack. The man fell inside and it slammed shut. Duuqua hammered it with the butt of his rifle.

"Cowards," he shouted at the enemy hiding inside the thick walls, speaking in their tongue. "Come out and fight like men." He yanked his horse onto its haunches to paw the door. "I, Duuqua, War Chief of the Quahadi, challenge you."

Rifles roared on either side of him. His ears rang and smoke stung his nostrils, but their bullets could not reach him. He was too close. He roared in frustration when the door held under his assault; he searched for another entrance. Pakawa, whooping and riding at full speed, sitting straight and tall, charged the rifles. He did not slip into the loop to hang behind the horse and shoot from beneath its neck. Duuqua watched him come, Pakawa's actions slowing as if in a dream.

"The loop," Duuqua cried, dread filling his heart. "Use the loop!" Rifles barked and the enemy's bullets blasted bloody holes in Pakawa's chest. The shots lifted him off his horse and threw him to the ground, where he lay still and silent.

Sorrow burning his heart, Duuqua stared at his dead friend, horrified. Isatai's paint was false! The *pahoute* had spoken truly. He raised his rifle, signaling two braves charging the building, calling out a warning. Immediately, they slid into their loops and fired from beneath their horses' necks. Ducking low, they each grabbed an arm and dragged Pakawa away, shouting a warning to others as they rode.

Fury burned through Duuqua's blood as the enemy's guns barked. Would the rest of the *pahoute*'s words be proven true too? Would they lose this fight? It could not be so. He would not let it be so. His warriors were many, the *taibo* hunters few but well protected inside their lodges. He must get inside and silence their guns. He glanced along the wall beside him. The holes in the wall were too narrow for him to crawl through. He would dig through the sod roof.

Duuqua tossed his lance and his rifle onto the building, jumped onto his horse's back, then onto the roof. He hammered at the thick sod with the butt of his lance, determined to make a hole big enough to shoot through. The enemy's guns barked at him from below. Their bullets thudded into the sod beneath his feet, but none came through.

Chikoba leaped onto the roof beside him. He, too, began digging. Smoke from the enemy's guns rose thick about the adobe lodge, drifting upward, burning Duuqua's eyes. He could barely see the roof beneath his feet.

"We can't get through," Chikoba shouted over the screams of charging warriors and answering gunfire. He coughed, choking on the heavy smoke. "I can't see in this smoke, let alone breathe."

Duuqua spun at a bugle signal coming from the hill. Sunlight flashed off the horn blown by a Mexican warrior under White Bear, the Kiowa chief. Again, the notes lifted over the sounds of battle, the signal for retreat.

"Fools!" he cursed, fury burning through him. "Do they think the enemy will not recognize their own signals?"

"Come. The battle is not going well." Chikoba pointed his lance at the hill far from the battle where Isatai sat on his horse watching, safe from the enemy's bullets.

Nodding, Duuqua gave the signal for retreat to the warriors surrounding the buildings, then whistled for his horse and leaped onto its back. Crouching low over its neck, he raced up the hill.

"Duuqua!" An urgent cry pulled him around. Quannah lay hidden by some brush. His dead horse lay a few feet away. He raised an arm and Duuqua circled, leaned low and pulled him up behind him.

"Isatai," Quannah hissed, as he settled behind Duuqua. Bullets slammed into the ground around them, kicking up dust as they raced to safety on Isatai's hill.

Quannah slid off the horse's rump and spat in the dirt. He glared up at Isatai, his eyes burning. "That for your medicine."

A Cheyenne warrior thundered up the hill, slamming his horse into Isatai's. "My son, Prophet!" He pointed down the hill to where a lone warrior lay sprawled on the ground. "Dead from the bullet of the enemy." He grabbed the rope on Isatai's horse. "Prove your paint is strong. Prove your medicine. Ride with me!"

Isatai yanked the rope from the warrior's hands. His gaze rose to the sky. He did not speak. The warriors who had gathered around him shouted their anger, but he ignored their cries.

"Do you look for help from the Great Spirit, Isatai?" Duuqua sneered, fighting the desire to knock him off his horse and stomp him into the ground. "Are you pleased with this day's work? Is your thirst to avenge the death of your uncle satisfied by the blood of your brothers?"

Isatai's gaze slid to him. Deep in the empty dark holes that were his eyes, a banked fire glowed, but he did not speak.

"Look at the warriors who believed your words," Duuqua hissed. "See the hate in their faces and know that it burns for you! Know that their hatred will never die."

Why did Isatai remain silent? Did he not understand? They must win this battle. They must destroy this enemy before the enemy destroyed the buffalo and the People's hopes along with them. Isatai's medicine had given their warriors confidence. They had believed they could not lose. But now? Overwhelmed by despair and frustration, Duuqua yanked Isatai off his horse and pressed his knife to his throat.

"No." Quannah's hand fell on his arm.

"He must die," Duuqua argued. "His lies have caused many deaths."

"We have fought without his paint before, we can do it again." Quannah walked away, signaling for Duuqua to follow. Duuqua tossed Isatai aside and followed his brother.

Quannah settled behind a rock to watch the enemy while he waited for the other chiefs to join him. "The enemy's medicine is strong. Their guns belch smoke that hides the buildings. I cannot see to take aim."

"They are only men," Duuqua spat. "We will kill them all and our women will dance around the scalp pole."

Something hissed past Duuqua, like a bee flying swift and fast. A bullet? An enemy rifle barked in the distance. Quannah jerked and groaned.

"What is it?" Duuqua caught his brother as he was flung forward.

"My back," Quannah groaned. "Shot."

"Where?" Duuqua shoved Quannah upright and searched his chest, his arms.

Quannah grimaced and tried to push him away. "Get Tabenanika."

Duuqua helped him settle on his side and swore at the bloody hole in his back. He sent a warrior to get the medicine man while he searched the trees behind them. No one was there; the ground was undisturbed. Again, the *pahoute* had spoken truly. She had warned that the enemy's bullets could travel long distances. But how could a bullet shot from somewhere before them change direction and shoot a man in the back?

"Did you find the man who shot me?" Quannah grunted when Duuqua returned.

"There was no one behind you." Duuqua kept the *pahoute*'s words to himself as he stared into his brother's startled eyes.

Quannah nodded. "Do not speak of this to the chiefs. They will think the enemy's medicine is too strong and give up. We must fight."

Duuqua poked at Quannah's torn skin. The wound was worse than he'd thought. Guilt filled him. If he had heeded the *pahoute*'s words, Quannah would not be wounded and Pakawa would still be alive. "This will keep you from the fight."

Quannah glared at him. "Only death will keep me from this fight." He jerked as Tabenanika rushed up and began probing his wound, looking for the bullet.

"We will lose many more warriors. We have already lost Pakawa." Pain ripped through Duuqua and the stones echoed the slow, heavy beat of his heart. "But we must kill this enemy."

"You know my heart," Quannah spat through clenched teeth. "I have come to fight."

Duuqua tossed a killing glance at Isatai where he sat on the hill staring into the sky. Another rifle barked from the buildings where the enemy remained hidden. Duuqua ducked, throwing himself over Quannah.

Isatai's horse screamed and fell heavily onto its side, dead. Isatai jumped free, crouching behind the horse's body. Duuqua stared in amazement, for the first time taking great satisfaction in the enemy's strength.

"Their guns have great medicine," Quannah whispered in awe.

Duuqua grunted agreement, then whispered. "The *pahoute* spoke the truth."

"You seek truth where none is to be found." Quannah glared at him. "The words of Isatai and your woman are like seeds blown by the wind."

"She warned us against Isatai's paint," Duuqua said, then left to prepare a pipe for the chiefs gathering to council with Quannah.

"She may have been right about Isatai's paint, but that does not make all her words true." Quannah shoved Tabenanika away and struggled to stand. "Help me go to the chiefs."

"Isatai's paint is false," Quannah said to the chiefs, seated in a circle, passing the pipe. "If we fight, more warriors may die. My brother has reminded me of his woman's warning that the bluecoats will come." The chiefs glanced between Quannah and Duuqua. "I have told him, I have not finished. We must kill this enemy."

"This fight will end only in death." Little Wolf spoke softly, but his words rang loud in Duuqua's ears. Though Little Wolf's words spoke of defeat, his eyes burned. Did he speak of this battle alone, or the fight of all the tribes to rid their lands of the hated white man?

"What will protect our warriors now that we have seen the

falseness of your medicine man's paint?" White Bear's voice boomed in the silence following Little Wolf's words.

Quannah stiffened at White Bear's sneer. "How many times have we fought with nothing more than our own medicine? The Quahadi are not afraid to fight without the promise of protection."

At once, the other chiefs rose to the challenge, shouting that their men feared nothing. White Bear's eyes narrowed and his hand tightened on his rifle.

"The *taibo* rifles have strong medicine." The calm voice of Little Wolf sliced the air. "Quannah, you were shot in the back, though no enemy was behind you. How can we fight it?"

Duuqua shot a questioning glance at Quannah, who gave a sharp, negative shake of his head, then fixed his narrowed gaze on Little Wolf. How had Little Wolf known?

"It is true. Their rifles are good." Quannah fixed each man with a hard stare. "But if we leave the fight now, the next sun will warm the dead bodies of our brother, the Buffalo, stripped naked and left to rot, shot by those same rifles." He waved an arm in the direction of the enemy. "If we are men, if we love our families and our People, we must fight."

"Duuqua's woman, the messenger from the Great Spirit, has said the white soldiers will come." Little Wolf said, turning to Quannah. "Do you believe her words?"

"I no longer heed the twisted words of medicine women, *or* men." Quannah threw a dark look at Isatai. "If we walk away from this fight, these hunters will tell others that the warriors of the Comanche, the Kiowa, the Cheyenne and the Arapaho are weak. Soon white men will cover the land, thick as the buffalo before the white men came with their long, shining rifles." He jerked his head toward the enemy's camp. "They will steal our land and slaughter the buffalo. The antelope and the deer will run from them. The Plains will be empty. Our People will starve and the bluecoats will force the People to move onto the reservations." He stared at each man in turn. "Is this

what you want? Is this how you want to live? Then go now."
No one moved.

Duuqua's heart filled with new hope. They would fight. Moments later, swift plans made, the chiefs gathered their men. Out came the warbonnets, the eagle headdresses, the buffalo, wolf and bear medicine. Moving quickly, the men painted themselves and their horses with their own, proven medicine.

Duuqua muttered under his breath as he tied swallow feathers in his horse's mane for speed. He glared at Isatai, mounted on another horse on a hill farther away from the battle. How could he ignore the shouted taunts of the warriors?

At Duuqua's signal, the Quahadi plunged back down the hill. The enemy's guns barked in answer to their war whoops and soon heavy smoke again surrounded the three buildings.

Again and again the warriors charged. Again and again, the bullets of the white hunters found their targets. Duuqua's hopes fell with each warrior that tumbled from his horse. No hair hung from his belt. Only the warriors who had killed the enemy beneath the wagon, before the battle began, had claimed scalps. Long before the sun began its slow walk toward the horizon, Duuqua signaled the retreat and rode to meet his brother where he waited on a high hill east of the battle, well out of range of enemy fire.

A shot rang out. "The white hunters have big hopes," Quannah laughed. "Their bullets cannot reach us here." His laughter died in his throat as blood blossomed on the forehead of the warrior mounted next to him. Slowly, he slid off his horse.

Duuqua leaped off his own horse and caught the man, pulled him to safety in a stand of nearby trees. He crouched behind a tree and stared down the hill at the building where the sun glinted off a lone rifle. Never had he seen a bullet travel so far. The man was not dead, only stunned. The bullet had traveled so far it lacked the strength to pierce his skull.

"We cannot win against this medicine," Quannah whispered, his face a bitter mask. "But we will not surrender and live like sheep on the reservation. We will find another place to fight."

"Death before surrender," Duuqua vowed. The fight was not over. The soldiers would come. That much of the *pahoute's* words he believed.

When they came, they would find the Quahadi ready to fight.

Chapter Thirteen

The new camp was much smaller than the old, and too quiet. A tense, expectant air hung over the tipis like a storm cloud. Children found relief from their mothers' short tempers in their usual games, but the women's hoops, wheels and darts lay unused. They were too busy gathering herbs and preparing medicines to play games. Though the tipis faced east, the People turned north in anxious anticipation.

One afternoon three days after they arrived at the new camp, several women jumped to their feet. Kris dropped the roots she'd been pulverizing and stared after them as they ran screaming, out of camp. Her breath caught as she spotted mounted warriors weaving through the trees, moving toward them.

He's back! Immobilized by a wash of intense emotion, Kris searched for Black Eagle. As the horses drew closer, she noticed the travois bearing the injured, then the bodies tied across other horses' backs. Six dead, two wounded too badly to ride. The warriors' hanging heads left her feeling hollow, bereft.

They had lost. She'd known they would, but the reality nearly sent her to her knees. As if born of her own emotions, a shrill cry began, swelling into keening wails.

With a shriek, Kiyani ran to the first travois where Quannah lay. Instantly, his other wives joined her, their wails and cries deafening as they directed the horse to Quannah's tipi.

Her tension mounting, Kris searched for Black Eagle and finally spotted him, bringing up the rear, leading two horses. One bore a body, the other pulled a travois.

Relief flooded her, leaving her so dizzy she swayed. Padaponi propped her up, clucking like a mother hen and patting her back. Kris clutched Padaponi's hand as Black Eagle rode nearer. Their gazes locked but he showed no emotion. Her tension drained away as she saw that he was uninjured. As he released the horses to several wailing women, her gaze swept over the dead man tied across the horse's back. That could have been him. She kept her emotions hidden behind the same calm mask he wore.

The women laid the dead man on the ground, then pulled their knives and began hacking off their hair and cutting their arms and legs, wailing themselves into a frenzy. One of the women caught Kris staring. She shrieked and ran at her, knife upraised.

Black Eagle leaped off his horse and grabbed the woman's arm. He whispered in her ear and held her as she sobbed. With scathing glances at Kris, the other women led the sobbing one away, followed by a group of men bearing the body of their loved one.

Kris suddenly became aware of the many angry faces turned her way. The People had remembered her predictions. They blamed her for their sorrow.

"Go with Padaponi," Black Eagle ordered in a low, urgent whisper. "Let them grieve." He turned to Padaponi with rapid-fire instructions.

Reluctantly, Kris did as he'd asked. Her questions would wait. She'd expected the People to blame her, had known they would need a scapegoat, but their suspicion stung.

It isn't their fault, she reminded herself. *They don't know the future. They're fighting for their lives.* Could she have done more to help? Doubt knifed through her, honed by the People's grief.

If only they'd listened to her and not to Coyote Droppings. He hadn't been among the dead or wounded, so where was he hiding? Of course, she realized. By now everyone knew his magic paint had failed, that he was a fraud.

Would grief cause the People's anger to grow? Did Black Eagle and Quannah also blame her? Her prayers that they would understand, that Coyote Droppings' actions would prove the truth of her words, seemed foolish now.

Dreading possible confrontations, Kris waited by the stream. She caught glimpses of Black Eagle, but he'd been busy directing the burials and comforting the grieving—things Quannah would have done if he hadn't been wounded.

"If I join you, will you push me in?" Kris jerked around, surprised to find Black Eagle smiling down at her. She'd been so caught up in her thoughts, she hadn't heard him approach.

She patted the brittle grass beside her. "Tell me about the battle."

"It did not go well from start." He stared out over the plains. "Isatai promised us the enemy would be sleeping. He say we sneak in and club them to death. But they were awake."

Kris couldn't help shuddering and longed to tell him to stop, but she needed to know what had happened.

"Lodge walls thick. They fire big rifles through narrow holes. We could not get to them. They shot three warriors before our first retreat, and six more before sun high in sky."

"And Quannah? How did he get shot?" Would Duuqua finally acknowledge that she'd told them the truth?

He gazed into her face, his own grim. "Shot in back as you say. No enemy behind him."

A strange sense of calm filled her. Nothing had changed; it had happened just like the histories she'd read; she hadn't been sent here to change history. Did that mean she could only predict calamity? Would knowing the horrors in advance help the People survive them?

"How many white men did you murder?"

"Mur-der?" Black Eagle stiffened beside her.

Kris gulped, seeing the fiery gleam in his eyes. Why couldn't she keep her foot out of her mouth today?

"Tell me this word's meaning," he demanded. "Chikoba will tell me if you do not."

"It means to kill someone wrongfully." Though she trembled in fear of his reaction, Kris could not retract the comment.

"We do not *murder* white hunters." His low voice vibrated with anger. "If white men continue to *murder* buffalo, my People die. White hunters *murder* my People every time they shoot buffalo."

He stood and glared down at her, his eyes burning. "Your skin Comanche, but your heart white. You have no love for the People. You keep to yourself, not wanting to be one of them. You even refuse my name for you." He turned to leave.

"Wait." Kris jumped to her feet and pulled him back to face her. "Please try to understand. It's difficult for me to accept that you have killed my people."

"Comanche also your people, Tomanoakuno." She winced when he flung her hand off his arm. "Where does your heart lie?"

"I don't know," she cried. Never had she felt so torn between her two halves. She loved both. Didn't she? His accusations stung.

"My people killed when I very young," he told her, gazing into the distance, as if he saw them there. "I watched Mexicanos murder my father."

She blanched, wanting to distance herself from the horror that had turned his eyes bleak. "They rape my mother, but Padaponi drag me away. We return later; bury their bodies. Not much left. Then Padaponi take me to live with Noconi.

"Pete Noconi, Quannah's father, chief. He adopted me,

raised me as son. Many of the People, chased from their homes by *taibo* and Mexicanos, joined the Noconi. Then *taibos* found our camp and stole Noconi's wife and baby daughter."

"Cynthia Ann Parker." Aching at his sorrow, Kris placed her hand on his arm.

His attention snapped back to her. "That her white name, but she Noconi's wife." Irritably, he shook off her arm and turned away from her. "Her white family killed her."

Kris recalled pictures of Cynthia Ann taken after her return to civilization. Her lifeless eyes and hopeless expression had touched a chord in Kris's soul. Cynthia Ann's white family hadn't literally done away with her, but despair had made her too weak to fight the disease that finally killed her and her tiny daughter.

"Pete Noconi and Quannah's younger brother died next summer of white man's disease. Padaponi brought Quannah and me here to join the Kwerherehnuh, where we became Quahadi warriors."

"Why Quahadi?"

"They live in secret, hidden places where no white man comes. She know the Quahadi are fierce warriors. If Quannah and I are to survive, we must learn to fight."

He turned his solemn gaze to her. "I became Quahadi warrior, then war chief, and now Great Spirit gives me you to help my People."

"What do you expect me to do?" she exclaimed. Jumping to her feet, she threw up her hands. "I don't have any *puha*. I'm not a medicine woman! If I were, I'd find my own way back to the Springs. I wouldn't need you. I'm just plain Kris Baldwin from Austin, Texas. How can I help your People? I can't even help myself."

"What do you need?" Honest concern replaced the heat in his eyes.

"I need to go home, but I'm afraid I might not be able to get there. I've lost something that—" She broke off with a frustrated sigh, her hand clenching into a fist over her breastbone. How could she explain about the stones? He'd never understand. Why try? He'd refused to believe her warnings about the battle. He'd laugh in her face if she tried to tell him about the stones.

"Look." He sat and motioned for her to join him. He opened his medicine bag and withdrew a buckskin-wrapped bundle. Very carefully, he folded back one side, revealing a clear, tear-shaped stone.

At first Kris could only stare in stunned amazement. Then hope and elation spiraled through her, leaving her lightheaded. "You found it!" She reached for it, but he stopped her.

"Gentle," he warned, and flipped open the buckskin. "There are two."

Kris gasped, almost overcome with relief. She pressed a hand over her breastbone. They weren't lost! He had both of them. Lying side-by-side on the rough buckskin, they seemed to gather light from the sky. She reached for her stone, knowing it by the fragment of gold chain caught in the tiny hole at the top.

"Very powerful," Black Eagle warned. "Could harm you."

"I wore this stone for years," Kris scoffed. "Other than a strange humming sensation every now and then, it never caused me any harm."

"Before its mate near."

Near? She pulled back, eyeing the stones. Almost a hundred-and-thirty years had separated these stones before they yanked her out of her own time and brought her to his. Was he right? Were the stones more powerful together? Was that power dangerous? She had to know. Since he'd revealed the stone to her, she'd felt a strong urge to pick it up, to hold it again. Was it joy at seeing it again, or was there more to it?

She picked up her stone and smiled at the familiar, comforting hum. Nothing dangerous here. She picked up its mate. Heat suffused her, sweeping through her body with incredible speed. Emotions flashed through her, until she was hard-pressed to identify each one, but the strongest was joy.

She smiled, turning to Black Eagle, feeling radiant, as if she glowed from within. Shadows stirred in the depths of her sub-conscious and he changed before her eyes, seeming younger, more carefree. She thrilled at the look in his eyes as he gazed at her. But then the look changed, turned questioning before it was transformed from disbelief to horror to sorrow. Each emotion swept through her, clear and more vivid than any she could ever recall feeling. Then she saw him again, as if in a scene from a movie, lying before her covered in blood, his pain-glazed eyes filled with regret and remorse.

With an anguished cry, Kris closed her eyes against the bleak images, but another nightmare tumbled her into the bowels of Barton Springs and the waiting arms of death.

She yanked away from the black abyss, dropping the stones. *Kaku?* A trembling voice rang in her head. *Can you hear me? Are you there?*

"Grandmother!" she cried, "I hear you! Grandmother?" There was no answer, only silence.

He was right. She didn't understand their power. "Put them back, please."

"You do not want yours?" He held her stone out to her.

"No," Kris said, still trembling. "Keep them safe, please." She wanted to add, "Until I'm ready to leave," but she couldn't bring herself to say the words.

"How did you find them?"

"I received this stone in my vision. Then I took it to the sa-cred waters and tossed it in."

She studied his face, trying to read his reactions as she spoke. "It almost hit me. I ducked into the water and picked it up. Then I saw you, standing on the ledge above me."

"Yes," he nodded. "You looked at both stones." He mim-icked her, holding both fists close to his face.

"After you disappeared"—Kris swallowed hard, remembering those terrifying moments as the bottom of the Springs disintegrated beneath her feet—"I couldn't let go of the stones! I couldn't get out of the water . . . I still had them in my hands when I . . . drowned." Her voice shook. "Where did you find them?"

"You start breathing, but you very cold. Hands like ice. I tried to warm you and found stone in each hand."

"Do you know what this means?" Kris asked, her voice rising. "The stones will take me home again!"

"No." His swift, decisive answer sliced through her elation. "You stay here."

"You can't keep me here," she protested.

"You belong with the People now," he said, firmly.

"Your People hate me. You hate me."

He leaned near, his voice low, almost menacing. "You wrong. I do not know what I feel for you, but not hate." He pulled her to him and his lips silenced her protests. She swallowed a squawk of alarm, reeling as his tongue thrust past her lips. With barely leashed hunger, he searched her mouth, learning her secrets. The crisp scent of sun and wind rose from his skin, engulfing her.

She braced to fight him but, as before, his lips gentled. His tongue teased a tentative response from hers. A thrill of heat swept her body at his deep groan. She waited for the warning screech of her conscience, but heard nothing more than the frantic beat of her own heart.

Bone by nerveless bone, she relaxed in his arms. Her mouth opened wider, hungry for more of him, as though he were nourishment and she were starving. She sank into his embrace, turning her head to accommodate his thrusting tongue, savoring his flavor—slightly salty, not at all sweet. She speared her fingers into the cool silk of his hair and clutched him closer.

All she needed was him, hot and hard against her, plundering her mouth. His lips seared her throat and his hands stroked up her sides. She moaned into his mouth when he cupped her breasts. Her nipples pebbled beneath his circling thumbs and desire lanced through her, loosing a flash flood of response that pooled between her thighs.

Abruptly, Black Eagle pulled away from her. Beneath a heavy scowl, his onyx eyes searched her face. "Who are you, woman? Why you make me do this? I want only to be war chief to Quahadi. You make me forget I am warrior."

Kris snapped upright, her mind instantly clear. "Make things easier for both of us. Take me back to the Springs."

He gripped her arms, turning her back to face him. "Why return? Someone wait for you? Another man?"

"No," she corrected, alarmed by the angry color rushing into his face. "That's not it."

"Then why?" He gave her a single sharp shake, his eyes raking her face. "Tell me!"

"I don't belong here," she shouted, trying to squirm out of his grip. How could she explain something she didn't fully comprehend? "My home is far away. I can't stay here."

"You cannot leave." His hands tightened on her arms. "My People need your *puha*."

"I can't help you." Kris struggled against his hold, but he held her firm. "The soldiers will come and if you fight them, they will kill you—all of you. You have to think of the women and children, the old ones. Their only hope of survival is surrender."

With an angry growl, Black Eagle thrust her away. "I die before I surrender, but they must find me first."

"General MacKenzie is relentless—"

"You know this man?" His voice changed.

Kris cursed her loose tongue. "Not personally. I've heard about him. At home. He'll come with his soldiers. In the fall."

"How you know this?" His hands closed over her arms, forcing her to face him. Fury etched chasms on either side of his mouth. "Tell me!"

Kris's heart beat so loudly, she knew he must hear it. What could she say? He wouldn't believe the truth—and he'd been a significant part of her journey into the past, perhaps even the cause. Her brain scrambled for explanations he could accept even as her mouth opened and she heard herself speak. "I've heard his name, okay? He's hard, relentless. And he's found the Quahadi before. He'll come again."

Black Eagle released her so abruptly, she staggered. His hands tightened into fists and she had to strain to hear his low mutter. "This time my lance will find his heart."

"*You* crippled him?" She felt suddenly queasy. "I thought Quannah . . ." Quannah had been credited with that crime in every book she'd ever read on the subject. MacKenzie would be looking for Black Eagle when he came again.

"I aimed for his heart but my horse stumbled." His gaze narrowed. "He rode away with my lance in his leg. Good lance." Regret etched his face. "I should have killed him."

"Perhaps he won't remember you."

"He not forget the man who lamed him." Black Eagle's lips pulled back in a feral snarl. "I kill him—"

"You can't!"

"—before his anger harms my People."

"No!" Horror swept her. "He'll kill you. Take me back first, before he comes."

His arms tightened around her and he pulled her to him again. The fire in his eyes held her immobile as his hands rose to her breasts.

"You don't want to do this," she protested, wedging an arm between them. "You're a warrior, remember? You don't need a woman distracting you."

His gaze fell to her lips, and he lifted her off her feet, raising her to meet his descending lips. His tongue slid along the seam of her lips as he settled her over the hard ridge nudging at the junction of her thighs.

She moaned into his mouth as the moist flood returned. Anger and fear dissolved in a wave of heat, incinerating resistance. She clutched his back.

He broke off the kiss as abruptly as he'd started it and stared into her upturned face.

Annoyed by his strength of will, she watched the heat die in his eyes. A cool mask of indifference settled over his face. "Make ready. Two suns, we leave."

"You're taking me home?"

"We go to *murder* more *taibo*."

With a soft cry, Kris sank to her knees, clasping her arms around them. Her body burned with shame—an entirely different heat from that aroused by Black Eagle's embrace. Why couldn't she resist him?

His kiss had probed deep and she had welcomed its intrusion! Were her dreams prophetic? Or had she known him before? Why was his name burned into her soul?

Nothing made sense anymore. Only desire and fear—the emotions warring inside her.

Coward! Duuqua called himself as he fled the *pahoute*.

By the Sun! Her medicine was strong. Even now he did not want to deny himself the pleasure of her arms. He wanted to make her his woman forever. And her body told him she wanted this too.

But he could not! He must not. His People needed him to be strong. Danger-filled days stretched ahead. MacKenzie was coming. He could not let her distract him. These feelings . . . Now he understood his warriors' reluctance to go raiding. How did they bear it? Better to take an arrow to the heart than let a woman rip it from your chest.

He must stay away from her until he could control his desire. But how could he do that and still protect her? Isatai had disappeared, but Duuqua knew he had not gone far. The worm would wait and watch for a chance to kill her. He had sworn it.

Duuqua must take her with him when he went raiding, though it would make him *pasa* to have her so near and not be able to take her to his furs. He must keep her close; he must protect her this time.

This time? His churning thoughts flew out of his head. *This time.* Again, his thoughts betrayed him. He had never seen the *pahoute* until he found her at the sacred waters, but he knew her face. The first night he slept with her in his arms, he had felt more content than at any other time in his life, and any time since. He could not bear the thought of her leaving. These feelings made him weak, not a warrior, but a *pabi*, an elder sister.

The Great Spirit had answered his prayers in the Sun Dance, had told him she was woman first, messenger second. But his People needed her. She could not be his woman. Not yet.

But she would be his, he vowed, if they lived through the dark days ahead. Until then he could not let her go. Until then he could not let himself love her.

"Stubborn man!" Powahe collapsed, sinking inward and curling her arms tight around her abdomen. Why wouldn't he listen to his heart?

If only Kris had accepted the stone. One hand tightened into a fist in Powahe's lap. If Kris had the stone, Powahe promised herself she'd make short work of enlightening the girl.

Powahe sighed and stirred up the fire, ignoring the wail of the wind outside her tipi.

She felt as if the marrow had been sucked from her bones, as if her body had lost the strength to press onward. She eyed the narrow bed of white-painted rock. How sweet it would be to lay these old bones down, knowing her work was finished, knowing that death would claim her while she slept. No pain, no suffering, only an end.

Suddenly, the wind screeched higher and its icy fingers slithered beneath the tipi walls to surround her.

"Be gone," she cried, recognizing that cold touch. The dark one had sensed her weakness. He had chosen this moment to challenge her! Too late, she realized he'd been waiting. Hurrying, she tried to douse the fire, but her sluggish body seemed reluctant to do her bidding.

Her heart raced, pounding against fragile ribs. *Put it out! Put it out!* Her fingers scratched the hard dirt around it, scrabbling for enough to bury the tiny flame.

The wind's screech became a moan, then writhed higher until she heard manic laughter, laughter at her useless frailty. The walls of her tipi bowed inward, the lodge poles creaked, bending from the pressure.

With a last mighty effort, Powahe flung herself over the pitiful fire. Not through her would the dark one find the two he sought. They must be given a chance to fulfill the promise.

A ripping sound made her gasp and arch off the fire. The entrance flap was being torn off. Horrified, Powahe gawked. Why would the dark one come in through the door? Not his style at all.

With a last horrendous wrench, the flap tore free and the wind whipped into the tipi, sending furs and blankets flying. In the confusion, Powahe thought she heard a man's voice, a deep, angry snarl. Was she imagining things? Had the dark one stolen a human body to do his evil work?

Powahe's world teetered precariously, dotted with flying debris, punctuated by male curses. Too weak to fight, she clutched for something to hold on to, something to balance her careening senses. Her fingers found it. Cotton. Spread over a wide chest, covering strong arms. Desperately, she clung, closing her eyes against the swirling maelstrom, shutting out the dark one's hideous screech as he found the fire.

Had she succeeded in dousing it? She peered around a broad shoulder and cried out. One last ember glowed in the darkness. As if someone blew on it gently, encouraging it to grow, the ember flared, then died. Evil laughter ripped through the night.

The dark one had found them.

Powahe had no time to chastise herself. Plunked on her

feet yards away from her suddenly calm tipi, she briskly tugged her buckskins back into place and prepared to give her would-be rescuer the sharp side of her tongue.

"What have you done with my daughter?"

Speech failed her at her first glimpse of the rugged face above her. Jacob Baldwin. She'd been rescued from the dark one by the devil himself.

"What do you think you're doing?" she demanded, glaring up at him. "Don't expect me to thank you. I didn't ask you to come here." His very face reminded her of the sorrows in their mutual past, the losses she still grieved. Did he miss her daughter, the wife whose death he'd caused?

Powahe rejected the sympathy that elbowed past her own grief. *He's come for his daughter*, she reminded herself and snorted, though she dreaded his reaction when he learned where Kris had gone—and that she had helped send her there.

"Where is she?"

"I've been fine. How are you doing?" She was in the mood for a good verbal sparring—the only form of aggression a sensible shaman allowed herself, the only form of aggression she could handle in her current depleted state. She shrugged and started to walk away, but her legs wobbled. Instantly, his hand appeared beneath her arm—warm, supportive, unexpected. But it didn't keep her from closing the door in his face.

He'd changed over the years since her daughter's death. But had he lost that arrogant, high-minded idealism that had led him to believe he could change her People, beginning with his own wife?

The door opened behind her. She braced for a slam, but he closed it without venting the anger that she knew must be riding him hard by now. Again she wondered how much he'd changed, then sniffed. Nonsense. With men, things only got worse.

"Where is my daughter, Powahe?"

"I'm too tired tonight." Powahe waved him away when he

tried to steer her toward the sofa and headed for her bedroom. "I'm going to bed." She suspected he wouldn't leave without an explanation, but that didn't mean she had to be gracious. Nor would she let him interfere with her attempts to reach Kris and her warrior.

But Jacob Baldwin wasn't a man to be put off easily. "I've traveled all day to get here and I want some answers. Now."

Powahe didn't bother to deny her involvement. "Kris is safe, for now, but I am exhausted. I want a bath, then bed, and tomorrow I will answer your questions."

She watched his stern face as he struggled to accept her words. How on earth was she going to explain things to him? She needed a night to think it over. Even that wouldn't be enough.

Finally he nodded, his reluctance plain in his suddenly drawn features. "You're sure she's okay?"

Powahe nodded. "I suppose you can stay here. You know where everything is; nothing's changed."

As she prepared for bed, the familiar thumps and bumps coming from her living room told her he'd opened the lopsided old sofa bed, preparing to reacquaint himself with its dubious comforts. She thought about offering him a pillow and a blanket, but squelched the urge. Men were like cats: feed 'em, you never got rid of 'em.

She sighed. She'd have to tolerate Jacob in her home. For Kris's sake.

Chapter Fourteen

It had been a long miserable day following Black Eagle and his warriors. When one of the women finally called a halt, Kris practically fell off her horse. She stared at their water source, a muddy circle on the face of the plains, hardly even a puddle.

Fatigue made short work of the process of erecting the tipis. Kris inserted the wooden skewers that held the tipi cover in place while Padaponi steadied her. Just as she thrust the last skewer into place and dropped to the ground, Black Eagle and his warriors thundered into camp.

Garishly painted in black, red and white, he preened astride his prancing horse, brandishing his lance and war shield and shouting some eerie chant. When he pulled his horse to a rearing halt then leapt off its back, she stumbled away from him.

His fathomless black eyes returned her stare from amid the black and white bars painted horizontally across his face with an intensity that set off rockets in her blood. In that moment she recognized the futility of her efforts to resist him. He overwhelmed her senses, left her feeling anxious, edgy, longing for something she couldn't even put a name to, and when he was gone—she felt bereft.

A warrior tossed Black Eagle a long, slender pole. He stabbed it into the ground and drums started beating. The women surged around him, forcing Kris out of the circle of firelight as they began chanting and dancing. Shadows flickered across Kris's face. She glanced upward.

Fresh scalps, stretched over hoops, dangled from the top of the pole, tangling in the dry wind and casting dancing shadows in the firelight. Kris tried to cover her scream.

She gagged. Racing around the tipi, she fell to her knees in the brush and lost her breakfast and her lunch. A hand settled on her shoulder and she screamed again.

"Sick?"

Black Eagle. She nodded, hoping he'd go away. She couldn't look at him, afraid she'd start screaming at the sight of his war paint and never be able to stop.

"Come." He picked her up and carried her into the tipi.

Kris kept her eyes shut as he laid her on her furs. How could he murder innocent people, then dance around their scalps?

"Drink." He pressed his water bag to her lips. The sight of

the unappealing bag opened a floodgate of images, reminding her of time spent on the trail with him, and the bizarre events that had brought her here. She'd thought she'd come to terms with them, with him. Until now. Until this.

He's a warrior, Kris reminded herself. *Even worse, he's a war chief. He doesn't just participate in these raids, he plans and leads them.*

"Better?" He knelt beside her, the concern in his eyes a glaring contrast to his war paint.

She gulped and nodded. "Thanks. I just need to be alone a while, t-to rest." To think. To come to terms with reality.

He shook his head, his loose hair flying, looking wild and untamed. How could she have been so blind? She should have known what he and his warriors intended when they snatched up their weapons and rode out of camp whooping and shouting. She should have felt it in the other women's tension, their anxious gazes glued to the horizon. She'd been so caught up in her own discomfort that she hadn't noticed.

"Rest later." He stood, beckoned to her to come with him, his head turning to the cacophony of chants and drums outside the tipi. His eyes lit and he gestured at the grotesque figures cast by the fire that danced on the tipi wall. "Come. Celebrate our victory. The warriors will count coup. I translate for you."

She stared at his hand and flinched away from the blood on it.

He glared down at her. "What?"

"Don't touch me." Kris couldn't help herself. Horror held her firmly in its grip. "You're hideous." The words burst from her. She trembled at the palpable tension that coiled around him, then reached out to swallow her.

He straightened, his eyes burning embers in his face. "Hid-e-us?"

She shuddered at his tone, praying that he'd satisfied his thirst for violence. "Y-you call yourself a warrior, but you're a murderer!" she cried, unable to control her horror and outrage, feeling her heart crack.

He became deathly still, his eyes glinting in the darkness. "Your Comanche skin hides a *taibo* heart."

He'd labeled her again, firmly drawing the line between them. The crack in her heart split open. She wrenched away, squeezing her eyes shut. She couldn't bear the sight of him. She clutched her fists over her ears, sickened by the crowing men and women outside. A wave of despair brought tears flooding into her eyes. She would never be able to help the People now. She gulped a deep breath, determined to get control of herself.

"Take me home," she said, turning to face him, dismayed at the effort it required. "I'm no use to you now."

He glared at her, then gave a sharp nod, spun on his heel and left. In moments, Black Eagle's voice joined the chanting—defiant, yet despairing.

Kris! A man's voice echoed in her head, clearly audible over the chanting.

"Dad?" she answered, but though she listened, she heard nothing more. She held her breath, wanting to hear a reply, needing to hear a reply. None came.

The dam burst then, accompanied by wrenching sobs that drowned out the chanting and drums, but brought no relief from the grief and guilt assailing her. Nothing could ease her pain.

She'd been betrayed by her own heart. It had lied to her, told her Black Eagle was worthy of her respect and admiration. Thank goodness she'd discovered the truth before it was too late, before she'd fallen in love with him.

Among the people, gossip traveled as fast as an August grass fire. Once word of her actions tonight spread, no one—including Quannah—would trust her. How would she ever persuade someone to take her back to the Springs?

Long after her tears dried on her cheeks, eerie silhouettes spun across the tipi wall. Her heart kept time with the pounding drums and stomping feet.

What would Black Eagle do with her now?

* * *

Powahe blew the hungry sparks of her new fire into a feeble flame. Gently, she nurtured it until it crackled brightly once again, chasing back the night's shadows. She sighed, turning her thoughts inward, preparing to again search out Kris and her warrior. She disregarded her weakness. Her puny strength must be enough. She needed more rest, but Kris's voice, a cry filled with horror, had awakened her, sent her stealing past a snoring Jacob Baldwin and outside to her reeling tipi.

The entrance flap opened, letting in a breeze that almost annihilated her infant fire. "Watch what you do, fool."

"Who are you calling a fool, old woman?" Jacob ducked inside, then secured the flap behind him. "What are you doing out here in the middle of the night? Trying to kill yourself? You're exhausted. You need to rest."

"And why should you care whether I live or die?" Powahe blew gentle encouragement to her feeble fire, hiding her surprise at his words.

"Because you know where my daughter is."

"And you're not leaving until you find her. Is that it?"

Jacob settled on the other side of her fire, his blue eyes turned dark with worry. "Where is she?"

Powahe studied him, afraid to just tell him outright. This man, though a man of faith, did not believe in the Great Spirit's power. He must see to believe.

"You want to see her?"

"Yes, damn it."

She watched him pull on the mantle of indifference that he maintained between himself and the world. What a man he would be if only he could learn to feel again.

Focusing on her granddaughter, Powahe reached deep into the darkness beyond her fire's light, searching, searching. Gradually, the darkness brightened, became another fire, a much larger blaze.

Chants and drumming rang in her tiny tipi and then she

saw Kris, staring at leaping shadows on the wall of the tipi where she sat.

"Kris!" Jacob's hoarse cry ripped through Powahe. Cursing herself for not anticipating just this, Powahe braced herself, expecting to be torn from Kris's side due to his interference, but to her amazement, that didn't happen. The flame burned brighter and the dancing shadows diminished. Powahe felt Jacob reach out to his daughter through the flames. They did not burn him.

How could this be? Only those of great faith could see the other side, could pass through the fire unscathed. Did his love for Kris give him unusual powers? Or had he grown in wisdom and strength?

No, Powahe decided, recalling the little Kris had said about life with her father. He was manipulative and controlling—selfish. Only his love for Kris protected him now. Perhaps, Powahe mused, she could make use of that power.

Kris turned toward them, her eyes searching the darkness. Powahe started, thinking she'd heard Jacob call her name, then realized Kris was only watching the warrior leave the tipi. Powahe recoiled at the agony in her granddaughter's soul as she watched him go. Powahe bit back a cry, sensing the growing chasm between them. How could she warn Kris if she were separated from Duuqua and the stones? What had happened? Why had Kris pushed him away?

Powahe felt herself pulled along as Duuqua left the tipi. The scalp pole loomed before her, and her soul echoed Kris's horrified cry.

Duuqua's chanting voice, the pounding drumbeat, swelled louder and louder as Powahe watched him join the dancers. Her tipi became hot, then hotter. Alarmed, she opened her eyes. Bizarre figures created by fire and shadow and the streaming hair that tangled about the scalp pole danced on her own tipi walls.

She gasped, astonished. Never had the images in her fire transferred themselves to her tipi; always they remained contained in the flames. She glanced at Jacob, sensing a new strength in her fire's images. Humbly, she acknowledged that his love for Kris had intensified the vision. Would his presence help or hinder her efforts to warn her granddaughter? How would he react to what he'd seen? She watched him, warily.

His blue eyes narrowed on Powahe, lit with anger. "What have you done with her?"

Powahe sighed and doused her fire. "Let's get comfortable. It's a long story."

Duuqua watched the *pahoute* ride away, bobbing along on the back of her horse until she became a small spot on the plains, a seed blown before the wind. He should not have brought her with him. He should have known she would not understand. But he had wanted to keep her close, to protect her.

He scowled, watching her struggle to keep up with Piyou, the young warrior chosen to take her and Padaponi back to the main camp. Piyou rode ahead, leaving the two women to eat his dust. Duuqua understood his anger. When Piyou returned three days from now, the other warriors would have taken many more horses and much hair, but he would have nothing to show for two days of hard riding. It did not help that he was the youngest and poorest brave in the war party. Duuqua sighed. He knew Piyou would protect Kris and Padaponi but he feared that the young man's anger would make him reckless when he returned.

Still, Duuqua could not pull his eyes from Kris's back. Why did his heart ache at the hard words that lay between them? How could he have feelings for this woman who called him murderer? He hated her white words, but this word most of all. Why did she not understand that he must fight? If he did not fight, his People would die.

He felt anger at her hard words and sorrow that she refused to help, but his sorrow ran deeper.

Swift and sure, his thoughts raced as he remembered her— skinning her first rabbit and laughing with him; standing up to his People when they hurt her that first day in camp. On and on the images ran, but always his mind brought him back to the image of her dressed in the white buckskins, seated on his furs, waiting for him. Even his anger at Padaponi's meddling could not cool the desire that image brought.

Firmly, he rejected it. As war chief, he would not take a wife only to leave her alone and helpless when he was killed in battle. He could not live like other men. Duty was his life.

And what man could love a woman who called him hideous, called him murderer? Still the words knifed deep, lancing his heart, wounding his tender feelings.

Duuqua sent his horse running after the warriors who had ridden ahead. For the first time in his life, he felt small, less than a man, less than a warrior. He had seen disgust in her eyes, disgust for him, for his actions. Did she not know it was his duty to lead the Quahadi war raids, killing any *taibo* he found on the land of the People?

Except the women and children. He remembered the horror of watching his mother die at the hands of the hated Mexicanos. A low growl escaped him. Never would he treat a woman so. Only when a woman pointed a gun at him did he kill her, and sometimes not even then. Most women could not hit a tree at five paces.

Did this make him better than his enemy? Kris Baldwin did not think so. Had she not seen that no women's scalps hung from the scalp pole? No. She had not cared enough to look that hard. Did she not understand that the men he had killed were trying to kill him? Duuqua had seen white men crush a child's skull against a tree or spear them like dogs and leave them to die slowly. Did she not know that the Quahadi did not kill children? They took them captive, made them one of the People, gave them to men and women who had none of their own to love.

Duuqua felt no shame. He could not give up this fight because of a woman and he would not let the disgust in the *pahoute*'s eyes make him weak. He was war chief to the

Quahadi, the most feared warrior on the Llano Estacado. And proud of it.

With a fierce cry, he dug his heels into his horse's sides, feeling its power leap through him as he raced across the plains to lead his warriors against his enemies.

"I need your help."

Kris jumped at the unexpected voice so close behind her, almost dropping the water bag she'd been filling at the tiny spring beside the People's latest camp. "Chikoba? Is something wrong?"

"Ekararo needs you." He took the heavy water bag and Kris followed behind, almost running to keep up with his long, hurried stride.

"What's happened? Is she all right?" She imagined Ekararo in labor, bleeding, dying—then stopped cold at the sight of her friend kneeling over a staked deer hide.

Ekararo glanced up as they approached, her gaze darting from Chikoba to Kris, then back again. Her cheeks pinkened. "What have you told her, husband, to make her face white as death?"

Chikoba shrugged. "Only that you need her help." He crossed his arms over his chest, his scowl settling deeper into the creases lining his mouth.

Kris bit back a grin, beginning to understand his problem.

Ekararo stretched over the taut hide, reaching for a far corner with her fleshing tool. "You should not have frightened her. I told you, I do not need help." Her eyes flashed and the color in her cheeks brightened. "A little work will not harm your child."

"You see?" Chikoba nudged Kris. "She works too hard and will not rest when I tell her to. By sunset, her feet are so swollen she cannot walk."

Touched by his concern, Kris laid a hand on Chikoba's arm, surprised to find the muscles tense, rock hard, beneath her fingertips. Over the last weeks, since her abrupt return from the war party, Kris had noticed Chikoba's increasing tension and had made a point of visiting while her friend's surly husband was away. She'd assumed that he chafed at the responsibility of caring for and watching over the women while the other warriors were away raiding. Was concern for Ekararo and their soon-to-be-born child to blame for his temper?

"Why don't you go hunting? I'll stay here and keep Ekararo from overdoing."

Chikoba huffed, glaring at Ekararo. When it became clear she had no intention of stopping her work to look up at him, he stomped away without a backward glance.

"He's right, you know."

Ekararo sat back on her heels again. "I cannot sit in tipi and watch belly grow. Must stay busy."

"Are you afraid of giving birth?" Kris mentally squirmed, feeling ill-equipped to handle a discussion on the birth process.

"Not birth; afterward."

"Afterward?" Did Ekararo's bleak mood have anything to do with Coyote Droppings' unexpected return the day before? It certainly explained Kris's own uneasiness and the persistent feeling that she was being watched. She wasn't at all surprised that he'd waited to reappear until Black Eagle was gone.

Ekararo rubbed a hand over her swollen middle, her expression brooding.

"Do you want to talk about it?" Kris laid a hand over Ekararo's. "Let me help you."

A tremulous smile brightened Ekararo's face and she squeezed Kris's hand. "Thank you, my friend."

Kris nodded at the partially fleshed hide. "You know, I've been nagging Padaponi to teach me how to do this, but she won't. I think she's afraid I'll screw it up."

"Screw it up?"

"Make a mistake. Ruin it."

Ekararo chuckled. "I surrender. Between you and my angry

husband, I cannot win." She leaned closer and whispered, "I not as fussy as Padaponi."

By the end of the day, Kris heartily wished she'd never seen a deer hide, although she suspected the finished product would greatly relieve the pain of her raw knuckles and aching back. The finely-tanned hide would be cut into mocassins and other items for the baby. Kris looked forward to making them herself with Ekararo's supervision.

She stepped out of Ekararo's tipi as sunset blazed across the horizon, turning all the tipis to a soft amber. Instinctively, she turned north, her gaze skimming the purpling ridges, searching for riders.

"You miss Duuqua."

She shielded her eyes against the sun's glare and Ekararo's scrutiny. "I tell myself I shouldn't worry, but it's no use." She turned again to scan the hills. "I know one of these days he's going to ride into camp. I dread facing him after our argument, but I look forward to it too. Crazy, huh?"

"Not so crazy." Ekararo smiled. "Not if you love him."

"Love him?" Stunned, Kris dropped her hand to stare at her friend. "No. There's too much between us, his culture, the distance between our homes." Kris grimaced. If her friend only knew! "We always seem to rub each other the wrong way."

"Those things are not important if two people love each other."

"As you should know, being married to a white captive. Has it been hard?"

Ekararo blushed. "Hard to love Chikoba?"

Kris laughed and slung an arm around Ekararo's shoulders. "Forget I asked." Again her gaze strayed northward.

"He come soon," Ekararo promised. "And then you see that I am right. Your heart will tell you its truth when you first see him." She turned back to her tipi, but stopped. "This time, listen to it."

* * *

Kris groused through the day, sure that everyone who giggled or chuckled or laughed was laughing at her. By evening, she couldn't stand any more. She made her excuses to Padaponi and Ekararo, telling them she needed to walk a while, to think. Ignoring their worried expressions, she wandered away from the camp.

As usual when Kris was troubled, her hand settled on her breastbone where her stone used to hang. More and more she missed its comforting presence. She was sorely tempted to ask Black Eagle to return it to her, but she still feared its power.

A group of children playing some silly game on the outskirts of camp burst into giggles. She watched them, letting their happy noises clear her troubled mind.

She started back to camp, feeling better, even smiling for the first time that day.

About a dozen painted, feather-bedecked warriors thundered out of camp. A newly recovered Quannah rode at the head of the group and led them straight at her. All of them bristled with shields and lances, bows and clubs. Another raiding party. Her heart pounded as loud as their horses' hooves as they galloped closer, screeching and whooping. What was he going to do to her? She braced herself, listening for the hiss of a rope swishing over her head.

Suddenly the men split, thundering around her in double circles that drew tighter and tighter until, if she dared, she could have reached out and touched the horses' flying manes.

Then the warriors riding the inner circle slid onto the loops dangling from their horses' manes. As they passed her, each man lightly tapped her shoulder. Kris stood frozen, not daring to breathe, let alone move, watching the blur of horses and faces sweep by as each warrior counted coup with a tap on her shoulder. Their horses never broke their steady, loping stride, even as they crossed into the outer circle. When every man had touched her, the circles broke and they lined up facing her.

Was this Quannah's way of putting her in her place? Couldn't she do anything right? Quannah rode forward, his gaze riveting, his full-length eagle headdress trailing over his horse's rump, almost reaching the ground. She held her ground when the horse reared as Quannah thrust his lance skyward. Throwing his head back, he gave a long, ululating cry that spiraled up Kris's spine to ring in her ears.

This magnificent warrior was her ancestor. Without a word, Quannah wheeled and galloped into the deepening shadows, followed by his raiding party. For the first time in her life, pride in her heritage swept over her, nudging aside the abhorence, the guilt.

Kris stared after him, seeing another, more handsome face. Black Eagle. With a shudder, she remembered him riding into camp at the head of the Quahadi raiding party. Horrified, she realized that her antagonism stemmed not from disgust at him, but from guilt at her fascination with the man.

Your Comanche skin hides a taibo *heart* he'd told her. He was wrong. The larger chunk of her heart was Comanche through and through.

She watched Quannah and his warriors streak across the dry, dusty plain. She couldn't sit this fence much longer, living as a Comanche but looking down her nose at them, holding herself aloof as if they might contaminate her, determined not to be like them.

How could she have been so blind? Even her goal to teach on the reservation stemmed from a desire to change them, to make them better, more fit to be a part of the white world. Shame made her cheeks burn.

Could she accept her People as they were? Could she forgive their failings and learn to love them? She wanted to, badly. But if she accepted their lifestyle, wholeheartedly became one of them, was she turning her back on her own life? If she stayed, she'd have to deal with her doomed fascination with Black Eagle. And if she lost the fight and succumbed, would she surrender the opportunity to return to her previous life?

Kris trembled, torn between the two halves of her soul, knowing she must find a way to reconcile the two. Before they tore her apart.

"It is as you said, brother." Quannah's voice rang with sorrow.

Duuqua only nodded. He could not speak. From where they stood, near the track of the iron horse at the Arkansas River, buffalo bones covered the plains. Stripped clean by scavengers, the bones lay naked, turned white by the sun. Silently, Duuqua mourned the senseless killing, knowing that the death of the buffalo meant death for the People.

Anger rose in his breast for the enemy who had done this. Stunned by the many sod huts that had sprung up on the plains, he fought to rid the plains of enemies—especially the hated buffalo hunters, but he took no more scalps.

He saw the desperation in his enemies' eyes and realized these people had nowhere else to go. He hated that understanding, that recognition of their need. Stubbornly, he refused to believe the People could not win this fight. But the farther he traveled, the more alarmed he became, for he found no buffalo, only rotting hulks left by the white hunters.

And now this. As far as he could see, the bones of buffalo covered the grass. So many had died here that a man could walk for miles, stepping from bone to bone, his moccasins never touching grass.

Then, suddenly, the scene changed. Bright images flashed through his mind and he saw this place filled with strange square lodges separated by flat, black ground with yellow streaks painted down the middle. Poles strung with wire stood everywhere. Overhead, high in the sky, the sun flashed off a silver bird bigger than any eagle he had ever seen. The images disappeared as abruptly as they had come, leaving Duuqua staring around him, almost relieved to once again see the bone-studded plain. He shook his head, clearing his mind of the strange vision, but his heart did not slow its pounding beat and the stones in his medicine bag took up the rhythm.

"Did you see that?" Duuqua asked Quannah.

"See what?" Quannah's voice was bleak, his eyes narrowed as he stared over the plains.

Despair swept over Duuqua. Had he just seen a vision of what this land would become under the white man's care? A chant of grief escaped Duuqua's lips. Echoed by the Quahadi warriors, the chant soon rose into a keening wail that brought knives flying from their sheaths to shine in the sun and slice gashes in arms, thighs, chests. The blood of Quahadi warriors blackened the grass beside their beloved buffalo.

But the bright flow did not dull the pain in Duuqua's heart. Without the buffalo the People could not eat. Naked they would run before the wind, only to die in its cold embrace. Without the buffalo they could not live on the plains they loved.

Duuqua turned his face south. His heart sought the woman who waited there, the woman who could tell him what they must do to survive.

Chapter Fifteen

Kris set the water bag down and rubbed her aching back. Since taking over Ekararo's heavy tasks three days before, her whole body hadn't been the same. Not one muscle moved without complaining.

Whenever the chores began to wear on her, she reminded herself she could be doing them while carrying twenty-five extra pounds around her waist, like Ekararo. The reminder always got her going again.

She trudged up the trail, picking up her pace. Besides, her efforts were paying off. The swelling in Ekararo's feet had gone down and she was smiling and laughing more. Mostly at Kris's bumbling efforts to "keep tipi."

If nothing else, this time with the People had taught Kris a healthy respect for the technology of her own time. She longed for large appliances—washers and dryers, stoves, refrigerators, microwaves—but they'd be hard to move by travois.

Head down, she trudged up a slight hill, taking the crest with a determined spring in her step. A man stepped into her path. Kris crashed into him headlong and bounced backward, almost losing her grip on the water bag. Bells tinkled, setting her nerves to jangling. Coyote Droppings.

"Why don't you watch where you're going? Or can't you see past that monstrous ego?" Kris sneered, and moved to step around him. Again he blocked her way. She set the water bag down. He hadn't bothered her since he'd come back. She'd even begun to think he'd forgotten about her. She snorted. She should have known better. Coyote Droppings seemed happiest when the people around him were miserable.

Not bothering to hide her contempt, she eyed him up and down. He seemed thinner, but more threatening. "So, the False Prophet has returned." She knew he couldn't understand her, but hoped her tone would make her meaning clear. "It's really a shame you don't speak my language."

His hand shot out and wrenched her wrist, forcing her to release the water bag. He twisted her arm and stepped behind her, slapping his hand over her mouth before she could scream. Pain shot through her shoulder as he shoved her arm high, forcing her off the trail and into a dense cluster of trees and bushes. He slammed her up against a tree, holding her prisoner with his whipcord lean body pressed firmly against hers, keeping his hand over her mouth.

"Yes, you are right. The Prophet has returned."

He spoke English! Kris controlled her breathing, but she couldn't keep her eyes from widening in surprise.

"Surprised?" he chortled. "I know many things. I know about the stones. Soon I steal them and your powers. Then I take back my honor among my People and use your power to destroy *taibos*." He released her and turned to leave.

Kris wiped at her mouth, scrubbing away the taste of his hand. "You're deluded, Coyote Droppings."

He spun to face her again, scowling. "My name Isatai."

"Which means Coyote Droppings in my language, or Rear End of a Wolf, as you should know." She knew that he could be violent, but her hatred of him ran deep. "Stay away from Ekararo."

"I cannot." His voice slipped to a taunting whisper. "Her child mine."

"You lie," Kris hissed. "She would never sleep with you."

His smile made her blood run cold. "Not willingly."

"You are evil." She longed to hit him, stab him, kick him. This man had raped Ekararo and must be taunting her with the horrible possibility that her child was his, not her husband's. "Stay away from her, you monster!"

He ignored her and sauntered away, disappearing into the shadows. He'd done what he came to do. Scared the heck out of her.

Trembling in rage and frustration, Kris searched for her water bag. Grumbling, plotting revenge, she returned to the stream, her whole body shaking in fury as she held it in the water. Where was Black Eagle when she really needed him? Not that she could imagine him doing anything as mundane as filling water bags. But if he were here, Coyote Droppings wouldn't be so bold.

Or would he? He'd accosted her in broad daylight this time and his threats left her shivering inside. He'd never before left her feeling chilled to her very soul, as if his touch had stolen some essence of her being, as if mere contact with him had harmed her.

A pebble rolled into the stream beside her. Kris spun on the balls of her feet and searched the shadows behind her. She saw no one, but felt eyes on her, watching. She tossed her head and turned back to her task. "Go find someone else to intimidate, Coyote Droppings." She hefted the water bag. "I'm not impressed."

A low chuckle started. She ignored it and kept walking, forcing herself to keep to a normal pace. But it grew, swelling out of the shadows to surround her. Heart pounding, Kris increased her pace but she would not run, no matter how hard her heart hammered. The pounding in her ears grew louder and louder until the very earth beneath her feet gave back the vibrations.

She topped the hill and pulled up, staring. It wasn't her heart thundering. It was horses, racing across the plain. The Quahadi rode toward camp, whooping in triumph, driving at least three hundred head of horses before them.

So many horses. And this herd didn't include those that had already arrived. How many innocent people had been killed for them? Kris hesitated, torn between outrage and anticipation at seeing Black Eagle again.

Your heart will tell you its truth . . . Ekararo's words whispered through Kris's mind. *Listen . . . listen.*

Several warriors cut in front of the galloping horses, sending them out onto the plain to join the existing herd. And then, there he was, riding beside Quannah at the head of the Quahadi.

Kris's stomach did a somersault and she listened, unable to do anything else. The feeling overwhelmed her, nearly driving her to her knees, so intense that she pressed a hand over her heart to slow its furious beating. He saw her and turned her way. She smiled, wanting him to come to her. But then Kiyani came running at him. Shrieking and crying, she leaped at him, forcing him to catch her and swing her up behind him or trample her beneath his horse's hooves.

The sight of her clinging to Black Eagle, her cheek pressed to his back, stopped Kris cold.

How could she have forgotten? Black Eagle had no interest in a would-be medicine woman from his future. She knew his obligation to the woman clinging to his back. She told herself to remember the scalps dangling from his scalp pole, to listen to her head and not her deluded heart.

No matter how wonderful its message.

Duuqua pulled Chikoba out of the line of dancers circling the fire. "Where is she?"

"You are not dancing?" Chikoba glanced at the sidelines.

Duuqua followed his gaze, smiling when he spotted Ekararo watching Chikoba with pride in her eyes. Envy stabbed through him. He had hoped to see Kris there, watching him dance. When he had seen her watching him ride into camp today, he thought she had looked happy to see him. Then, like dirt kicked onto a new fire, Kiyani's actions had doused the light in her eyes.

"I must speak to her." Duuqua ignored his friend's knowing grin. Let Chikoba think what he would. He only wanted to talk to the woman. Nothing more. He would not touch her again, not when she thought he was a murderer. He had tried to put her hard words from his mind, but they were written on his soul. He would continue to protect her, but he no longer desired her. He told himself he sought her only for knowledge to help his People.

"You are like a cloud on a sunny day," Chikoba muttered. "Go. She is in my tipi. She likes the quiet there."

Duuqua did not need Chikoba to tell him that Kris did not want to see him, but why had he not wanted to tell him where she was? Was she unwell? Alarmed, Duuqua hurried to the far end of camp, pausing before Chikoba's tipi, which glowed softly from within.

The fire cast Kris's shadow against the tipi wall. She sat so still, her head bent. Was she hurt or sick? He rattled the gourd hanging beside the tipi flap and ducked inside without waiting for her answer.

She started, her eyes flying wide in fear. "Black Eagle." She drew a deep breath and the fear passed. She looked away, but not before he saw pain flash through her eyes, pain that echoed in his heart. Was she remembering the angry words between them?

Jaw clenched, he sat and leaned on a backrest, not trusting himself to speak through his tight throat. Why did she make him feel as if his gut were tied in knots? Why did all his warnings to himself go flying out the smoke hole as soon as he saw her again?

"You are well?" His eyes ran over her, noting a new tear in her buckskins, the stains at the knees. His eyes went to her hands and the object she held. A tiny moccasin. Moccasins? For a baby. A red haze of anger blocked his vision. He felt as if a horse had kicked him in the chest. Throwing his shoulders back, he sucked in a deep breath. "You take husband?"

"What?" Her head came up fast and she stared at him, her eyes puzzled.

"You with child?" He motioned at the moccasin in her hands.

Kris looked down, then dropped it as if it were a hot rock. "It's for Ekararo's baby. Her fingers are swollen and she can't sew. I've been helping her."

Duuqua caught her hand, his thumb brushing the new calluses on her palm. He turned it over and cursed. Her knuckles were raw, some split and bleeding. "What have you been doing?"

She jerked her hand away, picked up the moccasin and continued her sewing. "I told you, I've been helping Ekararo. She can't do heavy work anymore."

"Humph." He took the moccasin from her, tossed it into the open parfleche beside her. "Chikoba can find someone else to do his wife's work."

Kris snatched up the moccasin. "I want to help. It beats sitting around all day watching everybody else work."

"I feared you would be gone." Duuqua watched her closely. Would she hear his regret? Would she understand that he had missed her?

She did not look up. "Kiyani seemed glad to see you."

Duuqua swallowed a curse. "I should have let the horse kick her," he muttered under his breath, remembering how swiftly all happiness had faded from Kris's face once Kiyani arrived. With shoulders stiff and square, she had walked past him, within arm's length, but she had not looked at him once.

"Why? Are you angry with her?" Still she kept her face turned from him.

He frowned, concentrating on his words. While he'd been gone, he'd been learning more English from another white warrior and wanted to impress her. "After you saw us together, I again asked Quannah to release me from duty to Kiyani." Duuqua watched Kris's reaction closely. He had said nothing before, but now he wanted her to know the truth. He wanted to see joy in her eyes once more.

"Why?" She turned a puzzled frown on him, letting the moccasin settle into her lap.

"Kiyani married Quannah because I refused her." He watched her face as his meaning became clear to her.

"You mean she only married Quannah to get to you?"

Duuqua shrugged. "I knew what she was doing, but Quannah loves her."

"But if you knew, why were the two of you . . . together that first night? I saw you . . ."

"Quannah is my brother. When he asked me to share his responsibilities for Kiyani, I had to agree. It is my duty."

She bent over the moccasin. "You don't have to explain yourself to me, Black Eagle."

Duuqua smiled at the hot color in her cheeks. "I want you to understand. Kiyani means nothing to me. I saw your face today when she climbed onto my horse. Was it anger or jealousy that stole the light from your eyes?" He tipped her chin up when she did not answer, forcing her to meet his gaze. "I have not shared my furs with Kiyani since before I found you."

"But that night, I saw you . . ." She frowned, her eyes searching his.

"I was tempted, but when I saw your face, I could not finish what we had started. I spoke to Quannah the next morning."

"What about Quannah's other wives? Do you share responsibilities for them too?"

Duuqua hid a grin at her sour tone. She was jealous, but he knew she would never admit it. He answered truthfully. "Yes."

She stiffened. "All of them?"

He sighed. "It is tiring, taking care of so many women, but someone has to help feed them. How could Quannah alone keep them all fed and dressed?"

Her gaze flashed up to his. "You tease." She ducked her head, picking up her sewing to hide her soft smile.

Duuqua cursed his stupidity. Why hadn't he said something sooner? Why had he let her believe that he was sleeping with Kiyani?

"But all those nights when you were gone," she asked, wanting so desperately to believe him, "if you weren't with Kiyani, where did you sleep?"

"Under the stars, with my horse." He grinned and once again took the moccasin from her, not letting her pull her hand away. "It was cold out there without you to keep me warm." He slid closer, smiling when her breath came faster and her cheeks heated. "Why are you not dancing with the People?"

She searched his face, cocked her head. "Your English has improved tremendously."

He grinned. "I practice."

"I have been practicing," she corrected.

"You have?" he asked, his eyes wide. "Why?"

"No, silly man," she said, laughing. "That's what you should have said. Not 'I practice,' but 'I have been practicing.' "

"I practice for you."

"Well, thanks. I'm flattered."

"What this word mean? Flat-terd?"

"It means, uh, pleased, surprised. Flattered." She blushed, picking at the tiny moccasin.

He lifted her chin. "What troubles you?"

"Who said I was troubled?"

"You do. Why do you stay in tipi?"

Kris shrugged. "I can't watch you dance around the scalps of my people."

"This not a scalp dance."

"It's not?"

"Tabenanika says the rains will come tonight. The People dance to welcome them."

She shook her head, the corners of her lips twitching. "That Chikoba. After all I've done to help Ekararo, he still plays tricks on me."

"He likes to play trickster. It means he likes you. He only fools his friends."

"That makes me feel so much better."

"Come with me?" he asked, extending a hand.

"I'd rather not." She looked down at her hands, plucked at a broken nail.

Duuqua frowned. Now what made her sad? "Why not?"

She stared at him, her gaze frank. "I thought you'd hate me after what I said to you."

"Your words were hard." Duuqua waited for her to say more. She had changed in the time away from him. This woman was not like the Kris he knew, the Kris who chattered like the squirrel, who laughed at Padaponi and smiled at the children. What had changed her? "I feared you would be gone."

"I can't go home until I convince Quannah to surrender."

"Then you will be with the People forever."

"Thanks to you." She glared at him, her hands clenching in her lap.

"Me?"

"Every day since you left I've tried to talk to Quannah, but one of his wives always chases me away. Then when I finally got to talk to him, he wouldn't listen. And do you know why? Because of you, and your successful raids, and the hundreds of horses you've sent him. How could you do this to your People?

They're the ones who will pay for the scalps you've taken."
Tears filled her eyes and she turned away from him.

He pushed back the anger that came at her words. He
would not punish her for speaking what was in her heart. Instead, he waited for her tears to stop. She hated to cry.

She furiously wiped away the last tear. "You're still here?"

He chuckled and with one finger lifted her chin.
"Tomanoakuno," he whispered, and kissed first one eye, then
the other, "you are a warrior in a woman's body."

Kris stiffened and pulled away from him. "No. I'm just
plain . . ."

". . . Kris Baldwin." He smiled down at her, and sighed. He
knew he should leave her, but he had to try once more to
make her understand. "The white man has broken the Medicine Lodge treaty. The White Father promised that no more
white men would come onto our land. Still they come with
their guns, their families, their iron horse. It is not enough
that they steal the land, now they kill the buffalo."

She frowned, concern crinkling her brow. "Did you see
many buffalo?"

Duuqua stilled. "I did not believe white hunters could kill
all the buffalo until we saw the rotting meat. Quannah's hatred burns ever brighter."

Taking Kris by the shoulders, Duuqua leaned close, watching her eyes, praying she would understand. "I fight people
who break treaty, and the buffalo hunters. They know when
they come here that they might die."

"But murdering women and children—"

He stopped her with a finger pressed over her lips. "Did you
see woman's scalp on my scalp pole? Have captives come with
the horses?" He held her chin, forcing her to look into his
eyes. "I no make war on women and children."

He searched her eyes, found them filled with questions. He
sighed. How could he make her understand? "What if soldiers
raid our camp? My warriors would shoot to draw them away
from our women and children. Would you want my warriors to

surrender without firing a shot? Do you not know what would happen? Do you know about Cheyenne at Sand Creek?"

"Yes," she whispered, and he knew by the sadness in her eyes that she did. "I wouldn't want the People to be massacred like that. I understand your reasons for fighting, but I'm connected to both sides. It's hard for me to choose one."

"You say you have no medicine powers, no *puha*, but you know things that have not yet happened. How can this be?"

"I can't explain."

He gripped her arms, shook her gently. "Tell me, woman. I want to understand."

She sighed and decided to take a chance, to tell him everything and hope for the best.

"You still have the stones?"

He nodded, reached for the medicine bundle.

"No, don't." Her stomach clenched as his hand tightened around the bag. "I just wanted to make sure they were safe. You told me once you believed they brought me to you. Do you still believe that?"

He nodded, his eyes searching hers, waiting. "Yes."

"I, too, believe the stones brought me here, not from another place, but from another time, almost a hundred and thirty years in your future. The things that are happening to you now, today, I read about in books."

"A hundred years? What are years?"

"That's how the white man measures time, the passing of days. How many summers do you have?" Kris asked, sure she remembered hearing a young woman give her age in that fashion.

"That is not important. I am a warrior. I count coup, not summers."

"Try to understand. The time between summers, the white man calls a year. I come from the future. That's why I know what's going to happen before it does. But, I can't seem to stop bad things from happening because no one will listen to me. I am not a medicine woman. I'm just—lost, out of place."

Why didn't he say something? Why did he just sit there staring at her?

"You've got to believe me. You're the one who brought me here, with your prayers and your vision quest and who knows what else. You and my grandmother," she murmured. "If you don't believe me, no one will, especially not Quannah. Don't you see? There has to be a reason for me to be here. Things like this don't happen for no reason." She couldn't bring herself to tell him that she suspected the other reason she'd been brought back in time was to be with him.

Black Eagle's hand settled over the stones and his eyes fell shut. Perplexed, Kris watched and waited, letting him think, letting him absorb everything she'd said.

Suddenly, his eyes flashed open again and he pulled her hand to the medicine bundle. "Feel the stones."

Kris tried to pull away, but he wouldn't let her. "Feel them."

Thunder surged into her bloodstream, racing to her heart and from there to her brain, until all she could hear was the stones. When Black Eagle released her hand, she settled slowly back to her furs. What was happening here?

Black Eagle's gaze locked with hers. "The stones tell me you speak the truth."

Kris sighed in relief. "You really do believe me?"

His lips twisted into a crooked smile. "I believe you, but I do not completely understand. Tell me about your home, the future? Do your people live in strange, square lodges? Do they travel in small, brightly painted iron horses that move on black trails between the lodges? Is there a large, silver bird in your skies that gives back the sun's light?"

"Yes! How did you know? Where have you seen these things?"

"I have seen many strange things since you came to the People. Sometimes I look at a meadow and it changes before my eyes. These visions do not last long, but they have made me lose much sleep."

"I can understand why," she laughed. Could her grandmother be sending his visions? How could Powahe do something like that? And yet, she'd heard Powahe's voice more than once since coming here. Was it really so unbelievable that a powerful medicine-woman could communicate with someone like Black Eagle, who was himself a very spiritual person?

Thank you, grandmother, Kris whispered mentally, hoping her grandmother could hear her thoughts. *Thank you for helping him to understand.*

"The visions," Black Eagle began, shaking his head. "They saddened me. Only white men filled my visions. Never did I see one of the People."

He caught her hands between his, his eyes searching her face, anxious, eager. "Tell me what will happen to my People. Can we save ourselves?"

Kris thought about telling him to pray, then remembered what he was only beginning to discover.

Prayer wouldn't help.

Duuqua knelt at the stream and scooped up a handful of water to splash onto his face. He had just left Kris to get some sleep. He had taken her back to his tipi and all through the night she had talked and he had listened. He sank onto a nearby rock and held his head in his hands. At last he understood, or hoped he did. His prayers had pulled her back through time to him, to his People.

He pressed a hand over his medicine bundle. At last the stones lay silent. So much pain, so much sorrow. But hope, too, after a time, when the People began to regain their pride. How he wished he might live to see that time.

Her words had strengthened his vow never to take a wife. He could not bring children to this sorrow. He trembled with anger, outraged that the government would take the People's children from their homes, send them far away. Mothers and fathers would not be allowed to see their children until they were grown. Then the government would return them, strangers dressed in white man's clothes, their hearts bleeding—not Comanche, not white, filled with shame instead of pride. Was this not worse than raiding and taking scalps? To steal a child and kill its soul?

How could the People bear it? How could he believe Kris's promise that Quannah could make it easier for his People? How could Quannah lead the Comanche in walking the white man's road? Quannah's heart burned with hatred for the white men who had destroyed his family. What could Kris say that would change Quannah's heart?

I need your help, she had said. What could he do? He, too, hated the white man.

Great Spirit, Duuqua prayed, *help me to understand*. He remembered Little Wolf's words in the sweat lodge. *Perhaps you should pray to understand her*.

At a stealthy sound behind him, Duuqua leapt up, spinning on the balls of his feet to face the young brave behind him, his knife in his hand.

The brave stepped back, his hands widespread, his eyes fastened on Duuqua's knife. "Quannah wants you."

Duuqua sheathed his knife. Would he forever be leaping at shadows? "Tell him I come."

How could he convince his brother to surrender? They would both rather fight. And die.

Quannah waited with a stranger at his side. Duuqua snorted, recognizing the marks on the man's buckskins. He was of the Tekapwi, who had settled on the reservation long ago and now rode about the plains carrying the words of their white masters to true warriors. Hatred boiled inside Duuqua. The last time he had seen this man, he was scouting for MacKenzie.

Quannah nodded at the stranger. "He brings a message from the Great White Father."

Duuqua's heart jumped. Not the Little Father, the weasel who ran the reservation, but the Great White Father who ruled the white man's government. "What message?"

"Our Father says . . ."

"Your father," Duuqua hissed. "Not ours."

The man gulped, then continued. "My Father sends word to our Comanche brothers."

Quannah cut him off with a slicing motion. "If we are not east of the Arkansas River by full moon, we are outlaws. The Great White Father will send his soldiers to find us and bring us to the reservation."

Duuqua gritted his teeth. Here was the sign he had asked for. Kris Baldwin did not lie. Already the moon was more than half full. What would Quannah say? What would he do? Duuqua saw the hatred burning in Quannah's eyes and knew what he would answer. He nodded. He could not heed Kris's warning.

Quannah turned to the messenger. "The Quahadi are warriors. If the soldiers want us, they can come and find us."

A jagged streak of lightning speared from the dark, turbulent sky, quickly followed by a booming clap of thunder.

Kris shuddered as she and Ekararo crouched at the tipi entrance watching the thunderstorm pound the naked plains. Rain, at last, but with such violence. She watched in fascination. She'd seen thunderstorms before from the safety of home or school, but she'd never experienced one with nothing between her and the storm's fury but a thin wall of buffalo hide. She found the experience exhilarating, yet frightening.

"You know, if not for that lightning, I might just go run around in the rain for a while," she said with a nervous laugh. The warm, driving rain would be the closest she'd come to a hot shower in a long time.

"You have strange ideas, Kris Baldwin." Suddenly, Ekararo laughed and pointed. "Look! Here come our warriors."

Kris laughed with her, watching as Black Eagle and Chikoba raced side-by-side for the tipi, a green deer hide stretched over their heads to keep them dry. "They don't look too fearsome right now, do they?"

The two women stepped aside to let the men dash in. Kris's laughter died with one look at Black Eagle's face. "What is it? What's happened?"

"Nothing." Black Eagle sliced a glance toward Ekararo, his gaze warning Kris to silence. "I come to take you back to our tipi."

Kris slapped on a bright smile and gave Ekararo a hug. "Looks like I get to play in the rain after all." Poised beside him at the tipi entrance, she let Black Eagle pull her up close with an arm about her waist. She felt the tension in his body. She shot him a questioning glance, then clutched her corner of the deer hide.

"Run!" he cried, and jumped out into the downpour, lifting and pulling her as he ran. Kris's feet barely touched the ground. They flew over the uneven ground. Suddenly, her foot slipped out from under her and she almost pulled him down with her.

Laughing, Black Eagle jerked her up against his side like a bag of meal. Kris lost her hold on the deer hide and it slapped over his face. The water that had collected drenched him. A laugh burst from her before she could stop it.

Abruptly, he set her down and pulled the deer hide off her head. Rain plastered her hair to her skull and streamed down her face to pool in the corners of her laughing mouth.

"Wheeee!" She flung her arms wide and spun in a circle. Her feet slid out from under her and she plopped down hard, shooting a geyser of mud at Black Eagle.

She laughed up at him, delighted at the unexpected retaliation and his futile attempts to wipe off the mud.

He stomped in a puddle beside her, grinning as she ducked the spray with a wild squeal. "You like mud, woman?"

She scooped up a handful and threw it at him. "Don't you?"

The gooey glob hit his buckskin shirt and slid downward.

Black Eagle followed its downward trail, then looked up slowly.

"No!" she cried, as he launched himself at her. "Don't you dare. Aaaaargh!"

Black Eagle landed on his side in the mud right next to her. Catching her in his arms, he rolled back and forth, coating them both with mud. He finally stopped, flat on his back holding Kris securely on top of him. She shook her head, flinging gooey droplets everywhere. Still, she couldn't see a thing. Using the sides of her hands like spatulas, she scraped her face then blinked warily. The mud in her eyelashes felt thick as a triple coat of mascara. Squinting, she scraped the mud off Black Eagle's face, swiping the worst of it from his eyes. When she freed his lips, a laugh burst from him.

Kris stilled, mesmerized by his shining eyes, his white teeth sparkling in his muddy face. Unable to resist the temptation of that laughing mouth, she planted a sticky kiss dead center.

Fusion. Heat. Explosive energy vibrated between them. Black Eagle captured her head between both hands and turned it, slanting her lips over his as his tongue thrust into her mouth. He rolled her beneath him, his tongue plundering. Heat, molten and fluid, surged through her entire body. He rolled, pulling her on top of him, thrusting upward and grinding against her.

Kris heard a deep rumble, but couldn't identify it. Was it thunder or her heart pounding in her chest? It came again. Horrified, she realized she'd made the sound deep in her throat—a low, needy moan.

She tore her lips from his and slid off him onto her knees in the mud, breathing hard. What had come over her? Hot color washed her cheeks.

Black Eagle scrambled out on the opposite side of the muddy hole they'd made and sank to his knees. Head hanging, he drew several deep, shuddering breaths, then looked at her.

Kris winced at his glum expression. "What is it? What's wrong?"

"A message from MacKenzie," he said, and told her the rest of it.

"What will Quannah do?" she asked, sick inside, knowing the end was quickly approaching.

"Run. Hide." He rose, helped her up. "We move tomorrow."

"In the rain?" Kris cried. "We'll leave a trail a mile wide. Any fool could follow it."

"We must." Black Eagle pulled her under his arm and together they trudged through the mud to the tiny stream where she hid under a small oak tree and stripped off her clothes, letting the rain wash her clean.

A different storm raged inside her throughout the night, gaining momentum every time she caught Black Eagle watching her, his eyes reflecting her torment. She lay listening to him breathe, knowing he did the same.

Both storms raged unabated the next day, through the mess of breaking camp in the mud and traveling all day. Her personal storm fed on glimpses of Black Eagle's broad back as he rode with Quannah, glancing back frequently, his mouth a taut line.

Her horse shied, snorting and dancing beneath her. "What's wrong, girl? What is it?" Kris clung to its mane, stroking its neck. The horse's eyes rolled back and it neighed, tossing its head.

Kris glanced around to find what was scaring the animal. About three feet ahead, something rattled in the dry grass. A diamond-shaped head appeared and flashed toward them. Her horse reared, hooves flailing. Kris clung to its back, alarm screaming through her. "Duuqua!" The cry escaped her before she even knew the thought had formed.

Its hooves hit the ground and the horse bolted. Kris clutched its flying mane and prayed, all the while calling to the animal, pleading with it to stop. The strap holding the travois to its hindquarters snapped, and Padaponi's household goods scattered across the prairie. Kris heard someone yelling, but she couldn't look up. All she could do was hold on and pray. Suddenly, she was yanked off the horse's back.

She clutched Black Eagle's waist, hiding her face against his chest as he brought his horse to a plunging stop. Hearing a high-pitched squeal, she looked up and watched in horror as her horse tried to stop, only to slide off a cliff she hadn't known was there. If Black Eagle hadn't snatched her off the horse's back, she would have gone over with it. She would have died.

Shuddering in reaction, Kris buried her face against Black Eagle's chest. His heart beat as fast and hard as hers. Beneath her hand, the stones pounded the same furious rhythm.

"What happened?"

Kris gulped, brushing away the tears she'd just noticed streaming down her cheeks. "A snake. The horse spooked and bolted . . ." She drew a shaky breath. "Is it dead?"

Black Eagle nodded. Kris followed his gaze, staring down into the huge chasm just beyond his horse's nose, down steep walls hacked out by a God-sized machete. Along the canyon walls, a narrow trail fell hundreds of feet to the canyon floor where a tiny ribbon of water beckoned. At the foot of that trail lay her horse, twisted and broken.

"Oh, God," she gasped, and pressed back against Black Eagle, turning her face into his chest. She clutched his arms, feeling faint and dizzy.

His arm tightened around her and he turned his horse away.

"What is this place?" she asked in a whisper.

"Palo Duro."

Kris's heart stopped beating, then resumed with a hard slam against her ribs. Palo Duro. This grotesquely beautiful canyon had almost been the end of the line for her. She shuddered, remembering the events that would take place here.

This was the end of the line for the Comanche.

Chapter Sixteen

"No pony soldier could find this place." Quannah glared at Black Eagle.

"At least post guards on the canyon rim." Kris threw Black Eagle a pleading glance, but he shook his head. He had agreed only to take her to Quannah, not to speak for her.

"Why you think I bring People here, through mud and rain?" Quannah continued. "This our safe place. No white man ever find this place."

Kris grabbed his arm. "Not this time. MacKenzie will find it!"

"No touch me, woman." Quannah flicked her hand off. "Go! Leave me in peace."

"Peace?" She stared at Quannah's closed face, knowing his mind was set against her. Still, she couldn't give up. "What about your people? When will they know peace?"

"The white man has stolen even that." Defeat rang in Black Eagle's voice. "Come." He pulled her away from Quannah. "My brother, your heart is a stone in your chest and your ears are filled with rock. But I cannot blame you." He stood unflinching, facing Quannah down. "We leave you in *peace*. Enjoy it while you can."

"You have forgotten, brother, who is chief here."

"No, my brother has forgotten." Black Eagle pushed Kris toward the tipi entrance.

"It doesn't have to be this way, Quannah." She struggled to keep her voice low. "Don't make the People suffer for your pride. If you surrender now, you can bargain with the soldiers for better terms."

"Bargain with blue-coats?" Quannah snorted. "I never bargain with my mother's killers."

"I pray you are right, Quannah," Black Eagle said.

"You grow soft, brother, listening to your woman. Do you fear MacKenzie?"

Black Eagle stepped forward, his lips set, eyes seething. He started to speak, but Kris laid a hand on his arm. "He'll understand soon enough."

"Out! Both of you!"

Drawn by Quannah's shouts, a crowd awaited Kris and Black Eagle outside the tipi. Black Eagle glared at them and stalked away. Kris watched him go. She needed time to think.

How could Quannah be so stubborn? What was it going to take to make him believe her? She wanted to scream in frustration. The People were like sitting ducks here. This canyon may once have been a safe haven, but she could see why it had become a death trap.

Caught up in her thoughts, she almost plowed into Chikoba, who waited beside their tipi.

"What did Quannah say?" he asked, catching her arms to steady her. "Where is Duuqua?"

"I don't know where he went," she answered with a heavy sigh. "He and Quannah argued. Quannah won't even post guards on the canyon rim. Why won't he listen to me?"

"Perhaps it is not what you say to him but the way you say it."

"What do you mean?" Had she been approaching Quannah the wrong way, defeating herself? Had Quannah sensed her dislike, her resentment? Of course, how could he not? She hadn't made any effort to learn more about him or try to understand him. Why hadn't she realized it? Kris shot Chikoba a grateful glance. "Thanks. I'll keep that in mind."

He shot her a surprised glance. "I am worried about Ekararo."

"Why? What's wrong?" Kris's thoughts flew to Ekararo, expecting the worst. "Has her labor started?"

"No, not yet," he sighed. "But with each day that passes, she becomes more withdrawn. She seems frightened."

Kris knew what troubled her friend, but Ekararo hadn't confided in her. She couldn't bring herself to repeat Coyote Droppings' gloating boast.

"Childbirth can be a frightening experience, especially the first time." She smiled, hoping he would find her naive assertions reassuring. "Tabenanika says everything is fine."

"I wish I could believe him." Chikoba shook his head, his gaze straying to the steep canyon walls, squinting as he followed the narrow track upward to the rim. "I have a bad feeling."

"I've heard that new fathers can get pretty tense, too," Kris teased and was relieved to see him smile. "Once the baby is born, you'll feel much better."

She couldn't tell him that she, too, was concerned for Ekararo, and not just for her physical health. Even if Coyote Droppings wasn't the father, he'd raped her friend. She couldn't begin to comprehend the agony Ekararo must have suffered, was still suffering. But Kris wasn't about to risk her friendship by telling Ekararo what she knew. Ekararo must have a good reason for remaining silent.

"I'll stay with her when you can't," Kris promised. "If the soldiers come, Padaponi and I will watch out for her. You and Black Eagle have to be free to defend the camp."

"Are you sure the soldiers will come?" Chikoba's stare was intense, questioning. "Many of the People say you lie."

"That's Coyote Droppings speaking through them. He's determined to discredit me. The soldiers will come, and after that—nothing will be the same."

"How do you know?" He caught her by the shoulders, shook her. "Why are you so sure?"

Kris shrugged off his hands, sick of the doubt, the questions in everyone's eyes, especially in the eyes of those who claimed to be her friends. "I know because I came here from the future." The words were out before she knew what was coming. She groaned and shook her head.

Chikoba stared at her, then laughed. "Woman, you will say anything to protect yourself. How far in the future? One year? Ten? Twenty?"

Indignant, Kris shot him an angry glare and tried to push

past him into the tipi. "Just let me by." She cursed the flaming blush that surged into her cheeks, knowing he'd see it as proof that he'd caught her in a lie. "Why should you believe me? Even I can't believe it."

Chikoba pulled her back. "Tell me more. I need a reason to laugh."

Kris jerked her arm out of his grasp, her chin snapping up as she faced him. "I lived almost one-hundred-and-thirty years in your future when Black Eagle found me."

"That is not possible." Chikoba caught her shoulders in a punishing hold, but Kris hardly noticed.

As if a dam had burst inside her, the words rushed out. "How do you think I know what's going to happen before it does? I'm no medicine woman. I have no *puha*."

"I knew you did not. I told Duuqua, but he would not listen."

"Sounds familiar," Kris huffed, remembering all the times Black Eagle had questioned her. "The things that are happening to the People now were my history. When I was studying to become a teacher, I *read* about it in books."

Chikoba crossed his arms over his chest. "Since you know what is to happen, you can do something to prevent it."

"What?" Kris demanded indignantly. "What can I do? You've seen how the People react to me. Consider your own suspicions. What should I do? Walk up to General MacKenzie and tell him to go away and leave the People alone? He'd lock me up in his stockade faster than Ekararo blushes."

Chikoba frowned as he considered her words.

Kris sighed. "All I've been able to do is spout warnings that no one heeds."

His weighing glance was filled with skepticism, doubt. "I knew from the first that you could not be who you said you were." His eyes burned as he shook off her hands. "But this!"

"You obviously don't believe a word I've said," she huffed. "Ask Black Eagle. Maybe you'll believe him."

"He will not lie for you."

"I wouldn't ask him to." Frustration made her voice rise.

His scornful laugh blasted her. "You'll say anything to cover your lie, won't you?"

"Laugh now, Chikoba," she said, indignant and defensive. "But one day very soon, you won't think it's so funny." She backed away from him.

"Do not point your evil tongue at me, woman."

"You've got more important things to worry about. Where will you go when the People are moved onto the reservation? Will you be properly grateful when the soldiers *rescue* you, a white captive, and force you to return to civilization without your beautiful wife and child?"

"Enough!" He glared at her over the bush, the veins standing out in his neck, a muscle jumping in his jaw. "I will die before that happens."

She blanched at the pain that lanced through her at his words. She couldn't explain her feelings, but this man had become very dear to her, in spite of his surly attitude and sly teasing. It had to be due to his tenderness with Ekararo.

Her anger evaporated and she recognized how childishly she was acting. "Do you remember how to pray, Chikoba?"

He stepped back, instantly subdued though still scowling. He gave a short, crisp nod.

"This might be a good time to practice."

A bitter, unseasonably cold wind swept across the Llano Estacado, keeping the People in their tipis. Wrapped in layers of warm blankets, Kris and Padaponi huddled beside a cheery fire in the center of the tipi, each of them beading baby attire. The weather perfectly matched Kris's mood.

Kris worried over her argument with Chikoba. All day long she'd had the strong urge to go to him, to try to reassure him. She shouldn't have told him. Not for the first time, she cursed her unruly tongue. He wouldn't understand. Heavens! She herself couldn't understand how such a thing as time travel could happen—and she was the one it had happened to.

When the sun finally set and she could no longer see the ridges above camp, Kris sank onto her furs, exhausted. She prayed for an end to the cold, drizzling rain, then remembered the summer-long drought. The night brought no peace. She slept in fits and starts, and bolted upright when Black Eagle entered the tipi deep in the night.

"What's wrong? Have the soldiers come?"

"No. They will not attack in the dark."

When he moved her to his furs, she couldn't find the strength to protest. He pulled several robes over them and stretched out behind her, holding her close, exactly as they'd slept those nights on the trail. With her head pillowed on his bicep and the comforting weight of his arm across her waist, she sighed. She snuggled closer and he pressed a kiss to her bare shoulder. How right it felt to lie beside him, safe and warm. For now she'd take the comfort he offered and face her conscience in the morning.

"Sleep, Tomanoakuno," he ordered gently, smoothing her hair behind her ear. "Nothing will harm you."

She searched his face, saw the need burning in his eyes, carefully banked as he watched her intently, waiting for some signal. Her body yearned for his touch, ached to bear his weight and share his passion. For a brief time, she could forget her worries in his arms, but in the morning, she would regret her actions. It was becoming harder and harder for her to remember the blood on his hands, the insurmountable obstacles of time and culture that would always lie between them.

He must have seen the regret in her eyes, for he eased away. "Sleep, woman," he muttered, and rolled away from her.

Kris lay staring at the broad back she ached to caress, shuddering in the chill that engulfed her.

Kris lurched upright, her heart pounding a staccato beat. The gray light of dawn cast eerie shadows about the tipi.

Alert, tense, Black Eagle crouched beside her, his hand resting on the haft of his knife.

"What is it?" she asked, clutching a robe to her chest.

He held up his hand.

A sharp sound, like a car backfiring, ripped through the silence.

"Gunfire?" Kris cried, recognizing the sound. She'd heard that sound when Black Eagle was shot by the Rangers.

"Get Ekararo." He turned to fire rapid instructions at Padaponi as he dressed and snatched up his rifle. He caught Kris to him and gave her one hard kiss. "Stay low." He slipped out of the tipi, leaving her staring after him.

Rifle fire punctuated the shouts of warriors, the shrill cries of women, the frightened wailing of children, the tardy warning howls of the camp's dogs. Kris and Padaponi yanked on their clothes, wrapped several blankets about their shoulders, then slipped out into the cold morning.

Soldiers lined the ridge above them, black against a lemon-yellow dawn. Like ants, they swarmed single-file down the narrow trail all the way to the canyon floor, then disappeared into the trees. People ran past—warriors pursued by screaming women dragging wide-eyed, terrified children. Gunfire sounded from the head of the canyon.

"Stop!" Kris tried to grab a warrior running past. "Shoot! Why don't you shoot?" She pointed at the soldiers stretched out along the steeply descending trail, like ducks on a shelf. Most could be killed before they ever got to the bottom.

What am I thinking? Those were white men. Kris stood frozen in the path of the People's retreat, her anguished gaze shifting between their horror-stricken faces and the menace that steadily approached.

Padaponi snatched at her arm, trying to pull her away, but Kris kept glancing behind her. A column of flame hissed skyward. The soldiers had reached the camp and they were firing the tipis. Seeing the flames, the People became hysterical, frantic to escape. The hysteria gave their feet wings.

Terror and sorrow warred in Kris's chest as she ran. Why hadn't they listened? At a frightening *whoosh* she glanced over her shoulder. Another tipi had erupted in flames. The acrid stench of burning hide reached them, searing their nostrils, pushing them faster.

Padaponi broke away, tried to turn back toward her home.

"No!" Kris pulled her toward the far side of the canyon where people had begun scrambling up the rocky walls. "We have to find Ekararo."

Padaponi nodded and led the way, slipping from shadow to shadow. Kris searched the frantic crowd, watching for her friend. She shuddered as more tipis went up in flames. Beneath the hysteria, hooves pounded, louder and louder. *They are coming this way.*

Hooves thundered closer. Or was that her heart?

"Kris!"

Kris spun and spotted Ekararo weaving toward her through the fleeing swarm, like a fish swimming upstream. A group of mounted soldiers rounded the nearest tipi. The People scattered. All but Ekararo. Eyes glued on Kris, she hadn't seen the soldiers.

"Look out!" Kris's cry went unheard, muffled by the thunder of pounding hooves.

Ekararo turned and froze directly in their path, terror turning her face chalky.

"Run!" Kris screamed, springing toward her, knowing she'd never reach her friend in time. "Run!"

Ekararo leaped into motion, but her advanced pregnancy made her slow, awkward. She glanced over her shoulder, stumbled, fell heavily onto her abdomen. Stunned, gasping, she lay helpless in the path of the oncoming horses. At the very last instant, she pulled herself into a ball, her arms cradling her child.

Uttering hideous whoops, the soldiers rode over her. Their horses' hooves pounded her into the dirt and they kept going. All but one. He gave a loud whooping cry and wheeled his mount, an ugly smile on his face.

"Nooooo!" An incredible red rage consumed Kris as she

reached Ekararo and gathered her broken body in her arms. "Ekararo!" It wasn't true. This still, crumpled woman was not her friend. A raging inferno blazed inside her as the soldier dug his spurs into his mount and turned to ride over Ekararo again.

As if in slow motion Kris watched him come, her heart echoing each beat of the drumming hooves. Dust filled her nostrils and the coppery scent of Ekararo's blood hung heavy on the air. At the last instant Kris sprang to her feet.

"Hi-yah!" She swung her arms at the horse, forcing it to veer. Its rider flew off in the opposite direction.

"Bastard!" Kris cried, then the horse's shoulder caught her, knocked her rolling in the dirt. The soldier staggered to his feet, winded, shaking his head. He saw her and his hand moved toward the gun holstered at his hip.

"You killed her!" Kris screeched. Rolling, she came up on her feet directly in front of him. Adrenaline pumped through her veins. The image of Ekararo's broken body driving her, she leaped at him, ripping his face with her nails. She brought her knee up hard, aiming for his groin, and connected. Surprise and pain etching his features, the soldier gave a loud groan and folded inward.

Once more Kris brought her knee up, catching him under the chin. The impact threw him backward with astonishing force. He landed hard. His head snapped back. There was a sickening crunch, then his eyes rolled back in his head. He lay still.

Kris fell to her knees, gasping for breath, trembling in the aftermath. A dark pool of blood was forming beneath the soldier's head. She checked for a pulse. There was none. He was dead.

I've killed him. She gagged, staggered to her feet, staring down at him in horror. She had killed a man, and she knew, given the same circumstances, she'd do it again. Buffeted by fleeing women and children, Kris heard nothing but the anguished cry of her soul *God, forgive me.*

"Kris! Kris!" Padaponi's cries shook her from the shock that held her immobile.

Kris searched the chaos and found her tugging Ekararo's body toward a clump of trees. With a last shuddering glance at the man she'd killed, Kris left him where he'd fallen and ran to help drag Ekararo's body out of the melee. Together, they pushed her beneath a jutting rock at the base of the canyon wall.

Mindlessly mimicking Padaponi's actions, Kris yanked up some bushes, but stopped short of throwing them over Ekararo. She sank to her knees and clutched Ekararo's hand, brushed back her tangled, blood-matted hair. Her tears bathed Ekararo's cheeks as she pressed a kiss to her forehead, then wiped the dirt from her face. With trembling fingers, Kris closed her eyes.

"Goodbye, my gentle friend." She laid Ekararo's hands over her unborn child and swiftly covered her.

"Kris," Padaponi urged, tugging at her and nervously searching the area around them.

Keeping low, slipping from shadow to shadow, Padaponi pulled Kris to safety. They climbed to a rock shelf several feet up the canyon wall where they huddled, stiff and silent, hidden beneath a pile of brush.

It was all her fault. Everything. Ekararo's death, the soldier, everything. Dear God, she wanted to run and scream and tear her hair out. She wanted to slash her body with a sharp knife in grief over the two deaths.

Had she caused Ekararo's death? The question screamed through her brain.

"Kaku." A rush of warmth suddenly enveloped her, protecting her from the horror rampaging through her. Her grandmother's beloved voice flooded her mind, stilling the turmoil.

Grandmother? her mind cried in response.

It was not your fault.

No, Grandmother? she answered vehemently. *You didn't see what happened. You didn't hear what I said to Chikoba . . .*

I heard, Kaku. I saw.

Kris trembled, her scalp tingling, as if a loving hand stroked her hair. *You cannot change their destiny.*

Then why am I here? Kris glanced at Padaponi, sure that she must have heard her anguished cry, but the little woman lay undisturbed, tears streaming from her eyes as she watched the destruction continue unabated far below.

To meet your own destiny.

My destiny? Kris frowned, pondering the enigmatic words only briefly before demanding, *What about the People? What about their destiny?*

Patience.

Patience? Kris clenched her teeth to keep from screaming in frustration. *Look around, Grandmother. For God's sake, use your powers to help these people.*

I have, Kaku, came the fading whisper. *I sent them you.*

Grandmother? The warmth disappeared, leaving her chilled from the inside out. She longed to close her eyes and return to the night before and the comfort of Black Eagle's arms. She tried to direct her thoughts, but in the darkness behind her eyelids, the dead soldier's face waited. Horror filled her again. She'd killed a man.

You did not kill a man, her conscience soothed. *You stopped the animal that had just murdered your friend.*

She shuddered, remembering the horrible, consuming rage that had driven her, remembering how she'd watched him ride closer, biding her time, waiting for the right moment.

Was this how Black Eagle felt when he fought and killed? He knew the face of death very well. And now she knew it too. Now she knew that rage and pain could drive a normal person to commit acts of violence, acts of war.

War. How many times had Black Eagle told her this was war? More than once. This particular war even had a name: The Red River War. But no name could convey the soul-wrenching horror, the absolute emptiness of soul Kris felt at being here, seeing the flames and the fury, hearing the gunfire and the pitiful wailing of the women and children, smelling the smoke and the fear and the blood.

Rowdy voices and loud laughter startled her. Soldiers. She squinted to see through the fire and smoke that engulfed the camp. She couldn't make out their words, but their laughter bounced off the canyon walls. Horrified, she watched them toss blankets, robes, anything they could find into a huge pile. Then they set it afire.

This was war. Death, fire, ashes, humiliation. At last she understood. At last she saw Black Eagle as he truly was—a passionate man driven to defend his own, just as she had been driven to defend Ekararo. He was a war chief of the Quahadi. War was his duty, his responsibility. He'd give his life to protect his People—and her.

But was that all she was to him? A duty, a responsibility to be fulfilled? Or did he truly care?

All through the day, she lay hidden, her eyes watering from the acrid smoke that filled the canyon, pondering Black Eagle's every look, every word, every kiss.

Her own feelings welled up, threatening to overwhelm her. Was this love? This pain that felt like it would tear her heart in two?

Yes, her heart whispered. She loved him. But he was duty-bound to Quannah's wives. Though he had assured her that Quannah had released him from responsibilities of a sexual nature, could she be sure he would never be required to take them up again? She could not, would not, share him.

Far from comforting, she found the realization of her deep feelings unsettling. How could she give herself to him freely, knowing she must eventually leave him? Could she give up hope of returning to her own time to stay here and share his life, his fate?

But what about the stones? She remembered their power throbbing through her. Was their power strong enough to take

Black Eagle back with her? As quickly as it was born, the hope died in her breast. He wouldn't come. He'd never willingly leave his People.

Rifles barked again in a deafening roar, firing volley after volley from somewhere near the head of the canyon, sending Kris's thoughts scattering. Padaponi's hand slapped over Kris's mouth, stifling the surprised cry Kris hadn't even realized she'd made.

What were they shooting at? The shooting continued, thundering through the canyon, accompanied now by the squeals and whinnies of horses. The horses. Only a few had run past their hiding place. Most of the herd had been picketed at the mouth of the canyon. The soldiers, finished burning tipis and everything in them, were shooting the horses. They wouldn't be satisfied until they'd destroyed everything.

Even the People's hope.

Duuqua and a small band of warriors circled back to the canyon late in the evening. Black clouds of smoke filled the once-sweet air, stinging his nose and throat. The only sound was an occasional keening wail. Heart pounding in his chest, Duuqua rushed from body to body, searching for Kris and Padaponi. He turned over a woman and cried out in surprise. For one heart-stopping moment he thought he saw his mother's face.

He fell to his knees. He should have guarded the canyon rim himself. Kris had warned him, had warned all of them that the soldiers would come. He had told her he believed her, but he had done nothing. Where was she? Had he failed her again? Did she lie covered with ashes, dead or wounded? Had the soldiers taken her? Where was Padaponi? Staggering to his feet, he renewed his search.

"Ekararo." Chikoba's cry echoed from the trees behind him, reminding Duuqua he was not the only one suffering. He rose and turned to his friend. His moccasin caught on some brush. He knelt and carefully moved the brush aside, revealing long, slender fingers folded over a pregnant belly. His heart jumped into his throat and he shoved away the remaining brush.

Ekararo. He hung his head, his heart aching for the pain he must bring his friend. He called Chikoba.

"Have you found them?" Chikoba staggered out of the smoke, his anxious face black with soot.

Duuqua blocked Chikoba's view of Ekararo's body and gripped his shoulders, wishing he could spare him this agony. "I am sorry, my friend." Then he stepped aside.

A strangled cry escaped Chikoba. He fell to his knees, clutching Ekararo's battered body to his chest. He threw his head back and screamed his anguish. Duuqua gripped his shoulder, feeling a matching cry build in his own chest.

Was this what love brought? Was this what he, too, would feel if he found Kris dead?

Chikoba gently laid Ekararo back in her makeshift grave, replacing her hands across their child, then rose and drew his knife. With a grim face, he drew off his shirt and slashed both breasts, then his forearms. He lifted the knife to his face.

"Enough." Duuqua stopped his hand. "You will need your strength."

"My wife and my child lie dead." Chikoba jerked his knife-hand free. "Who are you to deny my grief?"

"I am war chief to the Quahadi," Duuqua answered, "and you are one of my best warriors. Do you not want revenge?" He held his friend's arm until he saw the madness leave his eyes.

Chikoba sheathed the knife, knelt and again covered Ekararo with brush, all but her face.

Duuqua laid a hand on his shoulder. "Come, we must search for Padaponi and Kris." Fear rose up, stealing his breath. He refused to give in to panic.

Laughter rang in the creeping darkness. Duuqua's head snapped up. His smoke-stung eyes searched the shadows.

Quannah sat in the rubble that used to be his tipi, sharing some jerky that had escaped the fire with his four wives. Their laughter jarred Duuqua's aching soul. Seized by a blinding rage, Duuqua leaped upon Quannah, his fingers closing around his throat. Several warriors pulled him off, but not before Quannah's eyes rolled back in his head.

"See what you have brought the People?" Duuqua flung off their restraining arms. "You sit here laughing and eating as if nothing has happened."

"Do not make me forget you are my brother." Quannah rose, his voice shaking with anger. "What would you have me do? Sit in the ashes and cry like an old woman?"

"You are chief here," Duuqua reminded him. "Have you fed the children? Do you even hear their cries? You care for yourself before meeting their needs! Look around you." Duuqua swept a hand wide. "Take a deep breath, brother. It is the smell of death to the People."

A red flush climbed into Quannah's cheeks. "Leave us, *pabi*. I need no old woman to tell me what must be done. You think I am beaten?" He stepped close and jabbed his finger into Duuqua's chest with each word. "I will never surrender."

"I do not ask that you surrender, only that you care for your people." Duuqua turned his back on his brother. His heart like a stone in his breast, he made his way to the stream to wash off the stink of death. No one he passed on his way had seen Kris or Padaponi.

He stood beside the stream, staring at the moon shining on the water.

He could not find her and no one had seen her. He had brought her here, into danger, and had failed to protect her. The Great Spirit's anger would be fierce, but Duuqua felt no fear—only grief. Stubborn pride had kept him from realizing his love for her until it was too late. Now she would never fill his arms, never share his furs, never bear his children.

With an anguished moan he pulled his knife and bared his

forearm. His grief would flow out of his body with his blood. The blade glistened as he raised it.

But a sound carried on the night breeze, staying his hand. Laughter, innocent and free-flowing. The laughter of children.

Chapter Seventeen

"Ai-yeee!"

"Shhh-shh," Kris soothed the tiny girl in her arms as she cleaned a cut on her arm. "It will feel better soon."

Several older children waded in the nearby creek, cooling burns and washing injuries. Other children, wide-eyed and fearful, hovered close to Kris and Padaponi, starting at the slightest sound. Two fearless young boys played tag in the bushes nearby, their laughter a healing balm to Kris's battered soul.

Padaponi held a young boy who manfully refused to cry as she tended the injuries he'd sustained in a fall. The child's courage tore at Kris's heart. Would Ekararo's child have been a sweet little girl like the one she held, or a boy with his father's brilliant blue eyes? She couldn't imagine the child with Isatai's small, beady eyes. She met Padaponi's gaze, not surprised to find her eyes swimming with tears.

After the soldiers had left, they'd salvaged what they could from the charred remains of their tipi, then collected the children wandering the ruined camp, searching for their families. At the stream's edge, they had washed the soot from their tiny, troubled faces and tended to their burns and wounds. One by one, the children had been claimed by rejoicing parents or grieving relatives. Only a handful remained.

In a few years, they would be the blushing maidens and

strutting *tuibitsu*, young braves all dressed up to impress the girl of their choice. Together they would bear more proud, strong sons and beautiful daughters. Tears rushed to Kris's eyes. What did they have to look forward to now?

Instinctively, Kris's arms tightened about the child in her lap. She had to make Quannah understand before more children were hurt or injured.

Her heart clenched. No one had seen or heard from the warriors who had drawn many of the soldiers away from the camp, out onto the *Llano Estacado*.

Please, God, she pleaded, as the sun settled below the canyon rim. *Keep Black Eagle safe. I'll stay here and share his fate, whatever you want me to do. Just keep him safe.* Her hand went to her chest, seeking her stone, as it had done many times throughout the long day.

She needed to know he was safe, needed to share her sorrow over Ekararo's death, needed to explain that at last she understood.

She struggled to control her emotions, blinking back tears, but a fresh wave of despair rolled over her. *Why Ekararo?* She pressed her cheek against the shining hair of the child in her arms, letting her sweet, clean scent clear the lingering smoke from her brain. But she couldn't hide from the turmoil in her mind.

Why, God? she railed. *Why didn't You take me instead? Why Ekararo and her innocent baby?*

A twig snapped beneath a heavy foot. The children's laughter stopped. They sidled closer to her, staring as a man appeared in the shadows above the stream, his drawn knife glittering in the darkness. They watched as he strode closer. Not until he sheathed his knife did they move or breathe.

"I should have known I'd find you near water." White teeth flashed in a handsome, soot-streaked face as Black Eagle stepped out of the shadows.

For several long seconds, Kris could only stare, not trusting her own eyes. Gently, she set aside the child in her arms, but before she could gather her wits enough to stand, Black Eagle reached her. Uttering a loud whoop, he caught her up in his arms, holding her so tight she could hardly breathe. "I thought the soldiers had taken you away, or that you were . . ."

"Shhh." Kris pressed a finger over his lips, glancing down at the children watching them. "I'm fine. We all are."

"I search, but no one knew where you go." His whisper rang with agony as his hungry gaze traveled her face. "Then I hear children laughing and I knew where to find you."

He pulled her close, lifting her, then letting her slide down his length to rest on tiptoe. "Never frighten me like that again, woman." His lips seized hers in a breath-stealing kiss that curled her toes.

The children's giggles and Padaponi's shushing intruded. Grinning her delight, Padaponi gave them a huge hug and led the children toward the small fires twinkling in the heavy twilight. Kris heard them leave as if from a great distance, then forgot everything but the warmth, the hunger, the relief in Black Eagle's embrace.

"You're not hurt?" He pulled away to search her face, her arms and body.

"I'm fine." Her voice broke. How could she tell him? "Ekararo . . ."

He pressed a finger over her lips. "I found her. Chikoba is caring for her body."

A deep shudder racked Kris. "I killed one of the men who did it." She searched his face, hoping to find understanding there, not condemnation. "I didn't mean to, it just happened. But when it was over, I was glad," she said fiercely, her voice catching. "God forgive me, I was glad he was dead."

"Tell me." Black Eagle held her tight, as if his strength alone could wipe away her pain, while she related the events of the day in a tortured whisper. Reliving the horror drained her soul. Tears flowed freely, sobs punctuated every sentence.

"I understand now," she told him when the torrent finally

slowed. "I killed a man today because he attacked my friend, just as you have killed to protect your loved ones." She pulled back to search his dark eyes. "Even though I was too late," she whispered, forcing the bitter words past her tight throat, "I wanted to kill them. But even killing each one of them wouldn't bring her back or give her child life."

Black Eagle rocked her in his arms.

"Can you forgive me?" she whispered, as fresh tears started.

"For what?"

For not loving you enough, her heart cried, but she merely whispered, "For condemning you. For not understanding."

He kissed her forehead, then her eyes and lips, his own lips cool against her hot skin. His breath fanned her face. She sagged against him, glad of the solid strength of his body supporting hers, the smooth skin of his chest beneath her cheek, the steady beat of his heart, his thighs pressed tight against hers. The turmoil in her soul eased. She felt him tense. She pulled away to look into his eyes.

Twilight shadowed his features, making his cheeks deep hollows and turning his eyes into inky caverns. But a light burned deep inside those caverns with an intensity that made her breath catch.

"Come." He drew her with him, pulling her back toward the camp to where he'd left his horse. He leaped astride and lifted her into his lap. With her legs dangling off to one side, she snuggled deeper into his arms, not knowing where he was taking her, not caring. She felt no fear, only a giddy rush of breathless anticipation. Before this night was over, she would be his woman.

He hesitated before kicking the horse into motion and tipped her chin up to search her eyes. She smiled and answered his questions with a kiss, loving him for hesitating.

He didn't return her smile. His eyes darkened and she felt his heartbeat accelerate. He kicked the horse and settled her more comfortably between his thighs, tight against the pulsing hardness beneath his breechclout. Kris reveled in the feel of his hands exploring her body, grateful that he didn't need reins to direct the horse.

She didn't flinch from the proof of his desire. Instead, she rubbed against the hard ridge as she kissed his chest, tasting his skin—slightly salty and sleek as satin. He sucked in a breath and she kissed her way down to his nipple. Her tongue circled it slowly and it tightened.

"Don't stop," he growled against her hair. The rocking gait of the horse and the satin-salt taste of him stirred a warm softening deep inside Kris. She felt a hungry ache, an emptiness waiting to be filled. The sensations were so strong, she squirmed, needing something, but not knowing what.

Black Eagle bent her back over his arm, devouring her mouth. She opened and his tongue plunged deep. He kneaded her thighs, stoking the fires that burned deep inside her, sending hot bursts of desire spiraling through her. Her womanhood wept and when her legs parted, he stroked her intimately. He found her tiny, sensitive bud, sending shock waves cascading through her. She gasped into his mouth.

He swallowed her moans and she clung to him as his fingers parted her swollen lips. When he pressed deep, penetrating her, she cried out and arched against his hand, surprised at the intensity of her response, wanting more.

His kisses became fevered, his finger thrust deeper, rhythmically, his tongue copying the motion. Waves of pleasure rolled over her, stealing her breath. The horse moved into a trot that rocked her against his throbbing manhood. With a curse, he brought the animal to an abrupt stop. He ripped his lips from hers and glanced around them.

"Someday I will take you on the back of my horse," he whispered against her hungry mouth, "but tonight I want you beneath me." He jumped off the horse and pulled her into his arms, carrying her to a patch of tall, waving grass. With a lingering kiss, he set her down.

He pulled his knife and slashed handfuls of grass, tossing it into a pile, his movements jerky, urgent. She watched his muscles bunch and flex and longed to stroke his back, feel the motion beneath her fingers. Finally, he gathered her into his arms.

"I have nothing to offer you, no warm tipi, no bed of furs." His body, hard and hot against hers, trembled slightly. "Only myself."

"That's all I'll ever need."

A tremor ran through him. She felt it in his hands as he removed the blanket from her shoulders, saw it in his fingers as he smoothed the blanket over the bed of grass. Then he picked her up and her thoughts, her very reason scattered as he kissed her and stood her in the center of the blanket. She knew that the scent of fresh-cut grass would always remind her of him and this moment.

He stood facing her, his eyes locked on hers. His hand settled on the tie of his breechclout. He loosened it and let it fall.

Even in the darkness he saw her smile fade as his breechclout fell away. His manhood swelled with pride at her response. Her soft gasp echoed on the night breeze. He waited for her to look at him, to see his love for her shining in his eyes, to understand that he would never cause her pain.

When her eyes lifted, hunger stalked their depths. Desire flashed in them as she released the ties that imprisoned her beautiful body. As the buckskin fell away, his chest swelled and his manhood throbbed with need. She stood before him, clothed only in moonlight. His gaze swept up her long, beautiful legs to the dark nest of hair that adorned her womanhood. He longed to sink his fingers into the soft curls. He knew his hands could span her waist, and the dark nipples of her high, full breasts begged for his touch, his kiss. Awed by her beauty, he waited for her shyness to pass.

"Tomanoakuno." Her head lifted and her eyes widened as they locked on his. Her lips parted on a soft sigh and she took a hesitant step toward him.

"You are more beautiful than the first blush of morning."

"And you," she whispered, glancing downward, "are magnificent. More than I imagined."

"You have imagined me?" Color spilled into her cheeks as her gaze traveled over him. His blood pounded and his heart thundered in his chest. He must have her soon or die of the wanting.

"Mmmm, yes, I've thought of you." She stepped closer. Her tongue swept out, wetting her lips. "Often."

"Do not fear," he whispered, knowing he could not wait much longer. "You are made to hold me."

"I know." She stepped closer, her tongue tracing her lips.

Her innocent wisdom made his blood burn. Still, he held back. She was like the doe—her brown eyes curious, but watchful.

"Come." He smiled and held out a hand to her. "Touch me."

Her fingers curled around him, sending a flame flicking through him, lashing his loins. He moaned and sank to his knees, pulling her with him.

She followed, kneeling before him. Only his labored breath separated them as he let her explore his body. Her free hand settled on his chest; she tweaked his nipples while he cupped her breasts, taking their weight on his palms. He stared into her face. She seemed uncertain, but desire burned in her eyes. She was his. At last.

He kissed her softly, though he trembled with the need to throw her onto her back and sink into her hot, tight sheath. He would be gentle if it took all his strength. He trailed kisses across her hot cheeks, nibbled on her ear, rejoicing in her pleasured gasps. His thumbs teased her breasts into tight peaks as he kissed her neck and shoulder. Then it was his turn to gasp when her curls brushed him. He moaned and pressed into them.

His kisses became fevered, sweeping down her throat, along the high curve of her breast until he caught her nipple between his lips. She groaned and clutched him to her as he drew her into his mouth and suckled hungrily.

Her arms circled his back, slid to his hips. Her fingers explored him, testing the muscles of his thighs, slipping between them to cup his fullness.

"Use both hands." He wrapped her fingers around him and taught her how to please him, gasping as she quickly caught the rhythm. He settled back on his heels, bracing on his arms as he thrust his hips forward, his body taut as a bowstring as her hands worked their medicine.

"Oh, my!"

He smiled at her murmur of surprise as his manhood swelled, responding to the heat of her hands. He knew he could not survive this pleasure-pain much longer. Her fingers tightened and one hand slipped low to cup him again, driving him to the very edge of his control.

"Mmmm," she whispered, and a smile lit her face—an age-old smile of female satisfaction. "So soft, yet so hard. Like silk over steel." She licked her lips and he wrenched himself out of her hands.

"You will kill me, woman." He laid her down, pushed her legs wide and knelt between her knees. Shy again, she tried to hide her womanhood from his probing gaze. He drew her fingers away, kissing each one. Seeing her lying before him, her face glowing, her eyes filled with desire for him, he thought of the dreams that had awakened him night after night. The dreams and the woman before him blurred together as she smiled and reached out to him, exactly as he had dreamed so many times.

He shook his head, casting off the memory. This was no dream; this was real. This moment would fill his soul and change his dreams forever.

She moaned and arched upward, her breasts straining toward him. He kissed their tight nipples, trailing his hands down her sides, along her waist. He slid his hands beneath her, learning the curve of her thighs, filling his palms with her rounded softness. He lifted her hips and nudged her legs open, exposing her secrets.

"Oh, no, please. I . . ." Again shy, she protested his boldness.

"You are beautiful, woman." He tore his gaze from her beauty to stare into her eyes. "Everywhere."

He lifted her hips higher still, sinking his nose into her soft curls. Closing his eyes, he inhaled. She was like the breeze blowing across the plains, kissed with the breath of flowers, full of promise. He drew her scent deep into his lungs, filling his soul with her. He nuzzled past her curls, finding the tiny bud. He nipped at it, grinning when she cried out. Her hands clenched on his shoulders. Her nails pierced his skin.

"Duuqua," she moaned, her back arching still higher.

His Comanche name falling from her lips sent his heart racing again. "I am here," he whispered. "Let me teach you how to fly." He teased her swollen folds, dipping his tongue deep.

She tensed, and her fingers tangled in his hair, clutching him closer. "I-I need . . ." Her hips thrust upward, reaching, searching.

He gave her sweet folds one last, long stroke with his tongue, then pulled her hips onto his thighs and lifted her closer, pushing her legs around his waist as his manhood parted her hot, slick folds. She opened for him, her legs falling wider. He pushed inside, then stopped as her heat closed around him. Eyes closed, he took great, heaving breaths, waiting for his body to quiet. He wanted her with him when the stars exploded in the sky.

Her head lifted and she stared at the place where their bodies joined. He jerked, almost losing control when she reached down and touched him there, stroking his exposed shaft. "Fill me, Duuqua. Make me yours."

Her echo of his desire tore at his restraint. He pushed deeper, butting against her maidenhead. She tensed, her sheath closing like a fist around him.

"Don't stop." Eyes closed, her head thrashed from side to side. "Please, I need you—all of you—inside me—now." Her legs tightened and her strong legs forced him deeper.

He felt her tear, and then he was buried to the hilt, a captive of her hot, sleek folds.

Her eyes flew wide. She clutched his arms.

"Forgive me." He braced himself over her on trembling arms, fighting his body's urge to pound into her. His heart ached at the ragged breath she drew.

"There's nothing to forgive," she whispered. Her tongue shot out to moisten her lips. "I feel so . . . full."

His manhood jerked inside her, swelling.

She gasped and her hips strained toward him. "Give me all of you, Duuqua. Please." Her hands clenched on his legs.

He whispered encouragement, then kissed her again. With deep thrusts of his tongue, he drew her mind back to the pleasure. Her hips pressed upward. Responding to her signal, he lifted and sank deep into her sheath. A savage groan escaped and a shudder racked him as he fought to control the need to spill his seed.

"Love me, Duuqua." She writhed in his arms, clutching him.

He answered her plea, his hips lifting, pulling almost free of her heat, then plunging back into the fire. She answered him, hesitant at first then with growing confidence, until finally she met him thrust for thrust. Suddenly, she stiffened and her body clenched around him. Her eyes flashed open wide and he saw the wonder shining there.

"Don't stop," she cried, as she tightened around him.

He lost all control, thrusting faster, harder, racing beside her for the edge of the cliff.

Together they plunged over the edge and soared sunward on the arms of the wind. Duuqua flung back his head and the eagle's scream rent the night.

Duuqua held Kris close, protecting her from night's cold breath. She sighed. He kissed her lips and watched as sleep claimed her. How could she sleep? His body hummed like a tree full of bees. Never had *nameh'ehne* flung him into the very heat of the sun. Only his vision quests were more power-ful than what he had shared with this woman.

Would he, too, lose his desire to raid and hunt his enemies, too fearful to leave her behind? *Never*, he vowed. He was a war chief still, and no woman would ever control him.

Kris stirred in his arms and he smiled down at her as she snuggled closer, one knee wriggling between his own. He sighed, letting his eyes close. He need have no fears. A true warrior could love a woman in the night, and with the first light of the new day, ride away without a backward glance. Still, remembering the pleasures he had known in Kris's arms would make his nights on the trail much colder. His manhood reared its head at the thought. Unbidden, the memory of her heat sliding along its length rose up to tease him.

Duuqua's whole body arced in shock as once again he watched himself hesitate before entering her to stare down into her desire-darkened eyes, exactly as he had done earlier that night. What was this connection between his dreams and his life? Warm arms tugged him back into the dream, where he felt the stars burst first in her body, then his. And his release was as powerful as it had been with Kris.

Why? What does this mean? His mind whispered the question and he waited, tense and still, praying the voice would answer.

The two of you have loved before.

Shudders ran down his body. How could this be?

Tell her.

No! His heart cried the denial. *She will not believe it. I cannot believe it.*

The stones pounded, beating like drums against his chest. *Keep her safe.*

How? he cried. Hadn't this spirit whispering in his mind seen what had happened to the People this day?

Take her back.

No! Duuqua barely bit back the cry before it escaped his lips. *I cannot. It would tear the heart from my chest.* He froze, expecting lightning to strike him for daring to deny the voice's demand. But he heard nothing. Then he saw it.

Through the darkness came a light, growing brighter as it approached. Within it, he saw Kris's face, laughing, smiling. Then he saw her as she had been tonight, loving and giving in his arms. As the light hovered above him, Duuqua saw terror fill her face. He tried to shut his eyes, but he could not move, could only watch as her tears fell onto a bloody wound in his chest. He gasped and clutched a hand over his heart, feeling the sharp lance of pain. Another man lurked in the darkness behind her. The attacker twisted her hair and yanked her head back. A knife flashed.

No! Duuqua felt himself struggle to rise, to knock the knife away. Evil laughter filled his soul and he sank into a deep darkness.

Keep her safe. At the voice's soft whisper, Duuqua's eyes flashed open and his hand sought his knife. He was alone in the darkness. Feeling warmth against his side, he sagged in relief to see Kris still peacefully sleeping beside him.

Take her back.

Duuqua ignored the whispered command. The round face of Brother Moon smiled down as he cast aside the troubling images and woke Kris with a kiss, losing himself in her softness, drinking in the scent of her hair, her skin, their passion. Long before she awakened, her body responded to his touch and she opened for him.

Duuqua slid deep inside her on a sigh, ignoring the sorrow that made his heart bleed. He loved her long into the night, knowing it would not be enough. It would never be enough. Never would he lose his hunger for this woman. He would ache for her touch long after he died.

Powahe slipped out the back door of her trailer, closing the door quietly behind her. The moon lit the path to her tipi and she quickly built up her fire and began her chant.

Sleep had eluded her and a fine edge of tension had kept

her tossing and turning most of the night. Soon it would be dawn, but she could not wait to check on her granddaughter. Something had happened, and this time she believed it was something good. Not like the last time when she and Jacob had watched in horror, unable to stop the unfolding events as Kris's horse, terrified of the dark one, plunged ever nearer the canyon; the soldiers shooting and burning, Kris leaping in front of that running horse. Powahe shuddered. She felt as if she had aged years in a few hours.

The stench of burning buffalo hide still filled her tipi, but optimism kept her spirits high as she passed swiftly through the dark corridor, familiar now with the passage, moving easily along the path to her granddaughter. When she found Kris asleep, wrapped in Duuqua's arms, that optimism burst from her throat in a happy shout.

At last, Kris and her warrior had come together. Could it be that the promise would be fulfilled? Did she dare to hope that all might be well after all? Or would the dark one steal this joy from them, as he had stolen it before? She shuddered, remembering Kris's terror, her own terror, at the sight of Kris's horse at the bottom of Palo Duro. Fortunately, Duuqua had heard her cry and reached her in time. But what if he hadn't been close enough?

Powahe couldn't bear the thought. Jacob had been so shaken, he hadn't spoken for hours afterward. She had been right. His love for Kris, a vibrant force, strengthened her visions.

After two close calls at Palo Duro, Kris and Duuqua should be wary, but Kris must have dismissed the incident as a fluke, not realizing the danger. Would she and Duuqua now be too caught up with one another to recognize the threat to their lives? The new questions dimmed Powahe's joy at finding Kris and Duuqua together at last. She must show him all.

Slowly, so as not to startle Duuqua, she built up her fire, then lifted the images of his past into the smoke. This time, she did not interrupt them, though she knew the sorrow and pain they would bring. He must understand!

As the dreams unfolded, she watched, waiting for Duuqua's response. Then his eyes flashed open. Powahe started, forgetting he could not see her. Her thoughts whispered across the chasm, and his soared back to her. Stubborn man! She cursed his strength of will, his resistance to suggestion. He must agree; he must take Kris back to the Springs, to her own time. What could she do, what could she say to make him agree?

Suddenly, her breath froze in her throat. His gaze filled the flames and he was staring right at her.

"I will take her back," he said, his promise loud in the silence.

At last! She had succeeded, but the battle was not over.

She let the fire dwindle, sweat running down her spine. The dark one would try to separate the two lovers. Powahe prayed for strength—for herself, for Kris and Duuqua, and for the stones.

Chapter Eighteen

A delicious shiver trembled through Kris as she awakened, savoring her dreams.

Not dreams, she realized. The blanket still held Duuqua's warmth. The grass beside her still bore his shape.

She sat up too quickly and her body protested, aching in places she blushed to think about, places Duuqua had explored thoroughly. He'd kissed and caressed every inch of her, arousing her to fever pitch again and again. Just thinking about his hands and lips exploring her body sent tingles of pleasure humming through her. He hadn't said he loved her, but his control, his care for her told her more than words could ever say. He'd kept her breathless, denying her the opportunity to tell him she loved him. She planned to fix that immediately.

She found her buckskin skirt and blouse and blushed at their crumpled condition, proof of her haste to shed them the night before. She slipped them on, shivering as the cool hide slid over her skin.

Hearing a low chant, she followed the sound and soon found him praying to the rising sun. She paused several feet away to admire the play of muscles in his bare back and shoulders as he raised his arms, remembering those same muscles flexing and bunching beneath her hands as he moved over her. She'd unbraided his hair in the night and had enjoyed running her fingers through it as they made love. The morning breeze toyed with the glistening waves.

How did he feel this morning? When he turned to her would she see love shining in his eyes, or regret? What was he praying for so intently?

As if he'd heard her questions, his chanting stopped. Breathless, silent, she waited, but he didn't immediately turn to her. Denying her dark, brooding thoughts, Kris wrapped her arms around him from behind and pressed her cheek against his back.

The tightness left her chest when he clasped her arms to him, then turned and buried his face in her hair. She breathed in a deep sigh. She didn't know how long they stood there, just holding each other, but gradually her sense of disquiet grew into foreboding.

"Funny," she said, as a sharp pain ripped through her chest, "I thought the woman was supposed to have regrets."

He tipped her chin up and searched her eyes. The warmth shining there seemed carefully banked. "I regret nothing."

Confusion swamped her even as her heart soared. "Then why are you so sad?"

Before she could say more, he kissed her. Greedily, she returned his kiss. He smelled of the grass that had been their marriage bed and of love freely given, passion thoroughly savored.

"I am sorry, Tomanoakuno." Gently, he freed himself and

walked away from her. "I have nothing to offer you but grief and heartbreak. I must take you back where I found you."

"What?" Kris wrenched away from him. "Was I such a lousy lover? I know I'm inexperienced, but I'm sure I can learn to please you."

"Never have I known such joy as I found in your arms." His lips savaged hers, branding his words into her soul. Passion poured from him. Her body responded instantly and she sagged against him, hot, eager and weak-kneed.

His body bore witness to his words. His rigid sex pressed against her abdomen. With a low groan, she sank to her knees, pulling him with her. His hands seemed everywhere at once as he ripped off her clothes, but she didn't care as long as his lips remained locked on hers. He yanked off her blouse and skirt, spread them beneath her and laid her down. He kneed her legs wide, touched her intimately, teased her to readiness. Her heart raced as he ripped aside his breechclout and his manhood sprang free. She guided him home.

In two swift thrusts, he sank fully into her. She cried out in ecstasy, but he didn't pause. Bracing himself on one arm, he lifted her hips to meet his deep, swift thrusts. Her body raced to the pinnacle, paused for a breathless moment, then plunged into the sun. He stiffened against her and with a mighty shout, caught her and thrust her higher.

He collapsed onto her, his heart pounding like a drum, echoing her own. She welcomed his weight. Her arms tightened around him.

He loved her. She knew it, felt the echo in her own pounding heart, in the blissful satiation that robbed her body of strength as it reinforced her soul.

Groaning, he eased off her, then pulled her into his arms and kissed her.

"It will kill me," he whispered, his voice hoarse, "but I must take you back."

Kris knelt facing him. "I'm not going back."

"I must keep you safe." Duuqua sat up, adjusted his breechclout and tossed her clothes to her. "I have nothing to offer you here, not even a tipi to keep you warm in the night. I failed to protect you once. I will not fail again."

"All I need is you," she protested, focusing on the only thing he'd said that she understood. She struggled to control the rising hysteria that made her blood boil and her pulse pound. "I know what lies ahead for the People and I want to stay."

He shook his head, but said nothing, just leaned back braced on one arm.

"Are you so sure the stones will take me home?" Trepidation, like ice-cold black water, snaked through her at the thought of repeating that horrible experience.

"I am sure."

She searched his eyes, saw the doubt lurking there, doubt that he seemed determined to ignore. Anguish ripped through her. Stubborn, stubborn man. She must make him see reason. "Sure enough to risk my life?" She shuddered, feeling her blood freeze in her veins as she remembered the icy darkness surrounding her, swallowing then filling her.

He gripped her arms, his gaze intent, willing her to believe. "You will not die. All will be well."

"Then come with me." What was she saying? She didn't even know if she could return. How could she suggest that they both risk their lives?

"I cannot leave my People. Their need is too great."

"Their need is still great in my time." She knew it was a long shot, but she'd argue for the moon if she thought it would keep them together. "They've lost their pride. A man like you, a warrior who has counted coup, who knows the old ways, would remind them who they are, what they once were . . ."

He shook his head sadly. "I would be a stranger in a strange land. Your people would call me enemy."

"No," she protested. "The People long for the old ways. They would welcome you with open arms. You could teach them the things they've forgotten, help them rediscover their pride."

"In your time, do the men of my People wish to again become warriors?"

"No, but . . ."

"I am a war chief, not an old man to tell stories beside the fire." He rose to his knees and gripped her shoulders. "The soldiers have burned every tipi and killed all but a few horses. White hunters are even now slaughtering the buffalo, leaving us with nothing to replace our homes. Feel the cold breath of morning against your skin." He ran his hands lightly down her arms, leaving goosebumps in their wake. "It is nothing to the cold breath of winter."

Kris shuddered. "I can bear it, if you can." Knowing that he would have an argument ready, she tried to stop him by placing a finger over his lips.

He kissed it, then moved it aside and continued. "And if we were to have a child? Imagine ice and snow surrounding you and no warm tipi. Hear your child crying in your arms."

Tears clogged her throat at the cruel image, threatening to spill from her lashes. "But if I leave, I may never bear your child."

I don't want to lose you, her heart screamed inside her. *I couldn't bear it again.* Her breath caught. Once more the thought had sprung from nowhere.

He caught her hand and brought it to his medicine bundle. "Feel the stones."

Still stunned by her thoughts, Kris barely felt their strong pulse against her palm. "My stone always pulsed like this," she told him absently. "It seemed to reflect my emotions."

"They are very powerful." Duuqua removed the stones from the medicine bundle and took one in each hand. His body stiffened, the cords in his neck stood out as he braced himself against their power. She remained close, not touching him, yet the stones' energy seemed to leap between them. At last his eyes opened.

"When I first wore the stones," he whispered, "I had strange dreams." He reached for her hand and tried to put a stone in it, but she pulled her hand away.

"Take it," he insisted, and closed her fingers over it. Immediately, a surge of warmth coursed up her arm. It felt so good to hold it again!

"In my dreams, I have seen a woman," he answered, returning her smile. "Sometimes she is laughing, happy, content in my arms, then tears fill her eyes and I know that she cries for me. I know that the blood on her hand as she strokes my face is my own, for I am dying. Then I hear evil laughter and terror fills her eyes. Always I awakened before the dream finished. My mind fled the pain."

"How awful." Kris gave him back the stone, easing away from him and the foreboding his words evoked. "Do you know her?"

"You are the woman in my dream." His words fell between them like rocks in a pond, sending ripples of alarm through Kris.

"Me?" She'd known it, sensed it coming in his deliberate approach, but still alarm coursed through her. "You're just imagining it's me because we've been together so much."

"No." He shook his head almost sadly. "It is not so simple. The dreams started the first night I had the stones, the first night I slept with you in my arms."

Anxiety danced up and down her spine. "What are you trying to tell me?"

"I believe we have known each other before."

Kris choked back a nervous laugh. "Impossible."

"How did you come to be here? How did it happen?"

"The stones . . ."

"Yes," he agreed simply. "The stones."

Kris paused to consider his words, murmuring almost absently. "My grandmother gave me mine on my twenty-first birthday." Kris glanced away from him, her gaze unseeing as she looked back to that moment. "She said it had been waiting for me a long time. I wondered what she meant."

Her words startled him, but he recovered quickly. "I saw your face before I found you at the sacred waters. It happened at the end of my vision quest. You appeared exactly as I have seen you since in my dreams—laughing, happy, then sad and very frightened. Tears filled your eyes and one tear rolled down your cheek. I caught it, and then your face faded away. When I looked down at the tear, it had turned to stone—this stone."

Shivers coursed up and down her body. "What does it mean?"

"We have lived—and loved—in another life, another time."

"Are you saying that I traveled through time to be with you? That I'm not here to convince Quannah to surrender?" She searched his face, not trusting the fierce burst of joy inside her. She'd suspected the same thing but dismissed it as a wishful, romantic fantasy.

"Wear both stones." He lifted his medicine bundle over her head. "Both of them. Then you will know."

"I don't need to wear them," she said, backing away from the stones. "I've had dreams, seen things, just like you." She smiled up at him. "I thought I was just imagining them, that I wanted you so badly I'd created this fantasy in my mind. And now I find out that you've experienced the same thing and it's made you decide to send me away again." Her breath caught on a sob. "I'm sorry, but I don't understand."

"I must take you back to keep you safe," he told her, tense and edgy. "I sense danger around us, not just from the soldiers."

"Then we'll face it together," she cried. "You can't send me back now. Who knows how long it would be before we found one another again? What if we never did?"

"You must go back."

"Why?"

"I failed." The fear in his eyes was a live thing. It reached out and touched her, chilling, terrifying. "In the past, I did not protect you from our enemy. I will not fail again."

"But you said that in your dream it was you who was dying."

He pulled her into his arms and held her close. "Always before when I had the dream, I awakened before it was over. Last night, I did not wake up. I dreamed that I died and left you in his hands. I cannot risk that happening again. I must take you back before I fail again."

Kris held on to him, never wanting to let him go. At last his heartbeat slowed a little, and she pulled back and looked up at him. "I know you would not let it happen again. I trust you to protect me." She wrapped her arms around his waist and held her breath, praying he'd change his mind. If he set her aside now, she'd die.

She frowned. He'd mentioned an enemy. Hadn't her grandmother's voice warned of an enemy that first day? She'd chalked the warnings up to her own hysteria, but now that she recalled them, they seemed so much more ominous. "Just hold me," she pleaded, and sighed when his arms tightened and his lips pressed against her hair.

"I will not fail you again," he replied, his voice deep, filled with determination.

A tremor of dread snaked up her spine at his tone. She pulled back to search his face and didn't like what she saw— determination, stubbornness, pain. How could she get him to relinquish his plan? "What about the People, the children? I have to convince Quannah to surrender."

"He will not listen to you now." Duuqua shook his head, avoiding her gaze as a dull flush crept into his cheeks. "He is very angry."

"What aren't you telling me?"

"I found him laughing with his wives while the People grieved."

He shrugged. "I could not stop myself." At last he looked at her, his eyes filled with remorse.

"He won't stay angry." She truly believed her words, but she had a sinking feeling that Duuqua was right. Quannah would be more stubborn than ever. "I'll just have to be persistent," she murmured, keeping her voice steady. "I can't leave until he changes his mind. Don't you see?"

Duuqua frowned, but his lips twitched. "I see that I will have to gag you and tie you over a horse to take you back."

Kris grinned as relief sighed through her. "Don't even try it, mister."

"I will wait, but only until Quannah changes his mind." He pulled her close again, pressed another kiss against her hair. "Until then I will do my best to keep you safe. And warm."

"I'm counting on that." She rubbed her hips against his, smiling at his answering grin.

Several minutes later, Kris lay in the protective curl of Duuqua's arm, her cheek pillowed on his chest. She would convince Quannah. She had to. Her jaw clenched as she remembered the violence, the heartache and destruction of the previous day. She closed her eyes and once again saw the children, laughing and playing. Her heart ached, knowing the sorrow that lay ahead for them, knowing they were the People's true hope. She would succeed—for their sake.

But first she'd teach this stubborn warrior that he couldn't live without her.

Brother Moon lit the way as Duuqua and his weary braves rode among the brush shelters searching for their families. Glad cries welcomed their return, but all was silent when he found Padaponi and Tomanoakuno close to the tiny stream. Only Padaponi's snores broke the deep silence. He smiled, reassured by the noise, and hobbled his horse nearby, then rubbed it down with grass as it grazed. Its bones felt too close beneath its skin. His warriors' horses were ready for the soup pot. But the soup pots were gone and so were the herds of fat, healthy ponies. Duuqua sighed and hung his shield from the waiting tripod where it would catch the sun's first light. He scowled as he stroked the eagle feathers swaying in the night breeze. He needed every bit of power he could gather to stay ahead of the blue-coats.

He cursed as he stripped at the stream. The soldiers had found them in every place they had hidden—places no white man had ever before seen. How much more would the Great Spirit make the People suffer? What had the People done to make Him turn His face from them?

After Palo Duro, all the People had left were the clothes on their backs and their pride. But the bluecoats were teaching them a hard lesson: Pride does not fill bellies.

Exhausted and disheartened, he turned his thoughts to Kris. He longed for the warmth and comfort he knew he would find in her arms. Guilt made him linger at the stream. Each night the voice urged him to take her back to the sacred waters. Each night he promised, "Soon." And with the dawn he stole one more day, then one more night. He watched her grow thin as a willow branch from hard work and worry.

Yet he could not force her to leave, could he? He had given his word to wait until she convinced Quannah of the need to surrender, which she tried to do every day. Duuqua knew Quannah could not hold out much longer. The People could not bear much more.

Pain knifed through him. How could he take her back? It would be less painful to cut out his heart and end his life.

Each day as he rode the plains, leading soldiers away from the People, Duuqua saw many strange things. The Llano Estacado was no longer empty for him, but filled with people moving about in iron horses of all sizes, shapes and colors. He had seen more—many things he did not understand, like the homes of the People, not tipis but square lodges. Strangest of all, he'd seen a big square lodge with stars on the roof. He had laughed to see Quannah standing before it frowning, his hidebound braids looking strange over the white man's clothes he wore.

The images fascinated him, made him want to see more,

but he became angry at himself. His place was here with his People. He must keep his thoughts on their needs.

He shook off the troubling thoughts like drops of water, then returned to the brush shelter where Kris and Padaponi slept. Kris lay curled in the same blanket he had wrapped her in the night he found her floating in the sacred waters. His heart gave a frightened leap. How could he return her and let the waters take her again? How would he know she made it safely back to her home?

Come with me. Her words whispered on the night breeze. Excitement chased up his spine. He grasped his medicine bag where the stones pounded, drumming like hoofbeats against his chest. Was it possible? Could he bear to leave the People, his brother, his aunt? Sacrifice all for the love of this woman? His aunt would have a home with any one of Quannah's wives, and was needed more by them than by Kris or himself. The thought of a new world, a brighter future, drew him like a wolf scenting fresh meat.

Coward, he hissed at himself. *Do you fear the reservation so much?* He straightened, indignant at the thought. He did not fear the reservation, but the vision of his empty life without the woman he loved by his side left him aching and cold. He had touched the face of love and knew his heart could never again accept less. He could not give her up, yet he could not bear to see her suffer. Duuqua chased the troubling thoughts from his head, slipped beneath the blanket and pulled Kris into his arms.

Her warm body curled against his. She did not pull away, though she shuddered at the touch of his cold skin. He smiled as she settled her head on his arm and threw her arm across his waist, then he drew in a sharp breath as her knee pushed between his thighs. His thoughts scattered at her welcome. He buried his nose in the crook of her neck and drew in a deep breath that was all woman. His lips sought her throat, then the taut peaks thrusting against her buckskin shirt. He drew up her skirt and groaned, finding her wet, ready. He mounted her, rode her hard, swallowing her cries of ecstasy and snatching his name from her lips.

Head thrown back, he lifted himself over her and pressed deep as he spilled his seed. His arms gave out and he rolled, pulling her with him. He smiled. She had not opened her eyes, but her arms still held him to her. Was she, too, afraid to let go?

Her need for him matched his for her. He had thought that once he took her, that need would become less powerful. Not so. It drove him even now, fresh from release, to pull her close and kiss her hair.

What if their passion should create a child?

He squeezed his eyes shut, willing sleep to release him from his mind's torment. *Guard her well*, the Great Spirit had told him. *Keep her safe*, the strange voice warned. As sleep claimed him he wondered, how could he protect her from his love?

Kris yawned and snuggled closer to Duuqua. He was scowling in his sleep again. He scowled a lot lately. Not at her or any-one in particular, just at life in general, she supposed. He rarely smiled anymore. None of the People smiled. There wasn't much to smile about. But she smiled, remembering last night and waking to ecstasy only seconds before he entered her.

"Who are you?" His sleep-roughened voice startled her, but his lighthearted words warmed her heart.

"You've forgotten?" She pushed her hips forward to press against him. "Does that refresh your memory?"

His eyes heated and his manhood leaped against her thigh.

"You may have forgotten," she whispered against his lips, being careful not to disturb the rough rumble of Padaponi's snores on the far side of the brush shelter, "but a certain part of your anatomy has a long memory."

"Mmm," he groaned, as he nibbled on her neck. "And it is as hungry as I am."

Chapter Nineteen

A twig snapped on the trail behind her. Kris ducked behind a tree, holding her breath as she listened for the tinkle of bells.

A hand clamped over her shoulder. She dropped her full water bags, clawing at the hand.

"Stop, woman." Chikoba's low snarl brought Kris up short. "You need not fear me."

Clutching a hand over her thundering heart, she gasped for breath and glared up at him. "Why were you following me?" she finally managed to squawk. "Don't you have anything better to do than scare unsuspecting women?"

"I did not mean to frighten you, but when you ducked off the trail . . ." He looked away, his face grim. "Protecting you gives me something else to think about."

"Did Duuqua put you up to this?"

He bristled, and she gave him a warm smile. "Forgive me. I was being selfish—again."

He refilled her water bags, drew a deep breath, then faced her, his blue eyes searching hers. "Tell me what lies ahead for the People."

Dumbfounded, Kris studied his face. Not for the first time, she wondered what it was about this man that felt so comfortable, so familiar, as if she'd known him for years, not just months? Whatever, it made her disregard the gruff manners that kept others away. She shook her head. "What do you mean?"

"I have given your words much thought. Everything you have said has come to pass. I cannot explain your coming here from the future, as you said, but it must be so." He swallowed hard. "There can be no other explanation."

She considered pacifying him, but he'd asked a straight

question; she'd give him straight answers. "You must prepare to leave the People and make a place for yourself in the white man's world."

His eyes widened and his mouth fell open. "Leave? I could never live among white men, especially soldiers. Not after what they did to my wife and child." A shudder wracked his tall frame, grief bowed his shoulders. "I will never be able to see a soldier without wanting to kill him."

Kris's heart went out to him. "You won't be able to pass yourself off as Comanche, not with those blue eyes. And if you try to stay with the People, the soldiers will drag you away, return you to civilization. If one of your friends tried to defend you, there could be trouble."

He studied her for several long moments, his face becoming shadowed. "I'll leave, go west where no white man has ever been." A muscle rippled in his jaw as his gaze followed his thoughts.

"There's nowhere you can go to get away from them," Kris warned, then paused. "Except maybe Alaska." She frowned, trying to remember when Alaska was settled. "How about Oregon?" A sudden rush of excitement swept her and she clutched his arm. "If I remember correctly, there's land available there for homesteading. Lots of settlers took the Oregon Trail and established farms and ranches."

"Hor-ee-gun?" He sounded skeptical, but she caught a new light in his eyes.

"Oregon," she said, slowly.

"How would a man find this Oregon, if he were interested?"

"Just travel northwest until you hit the coast," she said. "You'd be safer traveling as a white man. You'll need to change your appearance to protect yourself."

He stared at her, disdain in every feature. "I must dress like a white man?"

"Cut your hair and grow a beard. If you don't fit in, they won't trust you." She gulped, suddenly realizing Chikoba could die if he took her advice. "You still have your rifle, don't you?"

"Since Ekararo died, I have thought of leaving many times. I cannot live here without her. I see her face everywhere. I hear her laughter and turn to find her, but it is always someone else. I cannot bear to touch the things she made that survived the fire." He turned away, swallowing hard.

Kris laid a hand on Chikoba's forearm and blinked furiously against the threatening tears. "I miss her too," she whispered.

Chikoba brushed a tear off her cheek. "She loved you. You were the sister she never had."

"I felt the same about her." Kris's lips trembled and the tears ran down her cheeks. Suddenly, she found herself crushed against Chikoba's hard chest, his cheek rubbing against the top of her head.

How long they stood there sharing their grief, she didn't know. "I tried to get to her . . ."

"It was not your fault. You did everything you could." Voice stern, he bent to look in her eyes.

"But it wasn't enough! She's gone and even killing that man didn't make her death any easier to bear." Kris jerked out of Chikoba's arms. "If I can't do anything to help the People, why am I here? What was I sent for?"

"What haven't you done? You have helped Padaponi and Tabenanika care for the sick. More than once I wanted to hug you for helping Ekararo those last two months."

"How could I do any less? Don't you see? I have all this knowledge, but it hasn't made any difference."

"Maybe you were sent here for yourself, not the People? Maybe you had to come here to learn something important. What a great teacher you would be if you went back to your time now."

Kris stared up at him, dumbfounded. His words left her cold, her heart pounding. "No! I don't want to go back. I can teach here. There's so much I can do."

"Easy, easy," Chikoba chided, gripping her arms. "I did not mean to make you angry. You have made a place for yourself here. But my place is gone."

Her panic subsided when he chucked her under the chin. There was something so familiar in the gesture that she couldn't help grinning.

"You see? There is still joy in our days, moments that chase away the shadows." He turned, drawing Kris along with an arm looped around her shoulders, easily toting her heavy water bags with the other hand.

She nodded, marveling that this man she'd thought so downright ornery could be so congenial, so comforting. "I suppose you're right."

"I will think about this Oregon," he said, then frowned. "But what should I do about my name? I suppose I can no longer call myself Chikoba."

"What was your name before you were captured?"

He hesitated, searching her face again. "I remember." He glanced away, staring off into the distance, his face troubled as if seeing, feeling, hearing bad memories. "But I never thought to use it again."

"What is it?" Why had her palms gone damp?

"My name is Jeremiah," he said, his cool blue gaze studying her face.

She laughed. "What a coincidence. That was my great-great grandfather's name."

He only shrugged and hung her water bags on poles beside the brush shelter.

"I will think about Oregon."

On a gray, overcast day several days later, Chikoba rode up to Kris's and Duuqua's shelter on a heavily laden horse. Tears filled Kris's eyes as he swung off the horse and approached. His leaving would be like losing Ekararo all over again.

Duuqua greeted him with a hearty slap on the back. "Ready to leave, I see."

Chikoba gripped his arm and they shared a long look. "Watch your back, my friend."

When he turned to Kris, Chikoba unexpectedly pulled her

into his arms and clasped her to him, holding her very tight for several seconds.

"I will not say good-bye," he told them. "You shall hear from me." Then he kissed her cheek.

He mounted and rode away without another word. Kris watched until the vastness of the Llano Estacado swallowed him. A tear rolled down her cheek.

"How far do you think he's traveled by now?" Kris asked several days later, snuggling deeper into Duuqua's arms as they huddled beneath the latest in a long line of crude shelters. "I hope he found some clothes to wear so he won't be mistaken for a Comanche and shot on sight."

Duuqua kissed her hard. "You lie here in my arms asking about another man?"

Kris chuckled. "Jealous?"

He nibbled on a sensitive spot between her neck and shoulder. "Should I be?"

Kris moaned, all thoughts of Chikoba vanishing. "Don't stop."

"I did not plan to."

Later, sated and content, Kris sat with the blanket tucked snugly around her as she watched Duuqua stoke the dying fire. His attempts to warm their three-sided shelter seemed as futile as the People's attempts to avoid the inevitable.

A sudden spasm of guilt racked her. She hadn't been persistent about speaking to Quannah. She felt like a thief, stealing hours of happiness at the People's expense. Surely, after what they'd shared the past few months, Duuqua wouldn't still insist on taking her back to the Springs. She couldn't bear the thought of leaving now, of never knowing what would become of him and Padaponi.

Loving Duuqua felt so right, so good. As if the two of them had known this bliss before. Sometimes as they made love, just before the ecstasy came upon her, she saw flashes of another time, another place. But always it was Duuqua holding her, loving her, sending her flying into the sun.

"I'm going to talk to Quannah tomorrow. Will you come?"

Duuqua turned to face her, suddenly tense. "Yes, I will come." He settled her between his knees and wrapped the blanket around both of them. "It is time."

She shot him a questioning glance, still uncertain of his mood.

"We cannot buy our happiness with the People's suffering." He kissed the top of her head. "You must tell him."

She let him avoid her questioning gaze. There would be time to question him later. For now she was happy that he understood and would be with her. "Will he listen?"

"He must."

A different Quannah faced Kris and Duuqua across a low fire. He'd agreed to their request to meet with him reluctantly and had sent his wives away. So far, he'd been pleasant, inviting them to share his fire, his food. Kris was shocked by his appearance. She'd seen him only at a distance since the raid at Palo Duro. Careworn creases marred his usual carefree expression. New, dark rings beneath his eyes made them seem deep and hollow, mysterious. He had lost weight and his broad shoulders seemed bowed under the great burden he bore. His gaze never left Kris's face.

"Tell me, Kris Baldwin," he said, without his usual arrogance. "What must I do?"

Kris blinked back tears. She searched her heart for the words to say, but her mind was suddenly blank.

Quannah looked at Duuqua, his eyes pleading for understanding. "I thought that the soldiers would come no more when winter came upon the Llano Estacado. But still they come. The People die of starvation and exposure." His eyes sought Kris's once more. "If we stay out here, none will be left. But I must know. What will happen if I surrender?"

Kris's mouth worked, but nothing came out of her tight throat.

Duuqua reached out and placed a hand on his brother's shoulder, speaking to him quietly in their tongue. When they turned back to her, Kris had regained control. She answered Quannah's questions candidly and in detail. She shared his pain when she explained what he could expect for his People in the coming years, the white man's theft of their culture, their pride.

"Your words are hard." Bitterness twisted Quannah's mobile mouth. "Much pain awaits my People. How can I surrender them into the white man's hands?"

"If you don't, everyone will die. Do you want to be remembered all through history as the man who was too proud to save his People? If you learn to get along with the white men, they'll say your white blood is stronger than your Comanche blood, and accept you. Because of your white blood, you can help your People in ways a full-blooded Comanche could not. Your People will need a strong leader, a chief and judge to guard their interests, to help them learn to live in peace with the whites."

"Will they thank me when their children are taken from them, when they can no longer dance or sing or pray without the white man's permission?" His worried gaze sought Duuqua's. "Could you do this?"

For long seconds, Duuqua returned his brother's anguished stare, then slowly nodded. "Better that some live, than that all die."

Quannah shook his head and turned from him. "It is too much."

"Please," Kris whispered in one final appeal for the future of the People. "You must do it. For the children."

His head whipped up and his tortured gaze scorched her. "This is hard enough, knowing the sorrow I will see in the faces I know and love. Do not ask me to think of others I will never know." His shoulders bowed and he held his head in his hands.

Quannah turned his bleak gaze on Duuqua. "We will have to find you different work." He smiled and Kris was warmed by the heart of this man and his concern for his brother. "The People will not need a war chief on the reservation."

"And you, Tomanoakuno?" Quannah turned to her, missing Duuqua's sudden stiffness, the tight line of his lips.

Kris blinked. He was smiling at her. He'd never smiled at her before, never called her by her Comanche name. Until now she hadn't been subjected to this man's potent charisma. Speechless, she basked in its warmth.

"Why have you been so determined to make me listen to your words?"

"I have a vested interest." She had not planned to tell him of their kinship, but the words were out before she could stop them.

"Vested?" Quannah's gaze sharpened, like a hawk spotting a fat rabbit. "What does this mean?"

Kris drew a shaky breath. "I'm one of those people you don't want to think of, one of those you will never see."

A deep frown creased Quannah's forehead. She was bungling this. Her hands twisted in her lap. "You're my great-great grandfather." She peeked up at him, watching his face, braced for his reaction. He'd probably throw her out of his tipi—again.

Quannah's eyes narrowed. His gaze traveled up and down her body and his frown deepened. She resisted the urge to clutch her arms over her chest, hoping he wasn't remembering the first time he'd seen her, stark naked and trembling. "This cannot be. My own children do not have as many summers as you, and I have no grandchildren."

Kris quickly explained how she had come to be there, with Duuqua filling in the gaps in her story. At first Quannah scoffed. Then they showed him the stones and shared a knowing smile as he held them and felt their power sweep over him. He returned them quickly, obviously shaken.

"You are my great-great granddaughter?"

Kris glanced away, shrugged, cursing the heat that rushed into her face.

He chuckled, then threw back his head and laughed. "This does not please you." He cocked his head, waiting for her to respond.

"My father warned me not to be lascivious like you." *Oh, God.* Kris kicked herself mentally. Why couldn't she control what came tumbling out of her mouth?

"Your father? A white man? But how can you be like me? You are a woman." His tone, still disbelieving, had taken on a defensive edge.

"Well, actually . . . My father, uh . . ." Dear God, how could she graciously tell this man that he was considered a rake, a womanizer?

"Tell me, woman," Quannah demanded.

"He said you had more wives than one man deserved."

Quannah cocked his head and frowned. "How many?"

"Oh, please." She glanced aside at Duuqua, not surprised to find him grinning, head cocked as he considered her, just like his brother. The rogue. No help there. He looked as curious as Quannah, and why not? According to Comanche custom, what was Quannah's was also his. Fighting down a surge of jealousy, she stared into the fire, fidgeting with a fringe on her skirt. "Seven."

"Seven?" Quannah bellowed.

She looked him square in the eye. "My father warned me not to become as lascivious as you." Too late, she realized the insult. Heat crept up her neck into her face. She had to distract him.

"I don't want you to think nothing good will happen for you once you surrender," Kris began. "You'll be made a judge over the Comanche and you'll travel a lot, even to Washington, D.C., I believe. And you'll be friends with Teddy Roosevelt, one of our most famous presidents. Oh, and you'll have a big house, for all your wives and children, built by the government. You'll move the bodies of your mother and sister, so they will always be close by."

"I would like that more than anything in the world." The hard lines in Quannah's face softened, and Kris squirmed under his searching gaze. Why was he studying her face? Was he looking for a resemblance?

"And your house," she babbled on, "your house will have twenty-seven rooms, two stories and a porch all the way around. Oh, and . . ."

". . . stars on the roof?" Duuqua asked, a frown creasing his forehead.

"Yes," Kris confirmed, surprised at his question. "How did you know that?"

"I have seen this in a vision." Wonder filled his voice as he turned to his brother. "And you standing before it, dressed in white man's clothes, black pants, a vest over a white shirt, and a black hat, but with your hair in braids that hung to your waist." He chuckled at the surprise on Quannah's face.

"You have seen this? In a vision? Did you see yourself at this lodge? What else have you seen?"

"Too much to tell you, brother. Some things that frighten me."

"Why didn't you tell me? What else have you seen?"

Quannah gave Duuqua a long look, then grinned and turned back to Kris. "Seven?"

Kris sighed and nodded, rolling her eyes.

With a shout Kris could only describe as triumphant, Quannah leaped up and circled the fire to scoop her into a bear hug that threatened to crack her ribs. "And what's this seventh wife's name?"

Kris's mouth fell open.

"Don't tell me," he whispered, plunking her down again before she could answer. "I want it to be a surprise."

"Quannah—" Duuqua began, but got no further.

"Brother," Quannah chortled, giving Duuqua a hearty slap on the back. "I may have work for you after all."

"Explain las-siv-eee-us."

Duuqua's request brought Kris up short. She burned a finger on the *yaps*, small, potato-like tubers she'd roasted for dinner. "You caught that one, huh?"

He waited patiently.

"Uh, it's kind of hard to explain," she hedged, cursing the creeping heat that scorched her cheeks, concentrating on brushing every bit of ash off the *yaps*.

He reclined beside the fire, smiling a very knowing smile. "I can wait while you think of an answer."

She tossed her head, hoping to appear nonchalant, hating the heat in her cheeks. After all they'd shared, why did he still have the power to make her blush like a teenager? "It's not important."

"I want to know." He looked determined, but his knowing grin set her blood to pounding.

"Where's Padaponi?" she asked, fussing with the fire. "Will she be eating with us?"

"She will stay with Quannah's wives while he is away. His children need their grandmother more than we need her company."

Kris glanced up, suddenly anxious. "He's gone?"

Duuqua nodded and took a careful bite of *yap*. "He went to sacred place to pray. Do not worry," he said, seeing the alarm in her face. "He will not change his decision."

"Do you ever change yours?" He hadn't said a word about taking her back to the Springs and she'd been hesitant to ask, unwilling to bring up the subject and remind him unnecessarily. Several times recently, she'd caught him watching her with a sad expression. She'd tried to show him how wonderful their lives could be together. Did he still plan to take her back to the Springs? Could she let him?

Kris glanced up, feeling his gaze. Why hadn't he spoken?

What caused the fire that burned in his eyes as he stared at her so intently? "Sometimes."

Kris's breath caught as she returned his stare. What was he trying to tell her? If he'd changed his mind about sending her back, why didn't he just spit it out? The sudden tension spiraled, winding her nerves tighter and tighter. She forced herself to be calm, to relax. He would tell her what was on his mind when he felt the time was right and not before.

Was he unsure of her? Was he waiting for some sign from her that she still wanted to stay? A soft smile curved her lips. After tonight, she vowed, there wouldn't be a shred of doubt left in the stubborn man's mind.

Reluctantly, she dragged her thoughts back to Quannah. "I suppose the other warriors will be more willing to accept Quannah's decision if he says it came from the Great Spirit."

Duuqua shot her a grin. "You should be chief."

"If I was, would you still sleep with me?"

He studied her, a very sober look on his face and a new expression in his eyes that she'd never seen there before. It set her heart to racing. His gaze traveled over her body, leaving a trail of fire. It settled on her face and the heat in his eyes scorched her. "Nothing on this earth could keep me from your bed."

His solemn avowal and the intent, searing look in his eyes left her shaken. She gulped, swallowing a bite of *yap* without chewing.

Duuqua ate with deliberate precision, peeling off the charred outer skin of his *yap* to reveal the tender flesh within, then devouring it in one swift bite. Kris's pulse jumped as his tongue swept out to lick his lips. His eyes locked on hers.

Mesmerized, she watched him eat, knowing the gentle strength of those long, supple fingers on her body, the sliding heat of his tongue coursing over her sensitive skin.

She felt like a rubber band stretched to its limit and about to snap. She wanted to show him exactly how much he meant to her. Her hands shook as she cleared away the remains of their meal, then carefully banked the fire.

She felt his gaze on her long before her eyes adjusted to the silvery moonlight. Before she could change her mind, she turned and slowly crossed the short distance to where he waited, reclining on their blanket. In her nervousness, she fumbled over the ties holding her buckskin blouse closed at her sides.

Why was her heart racing? This wasn't the first time they'd made love, but she wanted tonight to be different, special. Why didn't he say something?

His stare sizzled against her bare skin when she lifted the blouse over her head. Her skirt joined the blouse on the ground. She stepped closer, teasing him, wanting that hot gaze to sear her, all over. Placing her hands beneath her breasts, she lifted them, stroking upward over nipples already responding to his bold stare.

He hadn't even kissed her and she was melting, her knees weak. She stepped closer, sliding one hand down her belly and on down her thigh.

A low groan escaped him.

He knew. And with one swift glance, she discovered that his body was just as responsive as hers. Smiling, she knelt beside him and leaned low, letting her breast stroke the stiff peak in his breechclout. She smiled at his whisper of surprise, gaining confidence.

Opening her mouth, she hovered over the peak, blew on it without touching until a dark circle of moisture marked its summit.

He groaned again, deeper. His arm gave out and he fell back, those strong, clever fingers clenched into fists at his sides. His eyes closed as she leaned, claiming the peak through the buckskin, taking it between her lips in a long, sweet kiss as she slowly loosened the rawhide ties and lifted the breechclout aside, letting it drag over him.

All hesitation left her. He lay flat on his back before her, a male at his finest—hot, hard and ready—and hers to do with as she pleased. She let her gaze trail slowly upward, knowing he watched her every move. Pride filled her as her gaze took him in. All male, and all hers.

She dragged her hands down his torso, past narrow hips, skirting close to his proud erection. Her fingers spread wide and stroked down his thighs, then up again on the inside. Sinuously, she slid herself over one hard thigh, letting him feel the wetness at her core as she passed over his thigh to kneel between his legs.

She leaned over him, trailing her hair over the rippling muscles in his abdomen. Sliding lower, she blew gently on his straining manhood; touching him with nothing but hair and breath. She repeated the torture, smiling at his groans of pleasure.

Gliding forward, she let her breasts graze his abdomen, then swayed lower until the soft mounds caressed his taut belly. She glanced up to find him watching her, his eyes burning, his body on fire with desire.

She slid lower. He lifted onto his elbows. Exulting, her gaze locked with his, her tongue slipped out to moisten her lips as his engorged flesh passed between her breasts. She paused there, teasing him. He sank back with a low curse. The muscles in his legs tensed, trembling at the rigid control he exerted. Knowing he could toss her onto her back and finish this at any time, she reveled in her newfound power.

She pressed her breasts together, capturing him between them, casting another sultry look upward to find him watching again. His hips pressed upward. She licked her lips as the tip of his sex appeared between her breasts, blew a hot breath down. He withdrew and pressed upward again, straining toward her mouth. Her tongue flicked out to tease the tip, savoring the smooth texture, delving into the tiny opening. Again he retreated, then advanced, and her lips opened, taking him inside, closing about him as she savored his heat, his slightly salty taste and the pulsing strength of him filling her mouth.

His loud groan made the shelter shudder.

She inhaled deeply and his musky scent rose, filling her head with his essence. She suckled him, watching with pride and pleasure as his head fell back, his eyes closing tight, cords straining in his neck as his fingers clenched in the blanket. Her lips stroked his full length, her head lifting and falling, her tongue flicking over the sensitive tip. Sending him a challenging stare, she licked off the tiny drop of moisture that appeared at the tip of his shaft.

Her nether lips wept—so hungry for his touch. His head lifted, the gleam in his eyes promising retribution. Kris trembled, fast approaching the point of desperate need. Her body ached for his touch, his caress, the press of his weight upon her, his shaft filling her, but she prolonged the torment.

She sensed something new in him, something different. She hoped her instincts were right, prayed that he'd changed his mind about sending her back. But no matter what happened later, she wanted this night to be special.

Watching her through narrowed eyes, he again withdrew, then thrust upward. Again, she caught his length in her mouth, suckling hard, her tongue swirling as he thrust and withdrew, repeating the motion again and again. Gently, she massaged the full sack beneath his manhood, until his whole body trembled with the force of his need. Finally, she released him, sliding along one tense thigh, resisting the urge to press her throbbing core to his erection. Then, slipping past his hungry, seeking manhood, she spread her legs over his muscled abdomen, feeling his manhood press against her back. She rocked, her back arching, as she pressed her wet folds against his belly.

Duuqua groaned, his hands clenched on her hips, helping her find the friction she needed, gentling as they lifted to cup her breasts. It was Kris's turn to moan as he massaged her aching breasts, tweaking the tips. She gasped at the erotic ripple of his muscles against her weeping core as he lifted upward and drew a nipple into his hungry mouth. Then both his hands joined his ravenous lips and his mouth opened wide, sucking her breast in more fully. Shamelessly, she rode his tight abdomen, her buttocks burned by the insistent press of his shaft behind her.

He switched breasts, his eyes gleaming in the darkness. At last she pulled away from his sweet torture and lifted to one knee. She found his iron shaft, and she stroked it, positioning herself to take him.

Watching him, she rubbed the dewy lips of her womanhood with his tip, massaging her tiny, rigid button where every nerve seemed focused. She trembled at the self-torture, knowing she couldn't take much more. He steadied her, his hands hot on her waist, her hips. Then he pressed her downward as he speared upward.

"Duuqua," she moaned, as she sank fully onto his shaft, reveling in the feel of it parting her, thrusting deep. She pressed a hand over her lower abdomen, crying out at the sense of fullness from his penetration.

"Don't move!" He held her still as he fought for control. Cords of muscle stood out in his neck, his nostrils flared as he sucked in deep breaths. She waited, her body singing, a satisfied smile on her lips. When she felt his tension ease, she lifted and settled again, bringing his gaze snapping up to her as he sucked in a sharp breath. She grinned and repeated the motion, rocking higher, settling faster.

His answering groan made her pulse race. Then his sure hands helped her with the rhythm. Their gazes locked, but not a word passed between them. Kris braced herself, her palms flat against the solid wall of his chest as his hands roamed her body, stoking the fire burning inside her. Harder, faster the thrusts came. She caressed the abdominal muscles that tensed beneath her hands as he lifted almost to a sitting position and caught the bouncing fullness of her breasts, suckled. Clear thought eluded her. All she knew was Duuqua—his taste, his touch, his scent, his driving fullness deep inside her.

Then his fingers penetrated the dark curls above her womanhood and pressed. She cried out, his name exploding from her lips as she arched backward, thrust high by his straining hips—splintering, fraying. He echoed her cries as she burst into thousands of brilliant fragments that shimmered and spun away in a kaleidoscope of sensation. She felt the hot wash of his seed so deep inside her it touched her heart. She prayed that it also filled her womb.

"I love you," she whispered, when at last she could draw an even breath.

"I love you, too." His fingers thrust into her hair, tightened and pulled her head up for a swift, hard kiss, his tongue plunging into her moist depths.

Kris savored his kiss, her heart finally at peace. She pulled away to search his face. The truth was there in his eyes, in his smile, in the strong arms that held her. "Why didn't you tell me?"

"I will never let you go. You have wiggled your way into my heart, woman. I could more easily cut it out of my body than take you back"—his voice dropped to a whisper—"though it may kill me to watch your suffering."

For just a moment, the thought of her former life intruded. The faces of her grandmother, her father and her friends flashed through her consciousness. Doubts intruded, bringing stinging tears. Kris blinked hard to keep them back, but they escaped.

"Tears?" he asked, slipping from her body and settling her beside him. He gripped her chin and searched her face. "I love you, woman, not what we share between the blankets. Do you believe that? Can you stay with me? Can you give up your old life for me and my People?"

She didn't hesitate. "Yes, I will stay. Forget your worries, my love. Hold me."

He complied, pulling the blanket around them. Kris snuggled against him, feeling as though she could never get close enough, her heart soaring. He loved her. How incredibly, stupendously wonderful!

She sighed, settling deeper into his embrace, snuggling into her favorite position—next to one, or possibly two, she thought with a secret smile—the top of her head tucked beneath his chin, his arms holding her close. She blocked all further thoughts, exhaustion claiming her.

His deep voice rumbled in her ear. "What is lascivious?"

Kris blinked, suddenly wide awake. Then she grinned and ran a questing hand down his body, found his resting manhood and smirked at his sharply drawn breath.

"What we just did."

He grunted, his body responding to her touch. "I like the way you explain things, woman."

Chapter Twenty

Duuqua kneed his horse to a stop. He turned and watched the long column of his People winding toward him across the high, windswept plains like a snake in tall grass, slowly making their way to the hated reservation. This painful journey would not be swift. Each flower, each blade of grass must be noted. Each person would cling to the memory of this last trek, the sweet smile of the sun beaming down upon their heads, the nodding flowers wishing them safe journey.

The low moan of the wind echoed the People's sorrow, carrying their grief-filled chants. The sound was like a huge fist squeezing his heart, making it hard for him to breathe.

Bedraggled and weary, exhausted and hungry, disheartened by the long winter just passed, the Comanche trudged wearily toward their bleak future.

"What is it?" Quannah drew up beside him, facing the approaching column. In silence, he, too, watched the People's slow approach.

Even from this distance Duuqua could make out the words to the songs they sang as they walked—death songs. He did not need to see their faces to know their sorrow. He grieved as they did, but he would not sing his death song, not while Kris lived and loved him, not while there was hope. There would be children. Even now his child might be lying warm and safe beneath her heart. As long as there were children, there was hope.

"Your woman will be safe, brother. We will survive."

Duuqua's gaze swung to Quannah, sitting tall and straight upon his black horse, wearing his full eagle headdress, the only one to escape the fires of Palo Duro. Still Duuqua could not believe the changes in him. Over the long winter, Quannah had grown older, as if he felt the suffering of every one of his People. Worry had cut new lines into his face. His laughter no longer rang through camp, and his wives wore long, troubled faces. Day and night he sought Kris, asking questions, struggling to understand.

Duuqua clasped the arm Quannah extended to him. "We will make it so, my chief."

Quannah kneed his horse, turning slowly in a full circle. Duuqua watched, not needing to ask what he was doing, or why.

Duuqua turned his eyes to the distant horizon, sweeping the plains surrounding them as grief tore through him. Would this be the last time he rode free upon the face of Mother Earth? Would he never again know the kiss of the wind, the joy of the hunt? How could he live without this land he loved? He must find the strength to survive the grief, the loss, to endure the humiliation. He must keep his pride—well hidden, but alive and thriving—to pass on to his children, to give them strength. He tried to envision them. His eyes sank shut and the image came easily: two strong boys and one delicate, but very headstrong daughter, just like her mother. He smiled, the pain in his heart easing.

"Yes. We will, my brother." Quannah's words broke through Duuqua's sweet vision.

Duuqua turned his face eastward, toward the fort where the soldiers waited. He did not know what would happen there, but he would not let them see his fear. He would not let them steal his pride. They could take his freedom, but they could not touch his soul.

Kris shoved her way to the front of the crowd, but hovered behind Padaponi, shaking off her restraining hand. "What's happening? Why are they separating the warriors?"

Padaponi replied in Comanche and Kris struggled to understand as she watched soldiers shove Duuqua and his warriors into a line against the side of a half-finished building that, even when completed, would be as crude as the rest of the rough-planed plank buildings of Fort Sill. The People formed a huge half-circle facing their loved ones, anxiously watching the proceedings. Duuqua had made Kris swear she would keep quiet, stay in the background, keep her eyes down. Even now, his gaze found her despite the milling people. He sent her a warning frown. She nodded, forcing herself to watch in silence.

How she ached as she saw these proud men humbled, men who had kept their land free from white invasion with nothing but their meager weapons and their ironclad determination. Only when outnumbered almost a thousand to one were they forced to surrender, to endure this humiliation from men who never had been and never would be their equal.

A door slammed and the People turned as one to watch the general stomp toward them, dust rising in little puffs with every footfall. His hat brim shadowed his face, preventing Kris from seeing his expression, but the stiff set of his shoulders, his purposeful stride marred by a decided limp, told her he meant the People no good. The obsequious Quaker agent, Haworth, trotted along beside him, unable to match the general's long stride. Her trepidation increased as the general drew closer and the People moved aside to let him pass. Iron-gray hair, straight and stiff, poked from beneath his hat. His cold, granite eyes scanned the crowd before locking on the line of waiting warriors.

MacKenzie. Kris's heart thudded in her chest. Would he remember Duuqua, whose lance had given him that limp? She shot a frightened look at Duuqua, but he watched MacKenzie, who walked right up to him.

"We meet again."

Duuqua said nothing, didn't move or flinch, just returned MacKenzie's stare.

MacKenzie's smile was not pretty. "Where's your lance?"

Kris's breath caught in her throat and she prayed Duuqua would remain silent, though she knew it was too much to ask of any man, let alone her husband, the war chief.

She watched in horror as Duuqua's gaze slid to MacKenzie's right thigh, then back to his face. "I thrust it into my enemy and he rode away with it."

MacKenzie blanched. Angry whispers swept the troops awaiting the general's pleasure, rigidly at attention. Kris's uneasiness increased as they bristled at Duuqua's acknowledgment—in English—of the injury done their general. But nothing could stifle her surge of pride at his courage.

Bright spots of color appeared on MacKenzie's cheeks as he stared at Duuqua, a cold smile slowly turning up the corners of his lips. "Too bad you lost it."

Duuqua stiffened. Kris held her breath, willing him to keep his control, sighing in relief when the tension left his shoulders.

MacKenzie, through taunting Duuqua, turned to the man beside him.

"Quannah."

Quannah nodded, not one iota of expression showing on his face, not even surprise that MacKenzie recognized him. "Quannah Parker, General MacKenzie," he said stiffly.

Kris couldn't help a bright smile of pride as Quannah followed her advice. She'd told him to make his white blood known to the soldiers immediately, knowing he must remain close to MacKenzie and unfettered in order to benefit his people.

"Parker?"

Quannah nodded, short and sharp. "Cynthia Ann Parker my mother. She, my sister stolen by soldiers many summers past."

"Cynthia Ann Parker was your mother?"

Quannah nodded again, standing straight and proud as the general scrutinized his face.

"Orderly," MacKenzie barked. A soldier scrambled over to him, saluted. "Check out this man's claim, see what you can find out about Cynthia Ann Parker." He turned back to Quannah but Coyote Droppings stepped forward, drawing his attention.

"I am Isatai," he proudly proclaimed, "medicine man and healer to the People."

MacKenzie studied him briefly, his lip curling, then his gaze slid to Quannah, who gave a quick, confirming nod. MacKenzie glanced at a soldier, who grabbed Coyote Droppings' arm, pulling him away from the line of warriors, then reached to do the same to Quannah. Quannah jerked his arm away, freezing the soldier with a glance. With a nod to MacKenzie, he stepped over beside Coyote Droppings.

What was happening? Kris's heart lodged in her throat. She couldn't have spoken if she'd tried. She racked her brain, desperately trying to recall the specific incidents that would transpire.

"Bring them," MacKenzie barked and the order was crisply relayed from soldier to soldier. A door opened and five women and six or eight children emerged from a small building, approaching the line of warriors. Despite their military escort, Kris could smell their fear. The skinny children, clad in ill-fitting, ragged clothes, clung to their haggard mothers' faded skirts. The women's eyes, huge, sunken hollows in their pale faces, seemed frozen on the line of warriors ahead. Their steps slowed, but did not falter. Filled with dread, Kris watched them come steadily closer until they stood beside MacKenzie.

"I know how difficult this must be for all of you," MacKenzie began, and Kris's stomach turned at his patronizing tone of voice, "but you must look at these men. Do you recognize any of them? Are any of these men the ones who raided your farms and killed your husbands?"

The women turned frightened gazes on the line of warriors, their glances skittering from one man to the next and finally back to MacKenzie.

"Don't be afraid to point them out," MacKenzie urged, soothingly. "These savages are under my control. They won't hurt anyone again."

Kris couldn't breathe, could only stare in dread and horror, willing the women to be silent.

"Him," one woman croaked, lifting a trembling, bony finger to point at Duuqua. "He was there. He led them." Her finger shifted to another warrior down the line. "And him! He scalped my poor Joe." Her features crumpled and she sobbed openly.

Other women spoke up, all of them identifying one or two warriors in the line, but Kris couldn't hear their voices over the ringing in her ears. *No,* her heart cried in denial, *you're wrong. It wasn't him! He's the man I love. He would never . . .*

Suddenly, the crowd parted between them and Kris met Duuqua's gaze. She read the warning there, and worse, acknowledgment of the woman's accusation. Horror swept Kris's soul as she stared at the two whimpering children clutching the woman's skirt. She clasped her arms over her stomach, feeling sick and queasy. The man she loved was responsible for the death of those children's father. Her horror-filled gaze lifted to Duuqua.

He flinched, his eyes narrowing before he looked away.

This is war! Words he'd spoken earlier in his defense lost their potency in the presence of a weeping widow and her scrawny, orphaned children.

You, too, have fought and killed. The quiet voice rang in Kris's ears, bringing a flood of shame and remorse. What if one of these women was the wife of the soldier she'd killed?

This is war! The words came again and with them the horrible realization that she might have widowed an innocent woman, might have orphaned poor, defenseless children. Even the vivid memory of Ekararo's broken, bloody body, her arms clutched protectively over her womb, didn't stifle the painful flood of remorse. Kris's stomach clenched tighter and she swayed dizzily.

Men had fought and died on both sides. Who decided which man died a hero and which a villain?

Kris's gaze skittered feverishly over the line of soldiers, then the warriors as her thoughts rampaged. How did triumph become defeat, humiliation, retribution? Yes, the People had fought and died, just like the white men they had opposed. But the Great Spirit had turned His back on them, had made the white men heroes and left the People villains.

Now the People must endure the consequences of their actions, and so must she. She couldn't wallow in the dirt, wailing over her wounds. She must be strong, for her husband and for their People. Drawing a deep, calming breath, she shoved back the fear and remorse and braced herself to meet Duuqua's gaze with love and understanding in her eyes.

"Lock them in the icehouse." MacKenzie's order silenced the muttering crowd. Kris stared at the rough walls of the small building he indicated, no more than eight feet square, with no roof. He couldn't lock them in there with no shelter from the sun or rain. She glanced to Quannah, mentally urging him to do something. Why didn't he say something?

But Quannah wasn't looking her way. He stood beside Coyote Droppings, watching the six warriors walk by, his face an emotionless mask. Only the muscle that twitched in his jaw betrayed the depth of his emotion, the iron control required to remain passive.

Kris sought out Duuqua, struggling to control her expression. She must not let him see her fear. She felt his gaze slide over her, but his gaze did not meet hers. Her heart stopped beating. Did he think she was ashamed of him? She couldn't let him be imprisoned with that thought the last thing to pass between them. She had to let him know she understood, that she shared his grief, his pain.

"Duuqua!" she cried. He stiffened, but didn't look at her.

Padaponi hissed and pinched Kris's arm, trying to silence her, pulling her deeper into the watching crowd. Kris struggled, but someone grabbed her other arm. "No," she cried, "let me go! I've got to talk to him. He thinks—" A hard, callused hand slapped over her mouth, cutting off her words. Kris forgot they were acting for her own safety, forgot Duuqua's warning to be silent at all costs, forgot she must not draw attention to herself. All she knew was that her husband was about to be imprisoned and he thought she was ashamed of him. She couldn't let him go without explaining. She had to tell him she understood, that nothing had changed.

Desperately, she struggled against the person holding her, twisting her head, trying to escape the silencing hand. Then she remembered the trick she'd used on Duuqua when he'd first taken her captive, and bit into the hand, hard. It worked. The hand slipped away and, knowing she had only seconds to act, Kris sucked in a deep breath and cried the only thing she had time to say. "Duuqua!"

If only he heard and understood.

Duuqua!

Kris's cry rang in Duuqua's ears through all the long days that followed. He ached at the sorrow in it, the plea for understanding, the reminder of all that had come before and everything they had shared. He longed to hold her, to tell her he understood, that he loved her.

He paced the small square of their prison. What had become of his People? Were they safe, had they been fed and given new clothes and blankets as the white men had promised? Or did they, too, walk the walls of a wooden lodge with no roof? Were their women being abused?

A loud, rumbling squeak broke into his thoughts, growing steadily louder. Duuqua's jaw clenched and he moved toward the sound. The other five warriors jumped up and spread out, waiting, their eyes turned toward the noise, which grew louder, then abruptly stopped. They watched the top of the wall, tense, ready.

A chunk of raw meat flew over the wall and the closest man scrambled to catch it before it hit the ground. Another piece quickly followed, then another and another. The men lunged after each one, grinning at each other in triumph when they succeeded in keeping all the meat from touching the ground. One more piece sailed over the wall, hitting Masatawtap's head before landing in the dirt at the big man's feet.

Masatawtap scowled, uttering a low curse as he carefully picked up the bloody meat and brushed off the dirt. "They feed us like dogs."

"When are we going to be released?"

"What has happened to our wives and children?"

"Silence," Duuqua barked, cutting off the complaints of the others. "Eat. It does not matter how they feed us, only that they do, and that the meat is good."

"Will they hang us?"

Duuqua faced the circle of worried faces, keeping his own fears hidden. "No. Remember what Quannah said. They talk of sending us on the iron horse to a place called Florida, far away from here." He had spoken with Quannah briefly the night before, getting too few answers to his many questions.

"What about our wives, our children?" one of them asked.

Duuqua silenced the man with a slash of his hand. "They will be cared for until we return." He found the words hard to say, for the thought of being taken so far from his People, from Kris, left him feeling empty inside. How would he endure such a separation?

"How long will that be?"

Duuqua looked down at the raw hunk of meat, as big as his hand. "I do not know. But until then we must eat." He shook the meat in the men's faces. "We must remain strong." With a snarl, he bit off a chunk of meat and spit it out again, cursing.

"What is it?" Masatawtap stared closely at his own meat, then dropped it and kicked dirt over it.

"Maggots." Duuqua heaved his meat back over the wall, ignoring the jeering laughter that rose when it landed on the other side. He spat into the dirt again and again until he could no longer taste the rancid meat. Wiping his mouth on his arm, he faced the frightened men surrounding him.

"We will survive," he promised them.

The other men followed his example, heaving their meat over the high wall, then settling cross-legged in a shady corner. Duuqua stepped over to the wall, putting his eye to the small hole he'd made by prying the bark from between two boards. He saw no one but soldiers walking around the ugly, square lodges of the white chiefs. The soldiers slept in small tents behind the square lodges, or in larger lodges that held many men. His nostrils twitched, remembering the stink of the soldiers, like wild onions freshly peeled. The thought of so many of them sleeping inside the tight, airless wooden lodges made him draw a deep, clean breath. His stomach fisted, the reminder of that scent coming too soon after the taste of the rancid meat.

Where had the People been taken? How far away were they? He saw none of them, could not even hear their voices. The white men's lodges, running in straight lines from each side of his prison, blocked Duuqua's view of the land beyond the soldier camp. A large, open area lay between the lines of lodges, but no grass grew there and the wind played merrily in the dirt.

How were his People being treated? Were they, too, being fed rotten meat? Were the women being treated with respect and courtesy, or had they been forced to serve the soldiers' lust? Had Kris been discovered? Was she safe with Padaponi and Quannah and his wives? Duuqua's fears ate at his restraint.

A wolf howled close by, too close. No wolf would be that close to the camp. Duuqua strained to see through the small hole, peering into the shadows. He glanced to the side. He could not see the soldiers, but the smell of their tobacco drifted to him, teasing his nostrils. At a scrabbling noise, he jerked his mind back to the shadows.

A bird call this time. Someone, one of the People, was out there. But who? Inside, the other warriors had also heard and recognized the calls. They had found knotholes and were straining to see something, anything. Suddenly, an eye appeared at Duuqua's hole. He cried out and jumped back, his heart pounding. Hearing his brother's deep, familiar chuckle, Duuqua stepped back to the hole.

"Frightened, brother?"

"Never," Duuqua denied, whispering his answer. "If you were in here, I'd show you. What about the soldiers?"

Duuqua glimpsed Quannah's wolfish smile. "Trinkets buy much."

"Why did they not put you in here with us?"

"Your woman spoke truly when she told us what would happen here. MacKenzie likes my white blood. He uses me to keep the People happy. If not for her warning, I would have been inside with you. There would have been no one to speak for the People. Except Isatai, who speaks for no one but himself."

"What about the soldiers guarding us? They will hear you."

"I am short many trinkets."

"Kris? How is she?"

"Your woman is fine," Quannah assured him, then added on a sigh, "but difficult. She keeps telling me she must surrender for killing that soldier. Crazy woman."

Duuqua frowned. "You must not let her. MacKenzie would show her no mercy."

"What about my wife?" Masatawtap asked. The other warriors added their own concerns.

"Your families are well," Quannah reassured them. "Each man and boy has been given a suit of white men's clothes to wear." He sniffed. "The cloth is so thin the wind blows through it. Plus a shirt, pants, coat, hat and strange things the soldiers call 'socks.' The shirts and pants are all too big, but the women have cut the seats out of the pants to make leggings and ripped the sleeves off the coats to make vests. The women have new woolen skirts and bolts of fabric to make dresses and clothes for the children."

The men nodded, sharing their relief at knowing their families were not being ill-treated.

"What about food?" Masatawtap demanded. "They throw our meat over the wall, as if we were animals. Tonight it was rank, filled with worms."

Quannah sighed. "I will speak to the general. The People have been given a little meat, some sugar, even coffee. Much cornmeal." He gagged. "The horses like it."

The men snorted, chuckling in spite of their worry. Duuqua frowned, surprised that his brother could still find humor in their misfortune.

"Those blankets," Quannah snorted, speaking over the men's laughter at his joke. "Nothing but lint. Some white man is getting fat off the White Father's money."

"Why have you come?" Duuqua knew Quannah would not take such a risk to make them laugh. And only desperate need would make him part with his trinkets. He gave a sharp jerk of his head and the other men moved away, leaving him to speak with Quannah privately.

"Isatai."

Duuqua uttered a low curse. "What now?"

"He tries to make himself chief of all the People, but MacKenzie wants me."

Duuqua heard no pride in Quannah's voice, only a weary acceptance. "What has he done?"

"He has told the white chiefs he has great power. I am worried. His eyes are often on your woman. I overheard him talking to Kiyani about the stones."

The stones leapt to life against Duuqua's chest. "What about them?"

"He has said he will steal them."

"How?"

"I do not know yet, but be on your guard. When he comes, he will not be alone. You must not try to escape. They would hunt you down and the People would be punished. Haworth has said that if any of the young braves leave the reservation, rations will be held back from all."

Duuqua nodded solemnly. He would do nothing to bring the wrath of the white chiefs upon his People's heads. "I will not give Isatai the stones, Quannah. You know their power. I would give them to you to keep safe."

"No! I cannot take them."

"I will toss them over the fence. If you do not care to hold them for me, give them to Kris," Duuqua whispered back urgently. "She can hide them beneath her clothes."

"No!" Quannah hissed. "I will not touch your medicine. I will bring Kris to you tomorrow when the sun sleeps. You can give them to her."

"Do not!" There was no response, and Duuqua knew his brother had gone. "Quannah? Quannah!" Cursing, Duuqua slammed a hand against the wall. He did not want Kris brought here, did not want her to see him caged up like an animal, shamed, humiliated. The stench from the corner where he and the warriors were forced to relieve themselves rose up to choke him. He cursed his brother's unwillingness to take the stones to Kris.

Perhaps Quannah tried to solve two problems with one plan? Quannah might want to bring Kris here so that Duuqua could talk to her, persuade her to cooperate. Yes, that must be his reason. Quannah was no coward. Duuqua sighed and sat with his back to the wall, letting his head rest on his knees.

No good would come of Quannah's plan. He could feel it.

Kris crouched next to Quannah in the dark beside the crude, squat wooden building across from the icehouse where Duuqua had been imprisoned for over a week. "How will I talk to him? There aren't any windows."

"Hush." Quannah jerked his head toward the corner of the icehouse. "Look!"

Kris craned her neck to see past him and gasped out loud at the sight of Kiyani standing with the soldiers who guarded the icehouse where Duuqua was imprisoned. Quannah held a finger to his lips.

"What's she doing here?"

Kris stared in disgust as Kiyani coyly tossed her hair, laughing at something one of the soldiers said. The man's hand whipped out and disappeared beneath her skirt. Kiyani shrieked, but did not step away, instead her legs parted slightly, allowing the familiarity. Shocked, Kris glanced at Quannah, not surprised to find his jaw clenched, his eyes burning. She couldn't bring herself to look back at Kiyani again. She hung her head, thoroughly embarrassed at being forced to kneel beside Quannah while he watched an enemy fondle his wife.

"I will cut off her nose for this," he promised virulently, reaching for a knife that was no longer there.

"Wait," Kris cautioned, "Kiyani doesn't do anything without a reason. She's got to be up to something."

Probably nothing good, Kris thought, as her gaze scanned the shadows around the icehouse. She spotted someone edging closer and nudged Quannah. "There! Near the horse trough, now behind it. It's Coyote Droppings."

Quannah uttered a low curse and settled into a crouch. "Get ready to run back to camp."

"What's he after?" she demanded, laying a checking hand on his arm. Suddenly, realization dawned. "The stones! He's come to get the stones. Is he that desperate to be chief?"

Quannah shot her a derisive glance.

"You knew," Kris accused, instantly aware that Quannah had brought her here under false pretenses, with promises of speaking to Duuqua, solely to serve his own purposes—again. "You didn't bring me here to speak to Duuqua."

Quannah glanced down at her, no remorse in his gaze. "Duuqua does not want Isatai to get the stones."

"Over my dead body," Kris vowed.

"Never say such things." Quannah silenced her with a slash of his hand. "Watch."

Kiyani slipped a knife out of her mocassin. The huge blade glistened in the moonlight, sending chills up Kris's spine, as Kiyani maneuvered it between herself and the man playing with her body. Then his head lifted, his eyes wide, blood gurgling from a deep slash across his throat. Kris clutched a hand over her mouth and ducked her head, ignoring Quannah's satisfied chuckle. "Why didn't you try to stop her? Don't let Coyote Droppings—"

"There! They've done it. Isatai just got the other one." Quannah actually sounded pleased.

Kris gulped and looked up to find Kiyani and Coyote Droppings fumbling with the keys and the strange lock, two dead men at their feet. "The fools. Don't they realize the People will pay for those deaths? Don't they even know how to open a simple lock when they've got the key?"

"Simple for who?" Quannah whispered. "Do not worry. All will be well."

"How can you say that? They just killed two men! If anyone finds out we were here, we could be blamed. If one, just one of the men in that icehouse runs, they'll all be hanged."

"Watch." Quannah smiled as Kiyani produced a gun from under her buckskin blouse.

"Very resourceful woman, your wife," Kris whispered. "Too bad she can't put all that talent to better use."

Quannah sent her a questioning glance.

Kris ignored him as an alarming possibility occurred to her. "You don't think they're going to shoot Duuqua, do you?"

Quannah didn't answer, just slipped soundlessly across the

open space between their hiding place and the icehouse. Kris followed, not as quietly, arriving in time to watch Kiyani hold the other five warriors inside at bay, while Coyote Droppings gestured Duuqua outside, waving his knife threateningly.

Kris was thrilled at the sight of Duuqua, dirty, smelly, but whole. She wanted nothing more than to rush into his arms, but she hung back, waiting for Quannah to make his move.

Not until the icehouse was again locked and the two culprits were nudging their captive away did Quannah step forward.

"Too bad I don't need any more warriors." Quannah's grin widened when Kiyani uttered a frightened squeak and spun to face her husband. Coyote Droppings snarled angrily as Kris stepped up beside Quannah. "Release him."

"Never," Coyote Droppings hissed, and stepped closer to Duuqua. Duuqua jerked, then turned slightly. Coyote Droppings held a knife to his side.

"Kiyani." A firm warning rang through the single word Quannah tossed at his wife. She shrugged and dropped her weapons. She sent Kris a hate-filled look, then headed back toward camp, her shoulders slumped.

At that moment, something passed between Quannah and Duuqua. With lightning speed, Duuqua's elbow crashed into Coyote Droppings' face. Kris heard the crunch of bone, then Coyote Droppings' wail, smothered beneath Duuqua's hand. "We must not awaken our friends," he reminded the medicine man. Catching Coyote Droppings' arm, Duuqua squeezed his fingers until Coyote Droppings relinquished the knife, then Duuqua twisted his arm up behind him and propelled him deeper into the shadows. Kris and Quannah followed, Kris surprised at the intensity of her anger.

"I should kill you, but I do not want your blood on my hands," Duuqua hissed when they had traveled beyond earshot of the crude cabins. He shoved Coyote Droppings away from him. "Your thirst for power will bring death to the People."

"Leave us," Quannah ordered, his lip curling in disgust. Coyote Droppings slipped into the shadows, his eyes afire, hatred burning in his face. Kris caught the glance he shot at Duuqua as he slipped out of sight, a frightening, venomous promise.

"Are you sure he won't be back?" Kris asked, staring into the shadows. She didn't trust that man. She'd rather have him standing there under Duuqua's knife than skulking around somewhere in the darkness, waiting, watching for an opportunity to strike.

"He's a coward," Duuqua assured her. "He won't be back."

"You must go back inside," Quannah warned Duuqua, his gaze solemn but troubled.

Duuqua nodded. "I would not want MacKenzie to blame me for the deaths of his men."

"He'd shoot you himself," Kris whispered, her gaze darting between the two men. Had she come all this way only to look at him? Her gaze settled on Quannah, pleading with him to leave them alone, if only for a few minutes.

Quannah glanced down at Kris. "You must lock him inside again, then put the key back in the soldier's pocket. Can you do it?"

Kris gulped, nodded.

"I will wait for you."

"No," Kris said, nodding in the direction Kiyani had taken. "You have an urgent matter to attend to."

Quannah's face became grim. He gripped Duuqua's arm and thumped him once on the back. Then he disappeared into the darkness, leaving Kris and Duuqua facing each other.

Duuqua opened his arms, smiling when she walked into them without hesitation. He pressed his cheek to the top of her head, breathing deeply of her sweet scent, hoping his own would not make her ill.

"You're not angry?" she asked, pulling back to look into his face.

He remembered the look of horror in her eyes, felt her shame ripping through his soul, but he shook his head. "I was at first, but when I heard you cry my name . . ." Emotion clogged his throat and he could no longer speak.

"I wanted to tell you how sorry I was, that I understood."

"Shhh," he soothed, pulling her back into his arms and pressing her head to his chest while he stroked her hair. "It is no longer important." He kissed her cheek, startled by the taste of tears. "Do not cry."

"What's going to happen to us?"

"I will go to Florida," Duuqua said simply, hoping she would not argue. "I must. But it will not be for long. I will return to be with you."

He waited for her to say something, to tell him she would wait for him forever, but she remained silent.

Stiffly he said, "You could take the stones, return to your people if you do not wish to wait for me."

"How could you even suggest such a thing?" She jerked out of his arms, glaring up at him.

He shrugged, crossing his arms over his chest, delighted by her outrage, chuckling as she settled her fists on her hips. How he loved this woman!

Duuqua started at a sound behind him, a twig snapping under a careless foot.

Guard yourself! warned a voice, and Duuqua twisted. Lunging aside, he saw the flash of a knife arcing toward his exposed back, felt the grating slide of blade against bone, then the soft sucking sound as the blade was jerked free. He fell, bracing himself for another blow, sagging to his knees as the pain swallowed him whole—mind, body and spirit. Darkness swept over him, and he felt his strength flow out with his blood. He barely felt the tug on his neck as Coyote Droppings cut off his medicine bag.

"No!" he cried, struggling to rise, but the darkness pressed down on him, holding his body prisoner. Then suddenly the dream came and he saw Kris, kneeling beside him as tears streamed down her face. Blood dripped from the hand that stroked his cheek.

Coyote Droppings stood behind her, smiling. My *blood*, Duuqua moaned silently. My *blood on her hands*. He tried again to rise, but the pain pressed him into the dirt and he knew he wasn't dreaming. The knife in Coyote Droppings' hand was real, as was the blood dripping from it. He was not dreaming. Kris's tears were real. His nightmare had been brought to life.

Hatred burned in him, but the darkness swelled. Low laughter echoed around him and, as his eyes sank shut, Duuqua saw what his mind had shunned each time the nightmare brought him screaming from sleep. In one hand Isatai held the stones. In the other, her hair twisted cruelly in his fist, the woman Duuqua loved.

"Get her out of there, woman. Now." Jacob jumped to his feet, his hands clenched into fists, his eyes shooting enough sparks to set Powahe's tipi afire.

"I can't." Powahe's shoulders rounded beneath the burden of frustration. "Why didn't she take the stones when Duuqua offered them to her? I could have warned her about the dark one." Too late Powahe remembered she hadn't mentioned that particular problem to Jacob.

He spun to confront her. "When were you going to tell me about this 'dark one'? No, wait, let me guess. It's that shadow, right? The one that became a snake and frightened Kris's horse enough to send it running off a cliff."

Powahe nodded. "That first night you came, when you pulled me out of the tipi, *that* was the dark one."

"That foul wind?" He stared, obviously surprised. "I thought it was a big dust devil."

Powahe shook her head. "I don't know who it is, but it hates Kris and Duuqua, wants to destroy them. It's something from their past life, but when I've tried to pry information from the stones, Duuqua always blocks me. I don't know the whole story."

Jacob sank cross-legged on the other side of the fire. He ran a shaking hand over his face. "I don't know if I believe all this, but I do know that whenever I see that thing, that shadow, I feel cold inside, dead." He sighed. "This is getting too strange, but I'm not giving up until we get Kris back."

"We may never get her back," Powahe warned. "Didn't you hear her say she wants to stay there? She has to come back, but I'm afraid even that won't be enough now that the dark one knows where to find her. With Duuqua dead, the promise will no longer protect her."

"What promise?"

Powahe sighed. "Kris's stone has been passed down through generations of shamans. When I wore it, it guided me—helped me communicate with her, told me when to give it to her. Everything. Only the stones can fulfill the promise."

"Can you translate that to layman's terms?" Jacob frowned at her and leaned forward, his hands clenched between his knees. "What does it mean to my daughter?"

Powahe closed her eyes and searched deep for an answer. Not yet. She could not tell him the entire story without jeopardizing Kris's and Duuqua's safety. The dark one was too clever; he'd pluck it right out of Jacob's head.

"I cannot say. You must wait for answers until all has come to pass."

The bleak expression that crossed Jacob's face at her words turned a knife in Powahe's soft old heart.

"I'm sick of your mumbo-jumbo," he told her wearily, "but you're crazy if you think I'm going to give up and walk out of here. I'm not leaving until I have my daughter back on this side of that black hole, even if I have to stay at this fire until we starve or die of exhaustion. And neither are you. You got her there, but it's going to take both of us to get her home."

"It would kill her to leave Duuqua now."

Jacob placed a hand on either knee and leaned toward

Powahe. "She's lost him; he's dead! The sooner she's away from there, the better. She's my only concern."

"That's what I was afraid of," Powahe whispered, and quenched the fire.

She would have to manage Duuqua by herself.

Chapter Twenty-one

"Two more days and we reach sacred waters." Coyote Droppings jerked Kris off her horse, letting her fall. "Then I kill you and take your *puha*."

She scooted away from him, knowing she was too weak to stand. She tried to get warm under the moth-eaten robe he threw to her, but no matter how tight she curled, she couldn't cover enough of her. The wet grass turned her buckskins to icy sheets that stuck to her trembling skin. Though he hadn't hit or kicked her since beating her nearly unconscious that first night, her body ached.

She'd paid dearly for that bit of defiance. The swelling had gone down in her face, helped by long, bitter-cold days on horseback, battered by driving rain mixed with sleet; she could almost see out of her left eye again, but her split lip was still swollen and sore.

Coyote Droppings tossed a handful of grass onto the small fire he'd started. Kris inched away as he chewed peyote buttons and began dancing and chanting. He'd succumb to the nightly frenzy soon. She should try to sleep, but Duuqua lived in her dreams, handsome and commanding. Even there, the thing that Coyote Dropping became each night intruded, gloating over Duuqua's death and promising her own would soon follow.

Warily, Kris watched Coyote Droppings' macabre silhou-

ette, distorted by the dancing flames. Each night the ritual
lasted longer. He wasn't praying to the Great Spirit. At the
peak of his frenzy, the shadows swallowed him and his eyes
gleamed with an unholy fire that turned her blood cold. She
huddled under the ratty fur, desperate to conceal her fear.
Though he never touched her when in this trance-like state,
he often stood over her, menace emanating from him as he
chanted in a voice straight from hell.

As his dance became increasingly frenzied, Kris scooted
away from the fire, hoping to escape his notice. Odd how her
fixation on escape kept her mind off her grief and the empty
void her life had become, but nothing could erase the ache in
her soul and the ever-present knowledge that Duuqua was
dead. The awful ache swelled inside her, quickly becoming
unbearable. A low groan slipped from her unwary lips.

She felt the evil thing's gaze. Like a hot poker, it seared
through fur and buckskin.

"Aaaah," it gloated, and the air about her stilled as it drew
closer. "My prize is not sleeping after all."

"Leave me alone." Her cry fell flat.

It laughed, an evil hiss. "Ever have I been drawn to you."

Against her will, Kris rose to a sitting position and turned.
She felt suspended, inanimate, almost detached from her
body, but her mind was alive with questions. Slowly, she lifted
her gaze. She shuddered, finding no trace of Coyote Droppings in the blackness before her.

It drew closer, swallowing the ground between them.

"Don't touch me," she warned. She refused to shrink from
it, even as she marveled at her will to defy the creature.

"Grandmother!" she cried. "Help me!"

The fire flared high and the fiend turned, releasing Kris.
She fell forward onto her elbows and stared at the fire. Voices
came from the flames. She recognized her grandmother's, but
there was a man with her. A hideous wail filled the night and
a hot, sulfurous wind swept around the fiend, spiraling upward
until the blackness dissolved, leaving Coyote Droppings